THE VAGRANT KING

In Cornwall, farmer Joseph Moyle's stepson Ralf becomes page to the future Charles II. Britain is at war between the Royalists and the Parliamentarians. Ralf follows the heir to the throne through the western counties as he learns of court intrigue. When Charles begins the first of many affairs, Ralf also falls in love. But Brighid, an Irish Catholic, is also complicit in an attempt to kidnap Charles — a fact that Ralf discovers when he foils the plot . . . In 1645, when the conclusive Battle of Naseby marks ultimate defeat for the Royalists, Ralf follows Charles into exile. Desperate to return to Cornwall after years of loyal service to Charles, Ralf's dreams of the homecoming to his beloved Trecarne are shattered . . .

E. V. Thompson was born in London and spent nine years in the Navy before joining the Bristol Police. He moved to Hong Kong, then Rhodesia and had over 200 stories published before returning to England to become a full time, award-winning writer.

E. V. THOMPSON

THE VAGRANT KING

Complete and Unabridged

CHARNWOOD
Leicester

First published in Great Britain in 2005 by
Time Warner Books
an imprint of
Time Warner Book Group UK
London

First Charnwood Edition
published 2006
by arrangement with
Time Warner Book Group UK
London

British Library CIP Data

Thompson, E. V. (Ernest Victor), *1931 –*
    The vagrant king.—Large print ed.—
Charnwood library series
    1. Cornwall (England)—History—Fiction
    2. Great Britain—History—Civil War, *1642 – 1649*
    —Fiction 3. Historical fiction 4. Large type books
    I. Title
    823.9′14 [F]

ISBN 1–84617–314–0

Published by
F. A. Thorpe (Publishing)
Anstey, Leicestershire
Set by Words & Graphics Ltd.
Anstey, Leicestershire
Printed and bound in Great Britain by
T. J. International Ltd., Padstow, Cornwall

This book is printed on acid-free paper

Prologue

It was not yet noon but Ralf Hunkyn felt as though he had just completed a long and arduous day's work. Emerging from the high-banked track on the hill above the small Cornish waterside village of Polruan, a bundle of his belongings on his shoulder, it seemed that every fibre of his body was complaining.

However, he told himself there would be no more days like this now his work at Trecarne Farm for Oliver Pym, former captain in the Parliamentary army, was at an end.

Pausing for a few moments on the brow of the hill, Ralf glanced back towards the farm. One of the cornfields was just visible. The crop was ready for cutting and despite the recent bad weather it would be a good harvest and a tribute to Ralf's husbandry skills. He alone had fed and tilled the earth, planted and tended the corn.

Ralf surveyed the field of corn with mixed feelings. Chief among them was a reluctant pride. The crop should have belonged to him and not to Oliver Pym — as should Trecarne, the farmhouse where Ralf had spent his boyhood.

Those had been happy years, everything a boy could wish for — until the increasingly divisive

1

quarrel between King and Parliament had finally erupted in a bitter and bloody war.

But that had happened many years before. Now King Charles I was dead, victim of an executioner's axe, England had been declared a Protectorate under the iron rule of the late Oliver Cromwell and the martyred king's son, Charles II, was a monarch without a realm. Dead, too, was Joseph Moyle, the stepfather who had brought Ralf up as his own son, giving him and his mother those earlier, happy years.

Ralf fought back the sudden rancour that welled up in him as it always did when he thought of what might have been . . . what *should* have been. He wondered, as he often had, whether it had been a mistake to return to work on the farm that was rightfully his. If Oliver Pym had ever learned the truth it would have meant certain imprisonment — and possibly something far worse. Royalist sympathisers were harshly treated by an increasingly intolerant regime, and Ralf had been far more than a mere sympathiser to the exiled King Charles II who was presently living in penurious exile on the Continent.

There were still sporadic disturbances in Scotland, Ireland, Wales, Cornwall and even England itself, and such troubles provided the Protectorate with an excuse to round up and imprison known Royalists — even execute them if they posed a particular threat.

Oliver Pym was given to boasting that he and Cromwell had been close friends both before and during the time they were brother officers in the Parliamentary army. If Ralf had ever revealed his true identity, arrest would have been inevitable.

Besides, Ralf had someone else to think about now. Someone who also had much to lose, yet who had placed her trust in him.

Turning his back on Trecarne Farm and the thoughts it engendered, Ralf began the walk down the hill to Polruan from where he would cross the River Fowey and follow the river northwards to its source and beyond, heading for a new and uncertain future.

The brief rest had revived Ralf and, still thinking of all he was leaving behind, he walked briskly, heading for the ferry which would carry him across the estuary. Suddenly, the rays of the late-morning sun struck the glass panes of a window being closed in one of the Polruan cottages and Ralf came to a halt once more.

The brief flicker of reflected sunshine had brought back yet another memory of long ago. Of a particular day that was destined to change his life for ever . . .

BOOK ONE

1

'Leave what you're doing, Ralf, quickly now! Saddle the old mare and come with me. I'll show you a sight you're never likely to see again . . . Hurry!'

It was the year 1644, and Joseph Moyle's stepson was cleaning out the small barn where their four cows had been kept shut away since news had reached them some days before that the Parliamentary forces of the Earl of Essex were being beaten back towards Fowey by the armies of the King.

Essex's army numbered almost 10,000 men and it was common knowledge that they were desperately short of supplies, seizing upon any edible beast or bird they could find. The sound of cannon-fire had been coming from the direction of the far bank of the River Fowey for most of the morning, disturbing the tranquillity of the remote Trecarne farmhouse, and Joseph had ridden off to learn what was happening, concerned lest some of the Parliamentarians had crossed the river and were scouring the countryside in the Polruan area for food. If they were, it would be necessary to lead the cows down a hazardous cliff path to a smugglers' cave where they had already been hidden twice in recent turbulent years.

Now, hearing his stepfather's shout through the barn door, Ralf gladly put aside his bucket. 'Have the Roundheads crossed the river?' He used the derogatory term commonly used by Royalist supporters to describe soldiers of the Parliamentary army.

'No, and they're not likely to.' Joseph spoke excitedly. 'They're getting the beating of their lives. King Charles himself is on this side of the river with the young prince, ready to turn them back if they try to cross.'

The excitement in Joseph's voice was contagious and Ralf asked eagerly, 'Can we see them? See the King and Prince Charles?'

'Only if you move yourself. The King will have urgent matters to attend to today. Unless Essex means to allow his men to be driven into the sea he'll have to surrender — and on the King's terms.'

Ralf hurriedly threw a saddle on the back of the old mare which was shut in with the cattle. The task completed, he led the horse outside, hopping with one foot in a stirrup in his haste to mount the animal while it was moving. In the meantime, Joseph had called Ralf's mother from the farmhouse to tell her what was happening.

Grace Moyle did not share the excitement of her son and her husband. Addressing the latter, she asked, 'Haven't you had enough of war? It almost killed you once. Do you want to give it another chance — and take Ralf with you? Shame on you, Joseph Moyle.'

'You know I wouldn't put Ralf in any danger, Grace. He's coming with me to try to catch a glimpse of the King — and His Majesty is far too important for his officers to allow him close to any serious fighting.'

Grace was not convinced, but she had seen the expression on her son's face while she and Joseph were speaking. With a display of resigned indifference, she shrugged. 'Well, I can't stop you from doing what you want. You go off traipsing about the countryside and leave me to get the work done round the farm — but don't expect me to nurse you if you get hurt. Either of you.'

'We'll be careful,' Ralf said, with the eager sincerity of a thirteen-year-old. 'And I'll finish all the chores when we get back, I promise!'

'I've heard such promises from you before, young man. When the two of you are off together I swear you forget there's work to be done. Be off, both of you, but don't stay away too long. By the look of the clouds building up out at sea there'll be rain before nightfall. I don't want your wet clothes cluttering up my kitchen.'

Turning away from her husband and son, Grace went back into the house. Despite the disapproval she had voiced, she watched through the window with pride as Joseph and Ralf rode off together. Joseph might not be Ralf's true father, but he loved him as though he was his own, and his love was returned by the boy. She was lucky to have found such a man when she was left a widow with a baby son to provide for.

As the two riders passed from view the sound of increased cannon-fire rumbled from the direction of the river. She decided to go about her work and try not to think of what was taking place such a short distance away from Trecarne.

* * *

As they approached Polruan village it was obvious to Ralf and his stepfather that there was more than one battle taking place on the far side of the river. The sounds of cannon and musket-fire extended from Fowey to Lostwithiel, a few miles to the north, and was echoed in villages and hamlets to the west. Joseph guessed correctly that various Royalist armies which had been ranging the counties of south-western England had come together to trap Essex and his troops in the small peninsula that lay between Tywardreath Bay and the River Fowey.

For some days now Royalist cavalry had been patrolling the east bank of the river in increasing force to prevent Essex's men from escaping in this direction. On the previous day there had been great excitement at Trecarne when a large number of Royalist musketeers, escorting two brass cannons and numerous ammunition wagons, had made their way along the narrow lane adjacent to the farm, en route to Polruan. Here there was a fort, built some 150 years before, commanding the entrance to the strategically important Fowey harbour. With this in their hands, the Royalists could prevent the Roundhead army receiving succour from the sea and ensure there would be no escape in that direction for the trapped soldiers.

Before Ralf and Joseph reached the brow of the hill overlooking Polruan, the sea came into view to the south and Ralf could see Parliamentary ships cruising offshore, out of range of the Royalist cannons. A number of local people were lining the cliff top to watch them and Ralf and Joseph paused for a few moments too before renewed cannon-fire on land drew them onward once more.

As they topped the hill above the village, it was immediately apparent that something out of the ordinary was happening below them. Horsemen filled the narrow street and waterfront, the rays of the sun reflecting from the body armour worn by many of the riders, while a gay array of banners and pennants fluttered in the breeze that blew from the sea.

When Ralf commented on the many standards, Joseph said, 'Let's get closer and find out who they belong to, Ralf. Even if the King isn't among them there'll be some famous men there, for certain.'

Joseph's interest in the pennants was more than mere curiosity. He had served in the King's Cornish army as an ensign, his important duty in the heat of battle to carry the flag of a commanding officer and remain at his side, where the standard was a rallying point for the soldiers of that command, providing them with the reassurance that they were still part of a cohesive force.

Kneeing his unenthusiastic mount into motion once more, Ralf followed his stepfather along the faintly discernible sheep track that led down

11

through steep, unenclosed land towards Polruan and the Royalist gathering.

The importance of those in the party became evident even before Joseph was able to identify any of the impressive array of banners. A troop of half a dozen cavalrymen, led by a corporal, detached itself from the main body and cantered up the hill with the obvious intention of intercepting the newcomers. Behind them another horseman followed at speed. Joseph and Ralf brought their horses to a halt as the Royalist cavalry troop reached them.

'Where are you going, and what's your business?' The corporal put the question to Joseph, at the same time peering to see if they carried any weapons.

'I'm a farmer from Trecarne, over the hill. I've brought my son, Ralf, to see the army of King Charles — and unless I'm mistaken that's the standard of the King himself in Polruan. I'd like to take Ralf down there and allow him a glimpse of His Majesty.'

The cavalryman who had challenged Joseph looked at him with open suspicion. 'You're a farmer, yet you're able to recognise the King's standard — and at such a distance? What's your name, farmer?'

'I can give an answer to both your questions, soldier.'

The Royalist horseman who had followed the troop was Captain John Trevanion, a Cornish member of the King's bodyguard. He had arrived upon the scene in time to hear the corporal voice his suspicions. 'Joseph Moyle may be a farmer now, Corporal, but when he and I fought side by side at Lansdown he was an ensign, carrying the standard of Sir Bevil Grenville. Had he not been sorely wounded in that battle he might well have been the King's standard-bearer now.' Urging his horse past the corporal, he rode forward, saying, 'How are you, Joseph? I am delighted to see you did not lose your arm.'

Holding the arm in question awkwardly in front of him, Joseph replied, 'I still have it, Captain Trevanion, but I would it served me better.'

'I'll wager you are a better man with one arm than many who claim to serve His Majesty with two; but then, they are not Cornishmen.' Switching his gaze to Ralf, Trevanion asked, 'Is this fine young man your son? Will you be putting him into the service of the King when he's of an age?'

'God willing, there will be no need for young men to offer up their lives in His Majesty's service when Ralf is old enough to consider such matters . . . '

Even as he spoke there came the noise of cannon-fire from the far side of the river and Joseph added, 'Perhaps that peace will not be long in coming. It would seem you have the beating of Lord Essex.'

'Essex is a man of courage, but with little skill as a general,' Trevanion replied. 'He'll lose his army, but Parliament has many more up and down the country. Our battle here will soon be won, but I fear there are others yet to be fought.' Changing the subject, the Royalist captain went on, 'But what brings you to Polruan today? Have you business here?'

Joseph shook his head. 'As I explained to the corporal, I brought Ralf along to see what was going on. Now we're here I hope he might catch a glimpse of His Majesty. I doubt he'll ever again have such an opportunity.'

'Then we must not allow it to be wasted.' Turning to the cavalrymen who had been listening in silence to the conversation, Captain Trevanion addressed their leader. 'You did well to intercept strangers, Corporal. His Majesty has many enemies in the land — but Joseph Moyle is not one of them. I will accompany him to Polruan. You may return to your duties and maintain your vigilance.'

The cavalrymen turned their horses and trotted down the steep hill but before Joseph, Ralf and Captain Trevanion could follow, Ralf cried, 'Look! Everyone's leaving.'

The horsemen in Polruan were moving off to the right of the watchers on the hill, skirting the harbour and following the shores of a tidal creek that would take them inland.

'It seems His Majesty has had enough of war for today,' Captain Trevanion said. 'He's heading back to Boconnoc.'

A short distance from Lostwithiel, Boconnoc was a large mansion and estate owned by Lord Mohun, an ardent Royalist. The house had changed hands more than once during the conflict between King and Parliament, being used as headquarters by leaders of both opposing armies.

'If we take the path down the hill to the creek we'll get ahead of them and be able to see the King pass by,' Ralf said excitedly.

'Lead on then, Ralf,' Joseph said. 'Captain Trevanion will be concerned to rejoin the King's party. He's wasted more time with us than he can afford.'

'His Majesty would not agree with you, Joseph,' Captain Trevanion commented as he rode beside the farmer, both following in the wake of Ralf down the steep pathway. 'He can always find time for those who have served him well and he has a special fondness for his 'Cornish army'.'

The three horsemen reached the creek-side track well ahead of the royal party and sat their horses to one side, waiting for the King to pass by. Ralf found the colourful cavalcade strangely exciting.

The soldiers were men of the royal guard, dressed mainly in red uniforms, although there was a sprinkling of blue, yellow and white among them and many of the officers wore a variety of body armour over their tunics. There were also many flags borne high on pike-like staffs.

'There's the King in the centre,' Captain Trevanion pointed out. 'And Prince Charles is with him.'

The King and the Prince who was heir to the throne of England both wore gleaming breast and back armour decorated with tooled gold piping. In spite of the fact that the Royalist

15

forces were scoring a notable victory, the King had a sombre expression. Not so his son. The fourteen-year-old prince was clearly excited by the events of the day, his heavy features animated.

Although the King wore an expression of apparent preoccupation, he was keenly observant of things around him and had seen the captain of the royal guard ride after the small troop of cavalrymen sent to intercept the strangers. He was curious to know why Captain Trevanion now sat his horse alongside them beside the creek-side track. Urging his horse through the ranks of his escort, followed by the young prince, King Charles headed for the mounted trio.

Suddenly fearful that he and Joseph were about to get into serious trouble for daring to come so close to the monarch, Ralf held his breath. But, after a quick glance at him and Joseph, King Charles spoke to their companion. 'I saw your cavalry troop riding to intercept these two, Captain Trevanion. They obviously pose no threat, but I hardly expected to find them in your company. Are they known to you?'

'Indeed, sire. This is Joseph Moyle and his son, Ralf. Joseph was Sir Bevil Grenville's ensign and was at his side when he was struck down at Lansdown. I can assure Your Majesty that you have no subject more loyal than Joseph — and I venture to suggest none who is a braver man.'

It was high praise indeed and King Charles switched his attention to the suddenly embarrassed farmer. 'Captain Trevanion is not in the habit of bestowing such compliments, although

16

no man who fought at the side of the sadly lamented Sir Bevil Grenville has need to show proof of his courage. Why are you no longer with my army? Did you lay aside your weapons and return to Cornwall as did so many of my Cornish army when Sir Bevil was struck down?'

Raising his crippled arm to chest height with some difficulty, Joseph said apologetically, 'I took a sword blow which left my right arm useless. Were it not so I would have been proud to continue in Your Majesty's service.'

Satisfied, the King nodded. 'Spoken as a loyal subject, Joseph Moyle.' His gaze moved to Ralf, who had been rendered speechless by the attention of the King. 'What of your son? Will he one day serve me as loyally as his father?'

'He is my stepson, Your Majesty,' Joseph explained, 'but as dedicated to his monarch as am I. However, I trust that when he is of an age to serve you there will be peace in England.'

'I share your aspirations for the future, Joseph. Unfortunately, I fear there are still testing times ahead.' Again, the King turned to Ralf. 'How old are you, boy?'

Awestruck at being addressed by the King of England, Ralf managed to stutter, 'I . . . I am thirteen . . . Your Majesty — almost fourteen.'

Ralf was small for his age and, looking at him speculatively, the King was silent for a few moments before asking, 'Does your loyalty extend to royal princes?'

Startled, Ralf replied this time without hesitation. 'Of course . . . Your Majesty.'

Returning his attention to Joseph, King

17

Charles said, 'The Prince of Wales is to be given his own council and will need a court that reflects his importance. As he is also Duke of Cornwall it is fitting that some of his suite should be Cornish. I think your stepson might make an acceptable page. He would enjoy the usual privileges that attend on such an appointment, including tuition by Prince Charles's tutor. You may consider it a reward for your service to me and to the late Sir Bevil Grenville.'

It was a most unexpected turn of events. An honour for Joseph and an even greater one for Ralf. A page in the household of a prince would be constantly in attendance on his master. Although required to perform certain menial tasks, he would be taught the graces of a courtier.

Overcome by the King's generosity, Joseph said, 'How can I possibly thank Your Majesty . . . ?'

'You have already done that by your service in my army.' Suddenly brisk, and without another glance at the boy whose life would be changed for ever by his whim, the King said, 'Send the boy to Boconnoc tomorrow. He is to ask for Dr Earle, the Prince's tutor.'

Briefly inclining his head to Joseph, the King turned his horse away. Behind him, Charles, Prince of Wales and Duke of Cornwall, gave Ralf a fleeting glance in which Ralf imagined there might have been just the hint of a smile.

2

'These may be good stout clothes for *our* Sunday best, but I'm not happy that they're suitable for Ralf to wear in the court of Prince Charles!'

Grace Moyle might voice her doubts about the suitability of her son's clothes, but her misgivings went far beyond mere sartorial matters. In the privacy of their bedroom she had kept Joseph awake until the early hours of the morning, expressing concern for her son and the lifestyle upon which he was about to embark. Her husband had spoken of the great honour being done to the family by the King, but these were uncertain times. The increasingly bitter civil war had made the future of the monarchy uncertain.

Here, on Trecarne, Ralf's future would be far more predictable and secure. He and his stepfather, working together, could steadily improve the farm that would one day be his. It was a prospect that should have been more than enough to satisfy a young man in Ralf's walk of life.

It was certainly more than Grace could have expected when her first husband died, and when she and Joseph married she had been convinced that Ralf's future was assured. Now, the meeting of her husband and son with King Charles had thrown her world into disarray.

Grace *was* aware of the honour the King had done to the family, but she was dubious about its long-term benefit — especially for Ralf. It was all very well for Joseph to point out that the position of page in the royal household was usually held by the son of a gentleman. Ralf was *not* the son of such a man and she was doubtful about his ability to adjust to life in the court of Prince Charles.

'When our Ralf joins the Prince's court he'll be given clothes befitting his new status,' Joseph said in an attempt to reassure his unhappy wife. 'And I have some money put aside. He can take it and buy anything he's lacking. He'll not need to feel inferior to anyone else who serves the Prince.'

Grace was aware that Joseph had been saving money for many years in order that he and Grace should not be a burden to Ralf in their old age. This was what he would be giving away.

'It will take more than money to make a gentleman of a farming lad,' she retorted unhappily.

'Perhaps, but the King wants Ralf to join Prince Charles's court because he's Cornish. There are Cornish gentlemen in the court who will take an interest in Ralf and see he comes to no harm. Captain Trevanion himself has promised to keep an eye on him. No boy could have a finer protector.'

Grace was not convinced, but Ralf, who had kept silent until now, said, 'It will be all right,

Ma. I'm not happy about leaving you — either of you — but Pa's right: it's a great honour for me and a wonderful opportunity. I promise I won't waste it. I'll make you proud of me.'

Determined that Ralf should not see how deeply upset she was, Grace shrugged her shoulders and tried to appear nonchalant. 'Oh, well. Nothing I say is likely to change anything, so I might just as well save my breath. You'd better get yourself off, or you'll find the King and Prince Charles will have left Cornwall without you.'

★ ★ ★

Dr John Earle, tutor to Prince Charles, was a kindly and perceptive cleric. He suited his young charge so well that he was destined to be made a bishop when the throne was once more secure — but that would be in the far-distant future.

Before Joseph bade farewell to his stepson, the tutor assured the older man that good care would be taken of him.

'Captain Trevanion came to see me yesterday and told me about him — and about you too, Mr Moyle. Because of your close association with the late Sir Bevil, I have decided to place Ralf in the care of one of His Majesty's own senior pages, a kinsman of Sir Bevil and a fellow Cornishman. Ralf will remain with him until he is thoroughly conversant with his duties. I have no doubt at all that he will soon become a valued member of the Prince's household.'

After a moment of uncertainty, Joseph turned

to his stepson. 'It's time for me to go, Ralf. When I return to Trecarne I will be able to tell your ma that I have left you in very good hands.'

Ralf could not reply. Now that the moment had arrived when he would actually make the break with all he had ever known, he felt a sudden surge of panic inside him.

Aware of what was going through his stepson's mind, Joseph smiled at him affectionately. 'You will always be in our thoughts, Ralf, and we will think of you with love and pride. Serve Prince Charles well.'

Ralf felt an overwhelming urge to rush to Joseph and hug him, something he had not done since he was a small boy. Instead, he merely nodded, not trusting himself to speak lest he burst into tears and disgrace himself and Joseph.

Joseph found the parting painful too, but he left Boconnoc happy in the knowledge that he could inform Grace that there were a number of men in the court of King and Prince who would take an interest in the well-being of her son.

Watching his stepfather ride away, Ralf was far less certain. This was the first time he had left Trecarne since his mother had remarried, and although Joseph had been absent during the earlier years of the Civil War Ralf had come to love him and rely upon him in everything he did. Now he was among strangers and about to embark on a new and uncertain venture that had been thrust upon him with a frightening suddenness.

John Earle understood what was in Ralf's mind and, aware of his uncertainty, he said, 'You will like Piers Grenville, Ralf. He is the most knowledgeable of the King's pages and a very popular young man. He was devoted to his kinsman, Sir Bevil. Your link with him through your stepfather will endear you to him immediately. I will send for him to take you to the court tailors. You will need to be suitably attired before you are officially introduced to the royal court.'

What John Earle meant but refrained from saying was that if certain of the denizens of the court were to meet Ralf while he was wearing his farm-best clothes he would become the subject of their sharp-tongued derision and never be allowed to feel comfortable as a royal page.

★ ★ ★

Ralf liked Piers Grenville immediately. He had a ready smile and a quiet manner. When the two shook hands, Piers declared, 'I am delighted you have been chosen to become a page to the Prince, Ralf. There are too few Cornishmen in the court. One whose stepfather fought alongside my brave uncle Bevil is doubly welcome.'

When Ralf appeared surprised that Piers should know about the service of his stepfather in the Royalist cause, Piers explained, 'I was with Dr Earle when Captain Trevanion came to see him last night to speak on your behalf. He said your stepfather would have died for my uncle — and almost did. I hope I might meet him sometime. Captain Trevanion also told me to choose a horse for you from those captured at

23

Fowey. We'll do it together, then have the one that brought you here returned to your farm. I have no doubt your stepfather has need of it.'

'I have told Ralf we will also need to arrange suitable clothes for him as soon as possible,' John Earle said pointedly, 'I thought you might take him to visit the tailors before he is introduced to the court.'

'I can do better than that,' Piers declared. 'Ralf is not particularly tall for his age and I have a number of items I have outgrown. He can have them right away, before we go to see the King's seamstresses. They can make any alterations that might be needed and arrange for new clothes to be made, if necessary. They can also supply a tabard with the Prince's coat of arms so everyone will be aware that Ralf is employed in his service.'

'Good! I leave Ralf in your very capable hands, Piers. We will meet again soon, Ralf. You will be attending classes with some of the King's pages as soon as we reach a place where it is possible to have some semblance of a routine. Listen to all Piers has to tell you, learn well, and serve Prince Charles as your stepfather served Sir Bevil — with loyalty and devotion.'

As Ralf accompanied Piers to the pages' quarters in the great house of Boconnoc, the older boy chatted about the things that would be expected of Ralf. The new page was alarmed to learn that the duties were of such a wide and varied nature that it was quite impossible for Piers to tell him everything at one meeting.

Piers explained that in earlier years becoming

24

a page was the first step to obtaining a knighthood. A boy would first learn all the duties of a servant in a great house, including waiting at table, but would also be taught the attributes of a courtier and a gentlemen, including lessons in French, mathematics, chivalry, jousting and swordplay. In addition he had to be prepared to accompany his master into battle, having first dressed him in a full set of armour. These days, however, kings, princes and peers of the realm rarely went into battle dressed in full and cumbersome armour. What was more, the Civil War had thrown many of the strict rules of protocol into confusion. It seemed that a present-day page was expected to serve his king — or prince — in any way necessary, both on and off the battlefield.

'It may sound a little confusing,' Piers conceded, 'especially as a page is neither servant nor courtier. But you'll soon get used to what's expected of you. I've served Prince Charles while he's been accompanying His Majesty in his adversity and he's not difficult to get along with. He will expect total loyalty from you — and nothing less — but once he is satisfied he has that, he will treat you more as a friend than a subject. In fact, as his page, you will probably become closer to him than the members of his council.'

Piers told Ralf much more, especially whom he might trust and whom he could not, but Ralf found it increasingly confusing. It seemed a number of the courtiers were not the dedicated Royalists they would have the King and Prince believe. Although serving the royal cause, they would have no qualms about switching their allegiance to Parliament should they feel it was likely to emerge as the victor in the bitter Civil War that was tearing the country apart.

★ ★ ★

In the room shared by the court pages, it was apparent that much of Piers's cast-off uniform clothing was too large for Ralf, but the senior page shrugged it off, saying, 'Don't worry, it can be easily altered to fit you. We'll go along and see Molly O'Malley. She is in charge of His Majesty's seamstresses and has been widowed and remarried so many times that no one can ever remember her present name, so she's still called by the name of her first husband. She's a fearsome old harridan, but there's no better seamstress in the whole of the kingdom.'

Ralf was amazed to discover that even though the King was leading an army that was likely to be involved in battle at any time, he travelled with all the trappings of a royal court, taking with him tailors, cooks, washerwomen, personal servants — and seamstresses.

Molly O'Malley was a big-boned, pinched-faced Irishwoman with a fierce expression that Ralf felt might have intimidated King Charles himself. When Piers explained the purpose of their visit, the Irishwoman was openly scornful.

'Do you think I have nothing better to do than pamper to the whims of young popinjays who put elegance above necessity? We've uniforms to repair for officers who have had them torn and bloodied in battle — and themselves along with their clothes. Do you put your needs ahead of theirs?' Looking at him with a fierce expression, she added, 'Besides, they pay for the work that's done for them. There's very little comes our way from the keeper of the King's purse.'

'Ralf has just been appointed a page to His Royal Highness, Prince Charles,' Piers said patiently. 'He needs to be dressed for his position. I was hoping you might also be able to make up a tabard bearing the Prince's coat of arms. The only one I have bears His Majesty's, and I am wearing that.'

'And you'd best be taking good care of it,' Molly declared. 'Unless someone can find some money for us we won't be able to afford thread enough to stitch on a button, let alone make clothes.'

'Perhaps it is time His Majesty found himself a seamstress who puts her duty to her king above her greed,' Piers said, suddenly irritated by the Irishwoman's manner.

'Take no notice of Molly.' The intervention came in the same accent as Molly's from a slight, dark-haired girl who had been seated by a window, stitching, and had said nothing so far. Speaking to Ralf, she went on, 'Things aren't easy — for any of us — but they were worse in Ireland. As for the tabard, we had some made up ready with the Prince's coat of arms some time ago, knowing they would be needed before too long. I'll look one out for you before you leave and have it ready in no time at all. I'm a good

27

judge of size. As for the clothes you've been given, I'll alter them tonight — if Molly thinks we can afford the candles?'

'You do exactly as you like,' said a tight-lipped Molly. 'You always do anyway, but don't come crying to me for food when you can't sleep because you have an empty belly. One day you'll learn that gentlemen of the King's court need to pay their way, same as the rest of us. But why am I wasting my breath on you? You'll learn the wisdom of what I'm saying the hard way, just as you will with everything else.'

With that, the Irishwoman turned her back on them and busied herself with the cloak she had been repairing when the two pages had entered the room.

Talking to the girl, who was only a few years older than Ralf, Piers said, 'I'll have some candles sent to you by the house servants — and speak to the Prince's tutor about payment for your work on Ralf's behalf.' He ignored the scornful snort from the older woman that greeted his words.

Ralf allowed the girl to determine the extent of the alterations that would need to be made to Piers's uniform and, later that day, wearing his new tabard, he was both surprised and delighted when cavaliers of the King's army inclined their heads to him in acknowledgement of the coat of arms.

Perhaps for the first time, he really began to realise just how much of an honour he had been given.

3

The embattled Roundhead army in Cornwall surrendered on Sunday, 1 September 1644, but its commander-in-chief, the Earl of Essex, was not present to negotiate terms on behalf of his defeated and dispirited soldiery.

The Earl, together with Lord Robartes of Lanhydrock and a few other senior officers, had managed to commandeer a fishing boat and escape by sea to Plymouth, without telling Major-General Skippon, senior commander of the Parliamentary army, of their intentions.

Skippon had been wounded and was without his cavalry, which had broken through the Royalist lines and escaped capture the night before Essex's own flight to safety. Nevertheless, the Parliamentary general would have placed himself at the head of his remaining six thousand soldiers in a desperate attempt to fight his way out of the trap into which Essex had led them had not his council of officers, demoralised by the desertion of Essex, disagreed. They pointed out that their troops were exhausted as the result of a week of fierce defensive fighting and had no heart for heroics.

Reluctantly, Major-General Skippon was forced

to accept defeat. The following day he agreed terms that were extremely generous to his army, as a tribute to his courage in battle. Leaving the wounded behind for later evacuation by sea, the Parliamentarians would be allowed to march eastwards out of Cornwall, escorted by a small band of Royalist soldiers.

Late that afternoon, the King, the Prince and many of the courtiers were waiting beside the bridge over the River Fowey in Lostwithiel town to watch the dirty and dejected Roundhead soldiers tramp across the bridge on their way out of Cornwall. The vanquished army was jeered and taunted by the men and women of the town, who had assembled with a great number of the rank and file of the victorious Royalist host.

Bringing up the rear of the dispirited procession were a number of women and some children, the 'camp followers' who accompanied every army of the time, sharing the lot of their menfolk, both in victory and defeat. The jeers of the Lostwithiel women were particularly vociferous against this group, and trouble erupted when one of the Parliamentarians was stung into making an angry retort in return.

Stones were thrown from the crowd and then, without warning, it surged forward and fell upon the unfortunate women and their children. Some of the Parliamentarian soldiers turned back to come to their aid but Royalist officers immediately ordered members of the escort to draw their swords and drive them back into line.

It was a forlorn attempt to restore order. In the mêlée, the anger of the Lostwithiel women, fuelled by the pillage, insult and indignity inflicted upon them by the now-defeated army during their occupation of the area, was vented upon the camp followers, many of whom were severely beaten, their belongings stolen, and some even stripped of their clothing.

The King himself urged his horse forward and called upon the local women to desist, without any discernible result. Ralf was dismayed to see a young girl, aged about eleven or twelve, who had gone to the aid of her mother, seized by two of the angry Lostwithiel women and pitched into the river.

The water was deep here, and when the girl struggled to the surface it was apparent that she could not swim. Ralf ran to the river bank as the girl surfaced once more, arms waving frantically and trying desperately to shout for help. Reaching out, he managed to seize one of her arms and pull her to the bank.

A Royalist officer who had seen what had happened came to his aid and between them they succeeded in lifting the girl clear of the water. Once she was safe, the officer hurried away to assist the King in restoring order while Ralf stayed with the girl, who was sitting on the river bank retching and trying to suck air into her lungs.

When she had recovered, she looked up at him and suddenly burst into tears. At a loss as to what to do, Ralf said ineptly, 'It's all right. You're safe now.' He could see that the Royalist soldiers had succeeded in restoring some form of order. The angry, jeering townswomen had been driven

31

back and the camp followers were on the move once more. 'You'd better get moving or you'll be left behind.'

Still tearful, the girl wailed, 'They've stolen our money . . . food . . . everything — and we have a hundred-mile march ahead of us. We'll never survive.'

Ralf had seen that the royal party were moving off and was anxious to rejoin them. Round his neck, beneath the tunic, was a cord to which was attached a bag containing the money Joseph had given to him. Pulling out the bag, he opened it and extracted a silver half-crown.

'Here, take this and buy some food along the way.'

The girl looked as if she was about to question his generosity, but changed her mind. Rising to her feet, she dropped him a curtsy. 'Thank you, sir. Thank you for your kindness.' Then, turning away, she ran to join the camp followers who were still streaming across the narrow bridge.

When she had gone, Ralf hurried to where a soldier was holding the bridle of his horse. Mounting, he spurred after the royal party. When he joined them he looked back to see if he could spot the girl he had rescued, but could not pick her out. Turning forward again, Ralf was alarmed to find that Prince Charles had dropped back to speak to him.

Giving him one of his ready smiles, the Prince said, 'You are already learning your lessons well, page. Among the first things one should learn is the importance of chivalry — especially chivalrous conduct towards a defeated foe.'

32

His smile suddenly wider, he added, 'Of course, chivalry always comes more easily when a foe is as pretty as was that young woman, but well done.'

Riding back to join the King, the Prince left a very pleased Ralf behind him. He was almost as pleased by the fact that the girl had dropped him a curtsy and called him 'sir'. She must have believed him to be a gentleman.

4

After a few nights spent at Boconnoc, the King, Prince Charles and the Royalist army moved eastward out of Cornwall, following in the wake of the defeated army of Parliament.

It was not long before disturbing reports began to circulate of the sufferings of the Roundhead soldiers. It seemed their escort had been either unable or unwilling to protect them from the wrath of a vengeful populace as they passed through village and town.

The army of Essex had subjected Cornwall to a reign of terror during their earlier advance through the county, plundering and destroying property and possessions at will. Now the tide of war had turned against them the Cornish populace reaped a terrible revenge. Disease, starvation and exposure followed in the wake of the ill-treatment suffered by the defeated army and of the six thousand who started the long march, only one thousand survived to reach Poole, in Dorset, and ultimate safety.

Ralf heard the rumours and wondered about the fate of the young girl he had rescued from the river at Lostwithiel. However, he was given little time to think about her, despite the slow progress of the King and his army.

He was spending more time attending to the needs of Prince Charles now, sharing his duties with another, more senior page, Dominic Fulbrook, who had been transferred from the King's household. The transfer suited Dominic no more than the fact that he was now working with Ralf, whom he referred to, disparagingly, as 'the farm boy', when talking to Piers.

The two senior pages were riding together at the rear of the royal party when Dominic aired his dissatisfaction to his companion. 'What on earth was His Majesty thinking about, to appoint a farm boy to serve the future king of England?'

'It was the King's way of rewarding Ralf's father for brave service in his army. He was ensign to my kinsman, Sir Bevil, at Lansdown.' Piers spoke with more patience than he felt. He liked Ralf more than he did the arrogant and constantly complaining Dominic.

'An ensign in a foot regiment!' Dominic sneered. 'A future king should be served by gentlemen, not farm boys. Did you see him rush to the aid of that peasant girl when she fell in the river at Lostwithiel? He obviously recognised her as one of his own sort. When my father agreed to my becoming a page to the King he believed that because of the troubled times the position would entail performing the duties of a future knight, not carrying out servants' tasks with farm boys.'

'I don't know how you or your father came by such a notion,' Piers replied. 'It is an honour to serve the King in any capacity — and I have no doubt His Majesty is happy in the knowledge that his son is served by brave men, and the sons of brave men. As for foot soldiers . . . my kinsman's regiment, Ralf's father among them, scored a notable victory at Lansdown, holding firm when the cavalry broke.'

Dominic coloured angrily. His father had been an officer in the cavalry at Lansdown. Taken by surprise by an enemy charge, the cavalry had broken in disarray. Had the Cornish infantry not held firm, the battle would have been lost. It was an action the Royalist cavalry would prefer to be forgotten.

'I should have known better than to comment on the farm boy to *you*. You believe it's more important to be a Cornishman than a gentleman. Well, it's *not*.' With this heated remark, the angry page kicked back with his spurs and drove his startled horse forward, away from his companion.

Behind him, Piers smiled wryly. Dominic's father had been an unremarkable member of the House of Commons prior to Parliament's quarrel with the monarch. Siding with the King, Horace Fulbrook became *Sir* Horace and received a commission in the Royalist army. His son took both knighthood and commission very seriously and had been deeply offended when he had been transferred from the King's household to that of the Prince, sharing his duties with a 'farm boy'.

He would undoubtedly try to make life difficult for Ralf. Piers decided he should warn his fellow Cornishman to be on his guard.

★   ★   ★

36

King Charles and his army pursued a slow and erratic course through the west of England, generally in a north-easterly direction. Their progress was necessarily slow because they had commandeered a number of patient and slow-moving oxen to pull the baggage carts and artillery pieces.

They also had frequent long stops, some lasting for many days. On these occasions Ralf was obliged to attend the lessons organised by the patient Dr Earle. Joseph Moyle had taught Ralf to read and write, together with the rudiments of arithmetic, but at first he struggled with French, a language that was considered by the court to be important, particularly as the Queen, Henrietta Maria, was French and currently finding succour in the land of her birth. However, Ralf had a quick brain and before long was enjoying learning the unfamiliar language.

Sometimes Prince Charles attended lessons with the pages, but more often he was in conference with his father and the King's council, discussing the progress of the war, which was not going well for them elsewhere in the country. In the evenings he would often ask Ralf about the lessons and, before long, although Ralf never forgot his place in the Prince's household, an easy relationship blossomed between them.

Then, towards the end of the year, the King and his army clashed with a Parliamentary army at Newbury. It was the second occasion on which the opposing sides had fought each other in the same area. In September 1643, the army of Parliament successfully withstood an assault by the King's men in a hard-fought action that did not end until the Royalists quit the field under the cover of darkness.

Now it was the King and his army who were on the defensive, greatly outnumbered by three Parliamentary armies, led by the Earl of Manchester, Sir William Waller — and by Oliver Cromwell, who had taken over command of the army of the Earl of Essex when that Parliamentary nobleman was taken ill suddenly, shortly before the battle.

The Royalists held a defensive position in a narrow triangle of land, with Donnington Castle tucked in one corner. It was here that the Prince was placed, much against his will, protesting that he wanted to be part of the action with the King.

When the Roundheads attacked at dawn it was at the corner of the triangle farthest from the castle. Although the smoke from cannon and musket could be observed from the castle battlements, those watching anxiously could see nothing of the actual fighting. When word reached the castle that the Parliamentarians had broken through the Royalist perimeter there was great anxiety until another messenger assured the anxious prince that one of the King's generals had counter-attacked and driven the enemy back in some disorder.

There was jubilation upon the castle battlements, but the dawn attack had been in the nature of a diversion. For many hours the opposing forces were content to settle for an artillery duel until, at three o'clock in the afternoon, General Waller suddenly appeared at the opposite end of the Royalist defences. With him were Oliver Cromwell and General Skippon, courageous survivor of the Roundhead defeat in Cornwall.

The guns of the castle, together with other Royalist guns, opened up on the advancing Roundheads and Ralf was appalled to see the numbers of the men falling before the shot — but the advance continued determinedly and before long many of the guns outside the castle were overrun, the gunners struck down and killed.

It was the first time Ralf had seen a battle of this magnitude and he was horrified at the slaughter — but worse was to come. With Skippon were many of the survivors of the disastrous march from the debacle at Fowey and Lostwithiel. When they sighted the banners of Royalist Cornish troops an overwhelming desire for revenge overcame caution. They fell upon the westcountrymen with a fury that could not be contained. No quarter was given and Ralf and others around Prince Charles could only watch in horror as the slaughter progressed.

The King himself was caught in the midst of the fierce battle and for a few minutes it looked to the watching party, which included his son, that he too would be either killed or captured. Then two separate troops of Royalist cavalry came to his aid and, with the monarch in their midst, fought their way to safety.

The battle raged until darkness fell and

beyond. The Parliamentarian attack had been well planned. Had each of their commanders played the part designated to him, it would have ended in a decisive Roundhead victory. It might also have culminated in the capture of the King and thus brought the Civil War to an abrupt end. Fortunately for the Royalist troops, however, the Earl of Manchester failed to bring his army into battle at a vital moment. As a result, the King was able to successfully hold his defensive position — but only just.

Many good men had been lost and the King and his generals realised their army was now hopelessly outnumbered. A secret reconnoitre revealed a gap between the Parliamentary armies almost a mile wide. Taking advantage of this and aided by the darkness, King, Prince and Royalist army quietly decamped during the night, leaving behind them a garrison in the strongly built castle which would defy the Roundheads for many more months.

When dawn broke, the Prince and the bulk of the Royalist army were well on the road to Oxford and, as tension eased, men began boasting of the deeds done by themselves and their companions, speaking as though they had won a great battle instead of being fortunate to have averted a major defeat.

Amid all the bragging, Prince Charles remained markedly silent. So too did Ralf, who was unable to erase from his mind the memory of the carnage he had witnessed before night had cast a merciful shroud over the battlefield. He was particularly upset by the merciless slaughter of the Cornishmen who, in most cases, knew nothing of the politics behind the fighting. In common with those who killed them, they had wished for nothing more than to leave war behind and return home to their wives and families.

Such disturbing thoughts would haunt him on many occasions during the years ahead.

5

'The important thing at Newbury was not so much to win as to ensure that our army didn't *lose*. Had we suffered a crushing defeat it might well have been the end for the King and Prince Charles — and probably for us too. As it is, we live to fight another day.'

Piers's explanation was given to Ralf five days after the battle, when the two pages were relaxing in the room they would share in Christ Church, Oxford, where the King had set up his court. After the battle, the King and some of his cavalry had rendezvoused in Bath with his European cousin, Prince Rupert, one of the Royalists' most active generals. Meanwhile, Prince Charles and the remainder of the army had made their way to the safety of the Royalist city of Oxford, where the King would soon join them.

Piers was replying to Ralf's assertion that the great loss of life at Newbury had been in vain because neither side had either won or gained a significant advantage.

'Would you rather be fighting for the Roundheads, Ralf?' Piers, pale-faced and tired, was awkwardly trying to wrap a short bandage about his upper arm, where a musket ball had grazed him when he was attendant upon the King at Newbury.

'Here, let me do that.' Ralf adjusted the small pad covered with salve on the wound, then carefully bound the remainder of the bandage about his friend's arm, saying as he did so, 'I would rather there was no fighting at all. That King and Parliament could resolve their differences.'

'I doubt anyone would disagree with you, Ralf. Certainly not the King. It grieves him to see so many of his subjects being slain, but his cause is a just one, do you not agree?'

'I know little about 'causes',' Ralf admitted, 'but I enjoy serving Prince Charles and hope I may continue to do so for very many years to come.' Securing the bandage to his satisfaction, he added, 'Talking of the Prince . . . I need to take some of his clothes to the tailors and have larger ones made. The war has not stopped him from growing at a rate that is the despair of the Earl of Berkshire. He complains that the Prince's clothes bill would fit out a regiment of foot.' Berkshire was the current official governor to the Prince, although his young charge avoided him as much as was possible.

'Then both he and the Prince are in for a shock,' Piers said, carefully shrugging the sleeve of his shirt over the bandage. 'The royal treasury is desperately short of money and His Majesty has said that the needs of the army are to take precedence over all others. Let us hope the seamstresses have sufficient material for new clothes.'

★ ★ ★

The seamstresses had not.

'And just what am I supposed to do with these? Perhaps I should cut them up and make finery for the wives and daughters of His Majesty's Irish men-at-arms who haven't been paid for the last two months.'

Molly O'Malley, as disapproving and tight-lipped as ever, scornfully picked up each item of Prince Charles's expensive clothing between finger and thumb, raised it in the air for critical examination, then dropped it back on the table in the porter's room of Christ Church, which now served as workshop for the royal tailor and his staff. When the last garment had undergone her scrutiny, she said, 'Not that there would be any more warmth in these than they'd get from a peacock's tail-feather.'

Glaring at a slack-jawed Ralf, she snapped at him, 'I asked you a question. Has the cat got your tongue, or something?'

Gathering his wits together, Ralf said, 'His Royal Highness would like some new clothes the same as the ones I've brought to you — only larger. He's grown since these were made and they're no longer comfortable.'

'Comfortable! Comfortable, you say? Those of us who aren't so close to the King have forgotten what comfort is. All the time we were traipsing round the countryside we thought ourselves

44

lucky if we were able to share a rat-infested barn with the riff-raff of the King's western army, even though I would need to spend half the night stopping my stepdaughter from losing the only thing she'll ever have to offer a man in marriage.'

Ralf glanced at the younger of the two Irish seamstresses, who appeared quite unconcerned by what the woman was saying. He felt compelled by his position in the Prince's household to make some reply to Molly's comments.

'I doubt if His Majesty enjoys 'traipsing round the countryside' any more than you do. I'm sure he was far happier in his palace in London with his queen and the princes and princesses around him, but I don't think anyone in his court has heard him grumble about his personal discomfort, or the constant danger he is in.'

Ralf was expecting Molly to come back at him with one of her cutting remarks. Instead, and much to his surprise, she gave an exaggerated sigh before expressing agreement. 'You're quite right, of course, young sir. Hardships are a part of daily life for the likes of me and Brighid, but I'm just an ignorant Irish seamstress. It's not something that a king, or a prince — or even an educated young man like yourself — should have to put up with. Leave the Prince's clothes here and me and Brighid will have them ready for you some time tomorrow.'

The brief conversation marked an unexpected turning point in Ralf's relationship with the irascible Irish seamstress. There would even be occasions when Molly greeted him as though she was quite pleased to see him. Her unexpected civility towards him was commented upon by the other pages, all of whom remained victims of her sharp tongue.

Because of his acceptance by her, Ralf was delegated to call upon Molly whenever tailoring work was required by anyone in the Prince's household, and he soon developed a grudging respect for the Irishwoman. She did not hesitate to rebuke anyone in the court, whatever their rank, if she felt they were taking advantage of the seamstresses, yet she and her staff produced quality work under extremely trying conditions, plagued by a constant shortage of money and materials.

Ralf's popularity with her was secured once and for all when he was able to persuade the holder of the Prince's meagre finances to donate a hundred pounds to Molly to cover the considerable expenses involved in clothing the heir to the throne of England in a manner consistent with his status.

★   ★   ★

The royal courts had been in Oxford for a couple of months when Ralf had a rare free afternoon from his duties. Deciding to put on the clothes he had been wearing when he joined the Prince's household, he took a walk along the bank of the River Isis, which skirted the city beyond the college buildings.

The experience brought home to him just how much his life had changed since leaving

46

Cornwall. Wearing the everyday clothing worn by most of those in and about the city, he was not given a second glance, and when he was jostled aside by a group of drunken Royalist infantrymen he realised how much respect his page's uniform commanded.

Walking back to Christ Church, he suddenly saw Molly's stepdaughter, Brighid, coming along the road towards him, a satin-lined velvet cloak folded over her arm. The young seamstress never even glanced in his direction and would have passed him by had he not spoken to her.

'Hello, Brighid. Are you no longer talking to me?'

Startled, the Irish girl came to a halt and stared at him in disbelief, before saying, 'It's the Prince's page! What are you doing dressed like that? Are you on a secret mission for the Prince?'

For a moment Ralf thought of going along with her assumption — but only for a moment.

'No. I wanted to get away from the court and be myself for a while. I can't do that when I'm dressed up as the Prince's page. But what about you? Where are you going with that very handsome cloak?'

She held the cloak up for his inspection. 'Molly made it for a Lieutenant Muller. He's a troop commander in Prince Rupert's cavalry. I think the material was looted from a Roundhead lord's mansion in Devon. Muller served with Prince Rupert, the King's nephew, in Germany. He thinks of himself as a ladies' man, but he isn't. He's not liked very much by his men — they don't trust him. Mind you, I doubt if

47

there's one of the foreign officers who wouldn't join the Roundheads if he was offered enough money, for all that most are Catholics. Molly wants to make certain she gets her money for making this before he changes sides and she believes I'm more likely than her to wheedle the money out of him.'

'But . . . if she thinks he's likely to desert the King and join the Roundheads shouldn't she tell someone?'

Brighid looked at him pityingly. 'Who would believe a seamstress — an *Irish* seamstress — against the word of a lieutenant of cavalry? Besides, like I said, it's no more than soldiers' gossip and that's not in short supply among the King's men.'

'All the same . . . '

Ralf was concerned, but Brighid said briskly, 'I can't stand here talking to you all day. I have this cloak to deliver and there's more than enough work waiting for me back at Christ Church.'

'Would you mind if I walked along with you?' Ralf asked.

Brighid shrugged, and he could not tell whether she was pleased or displeased by his request. 'Please yourself, but there'll be no dawdling, Molly is a hard taskmistress.'

Lieutenant Hugo Muller was billeted in a large house tucked between two of the colleges farthest from Christ Church and, although Brighid had said she did not have time to waste, they found ample time along the way to exchange brief details of their backgrounds.

Ralf learned that Brighid's father was a

sergeant in one of the Irish regiments brought to England to fight for King Charles.

'My mother died when we were following the regiment, a couple of years ago,' Brighid explained. 'Molly and my pa were married a couple of months later. She's had two soldier husbands before and both were killed fighting for the King. She often talks of leaving this life behind and going home to Ireland, but I don't think she could. She's been following the drum since she was younger than me and knows no other life. She'll be with the regiment until the day she dies — and I've no doubt her spirit will stay with them for evermore.'

'Will you stay with the army too?' Ralf asked.

Brighid shrugged. 'Who knows? Even if I did, I wouldn't want to end up like Molly, living only for the regiment and prepared to take any man for a husband, just to stay with the army. But I've never known anything else in my life.' Giving him a wan smile, she asked, 'How about you? I suppose you'll stay in the King's service and grow rich and famous — or are you rich already? Most pages are.'

Ralf smiled. 'I'm certainly not rich, and I doubt if I'll ever be famous. I'll probably stay with the Prince until the war comes to an end, then return to our farm in Cornwall.'

'Is it a large farm?' Brighid asked. 'With lots of cows and sheep and the like?'

'It's not especially large, but we do have cows, bullocks and sheep, and we make a comfortable living. It's my stepfather's farm, really, but he's promised that I'll inherit it one day.'

'I spent a few weeks on a farm in Ireland once,' Brighid said. 'It belonged to an uncle, a brother of my mother who was still alive then. They had cows and sheep. I liked it. I think it's where I'd like to live, one day. But if that's where you belong, how is it you're a page to Prince Charles? I thought pages were the sons of gentlemen.'

'The others are,' Ralf said ruefully. 'In fact, I'm called 'the farm boy' by some of them.' He went on to tell Brighid how he had become a page.

When he ended, Brighid said indignantly, 'You're as good as any of the others — and better than most, I can tell you. They come round all smiling and friendly when they want something done for nothing, but you're the first page who's ever said so much as 'good day' when we've met up outside the sewing room. I know we're only seamstresses — and Irish at that — but we're as loyal to King Charles as anyone else who serves him — and we work a sight harder than most for him and those around him.'

Coming to a halt beside a large house, she said, 'This is where Lieutenant Muller is billeted. Thank you for walking here with me, and for talking to me as you have.'

'I'll wait for you,' Ralf said. 'Then we can walk back to Christ Church together and talk some more.' They had passed a number of stalls selling foodstuffs along the way and he added, 'I'll buy you some sweetmeats — as a small thank you for all you've done for the Prince.'

When he returned from his errand, the front

door of the house where Lieutenant Hugo Muller had his room stood open. The wind was quite keen along this particular narrow street, and Ralf stepped inside into the passageway for shelter. He could hear voices coming from a room farther along the passageway, and recognised one of them as being Brighid's. She sounded cross. Curious, Ralf moved down the hall in order to hear what was being said.

Reaching the room from which the voices were coming, he cast a quick glance about him before putting his ear to a narrow gap between door and jamb, where the door was slightly warped.

' . . . I don't need to earn any *extra* money — at least, not in the way you're suggesting. All I want from you is a half-crown, to pay Molly for the work that's been done on your cloak. Give me that and I'll be on my way.'

'You shall have the money, my dear, but I am offering you another half-crown for what . . . half an hour of your time? And for doing something you must find more enjoyable than sewing . . . ' The voice carried a strong Germanic accent and Ralf thought it sounded as though the officer had been drinking . . . but he had not finished talking.

'You have been with the army for a long time, so it is something you must have done many times before, surely? If you have not, then I will know — and I will give you another whole crown for yourself. Here . . . take it. It is yours.'

'Take your hand off me, or I'll scream!'

'That would be a very unfriendly thing to do. I want us to be friends. Besides, there is no one

51

else in the house to hear you. But there is no need for such measures, surely . . . ?'

Ralf was alarmed. He was a country boy, inexperienced in the sordid life, but he had been in Oxford for long enough to realise that licentiousness was not looked upon as a vice among those who fought for the King. However, he was not prepared to do nothing while Brighid became a victim.

Hammering on the door, he called, 'Brighid, are you there? If you don't hurry you are going to be late measuring the Prince for his new clothes.'

There was silence for a moment inside the room, before he heard the officer demand of Brighid, 'Who is that at the door?'

Brighid was quick-witted enough to realise that Ralf must be aware of what was happening inside the room.

'It's a member of Prince Charles's household. He came here with me to make certain I would be back at Christ Church in time to meet the Prince. His Royal Highness is having a new wardrobe made.'

A moment later the door opened. In view of what had been happening inside the room it was a very unflustered Brighid who appeared. Calling back over her shoulder, she said, 'Thank you, Lieutenant Muller. I am happy you are pleased with the cloak.'

'Wait a minute . . . ' The lieutenant appeared in the doorway and he was younger than Ralf had expected him to be. 'I gave a whole crown . . . '

'Yes, it is very generous of you. Come, Ralf, or we will be late for the Prince.' Taking his hand, she hurried him from the house.

Looking back as they walked quickly along the road from the house, Ralf saw the officer standing in the doorway staring after them. He appeared to be angry, but Brighid was smiling delightedly.

On the way to Christ Church they stopped at a market stall to buy more sweetmeats — paid for from Lieutenant Muller's crown coin.

6

For the King's courtiers, Oxford was a safe and comparatively comfortable city in which to endure their exile from London. What was more, the royal party had entered the seat of learning to such an enthusiastic welcome that King Charles might have been excused for believing he was still monarch of a loyal and undivided land.

However, the war was not going well for him elsewhere in the country — and, to a large extent, his flagging fortunes were due to the efforts of Oliver Cromwell, a stern Puritan general.

Until the quarrel between King and Parliament, Cromwell had been a little-known MP, with farming interests in Huntingdon. Now, actively engaged in the war on the side of Parliament, he had shown himself to be an exceptional commander of cavalry and he would soon reveal unexpected skills both as a politician and as a leader of Parliament.

The Royalists were in overall command of the west country, but there was great dissatisfaction with the King's soldiers among the populace. Not having been paid for many months, the

Royalist troops were looting the countryside around their garrisons. There was resistance too in the important towns of Plymouth, Taunton and Lyme, which remained in the hands of Parliamentary troops and were holding out against besieging Royalist armies.

The situation in the west was made even more difficult for the King because of growing animosity between Sir Richard Grenville and Lord Goring, the King's principal commanders in the area.

Prince Charles was now almost fifteen years old, an age when royal princes were expected to assume many of the responsibilities that went with their status, so, in a bid by the King to solve some of his problems in the area, the Prince was given his own council and nominal command of the armies of the west.

In addition, increasingly concerned lest both monarch and heir be captured by Parliamentary forces, the King decided that the future Charles II should leave Oxford and take up residence in the west country. As a result, in the first week of March, 1645, Prince Charles, accompanied by his court and council, left to set up his headquarters in Bristol.

★ ★ ★

'I wish this damned rain would cease,' Dominic Fulbrook grumbled to Piers Grenville as they sat their horses behind the coaches in which rode Prince Charles and the most senior members of his council.

Dominic's disgruntled mood was not entirely due to the admittedly abysmal weather. When it had been decided that the Prince's entourage should break away from the King, he had thought he would be the senior page — and he left the Prince's other pages in no doubt about what they could expect from him. Ralf, in particular, was informed that he could expect to be given the most menial tasks, 'as befitted his background'.

And then, much to Dominic's chagrin and Ralf's delight, twenty-four hours before the Prince set off for the west country, Piers was transferred from the King's court and placed in charge of the Prince's pages.

Replying to Dominic's complaint, Piers echoed the sentiments of Dominic himself, when he had told Ralf what he should expect from him when he was the senior page. 'If you don't like things the way they are, you can always resign from the Prince's household.'

Aware that Piers was repeating his own words, Dominic said angrily, 'Do all Cornishmen need a shoulder to cry on — or is it only farmers' boys?'

'Neither,' Piers replied evenly. 'You are a victim of your own indiscretion, Dominic. I believe you made that remark to Ralf when you were alone with him in the Prince's robing room and thought you could not be overheard. Fortunately — or unfortunately, depending how you view it — someone *did* hear, and I leave you to speculate who it could have been. I believe you also boasted to a great many people how things would be when you became Prince

Charles's senior page. As a result it was felt it might be better for everyone if I was placed in charge.'

'Who overheard me?' Dominic was genuinely alarmed. He felt it could only have been Prince Charles himself.

'That does not matter. Now, there is work to be done. We will be at our destination in an hour or so. You can ride ahead and warn Lord Stanford's household of our imminent arrival and ensure there are dry clothes, a fire and food ready for the Prince. You have permission to take a troop of the lifeguard with you — but make haste.'

★　★　★

That night was spent in the house of the Royalist peer, Lord Stanford, who was campaigning in the north of England. In his absence, every effort was made by his wife and servants to ensure that Prince Charles and his court were made comfortable.

The Prince's meal was served to him, as was customary, by his own pages, who later took their own food in another room. Afterwards, Ralf was on his way to the kitchen to make arrangements for the Prince's breakfast when he met Brighid carrying a tray of food.

Astounded to see her, Ralf said, 'Brighid! What are you doing here? You are the *King's* seamstress.'

'I was.' Brighid smiled at him. 'When the Prince and his council left Oxford we were told

57

that three seamstresses were wanted to become part of his household. I offered to be one of them and was accepted. It was a chance to get away from Molly. I've been around her for long enough.'

'But your father is with the King's army.'

'I'd been following him for long enough too. Besides, thanks to you I know more about the Prince's needs than any other seamstress so I was an obvious choice to come with him.'

'But . . . what does Molly think about you making the break from her and your father?'

Relieved that Ralf had accepted her explanation without question, Brighid said, 'Molly told me I'd been with her for long enough to know how to take care of myself, even though she doesn't believe I can. Besides, she feels she's shared my pa with me for long enough. She'll have him to herself now, so help him!'

Ralf was delighted that he had not seen the last of the vivacious Irish girl, but he had a word of caution for her. 'Did you know that Lieutenant Muller is a troop commander in the Prince's lifeguard?'

Brighid was momentarily disconcerted. 'No. I thought he was one of Prince Rupert's men.'

'He was, but he and his troop are part of Prince Charles's escort now, at least for the time being. I suggest you keep out of his way as much as possible.'

'He won't cause me any trouble — but what about you?'

'We've met face to face but he doesn't seem to recognise me. He never got a good look at me when I was with you in Oxford and I think he was too drunk to remember me anyway.'

'He was, but thanks for the warning. To be honest I'm surprised he's left Prince Rupert's cavalry. They have a reputation for plundering and that's the main reason most of Prince Rupert's men are fighting. There won't be much plunder for the Prince's escort . . . but I must go now. I came to the kitchen to collect the food for the seamstresses and it'll be getting cold.'

'I hope to see you again when we're more settled,' Ralf said, as Brighid was about to hurry away. 'Probably in Bath. We'll be there tomorrow night and the Prince hopes to stay for a few days.'

7

Although the royal party remained in Bath for ten days, neither Ralf nor Brighid had time to spare from their duties to meet each other for longer than a few minutes at a time. The Prince had been promised there would be men, money and supplies awaiting him in the ancient spa city — but none were forthcoming.

It was a blow to the hopes of him and his advisers. They had intended to spend the time in Bath preparing for a grand arrival in Bristol, the city that was to become the Royalists' western capital, headquarters for Prince Charles and his court and council. Instead, Charles was forced to spend his days touring the surrounding country-side in an increasingly vain attempt to recruit men for his dwindling army and arrange funds to support them and his court.

As a result of the Prince's lack of success, his seamstresses and washerwomen were worked hard to ensure that his existing wardrobe appeared as grand as possible when the royal party rode into the second largest city of King Charles's divided kingdom.

As if these problems were not enough, the

Prince discovered that he was nominal commander of a fragmented and disunified army. His generals neither liked nor trusted each other and each was stubbornly determined not to acknowledge another's superiority in rank, even if it meant their actions resulted in a defeat for the forces of the King.

One such general was Sir Richard Grenville, a kinsman of Piers and brother of the late Sir Bevil. He led the Cornish army and, fiercely proud of their Cornishness, his soldiers were reluctant to follow any other leader into battle. Capitalising on this, Sir Richard actively encouraged his men not to accept orders from anyone else.

Forced to listen to the bickering of his western generals, Prince Charles was also obliged to receive deputations from local residents, complaining about the depredations of rapacious and plundering Royalist soldiers who sought to make irregular pay an excuse for pillaging the homes of unfortunate westcountrymen and women.

One of the pages was always in attendance upon the Prince during these meetings and, as a result, Ralf gained an extensive knowledge of what was happening in the west of England, as well as an awareness of the parlous state of the royal finances. The general feeling among the more optimistic members of the Prince's council was that all would be well once they set up their headquarters in Bristol — but yet again they were destined to be disappointed.

The Royalists had captured the city from Parliament almost two years before and in that time had succeeded in milking Bristol's finances dry. The 'loyal citizens' had been made responsible for paying for the upkeep of the huge garrison quartered in the city. As a result, so impoverished were the city's corporation that they were obliged to borrow furnishings in order to accommodate the Prince and his household.

The Prince was little better off than his father's subjects. Setting a precedent that he would follow for many years to come, he was reduced to borrowing from those about him.

★   ★   ★

'Oxford was a much happier city than Bristol,' Brighid said. She and Ralf were walking together beside the River Avon. There were many ships moored alongside the quays here, but the port lacked the noise and bustle that should have been evident. Although the fort guarding the entrance to the river was in Royalist hands, there were usually a number of Parliament's men-of-war waiting beyond the range of the fort's cannons, ready to pounce upon any vessels attempting to enter or leave the port.

'Oxford is the King's capital now and has always been loyal to him,' Ralf replied. 'Bristol was taken by force and, by all accounts, suffered a great deal in the process. There is little love for the royal cause here.'

'I'm aware of that,' Brighid agreed. 'We've taken on a couple of Bristol seamstresses and they swear things were better when the city was held by the Roundheads.'

They walked on in silence for some moments before Brighid asked, unexpectedly, 'What will happen to the King and the Prince if they lose the war?'

Ralf felt unhappy because the question of defeat did not sound as improbable to him as it perhaps should have, but his reply gave no hint of his doubts.

'We won't lose. Something will be sorted out, sooner or later, you'll see.'

'You mean . . . all this fighting and killing is for nothing?'

Brighid's words brought back memories of Newbury to Ralf and he winced. 'I can't answer that, Brighid. I wish I could. All I can say is that I'm glad I'm a page and not a soldier.'

'I'm glad too,' Brighid said enigmatically, adding, 'there are many times when I wish I was a seamstress in some quiet little town where no one has ever heard of war. Where the only sewing I was asked to do was for a wedding gown, or perhaps for a christening. Where I was wanted to make happy things.'

'The war won't go on for ever,' Ralf said, 'so you might well get your wish. But where will you go?'

'I hope I'll still be working for Prince Charles,' Brighid replied. 'If not . . . ' She shrugged. 'I can't see there being much work for an Irish seamstress — a *Catholic* Irish seamstress — in a country ruled by Puritans.'

It was something that had not occurred to Ralf, but before he could comment on her statement a sardonic voice said, 'Well, well, well!

63

If it isn't the farmer's boy, and in the company to which he is best suited — an Irish sewing girl! I wonder what His Royal Highness would have to say about it.'

Ralf had noticed a horseman riding along the path towards him and Brighid, but had not taken any notice. Now he was dismayed to see that the rider was Dominic.

Before he could reply, Brighid said, 'No doubt His Royal Highness would say that there are a great many of his subjects who would like to become a royal page, but few who would — or could — serve as a royal seamstress.'

Stung by Brighid's forthrightness, Dominic said, 'You place a value on yourself that others might not share, girl.'

'I'll remind you of those words when you next come craving a favour,' Brighid retorted.

'Of that I have no doubt,' Dominic said. 'You certainly have more to say than His Royal Highness's Cornish page.'

Trying to appear nonchalant, Ralf said, 'I felt I could add very little to what seemed to be an evenly matched conversation, but perhaps you have something else you want to say?'

'Not me, farmer's boy — but others might. Meanwhile, I will leave you to the company of your friend.'

When Dominic rode away, Brighid asked anxiously, 'Will he get you into trouble?'

'For what . . . talking to you? I choose my own friends — and Dominic Fulbrook is most certainly not one of them. He makes that clear at every opportunity.'

They walked together in silence for a while before Brighid said, 'I'm sorry if I've caused you any trouble, Ralf, but I'm glad you think of me as a friend. I thought I'd be really glad to get away from Molly because she was always telling me what I should or shouldn't do, but I miss having her to talk to. I realise now that she meant well. I miss my pa too, even though I never saw very much of him.'

'If you want to return to the King's household I could probably arrange it,' Ralf said. 'I know what it's like to leave everyone you know and go somewhere you feel you don't really belong.'

It was the first time Ralf had aired such thoughts to anyone. Indeed, he had never honestly faced them himself. It both surprised and disturbed him.

In a moment of sympathetic understanding, Brighid reached out and took his hand. She squeezed it for a moment, saying, 'Well, we both have someone we can tell things to now that we're together serving Prince Charles — and I'll stay with him for as long as he needs a seamstress.'

★   ★   ★

'I met your fellow Cornish page when I was out riding yesterday,' Dominic said to Piers as the two pages made their way from their quarters to the dining room where they would serve breakfast to the Prince. 'He was with a friend of his own kind.'

Aware from Dominic's words that he was not

about to say something complimentary, Piers said, 'Good. I have no doubt that whoever it was is a nice person.'

'I would not know about that,' Dominic replied smugly. 'I have little to do with such people — but I believe she is quite a competent seamstress. She is also Irish.'

If Piers felt surprise, he did not allow it to show. 'Ralf has quite a knack of getting on well with people, be they prince, courtier, or seamstress. It is something of which the Prince is aware, I know.'

'The Prince will also be aware that by spending off-duty hours walking in public by the river with an Irish sewing girl, a page risks bringing scorn upon the royal court,' Dominic retorted.

'I doubt if he would consider it worthy of his attention,' Piers said, ' . . . any more than he would if someone told him that another of his pages is in the habit of paying for the favours of a soldiers' whore in the Shaven Crown.'

Startled, Dominic coloured guiltily. The Shaven Crown was a notorious tavern, frequented by foreign seamen, petty criminals, and the less-discerning soldiers of the royal army. Dominic had gone there with a group of university students who included his cousin. He had woken in the morning to find he was sharing a bed with a raddled whore more than twice his own age.

That in itself was bad enough, but he had consoled himself with the thought that it would never be known by anyone in the Prince's court.

'You would not say anything to the Prince?' he pleaded.

'Of course not,' Piers replied, cheerfully, 'any more than you would comment to him on the far more reputable company kept by Ralf. Now, I suggest you go to the kitchen and check that all is in order, while I speak to the Prince and ask when he will be ready for breakfast . . . '

8

Life in Bristol was less comfortable for the Prince and his household than they had been led to expect. Financially crippled by the fluctuating fortunes of war, the Bristol Corporation was unable to provide the many luxuries demanded by the Prince and his courtiers — and the heir to the throne was unable to provide them for himself. The royal coffers were empty and the Prince was forced to depend upon the charity of those members of his council whose lands, homes, or fortunes had not been seized by Parliament. Unfortunately, the numbers of those who fell into this category were diminishing as Roundhead forces brought more and more of the country under their control.

Aware of this, and seeing an opportunity to advance the prospects of her family, Christabelle Wyndham, wife of the governor of the Somerset town of Bridgwater and a wealthy woman in her own right, persuaded her husband to invite Prince Charles and his court to come to their town and use it as a base from which to raise soldiers for his army — and funds for his treasury. The offer was accepted with alacrity by the Prince and he and his council swiftly transferred the court the few miles to Bridgwater, where the Prince set up his household in the home of the governor and his wife.

Christabelle Wyndham was a renowned beauty who had once served at the royal court in London, in the nursery of the infant Prince Charles. One of the King's aims when sending his son to the west of England was to 'make a man' of him. Although more than twice the age of the young prince, Christabelle would fulfil the wishes of King Charles in a manner he could not have foreseen, but which was not particularly unusual in royal circles at a time when marriages were consummated at an early age.

The Prince was within a few days of his fifteenth birthday and had already earned rebukes from his tutors for the interest he was showing in young and attractive women. Now, taking a further and unanticipated step into manhood, the young Charles, Generalissimo of the Royal Army of the West, would earn the angry disapproval of Sir Edward Hyde, who had been appointed by the King to be his son's governor and guardian in place of the pernickety Earl of Berkshire.

With the court established in Bridgwater, Christabelle's increasingly familiar manner towards the Prince was frowned upon by older members of his council, although others were simply amused. Few seriously believed the two had become lovers.

Ralf knew better.

It was a page's duty to remain outside the Prince's bedroom when he retired for the night until it was certain he was asleep. One night, soon after their arrival in Bridgwater, most of the household had gone to bed and Ralf was performing this task when he was startled to see Christabelle coming along the dimly lit corridor towards him dressed in an exotic Indian gown, with slippers on her feet — and carrying a small dog!

He stood up from the chair on which he was seated, but, without saying a word, the governor's wife raised a finger to her lips. Then, giving him a conspiratorial smile and leaving the heady aroma of perfume hanging on the air behind her, she opened the door of the Prince's room and passed inside, closing the door quietly behind her.

Ralf was in a dilemma. His task was to keep visitors out of the Prince's room, but he doubted whether Christabelle would be regarded by his master as an unwanted guest. He decided he must remain outside the room until she left.

The long clock in the passageway had struck four before Christabelle emerged from the Prince's room with the small dog tucked beneath her arm once more. She still exuded perfume, but was considerably more dishevelled than when Ralf had last seen her.

Without appearing in the least embarrassed, she gave him a smile and, as she passed him by, said quietly, 'The Prince and I trust in your loyal discretion, Page. I will see that it is rewarded.'

'That will not be necessary,' Ralf replied, equally quietly. 'My duty will always be to the

Prince and his interests come before those of anyone else.'

* * *

Christabelle's regular nocturnal visits to the Prince's bedroom, accompanied by the small dog, soon became common knowledge among the royal pages, but Ralf was the only member of the Prince's household to enter the room when the governor's wife was inside — and it was brought about by the small dog.

It was about an hour after Christabelle had entered the bedroom when the dog began to yap inside the room. It kept up the noise for about ten minutes before Ralf, on duty outside the door, heard the Prince calling for him.

Entering the darkened room with some trepidation and aware of the dog bouncing excitedly about his feet, Ralf said, 'You called me, sire?'

Speaking from within the curtained four-poster bed, the Prince said irritably, 'The damned dog wants to go outside. Take it into the garden for a few minutes.'

'Yes, sire.'

Ralf picked up the dog and, tucking it beneath his arm, had opened the door before the Prince spoke again.

'Page!'

'Sire?'

'After the dog has been in the garden, keep it with you outside the room.'

'Yes, sire.'

As he left the chamber, Ralf could hear the voice of Christabelle Wyndham protesting to the Prince about his instructions to keep her pet out of the bedroom, but he closed the door before the Prince replied.

It was dark in the gardens surrounding the house and Ralf did not intend to take the risk of losing Christabelle Wyndham's dog. He had seen the house servants placing the cords which held the curtains back from the windows during the day in a cabinet at the top of the staircase which led to the hall. Finding the longest of the cords, he tied it to the small dog's collar before taking the animal into the garden.

When it seemed to him that the dog must have sniffed every inch of that section of garden, he picked it up and carried it back inside the house.

As he was about to take the animal upstairs, the door to the library opened and Sir Edward Hyde emerged, followed by a couple of titled officers of the Royalist army. He was the last person Ralf wanted to meet, but before he could escape up the stairs the Prince's governor called to him. 'Page! What are you doing with that dog? Does it not belong to Mrs Wyndham?'

'Yes, Sir Edward,' Ralf replied unhappily. 'I have just taken it for a walk in the garden.'

'But you are page to His Royal Highness. Is Mrs Wyndham with him?'

'I don't think so,' Ralf lied. 'His Royal Highness has taken a great fancy to the dog and is in the habit of having it in his room with him. I am taking it back to him now.'

Sir Edward Hyde looked at Ralf suspiciously.

72

'Are you telling me the truth? What is your name?'

'Ralf Hunkyn, Sir Edward.'

Before he could be questioned more closely, one of the other officers, who had the appearance of having drunk too much, said, 'Leave the page to go about his master's business, Edward — and what matter whether the Prince has a canine or a human bitch in his room? He has been sent to the west country by His Majesty in order to unboy him. It is a process that takes many forms.'

The other officer laughed loud and drunkenly at his companion's statement and Ralf took the opportunity to escape up the stairs with Christabelle Wyndham's dog.

★　★　★

The dog's owner left the Prince's bedroom an hour later and found Ralf seated on the chair outside the door with the dog curled up on his lap. Smiling at Ralf, she scooped up her pet, saying, 'Hesta seems to have taken a fancy to you. You are honoured — she does not take to everyone. Has she been good?'

'Yes, ma'am,' Ralf said. 'But when I came in from the garden with her we met Sir Edward Hyde. He asked what I was doing with . . . Hesta.'

'What did you say?' Christabelle asked sharply.

'I told him that His Royal Highness had become fond of her and was in the habit of sometimes having her in the bedroom with him.'

Christabelle looked at Ralf intently for a few moments, then smiled. 'You told him no untruth, which was very clever of you. What is your name?'

'Ralf, ma'am. Ralf Hunkyn.'

'I can tell by your accent that you are a Cornishman, Ralf. The Prince is fortunate to have so many of your countrymen in his employ. I shall commend you to him. Now, I bid you good night.'

Ralf watched Christabelle until she had gone out of sight, then sat down again and thought of the happenings of the night. The wife of Bridgwater's governor was a handsome woman, but she was much older than the Prince. He wondered what it was about her that Prince Charles found so attractive.

Before leaving his post and returning to his own quarters, Ralf had decided that, of the two, he preferred Hesta to her mistress.

9

It seemed to Ralf that he had been in bed for no more than minutes before he was being shaken into wakefulness by Piers. 'Wake up, Ralf . . . Wake up!'

'What is it . . . ?' Seeing who was shaking him, he said irritably, 'Go away, Piers. I'm lying in this morning. Dominic is duty page.'

'Dominic has received some bad news and has to leave the court for a while.'

Trying to shake off sleep, Ralf sat up in bed as Piers explained. 'Sir Horace Fulbrook, Dominic's father, has been wounded in a skirmish and taken prisoner by the Roundheads. It is not possible to say how serious are his wounds. Dominic has been released from duty in order to travel to Evesham, where his father was captured, to learn what he can of his father's fate. Meanwhile, the Prince is riding out of Bridgwater to meet with a delegation of Somerset clubmen. You are to go with him and take another page with you.'

The 'clubmen' were citizens who had banded together in opposition to soldiers who pillaged the country through which they passed in pursuance of the war, irrespective of their allegiance. They had initially been scorned by both sides in the civil war, but such had been the support for them in recent months that they had become a formidable force in the land and were now being wooed by Royalist and Roundhead alike.

It was Ralf's fourteenth birthday and he had been hoping to enjoy a day without duties, but he said nothing to Piers. He was a page to Prince Charles and his duty to the heir to the English throne came before all other considerations. He swung himself out of bed and began to dress.

It proved to be a long day. The clubmen went into their grievances in considerable detail and, had Prince Charles not arranged to have a private dinner with the Wyndhams, which he was determined not to miss, might have continued well into the night. As it was, Ralf was able to pass his duties to another page when the Prince had changed his clothes and been escorted to dinner.

Returning to his quarters, set up in one of the many outbuildings of the Wyndhams' house, Ralf was startled by a figure who suddenly emerged from the shadows just ahead of him. It was Brighid and she was carrying something bulky in her arms.

Holding her burden out to him, she said, 'Happy birthday, Ralf! I was beginning to think you wouldn't be back tonight.'

'It's been a very busy day,' Ralf said ruefully. 'But what's this?'

'It's a cloak. I remember how much you admired the cloak that Molly mended for

Lieutenant Muller and so I made this one specially for your birthday. I hope you'll like it.'

'You've made a cloak, for me? I'm certain I'll like it — but I didn't realise you knew today is my birthday.'

'You mentioned it a few weeks ago, and so on the days when I haven't had too much to do I've been working on it.'

Ralf was aware that Brighid was not being entirely truthful with him. The seamstresses had been kept extremely busy since their arrival in Bridgwater. She must have spent many late night hours working on his birthday gift and he was deeply touched that she had done so.

'I need to take it into the light to see it properly, Brighid.'

'Of course . . . I'll leave you to take it to your room.'

'No! I want you to be with me when I look at it.'

There was a light hanging just inside the hallway of the building where Ralf and the other royal pages shared a couple of rooms, and in the glow cast by this less than adequate illumination Ralf unfolded his birthday gift.

Dark blue in colour and made from a warm and expensive woollen material, the cloak was lined with silk of a paler blue. The collar and edges were decorated with silver thread and the fastenings were also of silver. Holding it up to the light, Ralf was more than ever convinced that many hours had gone into its making.

'I . . . I don't know what to say,' he exclaimed eventually. 'It's absolutely beautiful . . . the loveliest thing I've ever owned — or ever will, I don't doubt. Thank you, Brighid. Thank you very, very much.'

Delighted by his reaction, Brighid said, 'I'm glad you're pleased. It will prove useful to you, too. I noticed the other morning, when you rode out with the Prince, that you were the only one not wearing a cloak, even though there was a cold wind blowing. Now you have one that is as good as anyone else's.'

'It's far *better*,' Ralf declared vehemently. 'Better even than any the Prince owns. He's going to be jealous of me.'

'No he's not,' Brighid replied, 'but he might have been had I used gold thread and fastenings. That's why I chose silver. Besides, I think silver looks better with blue. The fastenings are *real* silver, too. They were taken from a cloak the King had Molly make for one of the Queen's French relatives. She sent it back to have gold fastenings put on it. I did the work and kept the silver ones. I knew I'd find a use for them one day.'

'It really is a wonderful present, Brighid. I just can't thank you enough!'

'Well . . . you could start by giving me a kiss, I suppose . . . as it's your birthday.'

Ralf had never before kissed anyone except his mother but, acting on the limited knowledge so gained, he did as Brighid suggested. It was the kiss of a happy but inexperienced fourteen-year-old.

Brighid was twenty and had spent her life with the army. Her response to his embrace quite

78

literally took his breath away and left him in a state of mild shock. She pulled him to her and he felt the urgency in her embrace . . . but did not know what to do about it. Just as his body began to respond in a manner sufficent to override inexperience a diversion came from an unexpected — and unwelcome — source.

There was the sound of raised and drunken voices calling to him from outside the building. It was Piers and two junior pages, come to collect Ralf and take him off to celebrate his birthday with them. In an instant, Brighid gave Ralf a last, quick kiss on the lips. Then, releasing him, she retreated into the shadows at the far end of the hall.

Clasped in the drunken embraces of his fellow pages and still holding the cloak Brighid had made for him, Ralf looked back seeking her as they hustled him out of the door, but she was nowhere to be seen.

He was left feeling utterly bewildered by what was an entirely new experience for him, but he was also greatly excited by the feelings Brighid had aroused in him and what they promised for the future.

10

'Charles . . . you poor darling! This has been a dreadful day for you. We have all heard about the latest defeat suffered by your army and the petty squabbles among those of your generals who ought to be uniting in your support. You poor dear, you should not have to endure such tribulations.'

The members of the Prince's council looked on in disbelief as Christabelle Wyndham swept into the chamber where they were about to go into session. Ignoring the shocked faces, Christabelle embraced the young prince and kissed him warmly.

'Really, madam, this is neither the place nor the occasion for such behaviour!' The Prince's governor expressed the disapproval of his fellow council members. He would have said far more, but he was hastily interrupted by Prince Charles.

'No matter, Sir Edward. I will take Mrs Wyndham off and speak to her. There are no matters of vital importance that need my personal attention. The meeting may proceed without me.'

As he hurried the governor's wife from the room it erupted in a hubbub of protest from the outraged members of his council. Christabelle Wyndham's affair with the young prince she had nursed as a baby was by now an open secret that certain courtiers found scandalous. Sexual liaisons involving those of royal blood were hardly unknown among the ruling families of England and Europe, but Christabelle's unprecedented lack of discretion shocked even the most broad-minded councillors.

It was also becoming a serious issue within the court. Not content with seducing the young prince, who was only just fifteen, it was known that the wife of the Bridgwater governor was pressuring her lover to grant favours and honours to her family and friends. In addition, she had been heard to criticise Sir Edward Hyde and other council members and it was believed she was also casting doubts on the manner in which the King himself was conducting the war against Parliament.

Ralf was well aware of the state of affairs. Christabelle was no more discreet when pages were present than on the latest occasion before the outraged council. Nevertheless, Ralf had learned his duties well enough to know that he should disclose nothing that occurred in the Prince's private quarters. Prince Charles expected his pages to be totally loyal to him.

Leaving the council, Ralf accompanied Charles and Christabelle to the Prince's chambers, averting his eyes when the familiarity of the governor's wife towards the Prince bordered on indecency. At the door to his room, Charles said, 'You will remain here,

Ralf. Allow no one to enter. Not even Sir Edward Hyde — *especially* not Sir Edward. Do you understand?'

'Yes, sire.'

Ralf's heart sank at the thought of standing guard outside the Prince's quarters all night — or until Christabelle Wyndham decided to rise from the bed of her youthful lover and return to her room. The situation could become extremely difficult if the angry Sir Edward Hyde decided to come to the Prince's chambers to take his young charge to task over his abrupt departure from the meeting of the Council of the West. Hyde took his duties as governor and guardian of the young prince very seriously. It was also well known that Sir Edward had a low opinion of the Bridgwater governor's wife.

It was with a feeling of great relief that Ralf was able to leave his post that night without meeting an irate Sir Edward Hyde, having seen Christabelle leave the Prince's bedroom without incident.

★　★　★

Sir Edward Hyde had declined to have a personal confrontation with the young prince over Christabelle Wyndham — but he took immediate action that was to bring the affair to an abrupt end. He wrote a letter to King Charles and despatched it to Oxford by a special messenger.

In his letter, the Prince's governor informed the King of Christabelle Wyndham's outrageous behaviour towards the Prince in public and detailed her attempts to promote the careers of her relatives and friends. He also told of her outspoken contempt of both monarch and council. Finally, he declared she was seriously undermining royal authority by making a laughing stock of Prince Charles.

The King's response was prompt and decisive. Prince Charles was to return to Bristol *immediately*. However, the monarch knew his son well enough to accept that he could be more easily led than driven. He used the advance of Parliamentarian armies into the west country as his reason, pointing out that they could achieve no greater success there than to have the heir to the throne fall into their hands.

Prince Charles obeyed his father's instruction with unusual alacrity and Ralf had the distinct impression that the Prince was as embarrassed as his court by Christabelle's increasingly outrageous familiarity. Indeed, such feelings were evident in the Prince's expression when Christabelle came from the house to bid her lover a tearful farewell.

Prince Charles had chosen to return to Bristol on horseback rather than ride in a carriage with his censorious governor. It also meant that when sitting his horse outside the Bridgwater governor's house he was beyond reach of the embrace of his outrageous mistress — but it did not prevent her from clinging to his leg until she became in very real danger of being trampled by the horses of the Prince's lifeguard. When the cavalcade set off, Christabelle continued waving until the royal party passed from view, but Prince Charles did not once look back and Ralf could not help feeling a little sorry for her.

Although it was now April, it was a cold day and Ralf was proudly wearing his birthday cloak, riding behind the Prince who was in high spirits, joking with his staff and officers — and confirming Ralf's belief that he was relieved to be free of Bridgwater and the wife of Colonel Wyndham.

At midday, the royal party stopped to eat at an inn on the Mendip hills, where an advance party had arranged for a meal to be made ready for the Prince. It was a magnificent setting with an expansive view over the surrounding Somerset countryside and the good humour of Prince Charles was still very much in evidence. When the royal household was on the move, mealtimes were very much more informal than was usual. Although the pages still served the food they were not required to kneel before their master, and Charles displayed some of the familiarity he would use towards them in private. Now he smiled at Ralf.

'That was a splendid cloak you were wearing this morning, Ralf. Indeed, it was superior to any others being worn by the court. Is it new?'

'It was a present, sire,' Ralf replied. 'Given to me only a few days ago, for my birthday.'

'By someone in the court?' The Prince was curious, knowing of Ralf's humble background and wondering who would give him such a present.

'No, sire, by an Irish seamstress. She was a

84

member of His Majesty's household, but is now serving Your Royal Highness. She made it for me.'

'A seamstress who can produce clothes of such quality as a gift for one of my pages? How old is this seamstress? Is she a motherly woman?'

'She is but twenty, sire.'

'Twenty, you say, and giving an extravagant present to a young man who is barely fourteen? There is more to you than meets the eye, my page. Nevertheless, beware of the wiles of older women, Ralf. They are likely to prove troublesome with the passing of time.'

The courtiers and senior officers dining with the Prince roared with laughter at what they realised had been a deliberate jibe at Christabelle Wyndham. Sir Edward Hyde did not laugh, but he realised, perhaps for the first time, that Prince Charles was probably far less gullible than he had believed. He would need to remember that for the future.

Addressing Ralf once more, Prince Charles said, 'You may tell your seamstress that I find your cloak most appealing. She must make one for me, but I would have it in red . . . yes, with a gold silk lining. I would also have gold fastenings and the whole stitched with gold thread.'

'She will be honoured to make such a cloak for Your Royal Highness. I will tell her to set to work as soon as we arrive in Bristol.'

Ralf was delighted that he had been given an opportunity to visit Brighid as soon as they arrived at their destination. He had grown very fond of the young Irish woman.

11

'Make a cloak like yours for the Prince? What am I supposed to use for materials? I have red cloth, that's no problem, but gold silk lining . . . and real gold fastenings? Do you realise the cost of such things?'

'I know it won't be easy, Brighid, but it was a command from His Royal Highness, and I promised him you'd make a start as soon as we arrived here in Bristol and were settled in.'

'I'd rather you didn't make such promises on my behalf,' Brighid said angrily, 'especially when I have no way of keeping them.'

'I'm sorry,' Ralf replied miserably. 'I do understand . . . but I don't know how I'm going to tell the Prince. He admired the cloak you made for me so much . . . '

'Well . . . you don't have to tell him right away. See what you can do about obtaining silk for the lining and gold for the fastenings and I'll probably be able to find gold thread — just this once.'

Ralf had asked her to carry out the impossible, but Brighid felt sorry for him. It was not his fault that times were so difficult, or that despite the events of recent years neither the King, his queen, nor the royal princes and princesses had yet learned to accept that they could not have everything they wanted.

★ ★ ★

'It's your own fault for attracting the attentions of such a generous young woman,' Piers joked, when Ralf told him of his predicament. However, aware that Ralf was genuinely concerned, he went on, 'Before we left Oxford, the King had seven hundred pounds allocated to Master Kirton, Gentleman of the Robes to the Prince. I fancy little has been forthcoming from him. I will speak to Sir Edward Hyde about it.' He smiled at Ralf. 'Sir Edward would be failing in his duty were people to suggest that a page of the court was wearing a finer cloak than the future king of England.'

Much to Ralf's relief, Piers was able to persuade the Prince's governor of the need for Prince Charles to outshine his page in sartorial elegance. Ralf hurried to the seamstresses' room and, opening the small pouch he carried, poured fifty golden coins on the table in front of Brighid.

Unable to hide the pride he felt, he declared, 'Here. This is for the cloak that His Royal Highness wants you to make for him.'

If Brighid was impressed by the sight of the coins, she was determined not to show it. 'Is this for everything? Cloth, lining — and fastening of pure gold?'

'No,' Ralf replied triumphantly. 'It's just for the cloak and lining, and any other expenses you might incur on the Prince's behalf. Some gold plate was among the 'donations' recently collected for the royal cause. Enough has been given to a Bristol jeweller to make all the fastenings and decorations that will be needed. I have left my own cloak with the jeweller for a while so he can copy the fastenings in gold.'

Brighid was silent for a few moments, before saying in a less belligerent manner than before, 'Thank you, Ralf. I . . . I'm sorry I got cross with you.'

'It's not important,' Ralf replied magnanimously. 'You had every right to be cross. You're very busy, and I had no right to put more work on you.'

'Nevertheless, we both work for the Prince, but if he is unhappy with anything I do it's left to someone else to tell me. It's different for you. You're much closer to him. Anyway, I wasn't really angry with you. It's just that the girls I'm having to work with here are not up to the standard of a royal court.'

'I told you, it doesn't matter. Now, I'm not on duty this evening. Would you like to come for a walk down by the river with me?'

'I have no time for walks if I am to finish a cloak for the Prince.'

Ralf's expression showed his disappointment, and Brighid relented — as she had always intended. 'Oh, all right then. It looks like being a fine evening and I couldn't have begun the cloak tonight anyway. I have to gather all the materials first. I would enjoy a walk away from everything for a while.'

When Brighid met Ralf on the riverside path her greeting was decidedly professional. Looking at his Sunday-best farm garb, she said, 'You've grown since joining the Prince's household, Ralf. You'd better let me have your clothes some time and I'll see if I can let them out for you.'

'Thank you.' Shyly, he added, 'I don't know what I would have done had I not met you, Brighid. Right from the very first day I became a page you've made my work very much easier than it might otherwise have been.'

Pleased by his praise, Brighid said, 'I'm glad, but I don't doubt that your life is very much easier now that Dominic Fulbrook has left.'

Looking at her, Ralf wondered how much she knew about the differences there had been between him and Dominic, but instead of agreeing with her he said, 'I feel very sorry for him. Having his father wounded and a prisoner of the Roundheads must be a great worry.'

'Soldiers know the chances they take in battle,' she said sharply. 'But don't let's talk about him. We haven't spent any time by ourselves since your birthday — and I seem to remember we were disturbed then . . . '

'That's right . . . we were.'

In her company, Ralf found it embarrassing to think about what they had been doing when they were interrupted. Brighid was aware of his embarrassment, but made no comment.

They walked slowly along beside the river, chatting ever more easily together, before climbing the hill behind Brandon fort, which guarded this section of the city's defences. They remained on the hill until the sun sank low in the western sky, plunging the narrow streets of the city into deep shadow.

'I think it's time we were returning,' Ralf said reluctantly. He felt very much at ease in Brighid's company.

'I suppose it is,' Brighid agreed, with a readiness that Ralf found disappointing.

Leaving the heights of Brandon Hill behind, they walked back to the heart of Bristol. Ralf was staying in the 'Great House', where the Prince had his chambers. The seamstresses were billeted nearby.

As they approached the Great House, Brighid said, 'Thanks to the money you gave me I was able to buy some very nice gold silk to line the Prince's cloak. It was very expensive, so before I cut it I'd like you to look at it and tell me whether you think it's suitable.'

'I'm quite certain it will be, if you think so,' Ralf said, 'and I don't know when I'll be able to inspect it. I'm on duty with the Prince all day tomorrow and we're out of the city the day after.'

'Then why not come and look at it now?' Brighid suggested. 'I have the key to the seamstresses' workshop.'

'I have no doubt the lining will be perfect,' Ralf declared. 'But I'll come and look at it, if that's what you want.'

At the workshop, Brighid produced a key and, inserting it in the lock, turned it and swung the door open. It was dark inside, but Brighid found a candle stub and lit it before drawing the curtains at the single window.

The inside of the workshop gave every indication that the women who worked here had abandoned the large room at the end of a very busy working day, dumping their various tasks where they sat. There were cuttings of cloth and half-completed garments strewn all over the tables and the floor.

Securing the candle in a holder, Brighid picked her way through the clutter and led Ralf to a small room at the rear of the workshop area. Here, he was surprised to see a bed made up on the floor and a quantity of material neatly folded upon a nearby table. Picking up the bundle, which glistened in the candlelight, Brighid said, 'This is it. This is the silk I have been able to get to line the Prince's cloak. Do you think he will approve?'

Fingering the sumptuous fabric gently, Ralf replied, 'It's beautiful. The Prince can't fail to be delighted. I think you are very clever to have found it.'

'Good! I'll start work on it tomorrow morning. It should be ready by the time the goldsmith has completed the fastenings.'

There seemed to be nothing more to say on the subject and, after a few moments' awkward silence, Ralf indicated the made-up bed on the floor. Vaguely embarrassed, he asked, 'Are you sleeping here?'

'Yes. The seamstresses have been given just one room for all of us, so I thought I would stay here. Apart from being more comfortable it means I can look after the workshop and all our things. Bristol has more than its share of villains.'

'Aren't you frightened being here on your own at night?' Ralf asked.

'Not really,' Brighid replied. Then she added, 'Mind you, there are times when it does feel lonely.'

There had been little opportunity in Ralf's life at the farm to gain experience with women, but he was not stupid. He had already realised that Brighid had not brought him here merely to approve of the material she had bought for the cloak she was making for Prince Charles. Nevertheless, he kept up the pretence.

'Surely one of the other seamstresses would stay here with you if you asked them?'

'They might,' Brighid agreed, 'but I have no intention of asking any of them. If one of them was here now can you imagine the scandal there would be about me bringing one of the Prince's pages in at this time of night? As it is, no one but you and me need ever know — and there will be none of your drunken friends to interrupt us.'

His mouth suddenly dry, all Ralf succeeded in uttering was a strangled, 'N-no!'

'You do like me, Ralf . . . as much as I like you?'

'I like you more than anyone I've ever known,' he replied truthfully.

Brighid gave him a delighted smile. 'I'm glad, Ralf. Very glad. I really am.'

Moving towards him she put her arms about him and kissed him and he felt his body reacting to her closeness.

Pulling her head back, but still holding him tightly, she said, 'You've never made love before, have you, Ralf?'

'No.'

He was afraid his truthful reply might earn him her scorn. Instead, she said nothing. Taking his hand, she turned to one side and blew out the candle. Then, his hand gripped firmly in hers, she led him to the bed in the corner of the workroom . . .

12

'Are you all right, Ralf? You look very tired. Not that I'm surprised — I heard you come in this morning, it must have been close to dawn. Did you spend the night partying with some Cornish friends?' Piers and Ralf were in the quarters they shared with the other pages, dressing ready to perform their duty with the Prince.

'I had very little sleep,' Ralf admitted, not wishing to tell an outright lie to his friend.

'Well, it should be a fairly quiet day,' Piers said. 'Prince Rupert has arrived to consult with the Prince and the council before he leaves for Oxford. They should be in secret session for most of the morning, at least. All that will be required of you is to sit outside the council chamber and ensure food is available for the Prince when the session comes to an end.'

It sounded as though Ralf would enjoy a quiet day, but all did not go as anticipated. The council had been in session for no more than two hours when messengers began arriving from various generals. Without consulting the Prince, or the Council of the West, King Charles had reorganised the western army. General Goring, a notorious drunkard, had been placed in overall charge — and the remaining western commanders were dismayed. Some protested to the Prince about the appointment, others threatened to resign. One of the strongest protests came from Sir Richard Grenville, who had been made second-in-command to Goring. The two men hated each other and now Grenville was threatening to withdraw his Cornish units from Goring's command and march them back to Cornwall.

To complicate matters further, messengers arrived from yet another of the Prince's generals, Lord Hopton, a very capable commander. Unaware that he had just been demoted to general of artillery, Hopton informed the Prince that he was engaged in fighting off a Roundhead army which appeared to be heading westward. Ralf soon found himself running between messengers and the council with commands and countermands until he was forced to call upon other pages to help.

This was to be the pattern of the ensuing week, during which time Ralf succeeded in spending only one more night with Brighid in the seamstresses' room. Then King Charles, under pressure from his advisers, changed his mind once again. Hopton replaced Goring as overall commander and the outgoing general was ordered to join the King in the Midlands, taking with him as many men as could be spared from the west.

Peeved at being, to all intents and purposes, demoted, Goring did not obey the King's orders. But even more serious matters quickly arose to divert the attentions of the Council of the West from the waywardness of their disgruntled general.

On a routine visit to the seamstresses' workshop, Ralf found the women there in a state of great agitation, and asked Brighid the reason.

'There's been an outbreak of the plague, down by Frome Gate,' she replied. 'One of the seamstresses we took on comes from there. We've sent her home, but we're all worried. It's a bad outbreak, by all accounts. A lot of the merchant ships are leaving the port. Their seamen say they'd rather be taken by Roundhead ships than stricken with the plague.'

Ralf was alarmed. The plague was something that was feared wherever it occurred. In Bristol, overcrowded as it currently was with the army and the Prince's court and council, it was a terrifying prospect.

'I've heard nothing about this at the court,' he said to Brighid. 'I'll go back there now and speak to Sir Edward Hyde. He'll no doubt want to do something about it.'

Sir Edward Hyde took action immediately. That same afternoon the Prince and his courtiers were riding out of Bristol, en route for Barnstaple, leaving the remainder of the royal household to follow — with an escort commanded by Lieutenant Hugo Muller.

When Ralf learned who was to be in charge of the escort he hurried off to warn Brighid. He found the seamstresses' workshop in a state of chaos. They had a great deal of unfinished work to pack and take with them. When Ralf asked

Brighid whether she was going to be all right, she replied testily, 'How should I know? Everyone is ordering us about and telling us to hurry and have things packed, but no one has told us where we will be going, or how long it will take us to get there.'

'We're heading for Barnstaple, a small seaport in north Devon. It will take the Prince's court about three days to get there but with your wagons and everything you'll no doubt be on the road for some eight or ten days. I came to warn you that your escort will be under the command of Lieutenant Muller. I thought you ought to know.'

Brighid was momentarily alarmed, but then she shrugged, 'He'll be far too busy to notice me. Even if he does he was probably too drunk when we met in Oxford to remember what happened then.'

'I hope so,' Ralf said. Hesitantly, he added, 'I'm going to miss you, Brighid.'

She was pleased, but would not show it. 'Away with you. I doubt if you'll even think of me — unless you have a button or two come loose.'

'That's not true,' Ralf said unhappily. 'I think of you a lot, and will until we meet up again.'

'Good! I'll no doubt be thinking of you too.' Suddenly brisk, she said, 'But I have a great many things to do if we're to get on the road at all. I'll see you in this 'Barnstaple' — if the Roundheads don't find us first.'

She turned away then, and began berating one of the younger seamstresses for the haphazard manner in which she was folding an unfinished garment.

Ralf left the workshop feeling vaguely unhappy. He suspected that Brighid would not miss him as much as he would miss her. He tried to tell himself she could not possibly have expressed her true feelings in front of all the other seamstresses, but did not quite succeed.

★   ★   ★

'You've been very quiet for the past half-hour, Ralf. Are you missing that little Irish seamstress of yours?' Piers's question was accompanied by a knowing smile.

The two pages were riding with the Prince and his lifeguard between Exeter and Tavistock. Although the court was officially based at Barnstaple they had spent very little time there in recent weeks. In fact, Ralf had not been to the seaport since the arrival of Brighid and the other servants of the royal household and he was not to see her again for another few weeks. He was about to deny that he had been thinking about her, but changed his mind. 'How do you know I've had anything to do with her?' he countered.

'You've been a page long enough to know you can't keep anything secret within the court, Ralf.'

'You mean . . . it's known by everybody?' Ralf was startled, even though he knew Piers was right. The court thrived upon gossip.

'The Prince is aware of it and most of the others know there is something going on

98

between the two of you. Not that it matters very much — just as long as things don't become too serious. She's a pretty little thing and good-natured, but she's Irish, Catholic — and a servant in the Prince's household. You are a member of his court.'

Ralf felt resentment but realised that his friend was giving him a gentle warning. If he revealed his true feelings for Brighid they could both be dismissed. It would be disastrous for her, and although he was still young he was aware of the effect it would have on his mother and stepfather — and it mattered to him. 'I'll try to be discreet,' he said.

'I never doubted it,' Piers said. 'But whatever you do don't upset the girl. I am quite jealous of the cloaks owned by the Prince and yourself. I would like one for myself as soon as things are more settled.'

★　★　★

The conversation had taken place soon after Piers had returned from an errand to Cornwall to speak to Sir Richard Grenville, who seemed to be the only man capable of holding the Cornishmen together. They formed an indispensable nucleus of the western army particularly since several detachments of that army had been sent to bolster the King's forces in the Midlands — but had deserted in droves after their leader was wounded and temporarily replaced by Lord Goring, who had never made any secret of his contempt for Cornishmen. It had been hoped that Piers might be able to cajole Sir Richard into persuading the Cornish soldiers to remain with the Royalist army and fight under the banner of the Prince in his capacity as Duke of Cornwall. His mission was successful but the compliance of Piers's kinsman would prove to be of a temporary nature.

13

When the court returned to Barnstaple, Ralf learned that the royal household had taken over a tailor's shop in the heart of the small town for the seamstresses and it was here he could expect to find Brighid.

He was eager to see her again but Piers had been sent on another errand to his kinsman who, although still suffering from his wound, had rejoined the army at Taunton to take command of the Cornishmen once more. As a result, the remaining pages were required to work longer hours than was normal and it was late that night before he was finally able to get away from his duties. He thought that in view of the arrangement that had proved so successful for Brighid in Bristol, he might find her sleeping once more in her workplace.

He was approaching the tailor's shop in the darkness when he thought he saw a Royalist officer coming along the street towards him. When the man passed by the lighted window of a noisy inn, Ralf was startled to recognise Lieutenant Muller. Having no wish to meet him face to face, he hurriedly crossed the road and sought the shadows of a deep doorway, intending to remain there until the Royalist officer passed by.

However, Muller stopped at the entrance to the tailor's shop and tried the door. It seemed to be secured, but as Ralf watched, the officer rapped on it with his knuckles. Moments later the door was opened, Muller entered and it was closed behind him.

Not wishing to believe it could have been Brighid who opened the door to Muller, Ralf hurried to the shop, his intention being to peer in through the window, but he found a curtain drawn across it. There was a very dim light behind the curtain, as though a single candle was burning inside the shop. For a reckless moment, Ralf considered knocking on the door which had no doubt been secured on the inside . . . but he stopped short with his fist raised. The only possible outcome of such an action would be that he would make a fool of himself. Besides, he could not be absolutely certain the woman who had opened the door to Muller was Brighid. Even if it was, he had no claim on her, and no right to question her actions.

Ralf walked around the quiet streets for more than an hour before eventually returning to the temporary quarters occupied by the court. He was not only confused, but unhappier than at any time since he had left the farm at Trecarne to enter the Prince's service.

When he reached the annexe where the pages were housed he found the courtyard crowded with men and horses. There seemed to be as much activity in the main house itself, so, after

102

hastily donning his page's uniform, Ralf hurried to the Prince's chambers. Here he met a travel-weary Piers, who told him he had been with Sir Richard Grenville at Taunton when a troop of cavalry had arrived en route to Barnstaple from the Midlands carrying news that the King and his army had suffered a disastrous defeat at the hands of Fairfax and his commanders, Cromwell and Ireton. Both Grenvilles had hurried to Barnstaple with the messengers bearing news of the defeat.

The battle had taken place at Naseby, between Leicester and Northampton, and it was being said that the indiscipline of the cavalry led by Prince Rupert had played a great part in the King's defeat. After slashing their way through a regiment of Roundhead horse they should have taken advantage of their success and turned on the enemy infantry. Had they done so they would most probably have won the day. Instead, they pursued the defeated enemy cavalry until they met the Parliamentary baggage train.

It was too good an opportunity to be missed, and Rupert's men began looting. By so doing they gave the advantage back to Fairfax and his army who, after some very hard fighting, carried the day.

Much of the Royalist cavalry had survived the battle, but virtually the whole of the King's infantry was either killed or captured. Charles fled the field leaving behind him a shattered army — and perhaps the last chance he would have of regaining his throne.

'What exactly does it mean?' Ralf asked a

weary Piers, who was not yet ready to take to his bed.

'It can best be summed up in the words of Sir Edward Hyde,' Piers replied. 'He told the Prince that His Majesty's cause is in tatters. We lost a thousand men killed, and four times that number were taken prisoner. Sadly, Parliament's army grows stronger with every passing day, while ours grows weaker. Our cause is being ripped apart by commanders whose loyalty to His Majesty takes second place to their pride and desire for self-aggrandisement.'

'Was Sir Richard present when Sir Edward said that?' Ralf asked. He was aware from his presence at numerous council meetings that Sir Edward was bitterly opposed to Sir Richard Grenville. He believed the Cornish commander was manipulating the men of the Cornish army for his own ends.

Piers nodded. 'He was furious, but it was not the moment to take Sir Edward to task. He had made no reply by the time I was sent away to summon the members of the council — but he will.'

A sudden thought struck Ralf. 'Was Lieutenant Muller one of the cavalrymen who came with news of the battle?' He had remembered that the Palatine soldier had been one of those sent from the western army to join the King.

'Yes. We travelled here from Taunton with him.' Piers replied, too weary to ask why Ralf was interested in the officer.

Ralf realised he might have misinterpreted what he had seen at the tailor's shop in the town centre. Brighid's father and stepmother were with the King's army at Oxford. If Muller was aware of this it could be that he had been visiting her with news of them . . . *bad* news.

★　★　★

The council meeting lasted for most of the night, with messengers being constantly despatched with orders for various Royalist strongholds and garrisons throughout the west country. Ralf remained on duty all night, but when he was relieved in the morning he went not to his quarters, but to the shop occupied by the seamstresses.

It was early, but there were already three seamstresses hard at work. Brighid, dry-eyed but taut-faced, was one of them. Her expression when she saw Ralf lacked the warmth he had been hoping for, but it would be quite understandable if she had received bad news.

She greeted him with, 'Oh, so you've decided to come to see me at long last, have you? I thought perhaps you'd forgotten I existed.' There was none of the discretion she had shown in Bristol when other seamstresses were within hearing.

'I wouldn't do that, Brighid,' he said, aware that the other girls were careful not to look up at him. 'I've been with the Prince all over the west country. We only got back yesterday and I didn't finish my duties until well after dark. Even then, I came looking for you. I came here . . . but a certain officer was here before me.'

'You saw Hugo Muller come here?'

He could not be certain whether her expression was one of surprise, or dismay — and he did not miss the fact that she spoke of the officer using his Christian name and not his rank.

'Yes. I couldn't imagine what business he had here at that time of night, but when I heard what had happened at Naseby I remembered that your father was with the King's infantry and thought that Lieutenant Muller might have come with some news of him.'

'Yes . . . that's right . . . that's why he came to see me. Why else did you think it would be?' Brighid glanced hastily at the two other girls, but neither of them looked up from their work.

'I didn't think anything,' he lied. 'What news did he bring? Is your father safe . . . and what about Molly?'

'Probably dead — both of them,' Brighid replied unemotionally. 'Hugo didn't actually see them killed, but one of the infantry officers who was captured managed to escape, and Hugo spoke to him. He said the Roundheads showed no quarter to the Irish regiment and killed every man they took. Then they rounded up all the women with the baggage train and slaughtered the Irish women too — and a few of the others.'

'Surely not?' Ralf was aghast at what Brighid had told him. 'Perhaps the officer was just listening to rumours. Even Roundheads wouldn't do that.'

'There was no mistake.' Brighid said, showing her bitterness for the first time. 'More men have

106

arrived since to confirm what was said. It doesn't come as any surprise. We were told long ago what our fate would be should we be captured by Roundheads. They hate us, both as Irish and as good Catholics.'

'I'm sorry, Brighid, I really am. What will you do now?' Ralf was deeply upset for her.

'What do you mean, what will I do? I'll do the same as I'm doing now and have been doing for more years than I care to remember. There's nothing else for me. Nowhere else to go.'

Ralf believed Brighid was keeping a tight rein on her feelings and he admired her for it. Dropping his voice, he said, 'Can I see you tonight, Brighid? I'd like to . . . very much.'

'And I'd like to have the time to do something other than sewing,' Brighid replied, stonily, 'but I don't. I have work enough to keep me busy for a couple of weeks even if nothing new comes in, so, if you don't mind, I'll get on with it. I'll no doubt see you again when the Prince wears out the seat of another pair of breeches gallivanting around the countryside.'

Ralf felt he had been summarily dismissed. After hesitating for a few moments, he turned and left the Barnstaple shop. Behind him, a tear fell upon the doublet Brighid was stitching and she rubbed her eyes angrily.

14

Their defeat at Naseby was a greater disaster than most Royalists realised. Not only were the dejected prisoners of the King's army paraded through the streets of London, jeered by their fellow countrymen, but the Roundheads had reaped an unexpected reward when they took the King's baggage train.

With it they captured the correspondence of King Charles and his council. It revealed that he had been appealing to Irish and French Catholics, as well as Scottish Presbyterians to help him in his fight against Parliament, and was quite prepared to promise anything to anyone likely to come to his aid.

Parliament gleefully made the revelations public as an example of the lengths to which King Charles was prepared to go in order to cling to his throne. Even to the extent of handing the Church back to the Pope — or whoever was prepared to make the highest bid on his behalf.

The defeat and its consequences cast a pall of gloom over the court of Prince Charles. Certain courtiers now seriously, albeit secretly, debated the increasing possibility that the royal cause was doomed, with all that would mean for them, their families and their estates. Indeed, a few, who had homes in the path of the advancing Parliamentary armies, decided they would not leave matters until it was too late. Resigning their posts at court, they hurried home, hoping they would be in time to enter into negotiations with the Roundheads to protect their properties.

Among those who took this course was the secretary to the Prince's council. It was an important post that needed to be filled immediately by someone the Prince felt he could trust implicitly. He appointed Piers Grenville.

Piers had been a page for far longer than was usual, and although it had never been in doubt that he would remain a member of the Prince's court it came as a surprise that he should be appointed to such an important post.

Piers gave Ralf the news on the evening of his appointment, adding cheerfully, 'I am to take over my new duties with immediate effect, Ralf, but there is nothing for you to be concerned about. It is a position of considerable influence and I have already been able to make use of it on your behalf. I have recommended that you be made the Prince's senior page — and it has been agreed.'

Ralf was taken aback by his newly acquired responsibility. He had been a page for a year now — but there were others who had been longer in royal service and he pointed this out to his friend.

'That does not matter, Ralf. There is only one of the Prince's pages who is your senior and he has made it clear that he intends leaving because the Roundheads are nearing his home in the north. Besides, the Prince has a high regard for your proven loyalty and the manner in which you carry out your duties.'

Still uncertain, Ralf said, 'But what if Dominic should return? He would never accept my authority over him.'

'We will worry about that when, or if, it happens. In the meantime you are going to be short of pages and will need to make out new duty lists. If you have any problems bring them to me. After all, there is no point having friends in high places if you don't make use of them!'

Piers was delighted with his new status, but Ralf was left uncertain about his ability to cope with his own increased responsibility.

* * *

When Ralf had time to return Piers's page's uniform to the seamstresses he discovered that Brighid was aware of his promotion.

'I suppose we'll be seeing less of you now that you're the senior page,' she said, as she took the uniform from him and began folding it carefully.

'If you do it will be because that's what you want, Brighid. I've asked you more than once to meet me when you're off duty. Each time you've made excuses for not coming.'

There was only the slightest hint of embarrassment in Brighid's reply when she said, 'Now you're in charge of others you'll find that, like me, you have very little spare time on your hands. Besides, the Prince and his court are so short of money that unless things improve they'll all be wearing patchwork clothes. As it is we're working our fingers to the bone trying to keep them together.'

'Is that the true reason for not meeting me, Brighid, or is there something else? I really thought you enjoyed being with me when we were in Bristol.'

'Yes, I did, and if I wasn't so busy I probably still would . . . even though things have changed.'

'What things have changed?' Ralf asked. 'Certainly not the way I feel about you.'

Although Ralf and Brighid were talking quietly together, one of the seamstresses was working nearby and was quite clearly listening in to their conversation. Aware of this, Brighid said pointedly, 'Let's go outside for a few moments. There are too many ears in here.'

Leaving the seamstresses' shop and closing the door behind them, Brighid said, 'You're right, Ralf. We *have* enjoyed each other's company, but I no longer have my father or Molly to fall back on should things go wrong in my life. I'm alone in the world now and need to think of my future, especially with things going so badly for the King. If he lost the war the Roundheads would treat me the same as they did Molly. I need to have a way to save my skin — and I can't see a page being able to do that for me.'

Taken aback by her bluntness, Ralf said, 'Even if the King were to surrender to Parliament — and there's very little possibility of that happening — even if he did, he would make certain Prince Charles was out of the country first, and his court would go with him.'

'Of course they would, and you are part of that court. I'm not. I'm just a servant in the Prince's household. An *Irish* seamstress. No one is likely to care what happens to me.'

'You're wrong, Brighid. *I* care and I wouldn't let anything happen to you.'

Brighid gave him a wan smile. 'You're sweet, Ralf, and I *am* fond of you, but your first duty is to the Prince. You wouldn't be able to take care of me too if the Roundhead army attacked us. I'd be captured and killed.'

'I'd find some way to get you to safety,' Ralf persisted. 'If things became desperate I could take you to our farm. My ma and pa would look after you there.' He was clutching at straws, and they both knew it.

Brighid shook her head. 'That would be putting them and their farm at risk. No, Ralf, I must make my own plans — and I am. I'll take care of myself. It's something I've grown used to over the years . . . but now I must go back inside. There's work to be done.'

She turned away from him, but before she entered the shop he said, 'Is Lieutenant Muller included in your plans, Brighid?' It came out on the spur of the moment and he did not even know why he said it, but it caused Brighid to turn back and her startled expression told him more than her words.

'I think it better that you know nothing of my

112

plans, Ralf — or who is involved in them. Goodbye.'

It sounded final, but Ralf determined that should the worst happen and the army of the Prince be overwhelmed, he would do his best to ensure that no harm came to Brighid.

15

The victory gained by their army over the King at Naseby had put new heart into the Parliamentary leaders. They now firmly believed not only that they possessed a superior army, but that God was on their side. As a result they were content to leave their Scots allies to deal with the remaining Royalist armies in the north of England and sent Fairfax and Cromwell to the south-west of the country to tackle the army of Prince Charles.

Their tactics were sound and before long the war was going from bad to worse for the Royalists. In a battle he should have won, Lord Goring was soundly defeated at Langport, in Somerset, and in the same month Bridgwater fell to the Roundheads, Christabelle Wyndham only just evading capture by the enemy. The town was a Royal arsenal and its loss was yet another disaster for King Charles.

Worse was to follow. Prince Rupert had promised that, come what may, he would hold Bristol for the King, yet, after a fierce but short battle, he surrendered the important port to Fairfax in order to lessen the suffering of the inhabitants. King Charles was furious at what he considered to be a lack of determination on Rupert's part and promptly relieved him of all commands.

Rupert protested in vain against such treatment. Not long before the assault on the city he had sent a carefully considered assessment of the Royalist position to his uncle. In it he had suggested that the only sensible course open to the beleaguered monarch was to surrender if favourable terms could be negotiated with Parliament. The letter still rankled with Charles. He believed such negative thinking might have had some bearing on Rupert's decision to surrender Bristol to Fairfax.

The following month it was Goring's turn to earn the wrath of the King and Prince Charles. As Fairfax advanced ever further westward, Goring promised he and his men would hold Exeter against the Roundheads. Within a fortnight, the erratic general had changed his mind and abandoned Exeter without a fight.

★ ★ ★

By the end of 1645, Prince Charles had retreated into Cornwall with his court and household, leaving his army to take up defensive positions on the banks of the River Tamar. For all except a few miles beyond its source in the north, the river formed a natural border with the remainder of England and was likely to be fiercely defended by the well-proven Cornish soldiers of the royal army.

Despite this, King Charles was deeply

concerned by the possibility of Fairfax and his Parliamentary army forcing the Cornish defences and capturing his son and heir. He wrote a letter to the Prince urging him to go to France.

The letter was discussed at a meeting of the council, at which Ralf was in attendance upon the Prince — and Sir Edward Hyde was vehemently opposed to his charge leaving the country. After an argument which went on for much of the morning, he addressed the Prince and council in uncompromising terms. 'If the heir to the throne flees the land it will be seen by the people as an unequivocal sign that the King's cause is lost. Furthermore, if he seeks the sanctuary of a Catholic country, those who oppose the monarchy will point to it as proof that His Majesty is a secret Catholic whose intentions have always been to have both throne and Church pay allegiance to the Pope.'

Turning to the Prince, Sir Edward declared, 'Your Royal Highness knows better than anyone that I would never suggest that you should refuse to obey an express command of His Majesty, but I beg you to support me — and, I trust, the whole of your council — in pointing out the grave dangers inherent in such a course of action.'

Seemingly exasperated by yet another of Sir Edward's speeches opposing the King's policy, the Prince said, 'My interpretation of His Majesty's letter is that he is urging me to avoid falling into the hands of Parliament at all costs and suggesting France as a possible haven. Tell me, where do you and my council suggest as a suitable alternative?'

There was an immediate babble of discordant voices from the assembled councillors, as Prince Charles had known there would be, each of the various members airing his own strongly held views on where it was best for the Prince to go for safe-keeping and at the same time to raise sufficient money to support an army strong enough to fight that of Parliament. The Scottish Highlands, Ireland, Wales, Holland, Denmark, the Channel Islands . . . each had its champions.

Eventually, rising to his feet, thereby causing the members of the council to follow suit, Prince Charles said, 'There would appear to be a difference of opinion within my council. I will leave you to discuss the matter. Inform me in due course of your conclusions.'

As Ralf hurried to the door of the chamber to open it for the Prince, Sir Edward Hyde frowned thoughtfully after the departing heir to the throne. He had no doubt at all that Charles had thrown the question open for debate, aware that the council would be totally unable to agree on a suitable destination. It had been a ploy to enable him to depart and pursue his own interests.

Sir Edward realised, not for the first time, that Prince Charles was quite capable of outwitting his councillors when it suited him to do so. He knew that, as the Prince's governor, it was likely to pose problems for him in the future.

Walking with Ralf towards his own quarters, Prince Charles said, 'The council will never reach agreement on where I should go if I need to leave the country. I am not at all certain

117

myself. Do you have any thoughts on the subject, Ralf?'

It was not at all unusual for the Prince to seek the opinions of his more trusted pages on a wide variety of subjects, though he seldom acted upon any advice that was forthcoming.

'I know very little about any of the places being suggested, sire,' Ralf replied honestly. 'But I do know the people of Cornwall. They would willingly give their lives in defence of Your Royal Highness should you decide to remain here.'

'I would like to think so, Ralf, but I fear my Lord Goring holds my Cornish subjects in less esteem than we do ourselves. He and his soldiers have treated them shamefully and lost much sympathy for our cause. Although I have tried to keep his army occupied elsewhere whenever possible, many of your fellow Cornishmen would as soon have a Parliamentary army occupying their land as my own. Indeed, even Sir Richard Grenville, whose family name embodies all that is honourable in Cornwall, is trying the people with the severity of his conduct here.'

'The people may resent individual commanders, sire, but you are their duke — the Duke of Cornwall. They love you as they do His Majesty.'

The young prince smiled sadly as he said, 'I trust you are right, Ralf. We shall surely learn the truth of it before many more weeks have passed.'

* * *

As Fairfax and his formidable army moved ever closer to Cornwall, the need for Prince Charles to make plans to take refuge out of the country grew urgent. France was no longer the subject of discussion by the Council of the West. The King had undergone a change of mind, even though the Prince's mother was there. He now felt Denmark might be a more suitable refuge for the heir to the throne.

With the area in the west country under Royalist control steadily diminishing, Prince Charles was spending a great deal of time travelling around Cornwall, rallying flagging support for the King's cause. When the court moved to Boconnoc, the Prince, remembering it was here that Ralf had joined the royal entourage, suggested his page might like to spend a few days with his parents.

'I will be remaining at Boconnoc for a while. How long is it since you last saw them?'

'I have not seen them since leaving the farm to become your page, sire. More than a year.'

'So long? Then you must visit them. I wish you were able to boast to them of our victories — but, as I recall, your father was a soldier, so will understand that in war battles are lost as well as won. Nevertheless, we fight in a just cause. The final victory will be ours.'

16

Ralf's excitement at returning home increased when the small cluster of buildings that composed Trecarne farm came into view. He needed to restrain an urge to put his horse to a gallop and effect a melodramatic homecoming. Instead, he chose to approach the farm so quietly that he succeeded in entering the farmyard without being observed and was dismounting from his horse before his mother appeared in the doorway of the farmhouse.

The winter morning sun was behind Ralf, shining in Grace's eyes, and it was a few moments before she realised who he was. Then, with a shrill shriek of delight, she ran across the farmyard, threw her arms about him, and promptly burst into tears.

Hugging her, he said soothingly, 'It's all right, Ma. There's no need to cry. I've come home to stay for a couple of days while the Prince is at Boconnoc.'

'I'm sorry, Ralf, I can't help it . . . it's such a surprise. A wonderful surprise.'

Behind her, Joseph Moyle appeared in the farmhouse doorway, wiping away the crumbs of a late breakfast from his lips. His face broke into a delighted smile when he saw who it was, but Ralf thought his stepfather looked older and more fragile than when he had last seen him.

'It's our Ralf,' Grace said unnecessarily, 'and just look at him! He's shot up like a beanstalk — and such clothes! You'd think it was a fine young gentleman come visiting us.'

'It is,' Joseph replied proudly as he reached out to shake Ralf's hand and grasp his arm affectionately. 'He's one of Prince Charles's courtiers, and I must say he looks the part.' Peering over Ralf's shoulder, he added, 'And that's a fine horse you have there, son. We don't see many like it in this part of Cornwall.' The animal had been captured from a Parliamentary officer in one of the rare skirmishes in which Royalists had emerged as victors.

'Never mind his horse,' Grace said happily. 'Come inside the house and sit yourself down, Ralf. Have you eaten? I've just cooked for Joseph and there's plenty for you. You'll have a million things to tell us, but it can wait until you've got something in your belly.'

Entering the farmhouse kitchen, Ralf thought how much smaller it appeared than he remembered. In fact, everything seemed reduced in size: farmhouse; yard; outbuildings; fields. Even Joseph. The only thing not smaller was his mother. She was, if anything, plumper than when he had gone away.

Breakfast was quickly cooked and placed upon

the kitchen table before Ralf. There was so much to talk about and so many questions asked about his life in the Prince's service that it seemed no time at all before Grace announced it was time she began preparing the noonday meal. Joseph said he needed to go to the cave on the cliff side where one of his cows was expected to calve at any time, and Ralf said he would accompany him.

Along the way, Ralf expressed surprise that Joseph still found it necessary to hide the farm animals, adding that there could not have been any Roundheads in the area since the defeat of Lord Essex at the time when Ralf had left home.

Grimly, Joseph said, 'We've had no Roundheads, but when Goring's cavalry were roaming the countryside they were worse than any soldiers of Parliament. I lost all our pigs and a half-dozen sheep that I was slow in hiding away. Not only that, but had I protested any more than I did I'd have lost my life too.'

Ralf was shocked, even though he was aware of the Royalist general's contempt for all things Cornish. However, Goring had recently resigned his command and fled to the Continent and Ralf gave this news to his stepfather, adding, 'I doubt if you'll see any of his cavalry hereabouts again. Sir Richard Grenville has given orders to the men under his command that they are to be kept east of the Tamar.'

Surprised, Joseph asked, 'Is Sir Richard commanding the Prince's army now?'

'No. Lord Hopton has been brought out of retirement to take over, but Sir Richard still leads the Cornish army. They refuse to take orders from anyone else. It's causing a great deal of concern to the Prince and his council.'

'They are wise to show concern,' Joseph said seriously. 'Sir Richard is a brave man, as are all Grenvilles, but he lacks the compassion and chivalry that set his brother Bevil above all others, and there are those who believe he values personal ambition more than loyalty to the Prince — or, indeed, to any other master. I would have willingly died for Sir Bevil, but would be as ready to face Sir Richard in battle as stand beside him.'

It was unusual indeed for Joseph to express such views about anyone, but Ralf was to remember his stepfather's words in the weeks ahead.

★ ★ ★

Ralf thoroughly enjoyed his couple of days at home and the hours spent working on the farm, but he was concerned to discover that Joseph was finding farm work more difficult than before, even with Grace's help. During the summer months he employed a lad from Polruan village to help him, but he felt he could not justify the additional expense in winter. Accordingly, Ralf was happy to be able to return the money Joseph had given to him when he left Trecarne to take up his appointment as a page to Prince Charles.

Joseph was reluctant to take the offered

purse, but it was not until he and Ralf were out of the house and beyond the hearing of Grace that he explained why. 'I would much rather you kept the money,' he said. 'I know things are going badly for the King and his cause. Should they worsen you might need to buy your way to safety.'

Ralf shook his head. 'Soldiers on either side would kill a man for far less, and I must take my chances with the Prince. The King is determined he will never fall into Parliament's hands. Where he goes I go too, and will always be certain of having food and shelter. I have little need of money.'

'I am proud of you, Ralf — proud *for* you, too. The money will be kept safe for your mother. Should my health fail she will be able to employ someone to work Trecarne.'

'You should take someone on now. You are working far too hard.'

Joseph shook his head. 'I am not as well as I would like to be, but I won't allow Trecarne to go to rack and ruin. It will be a farm to be proud of when it becomes yours, but you'll have need of a wife to help you run it — and I doubt if you'll find such a girl in the court of Prince Charles. No doubt you'll want to sell it, but whatever you do I know I can trust you to look after your ma.'

Alarmed at Joseph's pessimism about his own future, Ralf said, 'I expect both you and Ma to live out long and happy lives at Trecarne and hope to rejoin you one day. As for not meeting any ordinary girls at the

Prince's court, there is a girl in his household I would like to talk to you about. Her name is Brighid. She's an Irish seamstress whose father and stepmother were butchered by the Roundheads at Naseby. The same fate is likely to be hers if the Prince is forced to flee the country. Although the court will go with him, I doubt if he'll take his household too. I would like to be able to tell her she could find refuge at Trecarne.'

'An Irish girl? Is she a Catholic?' Aware of the views on Catholicism held by the Puritans among the Parliamentary party, Joseph was aware of the danger of having such a girl staying at Trecarne.

'She was certainly born a Catholic, but I'm fairly sure that religion plays very little part in her life.'

Joseph knew that in the present political climate it would make little difference whether such a girl practised her religion or not. The fact that she was Irish and had been a servant of the Prince would be sufficient to seal her fate and have serious consequences for anyone harbouring her. Nevertheless, he said, 'Catholic or not, if she's in need of help it will be here for her. We still have Irish boats coming into Fowey. They would take her back to her home country for a few shillings — unless you have other plans for her?'

Ralf hesitated, then shook his head. 'No. I wish it were otherwise, but she's a very independent girl. Her experience of life has left her disinclined to trust anyone but herself.' He shrugged. 'Who knows? She could be right. But she's made my life as a page with the Prince a lot easier than it might otherwise have been. I owe her a great deal.'

'Then your mother and I will make her welcome here and do all we can to help her. You can tell her that.'

17

Ralf returned to Boconnoc to find the situation had deteriorated rapidly. The war had already been lost in the north of England, where a Parliamentary army was successfully crushing all opposition. Meanwhile, other Roundhead forces were encircling the King in his Oxford stronghold.

In the west of England, Fairfax and Cromwell were advancing relentlessly despite inclement weather. Adding to the troubles of the Prince, Sir Richard Grenville was refusing to obey any orders he was given and constantly challenged the authority of the Prince's council. Rumours had reached the council that he was about to withdraw all his troops at present serving outside their home country, to take up position behind the River Tamar. Here, with an army of Cornishmen, it was his intention to hold at bay not only Roundheads, but non-Cornish Royalists too.

Prince Charles had sent his court ahead of him to Truro and it was here that Ralf was reunited with Brighid. He found her occupying a small shop in the heart of the town, with only one seamstress to help her.

When Ralf commented on the absence of assistants, Brighid said, 'No one with any sense is staying with the Prince. He'll be making his own escape any day now. When he goes most of his household will be left behind and at the mercy of the Roundheads — although I can expect them to show no more of it to me than they did to Molly.'

'That's what I would like to talk to you about, Brighid — in private,' he added, aware that the other seamstress was taking an interest in their conversation.

For a moment it seemed Brighid would dismiss the suggestion of a private conversation out of hand. Then, with a change of mind, she said, 'Mary, go and see if the tailor we spoke to yesterday will part with some more white thread. We're going to need some this afternoon for the Prince's table linen.'

'What am I supposed to use for money?' the girl asked insolently.

'Threats!' Brighid said sharply. 'If he doesn't give it willingly you can tell him that soldiers of the royal bodyguard will come and take it from him — together with anything else that takes their fancy. Off you go, and no dallying along the way.'

The girl petulantly threw down her work and left the room, casting a malevolent glance at Ralf as she passed him.

'She doesn't seem very happy,' Ralf commented, when the girl had gone.

'She isn't,' Brighid agreed. 'Her sweetheart was one of the Prince's farriers and she believed he was going to marry her. Instead, he ran off when we were on the road to Truro, taking a fine horse with him. If he's found he'll be hanged. If he's not, then she's lost him anyway — and I suspect he's left her in trouble. But I didn't send her off just so we could talk about her. You said there was something you wanted to say to me in private.'

'Yes. When the Prince was staying at Boconnoc I managed to spend a couple of days at home on the farm. My mother and stepfather are aware that things aren't going well for the King and the Prince and I spoke to them about you. Should the Prince leave the country without taking his household with him, they are willing for you to go to Trecarne and stay with them.'

Brighid was startled. 'That would be as dangerous for them as it would for me! You know that. I've told you so before.'

'It wouldn't be as dangerous as you might think. Trecarne is very isolated and has no near neighbours to see who is there. Besides, if danger threatened, my pa says that Irish boats come into Fowey. He would arrange a passage back to Ireland for you.'

Ralf had been expecting Brighid to show some gratitude, but instead she demanded angrily, 'And what would I do in Ireland? I know no one there any longer, and have no money. I might as well allow the Roundheads to kill me in Cornwall as starve to death there.' Aware by Ralf's expression that her response had hurt him, she relented a little. 'I'm sorry, Ralf. I know you mean well and I believe you really care, but I'm never going to be safe if I stay anywhere that's likely to come under the rule of Parliament, and when the King is beaten they'll turn on Ireland. No, I need to go to a place where they'll never catch up with me — and I have already made plans for that.'

'What sort of plans? How can you be certain of staying out of Roundhead hands?'

Brighid hesitated. Ralf probably deserved to know the truth, but she was reluctant to give him any details of her intentions. 'I shall probably be leaving Prince Charles's service very soon. As you'll know, the King has relieved Prince Rupert of all his commands and the Prince is applying to Parliament for permission to return to Europe with some of his men and household servants. I hope to be one of them.'

'Travel to Europe ... ? But Rupert's household is not English. Besides, he's in Oxford. How will you reach there without being picked up by Roundhead soldiers?'

'I can't give you any details, Ralf, because I don't know them myself yet, but some of the officers of Prince Charles's bodyguard came from Europe with Prince Rupert. I will be travelling with them.'

Ralf was about to protest that he doubted very much whether Prince Rupert's countrymen would be particularly interested in the welfare of a seamstress when he remembered the officer who had brought her news of the death of her father and Molly.

'You mean you will be travelling with Lieutenant Muller? You hardly know him,

130

Brighid, and he's a mercenary. He'll go to Europe only to join someone else's army.'

'How well I know him doesn't matter. He can take me to safety and has promised he will. It's the best chance I have of staying alive.'

Trying very hard not to allow his feelings to show, Ralf asked, 'It sounds too good to be true, Brighid. Can you trust him to do what he says?'

'Trust doesn't come into it, Ralf.' Looking him defiantly in the eyes, she added, 'I have something he wants — for now, at least. In return he is prepared to offer me something I *need*. It may be only a temporary arrangement, but it's a life-saving one.'

Trying very hard not to accept what she was saying as inevitable, Ralf said, 'I can't guarantee a safe passage out of the country for you, Brighid, even though I would move heaven and earth to keep you from harm, but have you thought how things are likely to end for you if you put yourself under Lieutenant Muller's protection? *Really* thought about it?'

'It's my *life* we're talking about, Ralf. I've weighed what I'm doing against all the possible options — including yours — and have no alternative. It's my best chance of staying alive. I'm taking it.'

'Then there's nothing more to be said,' Ralf said unhappily. 'But if things don't go the way you've planned I want you to remember that you'll be taken care of at Trecarne.'

'I'll remember, Ralf. I'll remember a great many things . . . '

At that moment the other seamstress returned

131

and Brighid stopped what she was saying and turned to listen to the girl's complaint that the tailor had refused to part with any thread. After waiting in vain for her to turn back to him, Ralf left the premises and made his way back to the royal quarters.

18

'Piers, I want you to go to Launceston to speak with your kinsman once more, before the council meets to discuss the rumours reaching the court about his extraordinary conduct and continual disobedience of the orders issued by Lord Hopton. I would like to know whether he has a particular grievance against Hopton. Matters between them need to be settled — and swiftly. An army can have only one commander, and the King has appointed Lord Hopton as commanding general. His authority must be absolute.'

Sir Edward Hyde had called Piers to his room for a private meeting to discuss the worrying and inexplicable conduct of Sir Richard Grenville.

'Yes, Sir Edward. Will I be taking a written reprimand from His Royal Highness, or a note from yourself?'

Piers had been aware that some action would need to be taken by the Prince's council. As secretary he had read the many reports reaching the members, complaining of Sir Richard's lack of co-operation with Lord Hopton, the commanding general of the Prince's army in the south-west. It seemed his kinsman was not only operating his Cornish infantry as a separate army, but also directly opposing the remainder of the Royalist force, with particular animosity towards the cavalry units. One disgruntled cavalry commander had complained to the council that it was as though there were now not two but *three* armies in the field, each at war with the others.

'There will be nothing in writing from anyone here,' Sir Edward said firmly. 'And I demand no written reply from Sir Richard. All I ask is his assurance that he will affirm his loyalty to the King and obey the commands of his superior officer. I am fully aware that Sir Richard has great authority over the Cornish infantry — and Prince Charles has desperate need of such proven fighting men — but they should be fighting Roundheads, not our own soldiers. I had hoped relations between Sir Richard and his superior officers might improve after Lord Goring resigned his command and fled abroad. Instead, they have worsened.'

'I think Sir Richard was expecting to take command of the Prince's army when Goring resigned.' Piers put forward the theory of many Royalists as a reason for Sir Richard's wayward behaviour.

'Had his loyalty to His Majesty been beyond question, and he displayed an unquestioning willingness to carry out the wishes of the Prince and the Council of the West, the command would have been his,' Sir Edward replied. 'As it is . . . But, enough. I have no wish to take matters any further. However, unless Sir Richard is prepared to give his full and immediate support to Lord Hopton and the orders issued through him by the council, then I will be forced to call a meeting of the council to decide what action will be taken. I think you are aware what that is likely to mean for Sir Richard, so I need say no more.'

Piers *was* aware what it would mean for his kinsman and, as he went away to prepare for the ride to Launceston where he expected to find Sir Richard, he thought uneasily of the task ahead of him. Piers had adored Bevil Grenville, Sir Richard's elder brother, but had never taken to Sir Richard.

Richard had fallen out with Bevil many years before and, after making a disastrous marriage as a young man and spending time in a debtors' prison, had gone to Europe to become a professional soldier.

At the time the Civil War began between Parliament and King, Sir Richard was involved in the bloody war against Catholic rebels in Ireland. Resigning his commission when Bevil was killed, he returned to England where he was promptly arrested by Parliament on suspicion of being a Royalist supporter. However, convincing his captors that he had no Royalist sympathies, he was not only released, but made Lieutenant-General of Horse in the Parliamentary army of Sir William Waller. In 1644 he defected to the King's cause and Parliament promptly sentenced him to be put to death should he ever be unfortunate enough to fall into their hands again.

In the King's army, Sir Richard proved himself a brave warrior and a skilful commander, but he also gained notoriety for the harshness he displayed towards the Roundhead soldiers who fell into his hands. There were also many who complained that he put his own interests and ambitions before the needs of the cause for which he was fighting.

Such thoughts troubled Piers on the journey from Truro and were still with him when he entered Launceston, and found his way to the large mansion where the recalcitrant lieutenant-general was sitting down to an evening meal with his senior officers at a long and crowded table.

Sir Richard was dining well in the vast medieval hall, but he broke off to greet Piers with a warmth that owed more to the wine he had consumed than to family affection. 'Piers! What are you doing here among rough fighting men? You are a courtier, more used to the pampering of a royal court! Are you accompanying the Prince? No, of course you are not; my guards would have informed me of his approach. But, come, seat yourself beside me. This calls for a celebration.'

Waiting for Sir Richard's officers to make room for him, Piers felt ill at ease. Taking a seat beside his kinsman and keeping his voice low, he said, 'I fear this is not a social visit, Richard. I come with a message from Sir Edward Hyde. Perhaps it should be more accurately described as an ultimatum . . . '

Piers's discretion was wasted. Raising his voice, Sir Richard addressed his fellow diners. 'Gentlemen, most of you will have met my kinsman, Piers. He is a courtier at the court of Prince Charles, Duke of Cornwall. He is joining us for dinner, but I fear the news he brings may prove indigestible for many of us. He is here at the bidding of Sir Edward Hyde — and brings with him an ultimatum, no less! Pray tell us, Piers, what is this ultimatum?'

Embarrassed, Piers realised that he knew many of those seated at the table, most of whom were Cornish landowners: men who had represented Cornwall's minor gentry before the start of the Civil War, when their status in society would have been of a mainly parochial nature. Now many had been rewarded with knighthoods, baronetcies and even peerages for their support by a grateful and increasingly desperate monarch.

'Now is not the right moment to discuss official business, Richard,' Piers said. 'I have ridden far and am hungry and thirsty. Let us enjoy our reunion and talk business in the morning. In the meantime I would be grateful for news of the family at Stowe. You will have visited them more recently than I.'

'As you wish.' The look that accompanied Sir Richard's acceptance of Piers's suggestion was not that of a man who was the worse for drink and Piers felt increasingly uncomfortable. 'But first I must reunite you with an old friend of yours. He arrived only shortly before you and is on his way to rejoin the Prince's court. You can

137

travel together in a day or two. There he is, farther along the table.'

Looking in the direction pointed out by Sir Richard, Piers was startled to see Dominic Fulbrook.

19

Piers left the headquarters of Sir Richard
Grenville two days later, in company with
Dominic, whose father's wounds had been so
slow to heal that his captors had eventually
released him and allowed him to return home. In
a pocket Piers carried a letter from Sir Richard
to the Prince, tendering his resignation as
lieutenant-general of the Army of the West.

In the letter, Sir Richard declared his
conviction that he could best serve the cause of
the King by commanding his Cornish army in
defence of their homeland, thus securing
Cornwall as a base from which to negotiate with
Fairfax and the forces of Parliament.

Piers had conversed with his kinsman at some
length on the subject of the progress of the war
and listened to Sir Richard's views on what the
future held for the royal cause. The talks had left
Piers deeply disturbed.

He was mulling over his thoughts when
Dominic, riding beside him, asked, 'How many
pages does the Prince have now — and is the
farm boy still one of them?'

Piers drew his thoughts back to the present. 'If
you are talking of Ralf, then yes, he is still with

the Prince and he is now in charge of the other pages. That means you will be taking orders from him if you resume your previous position. However, you have reached an age when you might prefer to take up other duties in the Prince's court — as have I.'

There was silence from Dominic for a few moments before, much to Piers's surprise, he said, 'I would prefer to stay on as a page — at least, for the foreseeable future.'

'Are you quite certain? I would have thought you might resent having a 'farm boy' giving you orders. You have always made your opinion of him quite clear to everyone.'

'As I said, I will give it a try. I have been away from the court for a long time. Things will have changed. I need time to learn what has been happening and where I might best serve the Prince.'

This was certainly not the attitude Piers had expected from a page who had taken every opportunity to question Ralf's right to be at court. Suddenly curious, he asked, 'Are you declaring that you are content for Ralf to be your senior and are willing to take orders from him?'

'I am not saying I am happy about it, but it will be enough for now to be part of the Prince's court once more.'

'I am very pleased that you are adopting such an attitude, Dominic, but I dare say you will not be working with Ralf for very long. You are both of an age when you would normally be moving on to greater things. Unfortunately, these are not normal times.'

'We are all aware of that,' Dominic retorted. 'But tell me all that has been happening during my absence. How is the Prince reacting to the collapse of the royal cause . . . ?'

★ ★ ★

Piers delivered Sir Richard Grenville's letter to Prince Charles in the presence of Sir Edward Hyde and the Prince read it aloud. By the time he reached the end, he seemed bewildered. 'What does Sir Richard mean by saying he can best serve me by retiring west of the Tamar and keeping Parliament's army out of Cornwall? He is a general of the King who can best serve his master by following orders and deploying his Cornishman wherever I and Lord Hopton see the need for them.'

'I wish I could throw some light upon his intentions for Your Royal Highness,' Piers replied, 'but Sir Richard has never deemed it necessary to confide in others, even though they be family.'

'No one would dispute that,' Sir Edward Hyde snapped, 'but you must have formed an *opinion* about his motives. What are they?'

Reluctantly, Piers said, 'My kinsman was no more forthcoming to me than he is to Your Royal Highness in his letter. However, my opinion — and it is no more than an opinion — is that Sir Richard is convinced that the best course for Your Royal Highness to take is to negotiate with Parliament in a bid to have all hostilities cease in the west country, with Cornwall remaining in

141

your hands, while Parliament negotiates a separate peace with His Majesty.'

'Leaving the Puritans to pursue the war against His Majesty with the whole of their army and, no doubt, enabling Sir Richard to become a very powerful figure here in Cornwall,' Sir Edward Hyde commented scathingly. 'The man is pursuing his own aims, not that of his king.'

'I fear you are right, Sir Edward,' Piers said unhappily. 'I sincerely wish I could put another interpretation on his conduct.'

'You have done well in a very difficult situation,' the Prince said appreciatively, 'but I think we will need to call a meeting of my council to discuss what action needs to be taken on the matter. Thank you, Piers. You may go.'

★ ★ ★

In the days following the return of Dominic to the court, Ralf became increasingly puzzled by his deferential attitude. He accepted the orders he was given without question and took on any task, no matter how menial, without complaint. Ralf thought he was *too* uncomplaining. It was out of character.

He would have liked to discuss his thoughts with Piers, but the secretary to the Council of the West had other matters of more personal concern on his mind. He was present at a meeting of the council where the behaviour of Sir Richard Grenville was described as 'highly suspicious'. After a heated debate, it was decided that the recalcitrant Cornish leader should be dismissed from all military commands and arrested.

The orders of the council were carried out and Sir Richard was taken into custody and imprisoned in Launceston castle. His officers, showing that their loyalty lay with the Cornish baronet and not with the Prince, were ready to lead their men to his rescue and follow wherever he cared to take them, even if it meant direct opposition to the monarchy and the Council of the West.

Fortunately, Sir Richard was not prepared to take his dispute with the Prince and his council to such lengths, possibly out of loyalty to Prince Charles, Duke of Cornwall, or because he was under sentence of death from Parliament because of his earlier treachery and could not expect them to reach any agreement with him alone.

The result was that, without a prominent Cornishman to lead them, the men who had been under his command deserted in ever-increasing numbers. When General Fairfax scored another resounding victory against the Royalist army in the south-west at Torrington, it was apparent to the Prince's council that their cause was lost. Their thoughts now turned to ways of keeping Prince Charles from falling into Parliament's hands.

The first move was to take Charles down to Pendennis castle, a stronghold on the coast, south of Truro. Before they did so, Piers pleaded successfully for his kinsman to be moved too, in order to stay out of enemy hands, and he was

143

transferred to the castle at St Michael's Mount, a Cornish stronghold even farther west than Pendennis.

There was a sense of urgency in moving the Prince, but it was not an easy operation. The combined court and royal household numbered some five hundred men and women and they carried with them household goods that filled a great many wagons. Eventually, the royal cavalcade reached Pendennis where there was ample room behind the extensive earthern ramparts of the fortress for both the Prince's household and a garrison of more than a thousand soldiers.

The knowledge that Fairfax and his formidable army would eventually arrive provoked a siege mentality within the fortress, but reports began to filter through suggesting that Fairfax was behaving with unexpected generosity and compassion, releasing all his Cornish prisoners and sending them home with more money in their pockets than most ordinary soldiers had seen for many months. It was a shrewd move, coming at a time when hungry and penniless Royalist cavalry were roaming the Cornish countryside, taking what they needed from an already impoverished populace.

20

The Prince and his court had been at Pendennis for a week when Ralf took a walk to the farthest point of the headland on which the castle stood. Here there was a small fort with a blockhouse and fortifications that pre-dated the other buildings by many years. Ralf was interested, and fell into conversation with the artillery officer in charge of the blockhouse which lasted longer than he had intended. It was dusk when he set off to return to the castle.

A cold north-easterly wind carrying a hint of rain with it had blown up while Ralf was in the blockhouse and he pulled the hood of the cloak he was wearing up over his head, where its generous cut also protected much of his face. This was not the elegant cloak made for him by Brighid, but an old hooded one that had been given to him some months before by an elderly cleric when he left the court to return to his home.

Ralf was on a path that would soon join the track that encircled the outside perimeter of the castle when he saw a horseman approaching the junction from the direction of the castle gatehouse.

Much to Ralf's surprise, as the horseman passed by, he saw it was Dominic. Grateful for the fact that he was wearing the hooded cloak, Ralf pulled the hood farther over his face and slowed his gait, allowing Dominic to ride past the junction casting no more than a brief glance in his direction.

Curious as to why Dominic should be out on a day that was not best suited to riding, Ralf did not turn left when he reached the perimeter track. Instead, he turned right, following Dominic at a discreet distance. Horse and rider were still well in view when they turned off the track and the horse began picking its way along a path which led to the shore at a spot known as Crab Quay. Ralf waited until Dominic had dropped out of sight behind a number of dilapidated wooden huts before leaving the track to take a short cut across the rough ground to the quay. He had reached the first of the huts when he heard voices coming from the quay, and he proceeded with considerable caution until he was able to peer round the side of the hut without being observed.

Dominic had dismounted and was talking to a group of men standing at the water's edge. Unfortunately, the light was too poor for Ralf to identify them, although he counted eight men and was able to see that some were dressed as seamen and there was a boat drawn up on the foreshore. The men remained in discussion for some twenty minutes, by which time it was too dark to discern anyone, despite a three-quarter moon that was beginning to show itself above the land on the far side of the entrance to the anchorage guarded by Pendennis castle.

When the conversation came to an end, all except two of the men turned away to make their way to the boat. Both the remaining men had horses and, collecting them, they mounted and made their way together along the path that passed by the hut behind which Ralf was concealed. Ralf knew that one of the two mounted men must be Dominic, but he wished it was light enough for him to identify the other. Then, when the men were level with the hut, one of them used a tinder box to ignite tobacco in the pipe clenched between his teeth and Ralf was able to see his face.

It was Lieutenant Hugo Muller!

★ ★ ★

Returning to the castle, Ralf's first thought was to hurry straight to Piers and inform him of what he had seen. But when he thought about it, what exactly *had* he seen? Dominic had met an officer of the Prince's lifeguard and they had been talking to some unknown seamen down by the shore. It might have been an accidental and innocent meeting. Ralf was convinced it was not, but even he had to admit that he was prejudiced against both Dominic and Muller for reasons of which Piers would be fully aware.

Inside the fortress, he made his way to the building that housed the royal pages and was still pondering on the action he should take when a figure came out of the shadows of a nearby outbuilding and called softly to him. It was Brighid.

Before he could greet her she pulled him from the lamplight shining from the building's hallway. When they were both enveloped in darkness, she said softly, 'I wanted to say goodbye to you, Ralf, just in case I need to leave suddenly and have no opportunity to speak to you again.'

'You are leaving the Prince's household? Is Lieutenant Muller going to take you away?'

'Yes, but he's not sure when it will be. He's said I'm to have everything ready in case we need to leave in a hurry.'

As far as Ralf was aware, Hugo Muller had not submitted his resignation to the Prince, but it would not be at all unusual for him to leave without giving any notice. Desertions from the royal camp were becoming commonplace, even among the Prince's lifeguard — and Hugo Muller was a mercenary. His loyalty was with whoever could pay for his services, and there was very little money remaining in the royal coffers.

'I would feel much happier if I knew you were going to my parents' farm, Brighid, but it's your life. I only hope that everything works out well for you.'

'Thank you, Ralf. I'm sorry if I haven't turned out to be all you would have liked me to be, but I am what life has made me. Nothing can change that.'

Ralf began to protest that she was wrong, but Brighid cut him short. 'No, Ralf, there is nothing more to be said now but goodbye. I'll always think kindly of you. You will grow up to be a good man.'

She stepped forward and kissed him full on the lips, but before he could react to the gesture she turned away. She had gone no more than a few paces before, halting, she turned and said, 'Oh, by the way, you can tell Dominic Fulbrook that the seaman's clothes he had me make up to fit the Prince are ready to be collected. But if the Prince intends to escape the country disguised as a sailor he'll need to cut his hair and do something about that moustache he's trying to grow. Once they're gone no one will look twice at him in such clothes.'

With this final remark Brighid disappeared into the darkness. Neither she nor Ralf was aware that they had been observed by Dominic, who had been in the process of drawing the curtains in his unlit room only a few paces from where Brighid had first accosted the senior page.

* * *

Piers was bewildered when Ralf came to him with the story about the sailor's garb that had been made for Prince Charles, and told him of the meeting at Crab Quay between Dominic, Hugo Muller and the unknown seamen.

'There *is* no plan to smuggle the Prince out of the country,' Piers said. 'If there were I would certainly know about it. Besides, there is no need of such subterfuge. There is a Dunkirk privateer waiting offshore to take the Prince on board should the need arise. So why would Dominic have your seamstress make up a set of seafaring clothes for the Prince and what — if anything — does it have to do with Dominic's meeting Lieutenant Muller and the seamen you saw them with at Crab Quay?'

'I don't know any of the answers,' Ralf replied, 'but I can hazard a guess — albeit a far-fetched one.'

'Then tell me what you suggest,' Piers said. 'A far-fetched speculation is better than none at all.'

'What if Dominic and Lieutenant Muller plan to somehow abduct the Prince and take him to Crab Quay dressed as a seaman, then have him taken out to a waiting Parliamentary ship?' Ralf was aware that, when voiced, his theory sounded even more incredible than when he had first thought of it.

'No, Ralf. I could perhaps be persuaded that Muller might become involved in such a scheme — after all, he is a mercenary, ready to sell his services to the highest bidder. For delivering Prince Charles to Parliament he would be rewarded with riches beyond his wildest dreams — but for Dominic to be involved in such a plot is unthinkable. He has been a page for almost as long as myself and his father was seriously wounded in the King's service . . . '

'We have only Dominic's word that his father was *seriously* wounded,' Ralf said doggedly. 'Before Dominic's father became an officer in the King's army he was a Member of Parliament and would have known the most senior of the officers who captured him. What if he was persuaded to change sides . . . or even threatened? They could have taken Dominic prisoner when he visited his father and said they would execute them both if he didn't agree to do what they wanted. And who better to help abduct the Prince than one of his trusted pages?'

Piers was openly sceptical. 'How would they carry out such a bold plan while the Prince is secure in one of the best-guarded castles in the land?'

'Secure in whose hands?' Ralf became increasingly excited as his theory gained substance in his mind. 'On many occasions Dominic will be the one to ensure the Prince's bedchamber is secure for the night. The guard is not set until the duty page declares the time to be right. What if he were to drug the Prince — a simple matter for someone in his position of trust — then dress the Prince in a seaman's clothes with a sailor's hat hiding his hair — or even a wig? In a drugged state he could be supported between two men through the gate — the sally port. The light is poor there. It would be easy to pass him off as a drunken sailor being returned to his ship. You and I know that to be a regular occurrence. They could take the Prince to Crab Quay, and long before it was discovered the Prince was missing they would be on a Parliamentary ship bound for London.'

Piers still thought the suggestion was far-fetched. 'Where does Lieutenant Muller come into this? He is one of Prince Rupert's men.'

'A *countryman* of Prince Rupert, not a friend,' Ralf corrected Piers excitedly. 'And he intends to leave the country in the next few days!'

Ralf did not disclose that his information had come from an Irish seamstress and had not been obtained entirely on behalf of Prince Charles, but he persisted. 'We've already agreed that Muller is a mercenary, Piers, willing to sell his services to the highest bidder — and there will be no higher bidder than a party that would desperately like to have the heir to the throne of England in their hands. What's more, I have already asked the Prince whether he would consider having clothes made in order to disguise him if he intended escaping from Cornwall.'

'And what did he say?' Piers was still not convinced.

'He was amused at the thought of it but said that he is the heir to the throne of England and if he is going to be taken by Parliament it will be as the King's son and not as a skulking fugitive.'

'So the Prince has no knowledge of the seaman's clothes that have been made for him?' For the first time Piers began to take Ralf's information seriously.

'None at all,' Ralf declared emphatically.

Piers was thoughtful for a long time, then said, 'I will arrange a meeting with Sir Edward and Colonel Trevanion. I will see what they think about all you have told me. In the meantime say nothing to anyone about your suspicions, Ralf — but keep both the Prince and Dominic under close surveillance.'

21

'I tell you I saw them talking — and it was more than just a casual meeting. Far more.' Dominic was telling Hugo Muller what he had seen the previous evening. 'Besides, she was Hunkyn's whore when I left the court, and probably still is.'

Muller had not been aware of Brighid's affair with Ralf, but his start of surprise passed unnoticed by Dominic, who was still talking.

'What if she's told Hunkyn? What can we do about it?'

'Do you think she was telling him about the seaman's clothes you asked her to make for the Prince? I thought you told her to keep it a secret,' Muller said.

'I did, but I don't suppose she thought the secrecy extended to Hunkyn. After all, he's supposed to be the senior page now. But what if she *has* told him? What can we do about it?'

'Did he or the girl know you saw them talking together?' Muller asked.

'No. I saw them from my window, but the room was in darkness.'

'Then think of some story to tell Hunkyn, just in case she has mentioned the clothes to him. Say that with the Roundheads advancing so rapidly you thought it might be necessary to have the Prince taken off by boat and he could best pass unnoticed if he was dressed as a seaman. In the meantime I will seek out the captain of our ship and tell him he must be ready to sail tomorrow night.'

'Tomorrow!' Dominic paled now that the execution of the plan to abduct the Prince was imminent. 'But I am not on duty tomorrow night.'

'Then you must find some excuse to change your duties,' Muller said firmly. 'There is much at stake — not least our lives. We need to act swiftly before anyone becomes suspicious. I, my men, and the boat, will be ready. Do not fail us.'

★ ★ ★

'I told Colonel Trevanion about your fears and he took them very seriously. However, since then Dominic has been to see me. He explained about the clothes he had the seamstress make for the Prince and I think he has shown admirable forethought.' Piers was talking to Ralf in the privacy of the council secretary's room.

'If he's telling the truth,' Ralf retorted. 'I think he is merely trying to allay suspicion should anyone query what he's doing.'

'Well, let's go and speak to Sir Edward and see what he has to say about it,' Piers said. 'I felt it incumbent upon me to inform him of your suspicions. In truth, he was inclined to dismiss them out of hand, but said he wished to be informed of any new developments.'

They found Sir Edward Hyde in his chambers, and with him was John Trevanion, now colonel of the Prince's lifeguard. When Sir Edward said he had discussed Ralf's suspicions with the colonel, Piers said, 'What I have to say might change your thinking. Dominic has been to see me and, without being prompted, has told me about the clothes he ordered for the Prince, and given me his reason for doing so. I applaud Ralf's concern for His Royal Highness's well-being, but I believe that on this occasion he may be mistaken.'

'Dominic may have come to you voluntarily and given a plausible explanation, and had you come to me no more than half an hour ago I would have agreed with you, Piers. However, there has been a new development.'

'There has indeed,' Colonel Trevanion said grimly, nodding acknowledgement to Ralf. 'As soon as Sir Edward informed me of Ralf's suspicions I had Lieutenant Muller report to me. I told him I wished him to carry despatches to the King, in Oxford. He declared he was unable to undertake the journey, saying he is trying to shake off a fit of ague and feels it would be unwise for him to make such a journey, lest the attack worsen and allow the despatches to fall into Parliamentary hands. I was watching from a window as Muller approached the castle in response to my command and he looked as fit as any man in the lifeguard. It would seem the lieutenant has no wish to leave Pendennis, possibly because he has other business to attend to.'

'I too have information bearing on the situation,' said Sir Edward. 'As we all know, Page Fulbrook was granted leave from the Prince's service because his father had been wounded while serving as a cavalry officer in the King's army. Fulbrook has recently come back to take up his post again and received sympathy from one and all. It was believed that Parliament allowed his father to return to his home without further action being taken against him because his wounds were serious. I have, within the last half-hour, received a letter from a cousin who is one of His Majesty's most loyal supporters, but whose poor health prevents him from taking an active part in the present conflict. He is a near neighbour of Sir Horace Fulbrook and felt duty-bound to inform me of the rumours that are circulating in the area. It would appear that Sir Horace *was* wounded, but not as seriously as we have been led to believe. Indeed, it would seem that Sir Horace has transferred his allegiance to Parliament and been rewarded with a senior commission in their army — not as a fighting soldier, but as an adviser on policy matters. As I say, these are merely rumours, but my cousin says that all who know Sir Horace are in no doubt about their veracity. They say he was always a better parliamentarian than a soldier.'

'If all this is true, why would Dominic return to the court?' Piers asked.

'Why indeed?' Sir Edward said. 'Unless a plot *has* been hatched to abduct His Royal Highness and deliver him into the hands of Parliament. Such a daring coup would assure the future of a

Parliamentarian — and his son — and also reward a mercenary soldier far more handsomely than a lifetime spent fighting other men's wars.'

'So you really do believe that something is being planned by Dominic and Lieutenant Muller?' It was Piers who spoke.

'I think we have cause to be grateful that Ralf was astute enough to take note of the meeting between Fulbrook, Muller and the unknown seamen,' Sir Edward replied. 'Unfortunately, we do not know when the move against His Royal Highness is likely to be made.'

'I think I might.' Ralf's words startled the others and he explained, 'Dominic said there was something he particularly wanted to do tomorrow and has changed places with the page who should be on duty with the Prince tonight. If anything is going to happen, it will be tonight.'

22

Had Ralf's suspicions not been aroused, the plan of Muller and Dominic might well have succeeded. Shortly before midnight Prince Charles had Dominic fetch his late-night drink of brandy-wine from the small kitchen which catered exclusively for the Prince and bring it to him in his chambers on the first floor of the tower, which would in more normal times have been occupied by the castle's governor.

Carrying the brandy-wine in a silver beaker, Dominic paused on the spiral stone stairway. Although he could not possibly be overlooked here, he was nervous as he withdrew a small silver box from a pocket. Lifting the lid with shaking fingers, he emptied the white powder it contained into the beaker. He did not know what the powder was, but it had been given to him by Muller and told it would render the Prince speechless. Although not completely unconscious, he would be unable to walk, or even stand, without aid and would show all the symptoms of acute intoxication.

Until now, the whole scheme had carried about it an air of unreality, but the very act of putting the drug into the Prince's drink brought home to Dominic the degree to which he was involved. He had become the prime mover in an act of treason for which there could be only one punishment should the abduction fail.

Entering the Prince's bedchamber, Dominic proffered the beaker to his master. 'Sire, your brandy-wine.'

'Thank you, Dominic. Place it on the bedside table. I shall prepare for bed and drink it shortly. You may go now and set the guard.'

'Is there nothing else you require, sire?'

'Nothing. You may go.'

Dominic imagined the Prince was particularly short with him tonight, but put it down to his own sensitivity because of what was planned. Bowing to the Prince, he backed out of the chamber.

Once outside, he had a brief moment of indecision. Should he go through with the plan? If so, how long should he wait before summoning Muller, who was waiting outside the gate of the tower, as planned?

The next half-hour seemed a lifetime, but then, in a highly nervous state, Dominic ventured back inside the Prince's bedchamber.

'Sire, are you awake?'

He addressed the still form hidden beneath the bedclothes. When he received no reply, he tentatively placed a hand on the blanket covering the royal figure and received only the faintest of responses. It seemed the potion he had administered had succeeded in the purpose for which it had been intended.

Hurrying from the Prince's quarters, Dominic

made his way from the tower and crossed the drawbridge. A figure emerged from the shadows beside the wall, with others behind him: Lieutenant Hugo Muller and some of his fellow mercenaries.

Relieved, Dominic said, 'It's worked. He's ready for us. Do you have the clothes?'

'One of my men has them,' Muller said. 'Come, lead the way. We must waste no time.'

With Dominic leading the way, a group of half a dozen foreign members of the royal lifeguard, with Muller in the van, hurried up the stone staircase in single file. Entering the bedchamber, they arrived at the Prince's bedside.

Hugo Muller pulled back the bedclothes — and sprang back, startled. The figure in the bed was not Prince Charles, but a Royalist officer. Fully clothed and holding a cocked pistol in his hand, the officer rolled off the bed on the far side from the would-be abductors and called, 'Stay where you are and drop your weapons.'

At the same time, the door to the Prince's daytime quarters was flung open and soldiers led by Colonel Trevanion burst into the room.

The first man to escape from the bedchamber was Hugo Muller, but not before he had received a sword-slash across his back from one of his erstwhile comrades-in-arms. A couple of his fellow countrymen were close on his heels. Dominic would have followed them, but as he turned away the officer who had been lying in the Prince's bed pulled the trigger of his pistol and the ball struck Dominic in the back of the head. Fatally wounded, he fell to the floor.

The next few minutes were chaotic. Shots were fired and there was the clash of steel upon steel as swords came into play. The brief but fierce fight lasted for no more than a few minutes, by which time two of the would-be abductors were dead, as was Dominic. The remainder of the intruders who had been trapped in the bedchamber were captured.

Muller and two of his countrymen escaped, pursued by a hue-and-cry.

Loyal officers of the Prince's lifeguard had been hiding with the Prince in an adjacent room in the governor's quarters. Colonel Trevanion had set a guard at Crab Quay. His men had already arrested the crew of a boat sent inshore from the waiting ship.

The lifeguard officers lying in wait at the quay captured Muller's breathless companions when they reached the spot where the boat should have been waiting to carry them to safety. But there was no sign of Hugo Muller.

Not until the early hours of the morning, after a thorough search indicated that Muller had escaped, did the excitement die down. After seeing Prince Charles safely settled in his bed, with a much strengthened guard posted on the chambers and the tower, Ralf went to his own quarters. Here he found Piers and Colonel Trevanion awaiting him.

In answer to his question, the Cornish colonel said, 'There has been no sign of Lieutenant Muller. The officer in charge of the guardhouse was alerted to look out for him and I had the sally port drawbridge raised, but Muller is a daring and resourceful man. He probably escaped over the ramparts. It has been raining for much of the night and I doubt whether the sentries will have spent as much time as they should have outside the guardhouse.'

'There is one place that probably won't have been searched,' Ralf said. 'Muller has been sharing the bed of Brighid, the seamstress. He had promised to take her with him to the Rhine, in order to escape the fate that was suffered by her father and stepmother at the hands of the Roundheads. I've always believed he had no intention of keeping such a promise. Tonight's events would seem to prove I was right, but if she still believed him he might have persuaded her to hide him.'

Ralf's words took Piers by surprise. He had thought Ralf was Brighid's lover. But it was Colonel Trevanion who spoke. 'Where are the quarters of this seamstress?'

'She sleeps in her workshop,' Ralf said. 'The servants' quarters are too crowded to allow for liaisons. I'll show you the way.'

'Do you think this seamstress would have had any knowledge of what was going to happen tonight?' Ralf shook his head emphatically.

'How can you be so certain?'

'It was Brighid who aroused my suspicions when she told me about the seaman's clothes she had made for the Prince. She would never have mentioned them had she been part of the plot.'

'We'll gather a couple of guards and a lantern before we go,' the colonel said. 'Muller is not a man with whom to take chances.'

162

The seamstresses' shop was unlocked, but before the soldier with the lantern opened the door Colonel Trevanion drew and cocked his pistol.

Such caution proved unnecessary. The shop was empty. There were signs that it had been vacated in a great hurry: garments were strewn about the room and, in a corner, Ralf found a bloody shirt.

'It seems that Lieutenant Muller has been here,' said Colonel Trevanion, 'but both he and the girl are long gone.'

'How do you think they could have got past the guard?' Piers asked.

'There's only one way to find out,' Colonel Trevanion said. 'We'll ask the sergeant of the guard if he and his men have checked everyone who has passed through the gate.'

The sergeant of the guard was adamant that his men had checked every man who had left the fortress that night — and Lieutenant Muller was certainly not one of them.

'Then he must still be in Pendennis,' Colonel Trevanion declared.

Not convinced, Ralf questioned the sergeant. 'How about women? Have many of them passed out of the castle?'

'Not for a while,' was the reply. 'In fact, I think all the women who had no right to be in Pendennis overnight left more than two hours ago . . . maybe longer. It was at the height of the storm. Some twenty or more were huddled right here in the gateway for ten minutes or so. When

163

the rain eased off they all hurried back to their homes.'

'Were they well wrapped against the weather?' Ralf asked.

'Of course,' said the sergeant. 'The rain's been threatening all day. Most of the women were wearing cloaks and hoods. They wouldn't have got too wet, and the ale most had been drinking would have kept out the cold.'

'I think we have the answer to how Muller managed to escape from Pendennis,' Ralf said. 'My guess is that, disguised as a woman, he left with Brighid. If there was a ship waiting offshore for him he will be on it. We'll not catch him now.'

Ralf did not voice the thoughts that were troubling him. He had no doubt that Brighid had helped Muller to escape from Pendennis. He hoped the mercenary soldier had not got rid of her along the way . . .

Three days after the failed abduction, Prince Charles set sail from Pendennis in a Dunkirk privateer, bound for the Isles of Scilly. It would be more than four years before he set foot on the soil of mainland Britain once more. In the meantime, he would know exile on the Continent during which he would suffer penury, humiliation and frustration — and experience the agony of a loving son whose father had been brutally executed.

In short, he would become Charles II. Uncrowned king of the British Isles.

BOOK TWO

1

'Here we are at last, Ralf. Safely at anchor in home waters. It may not yet be England, but I am monarch of Scotland too. God and Covenanters permitting, we may soon be setting foot in my kingdom.'

King Charles II and a small group of courtiers were standing on the deck of the Dutch ship *Skidam* which had carried them to Spey Bay, on the Moray Firth. The group included Ralf, who had long since put his days as a page behind him and was now a valued personal secretary to King Charles, Piers Grenville, and John Trevanion, now the officer commanding the Royal body-guard.

It was June, 1650, and after protracted and at times humiliating negotiations with emissaries from the Scots Covenanters, Charles — pro-claimed King Charles II by Scotland when his father had been beheaded in the previous year — had arrived by ship from the Continent, intent upon wresting his throne from the Parliamentarians and avenging the brutal execu-tion of his father.

The Scots were to provide him with an army — but the uncrowned king had been forced to pay a heavy price for its services. The government of Scotland was now in the hands of the more fanatical Presbyterian elements and in order to secure their backing Charles had been forced to sign increasingly stringent conditions which had lost him much support among those in England most bitterly opposed to the Puritan regime.

Charles had originally only agreed to allow Presbyterian worship in Scotland, and when the Scots negotiators had suddenly insisted that he support imposition of the same system upon the whole of his kingdom he had objected strongly to making such a promise. However, there could be no turning back from his declared aim of securing the throne of England, and in the end he had reluctantly put his signature to a covenant agreeing to the conditions imposed by the Scots in return for their support.

There were few in the King's immediate circle who believed he would keep his word once he was monarch of Great Britain, but the young king was an unknown quantity to others of his supporters, and they were appalled that he should have agreed to such conditions.

'I would that we had an army of Cornishmen awaiting us on shore, instead of Scotsmen,' said Colonel Trevanion. 'The Scots served his late majesty ill when he placed himself in their hands.'

Trevanion was referring to the fact that Charles I had been handed over to the Parliamentarians by a Scots army when he had thrown himself upon their mercy. As a result, he had been put on trial, found guilty and executed by his captors.

'Your Cornishmen served my father well, Colonel Trevanion, but now it is time for all loyal Scotsmen to show what they will do for me.' Suddenly shaking his head, Charles went on, 'Mind you, I doubt very much whether Cornishmen would have forced me to swear so many oaths before agreeing to fight for me.'

'I fear there will be more demands made upon you before you sit on your throne in London, sire,' Ralf said. 'And unless I am mistaken some of my Lord Argyll's men are on their way from the shore now.'

The Earl of Argyll, a staunch Covenanter, was one of Scotland's most powerful men. It was he who had conducted many of the negotiations which had forced the King to accept the most humiliating of all the conditions imposed upon him.

'Then I shall go to my cabin,' Charles declared. 'They can come and find me, if they must. I will not wait on deck to welcome them.'

The King departed with Colonel Trevanion and a number of others, leaving Ralf and Piers to greet the men from the shore.

The party welcoming Charles to his northern kingdom consisted of a small number of Scots dignitaries, two members of the Earl of Argyll's household, and three members of the Kirk, bearing new demands from their elders. Ralf's first impression was of the lack of humour in their expressions. It was a foretaste of the weeks and months ahead.

He led the five men to the King's cabin, where they greeted the young monarch with a lack of deference that Ralf found disturbing. He was aware, too, that Charles was unhappy with his reception. It was not the welcome he had been expecting.

Reading through the written demands, Charles was dismayed, and he immediately made his feelings known. 'I cannot agree to these! To do so would be to declare that everything the King, my father, fought and died for was wrong. That is not so!'

'The elders of the Kirk have no wish to depict the late king as an evil man,' said the leader of the Scots churchmen sanctimoniously, 'only as one who was mistaken in his beliefs.'

'I do not agree,' Charles declared. 'My father was an honourable man who served God and his country as diligently as any monarch the world has known.'

'You too would be serving God and your country by agreeing to the additional terms offered by the General Assembly of the Kirk and the Parliament of Scotland,' came the reply.

Ralf knew by the expression on the face of the young king that he was in one of his stubborn moods, likely to say something he would later regret. Yet the future of his monarchy could well lie in the hands of these intransigent and arrogant men.

'Gentlemen, His Majesty has had a long, exhausting and dangerous sea voyage to Scotland, beset by storms and pursued by the ships of his enemies. He needs to rest before

170

discussing such important matters of state as you have placed before him.'

'Then we will take him ashore, where prayer and humility will refresh both body and soul . . . '

'No!' Ralf realised he was exceeding his authority, but he was aware that these men were trying to bully the King into submitting to their demands. 'We have had a rough crossing. His Majesty needs to rest for a day or two before he undertakes any duties.'

'And who might *you* be?' The question was put to Ralf by a glaring and heavy-browed representative of the Kirk, but it was the King himself who replied.

'Ralf is my secretary, my companion, and a courtier whose advice I value highly. He is right: I need to rest, in order to contemplate your latest demands on me. Thank you for coming aboard to welcome me home to my kingdom. We will meet again the day after tomorrow, in the forenoon, and discuss matters that are of importance to us all.'

The Scottish commissioners were not happy with the course of events, but there was little they could do. When they had left, escorted from the cabin by Piers, King Charles turned to Ralf, and after expressing gratitude for his intervention added, 'I find these Covenanters alarmingly daunting, Ralf, but they hold my future in their hands. Indeed, the survival of the monarchy depends upon their support.'

'They are well aware of their importance to you, sire. Unfortunately, it is becoming increasingly apparent that they intend to use this power to the full. My feeling is that you must play their game for the moment, but never allow them to forget that *you* are the ruler of Scotland, as well as of England, and that they are subject to your commands, not the other way round.'

'You are quite right, of course, Ralf, but at the moment I am more in need of them than they are in need of a king.'

'Perhaps that is so, sire, but they have a mission too. They wish to impose their religion upon the whole of your kingdom. It cannot be done without you.'

'You are right again, Ralf, but I feel uncomfortable in their presence. Should they continue to extend their demands I will be required to atone for the sins of everyone in the royal household, from myself down to the kitchen dogs. And I swear they have a longer list of sins than the devil himself!'

Ralf felt sympathy with the King. The Covenant commissioners had subjected him to intense pressure, well aware how desperately he needed their armed support. However, Ralf believed his young sovereign possessed a resilience that would surmount all the problems posed by the Scots officials.

2

Despite the reluctance of King Charles to make more concessions to the Scots commissioners, when he went ashore to the small village of Garmouth he was obliged to swear yet another solemn oath, this time to bind himself and future generations of his family to adopt the Presbyterian practices and customs of the Church of Scotland.

It was an oath taken under duress, as a matter of expediency. Few of the Scots nobles who were present at the signing believed he would adhere to it if ever he regained the throne. The Scots clerics were less sceptical. Naively, they were convinced that if Charles were restored to the throne Presbyterianism would become the religion practised throughout the British Isles, to the exclusion of all others.

If the young king thought the demands of his hosts were now at an end, he was to be sorely disappointed. No sooner had he signed the Solemn League and Covenant, as the document was called, than the elders of the Kirk declared the majority of his courtiers to be unacceptable to them. Piers, Colonel Trevanion and Ralf were among their number.

Being in the hands of the Scots and fully aware they had changed their allegiance on more than one occasion in the recent turbulent years, it was difficult, if not actually dangerous, for the uncrowned king to defy them — but he did. Although forced to accept the purge of a great many of his most trusted and loyal courtiers, he managed to retain both his particular friend, the young Duke of Buckingham, and Ralf.

Over the next few weeks, Charles was in sore need of such friends. The Scots seemed determined to humiliate him in every way possible. He was constantly required to publicly beg God's forgiveness for the sins of his late father — something he found particularly hurtful — and on Sundays was forced to listen to a series of bigoted sermons given by breast-beating ministers.

Referring to the latest, as drinks were poured for him and Ralf in their temporary abode in the palace at Falkirk, which had been built as a hunting-lodge by James V of Scotland, Charles said, 'We have listened to some powerful sermons today, Ralf, but I doubt the Round-heads will be defeated by words, no matter how pious the speaker. I came to Scotland because I was promised an army that would help me recover the throne. I have seen little evidence of such a force, have you?'

'No, sire, and I fear that by the time such an army is placed at your disposal it will be more skilled in sermonising than in fighting. I heard only today that the Covenanters have ordered yet another purge of their army, to remove more of

174

the 'ungodly' fighting men. The officer who told me about it said that thousands of battle-hardened infantrymen have been sent home. They are being replaced by men of piety, but this officer is a professional soldier and he commented that he has yet to witness a single instance of a musket ball being stopped by even the most fervent of 'Allelujahs'!'

The King groaned. 'What have I let myself in for? Where is the army I have been promised? What is it *doing* — it is certainly not fighting!'

'Perhaps the Earl of Argyll can give you an answer, sire,' Ralf replied. 'He seems to be guiding the actions of the Covenanters.'

'Argyll?' Charles was scornful. 'He and his retinue spent almost an hour last night rolling on the floor, beating their breasts and calling on God to grant them forgiveness for their sins. Can you imagine even the most understanding God taking such behaviour seriously? Then, when Argyll rose to his feet once more and was brushing away his sins with the dust on his clothing, he suggested that I might consider marrying his daughter, the Lady Anne Campbell. A young woman I have never even met. Have you?'

'I have, sire. She is a handsome young woman.'

'So she may be, but she is not a future queen of England. Under no circumstances would I accept my Lord Argyll as a father-in-law. I neither like nor trust him. As for his devotion to the Covenant . . . It suits him to be seen acting the part of a most devout Presbyterian, but

Argyll's first loyalty is to Argyll. Like a weathervane, he turns in whichever direction the wind blows strongest.' The King heaved an exaggerated sigh. 'Would that we had some of the court back with us again, Ralf. We could set Trevanion's men to stand guard while we enjoyed a game of cards, and had an occasional laugh, without the threat of a dire penance if we were caught.' Suddenly Charles threw up his hands in exasperation. 'Listen to me, Ralf. A monarch, afraid to play a game of cards lest he is caught and made to do penance, like some naughty child! Such a situation cannot continue. It is quite preposterous.'

★　★　★

Shortly after this conversation with Ralf, it seemed that the trials of the King might soon come to an end. Alarmed by the presence of Charles on the British mainland, the English Parliament in London decided to send an army against the Scots as a warning not to give the uncrowned king their support. Oliver Cromwell was appointed to lead the English army and commissioned as 'Captain-General and Commander-in-Chief of all the forces raised, or to be raised, within the Commonwealth of England.'

On 22 July 1650, Cromwell crossed the border into Scotland at the head of a formidable army. Opposing him was the experienced Scots General David Leslie with a force that considerably outnumbered his adversary — but

176

owing to the many purges initiated by the Covenanters, most were untried troops. Accordingly, Leslie decided against attacking the English invaders. Instead, he put his men in an impressive defensive position around Edinburgh, in a bid to halt the Roundhead advance.

King Charles was invited to Leith, Edinburgh's port, by Argyll and the elders of the Kirk, to witness what the Covenanters were convinced would be the inglorious collapse of Cromwell's Roundheads before the might of the Scots opposition. Excited at the possibility of going into action against a man whose signature had been on his father's death warrant, Charles was heartened by the enthusiastic welcome given to him by soldiers of the Scots army.

Unfortunately, such enthusiasm for the King alarmed the Covenanters. Fearing that he might take advantage of his popularity to assume command of the army, they ordered him to leave Edinburgh again — a ride north, to Perth. It was also felt necessary to purge Leslie's army of a further 3,000 valuable fighting men, who might possibly have supported Charles in any test of strength.

Meanwhile, Cromwell was having problems too. The wet Scots weather was seriously affecting the health of his army and when its strength fell to 12,000 the Parliamentary commander realised that unless he could provoke a fight with the Scots very soon, he would be forced to make an ignominious retreat back across the border into England.

When the opportunity to do battle occurred,

Cromwell seized it with both hands — and succeeded beyond all expectations. He moved his army to a more strategically advantageous position at nearby Dunbar and the Scots, mistakenly believing he was retreating, relaxed their guard.

Shortly before dawn on 3 September, they discovered their mistake. Cromwell attacked, taking the inexperienced Scots soldiers completely by surprise.

Adding superb tactics to the advantage of surprise, Cromwell had effectively won the battle of Dunbar within an hour, although the slaughter would continue for a great deal longer. As a result 3,000 Scots soldiers died, 10,000 were taken captive and only 8,000 managed to flee to safety. The Scottish army of David Leslie was no more and Cromwell led his triumphant soldiers into Edinburgh unopposed.

3

When news of the crushing defeat was brought to King Charles by Ralf, the young king was torn between delight that his tormentors had been humiliated, and despair at the defeat of the army he had hoped to lead into England to claim his throne. It seemed that all he had endured at the hands of the Scots Covenanters had been in vain. To add insult to injury, instead of accepting that their emasculation of the army was to blame for the defeat, the Covenanters claimed it was God's way of punishing King Charles for the sins of his father.

Charles decided he had suffered enough at the hands of those who had become his virtual captors and many secret letters were exchanged between the King and those Scots nobles who planned for a separate army which would be commanded by the King. Matters were precipitated by the arrival of a deputation of hardline Covenanters who spent two hours closeted with Charles in a stormy meeting from which all his own courtiers were excluded. The Covenanters informed the King that there was to be a new purge, as a result of which the remaining members of his household would be replaced by servants of their choosing.

When Charles refused to accept such an arbitrary decision, he was told that unless he co-operated with them they would withdraw their support for him and sign a treaty with Cromwell — one that would give a guarantee that the Parliamentarian general would leave Scotland, but would put the King in great peril.

Agitatedly telling Ralf of their demands, Charles said, 'There is only one thing that might persuade Cromwell to leave Scotland. The Covenanters must be intending to deliver me into the hands of Parliament, just as they did my father. I should never have placed my trust in such a band of narrow-minded bigots. Far from helping me to claim my birthright, they would deprive my country of its rightful monarch.'

The King's concern was shared by Ralf, but he tried to allay Charles's fears. 'I doubt if that is the Covenanters' intention, sire — but it might be wise to seek refuge with men who have less ambition than Argyll, and more understanding than the elders of the Kirk.'

'I agree wholeheartedly,' the King replied bitterly. 'But where am I to find such men?'

'You have spoken to my Lord Airlie, sire. He has assured you of his own support and given you the names of Scottish nobles who can be relied upon. And I know Piers and Colonel Trevanion intended to join him at his castle in Cortachy at the earliest opportunity. We will send a message seeking his help . . . '

'No!' the King interrupted. 'There have been too many letters and unfulfilled promises. We will ride to find Airlie and speak to him in person.'

Startled, Ralf nevertheless said, 'Very well, sire. I will make arrangements for tomorrow ...'

Once again he was interrupted by the King, who was now pacing the chamber. 'Tomorrow may be too late, Ralf. I have a bad feeling about the meeting I had with the Covenanters this morning. We will go today ... this instant!'

It was now after noon and Cortachy was more than forty miles distant. 'But what of the guards? They will never let us ride so far.'

'When we go hunting we are allowed to leave the guards behind because their noise would frighten all the game for miles around. Very well, go and fetch a hawk and have horses readied — good, sturdy horses. We have far to go before sunset.'

Ralf never expected the impromptu plan to succeed, but the ruse worked perfectly. Charles left the house that had become a virtual prison for him, accompanied by Ralf and five servants, and with a blindfolded hawk on his arm. The officer on duty allowed them to head for the nearby forest without insisting that the King be accompanied by guards.

Once out of sight of the soldiers, the jesses were removed from the hawk's legs, the hood came off, and with a quick flick of an arm the hawk sped off to freedom — and so too did the King. He and Ralf headed north-eastward to the home of the Earl of Airlie, while the servants

181

were told to make their way back to Perth . . . slowly.

★ ★ ★

The first halt made by the two horsemen was at the home of Viscount Dudhope, one of the Royalist supporters named by Lord Airlie. He was startled to see the King and dismayed to learn what he had done. However, he agreed to accompany him and Ralf to Cortachy. They set off again immediately and on the way collected the Earl of Buchan, another of the King's supporters.

When the horsemen reached Cortachy castle, weary but elated, they were greeted with disbelief by the Countess of Airlie and the women of the Earl's family. Airlie was not on his estate. Neither was his son, Lord Ogilvy, another of the Royalist conspirators upon whom the King was relying. Word had reached the Covenanters that he and Lord Airlie were seeking support for Charles and they had felt it advisable to absent themselves from their family home for a while, taking Piers and Colonel Trevanion with them after the two King's men had enjoyed no more than an overnight stay at Cortachy. They had ridden off that morning, heading north.

The Countess of Airlie was dismayed that Charles and his small party had chosen such a time to put in an appearance at Cortachy. If Covenanter soldiers came to the castle and found him here it would mean certain death for the Earl and his heir.

Charles too was alarmed. His spirits had been rising with every mile he put between himself and his captors. Now his hopes had collapsed yet again.

It was Ralf who responded to the Countess's fears. 'You are quite right, of course, the King dare not remain here — but where can he go? Where are we likely to find the Earl?'

After a whispered conference among the women, one of them said, 'If you go to Clova and ask for Fergus Findlater, he may be able to take you to him.'

'Findlater . . . ? Clova . . . ? Where is Clova?' Charles asked.

'About ten miles to the north,' the Countess replied. 'Ride through the glen and you'll find it.'

'I doubt my horse will last another ten miles — and Ralf's is little better. Do you have others we may take?'

Again there was a whispered conference before the Countess replied once more. 'My lord and his escort took all the horses . . . Please, if we give you food for the journey, will you leave right away? If you are found here . . .'

There was no need to complete the warning. The King was in no doubt about what would befall the family of the Earl of Airlie if he were found in the castle. It was quickly decided that while food was being prepared Buchan and Dudhope would ride ahead to Clova, find Airlie and tell him what was happening. In the meantime, Charles and Ralf would satisfy their immediate need for food and drink.

When he had eaten, Charles was at his

charming best when thanking the Countess for her hospitality, adding, 'Now, I would be grateful if someone could be found to set me on the road to Clova in order that I may meet my Lord Airlie and some of the men who I hope will help to form my new army.'

One of the younger women, who had until now remained in shadow at the rear of the room, and was dressed in a more simple fashion than the other women surrounding the Countess, now stepped forward. 'The way to Clova is not quite as straightforward as Lady Airlie made it appear. I will take you there. All the way.'

'You? You don't know the way to Clova.' This from the Countess of Airlie.

'I know it as well as anyone in this house. Indeed, *better* than anyone else. I travelled these hills many times with Lord Montrose, when he and my father fought for the King with Lord Airlie. I'll go and prepare for the journey. It will take only a matter of minutes.'

Not waiting to listen to any further objections that might be made, the young woman turned and hurried from the room, leaving behind an embarrassed silence.

It was broken by the Countess. 'I apologise for Frances, Your Majesty. She is not one of my own family.'

'Indeed? Tell me more of her.' The King was intrigued.

The Countess of Airlie looked pained, but said, 'Frances is the natural daughter of my late brother, Sir Douglas Skene, who went to England in 1625 to join the court of King James.

When the King died he remained to serve your late father, and became enamoured of a Lady Elizabeth Jermyn. As a result of that liaison they had a daughter . . . Frances. When her mother died my brother acknowledged Frances, gave her his name, and brought her to Scotland. She was then seventeen years of age. Unfortunately, she is more tomboy than girl, and because she was of a wild disposition and my brother encouraged such behaviour, he permitted her to go to war with him. I believe Lord Montrose also humoured her by allowing her to think she was in command of a troop of cavalry and the Covenanters put a price on her head. Unfortunately, my brother was killed fighting the Covenanters and when Montrose fled to the Continent I agreed she might come here to live with my daughters in Cortachy, where she was unknown — but she has been nothing but trouble. I am not at all certain she is the right person to accompany Your Majesty on such a difficult journey.'

The King smiled. 'On the contrary, I have no doubt she will prove as loyal to me as her father and the family to whom she belongs. I am grateful for the assistance she has offered me.'

★   ★   ★

When Frances Skene returned to the room and declared herself ready to guide King Charles and Ralf to Clova, Ralf asked if she had a horse.

'No. I will ride behind you,' she said.

Startled, Ralf asked, 'Do you have a double saddle?'

'I have no need of a saddle. I will straddle the horse and cling to you for support — if I need it.'

When Ralf looked uncertain, Frances boldly lifted her dress to reveal that she was wearing breeches beneath her skirts.

As the women of Airlie's family gasped in shocked disbelief, Frances said scornfully, 'It is only in deference to His Majesty that I am wearing a dress. When I rode with my Lord Montrose these breeches were sufficient to protect my modesty.'

King Charles made a sound that might have been stifled mirth, but when he spoke it was to say, 'I am delighted to have you guide us, Frances, but should we not be on our way if we are not to risk our necks in the dark?'

'Of course. I'll go and fetch the food we are to take,' Frances said. Turning to Ralf, she added, 'I will meet you outside.'

Outside the castle both King Charles and Ralf were mounted before Frances put in an appearance carrying a muslin-wrapped bundle containing a quantity of foodstuffs. There were mounting steps close to the castle entrance and, directing Ralf to them, she handed her bundle to him before springing nimbly up behind him, the display of her linen breeches earning a murmur of disapproval from the Countess and a smile from the King.

Settling herself comfortably on the horse's back, Frances placed her hands lightly on Ralf's waist. Making no attempt to retrieve the bundle of foodstuffs held before him on the saddle, she said, 'We can go now. I will give you directions when we leave the castle grounds.'

She left Cortachy with no words of farewell.

4

With Cortachy castle little more than an hour behind the small party, the horse carrying Ralf and Frances became lame. The glen was already in deep shadow and it was obvious they would not be able to reach Clova before nightfall.

'Is there anywhere we might spend the night?' asked the King. 'I have seen no houses since we left Cortachy.'

'There would be little to support anyone who built a house here,' Frances replied. 'But if we cross the ridge between the two hills over there we'll be in Glen Cally.' She pointed to a high gap between two rocky heights. 'There's a shepherd's cott on the far slope. It's little enough, but it's all there is — and the shepherd was in my father's command in Montrose's army.'

'Then we will seek his hospitality and share our food with him,' the King said. 'Please lead the way, Frances.'

*   *   *

The home of shepherd Angus Gunn was the meanest of hovels with a dirt floor and three rooms — the centre one for the use of sheep when shelter was needed. The outside door opened on to this byre, with crude interior wood doors leading to the rooms on either side.

The primitive cott was occupied by the shepherd, his pregnant and careworn wife and five dirty and hungry children.

Recognising Frances, the shepherd doffed his bonnet and dropped to one knee, but she called on him to rise to his feet and, without formally introducing the King or Ralf, said, 'These are friends of the Earl, Angus. We are on our way north, but a horse has gone lame. We need shelter for the night.'

'My home is yours, Mistress Skene, but we have little food and will need to gather fresh rushes to make up beds.'

'A rush bed and a roof above our heads is all we need,' declared the King. 'As for food . . . is there enough for all, Frances?'

'It will suffice,' she replied.

'Good! We will eat now, then rest. If Ralf's horse is better we will resume our journey at daybreak.'

'And if it is not?' Frances asked boldly. 'We can hardly remain here.'

'We will consider that in the morning,' Ralf said. 'I think we should eat as soon as we can. This is a poor family. I doubt whether they have very much with which to light their home.'

It was an unusual but memorable meal. The furniture of the cott consisted of two home-made chairs and a single rough-wood table, while the only candle stubs they were able to find were made from sheep's tallow, giving an indifferent and pungent light with which to illuminate a feast the like of which had never before been seen in the humble home.

It was dark by the time the meal was over. Although the shepherd had not been told the identity of the King, it had become increasingly apparent to the simple man that he was someone of great importance and so he was given the room at one end of the cott which usually served as a bedroom for the whole family.

Hastily prepared beds of reeds were made for Ralf and Frances on either side of the table in the living room, leaving Angus Gunn and his family to share the centre section of the cott with the two horses. In winter they would have also been sharing it with the sheep.

In the darkness of their section of the cott, Frances called softly, 'Ralf, are you awake?' It was necessary to speak quietly because the walls dividing the rooms did not reach the roof and were little more than stone-built partitions. Sounds would travel freely between the three rooms.

'Yes.' He was finding it difficult to sleep, thoughts of what might happen to the King occupying his thoughts. He also found sharing a room with Frances vaguely unsettling and wondered what she wanted.

Still speaking softly, Frances said, 'Things aren't going well for the King, are they?'

The question was not one he had been expecting, but there was no sense in lying to her. 'Things haven't gone well from the first day he set foot in Scotland. If he hadn't been so

190

determined to claim his throne he would have been better off staying in France or Holland.'

'What sort of man is he?'

'I like him far better than any of the kings or princes I met in Europe,' Ralf said. 'He cares for people — too much, sometimes.'

'What do you mean by that . . . are you talking of all the women we've heard about? His mistresses?'

'I doubt whether he's had any more than most men of his rank,' Ralf said defensively.

'He'll have no more mistresses when he marries Argyll's daughter. Argyll will see to that,' Frances commented.

'The King has absolutely no intention of marrying a daughter of Argyll,' Ralf retorted.

'That isn't what's being rumoured,' Frances persisted.

'You can believe me that it is no more than rumour,' Ralf said. 'There's not a jot of truth in it.'

'Well, you should know, I suppose,' Frances conceded. 'I heard Piers say that you are as close to the King as any man, and could be trusted implicitly.'

'Piers said that?' Ralf felt a warm glow inside him at her words. Such a statement from Piers was praise indeed, but he wondered about the meeting between Frances and his friend. Before he could ask her, she explained.

'I was listening to the men's conversation during dinner before the messengers came to warn Lord Airlie that the Covenanters believed he was one of the Scots nobles raising troops for

191

a Royalist army. As Countess Airlie told you, they should both now be in Clova with my lord. Unless Buchan and Dudhope found them right away, which I doubt very much, they will not be able to start back until dawn, by which time they will be very concerned that the King has not found them.'

'We will leave at first light and meet them on the path to Clova,' Ralf said. 'It will be good to see Piers again. He was declared by the Covenanters to be a 'malignant' as soon as we came ashore in Scotland. I miss being able to turn to him for advice. The King will be pleased to have him with him again too. He trusts Piers more than any other man at his court.'

'The King must trust you too,' Frances said. 'I doubt he would have ridden off in such a manner from Perth with just anyone. But . . . Piers? Is he someone very important?'

'Very!' Ralf replied. 'He is secretary to the King's council and one of King Charles's closest advisers. The Covenanters were aware of this — that's why he was one of the first to be removed from the King's court.'

'He's young to be so important,' Frances said. 'But then, so are you.'

'We have both been at the court for many years — Piers for longer than me.'

Ralf was aware that Frances was taking a more than polite interest in Piers. He wondered whether Piers had said, or done, anything to encourage her during his brief visit to Cortachy castle. He doubted it. Piers had enjoyed a number of casual affairs with women in the

192

French court — as he had himself — but he was not a libertine. Ralf decided to tell her more of his friend.

'He was a senior page to King Charles the First, when I came to the court as a page to the then Prince Charles. We became friends immediately, because my father had been ensign to one of Piers's kinsman who was killed at Lansdown, a man Piers idolised. Mind you, I have never met anyone who had a bad word to say about Bevil Grenville.'

It was dark in the windowless room of the cott, but Ralf sensed that his words had caused Frances to sit up on her reed bed.

'Piers was related to Sir *Bevil* Grenville?'

'Indeed he was.'

Excitedly, Frances said, 'My father was at Lansdown too. He spoke highly of Bevil Grenville and said there was no more honourable man in the whole of the King's service.'

'You must tell Piers,' Ralf said. 'He's convinced that had Sir Bevil not died at Lansdown, the Royalist cause would have prevailed and King Charles the First would still be monarch of England.'

'I *will* tell him, when we meet up with him and my Lord Airlie.'

In the darkness, Frances lay back on her bed of reeds and Ralf, acutely aware of her presence in the same room, found himself secretly wishing that Frances had shown as much interest in him as she appeared to have in Piers.

5

Events did not go to plan for the young King and the morning brought only more humiliation and despair.

When the light of the new day finally filtered through to the occupants of the windowless hovel, Angus Gunn emerged to see a small troop of Covenanter cavalry filing down the hillside towards the cott. He hastily woke the others.

Ralf's first thought was to saddle the horses and try to outrun the Covenanters, but Charles shook his head. 'I'll not be made a fugitive in Scotland, Ralf. Besides, I doubt your mount would be capable of outrunning those of the cavalrymen. We will remain here and maintain as much dignity as my present situation will allow.'

Frances had not left the cott, and speaking now from the shadows inside the door she said, 'They must not find me here. There is a price on my head because of my support of Lord Montrose. If I am recognised . . .'

There was no need for her to complete the warning. Argyll's bitter hatred of anyone connected with the late Marquis of Montrose was well known. His power within the hierarchy of the Covenanters would ensure that she could expect no mercy from her captors.

Angus Gunn said, 'Go to the back of the byre and climb the wall there. You will find a space between wall and thatch where you are completely hidden from view. It's where I keep meat — if I am lucky enough to have any.'

He did not need to explain that by 'meat' he meant either an occasional illegally killed sheep, or an equally illegal poached deer — both offences punishable by death.

'I'll help you up and make certain nothing of you can be seen . . . ' Ralf hurried inside the byre and, after providing her with a step by linking his hands and helping her on to the freestone wall, he ensured that none of her dress was hanging down in the view of anyone entering the cott. Then, with a hurried, 'Good luck!' he walked outside as the leading horseman reached them.

Showing little deference to the person of the King, the Covenanting officer in charge of the troop said, 'You've led us a merry chase, I must say. There have been men out searching for you throughout the night. What were you thinking of?'

'You were under no obligation to follow me,' King Charles said frostily. 'As for my thoughts . . . they are mine alone.'

Aware he had offended Charles, who *was* King of Scotland, despite his present situation, the officer said, more respectfully, 'I must ask you to return with me to Perth, sir.'

'I will return when I have bathed and eaten,' the King said haughtily, aware that he had won a moral victory, at least. 'Is there somewhere

195

within easy riding distance where I might satisfy my needs?'

'My orders are to return you to Perth as soon as you are found ... ' the officer replied uncertainly.

'And *my* orders are that you should take me to a place where I might bathe and eat before I return to Perth,' the King declared autocratically. 'Only then may you escort me to Perth — but I shall need a horse for my secretary. His is lame.'

'I have no orders to return anyone other than yourself,' the officer replied, 'and I have no horses to spare. As for somewhere for you to eat and bathe, we could either call in upon Lord Airlie at Cortachy, or perhaps Lord Gray at Huntly.'

Charles was about to argue when Ralf spoke, his thoughts with Frances, hiding inside the cott. 'You return to Perth, sire. I will remain with the horse and catch you up later, either along the way, or in Perth.'

Guessing the reason for Ralf's unexpected suggestion, Charles agreed. 'Very well, Ralf, but do not delay any longer than is necessary. In the meantime, here is my purse. Please recompense the shepherd for providing us with a night's lodging. Tell him that although he was unaware of the identity of his guest he could not have been more hospitable.'

Having done what he could to ensure that the shepherd would not be accused of knowingly harbouring his king, Charles turned to the officer of the cavalry troop and said, 'If you will have one of your men saddle the chestnut he will find in the byre, we can be on our way.'

★ ★ ★

Not until the King and his Covenanter 'escort' were topping the rise of the hills that separated Glen Cally and Glen Clova did Ralf re-enter the cott and help Frances from her hiding-place.

Her first words were for Angus Gunn. 'Thank you for not betraying me to the Covenanters, Angus. You can be certain that Lord Airlie will hear of your loyalty.'

'It has also been recognised by His Majesty,' Ralf said. 'He has left me his purse to reward your loyalty, Angus. Here, take it — take it all. It is what His Majesty would wish.'

'Why did you not tell me it was the . . . King Charles?' the Scots shepherd asked as he took the heavy purse from Ralf.

'It was better that you did not know, Angus,' Ralf replied. 'But he will always remember your loyalty.'

'It will be recognised by Lord Airlie, too,' Frances said. 'The Covenanters are out of sight now, Ralf. Check the horse and if it's fit to ride take it back to the track we were on when it went lame. Head north, following the river, and it will lead you to Clova. If you haven't met the others by the time you get there ask for Fergus — Fergus Findlater. Say you come from me and need to be taken to Lord Airlie right away. If he asks, you can tell him what it's about. Fergus is absolutely trustworthy.'

197

'What about you? What will you be doing?'

'I'll be all right. I would come with you, but we can't rely on the horse to carry two.'

'I'll try to get a horse to you as soon as I can . . .'

'Don't worry about me. I'll make my way back to Cortachy the way we came — but go now and find Lord Airlie. He'll want to set off after the King right away.'

6

Riding the horse that was still favouring a foreleg, Ralf topped the line of hills dividing Glen Cally from the great Glen Clova, and had almost reached the track when he saw a large body of men riding hard towards him from the direction of Clova.

At first he thought it might be more of the Covenanters. One of the officers taking King Charles back to Perth had boasted of being supported by two regiments of cavalry. However, as the group drew closer Ralf recognised Lord Airlie in the lead, with Piers and Colonel Trevanion hard on his heels. The Earl of Buchan and Viscount Dudhope followed with a force of some eighty heavily armed Highland warriors.

As the leaders urged their horses forward to meet him, Ralf brought his horse to a halt to await their arrival. When they came within hailing distance, Colonel Trevanion called out anxiously, 'The King . . . where is the King?'

Saving his reply until the horsemen reached him and brought their mounts to a halt, Ralf said, 'The Covenanters found us in a shepherd's cott Frances Skene led us to when my horse went lame. They've taken the King back to Perth.'

'Did someone at Cortachy tell them in which direction you were heading?' Airlie asked angrily.

Ralf shook his head. 'I doubt it. The Covenanters have had at least two regiments of cavalry out searching for the King. There can't be too many strangers travelling in these parts and we would have been seen by someone.'

'Aye, and the Covenanters would have gathered one or two deer-trackers along the way,' Buchan said. 'Some of them can track a deer — or a horse — as easily as you and I read a book.'

'Why didn't they take you with the King?' Airlie asked suspiciously.

'My horse won't stand up to travelling any distance. Besides, the Covenanters said their orders were to take the King, not me.'

'What of Frances?' Airlie demanded. 'There's a price on her head. What did they do with her?'

'They didn't find her,' Ralf replied. 'Angus Gunn, the shepherd, showed her a hiding-place between the roof and the wall of the cott.'

'Where is she now?'

Pointing to the saddle between the two peaks of the hills behind him, Ralf said, 'She's probably on her way up the slope behind there. We thought it important that I come on ahead to find you and tell you what's been happening.'

His suspicion allayed, Airlie said, 'She's as good as any man when there's the need for a cool head.' Turning his attention to Piers, he said, 'You and Colonel Trevanion make your way

200

to Cortachy and inform the Countess what is happening. Half a dozen of the Highlanders can go with you, just in case you run into trouble along the way. Lords Dudhope and Buchan can return to their homes while the rest of the men come with me.'

'I would prefer to stay with you,' declared Colonel Trevanion. 'I may be a malignant to the Covenanters, but I still consider myself to be commander of the King's bodyguard.'

'For that very reason you must avoid trouble at all costs,' Airlie declared firmly. 'I don't anticipate there being any fighting when we catch up with the King and his captors — and that is what they are — but should there be any bloodletting it is better that it is between Scotsmen and not Scots and Englishmen. Besides, as you say, you are a malignant. It would need to be explained why you and Grenville are in my company. We could all lose our heads and set back the cause of King Charles. With Hunkyn it is different. My castle is nearby, so it is perfectly natural he should have come to me for help — and equally natural that I should be concerned for the King's well-being.'

'I will need a new horse if I am to come with you,' Ralf said. 'I doubt this one will carry me as far as we will need to ride.'

'Choose one from the Highlanders who are returning to Cortachy,' Airlie said. 'They can double up for that distance, and lead your mount into the bargain. You'd better pick one out for Frances, too.'

'I'll do that,' Piers said unexpectedly, 'and I'll

take it to find her. I would like to feel I was doing something useful. Colonel Trevanion and the escort can ride to Cortachy and let them know what is happening, and we will follow you to Perth later.'

'No, remain at Cortachy until I return,' Lord Airlie said. 'When I find out what is likely to happen as a result of the King's escapade we will need to make new arrangements. The Covenanters are aware that something is being planned; that is why they were able to find him so quickly. We can afford to take no chances. There are more than our lives at stake here. The future of a king and of our two countries is in our hands.'

★ ★ ★

Bringing his own horse and the one he was leading to a halt when he reached the saddle between the two peaks, Piers looked down into Glen Cally and saw Frances climbing the slope towards him. She seemed in no hurry. As he watched, she reached down and plucked a small flower that was growing among the sparse grass, unaware of his presence.

It was not until she carried it up to her nose that she saw him. Piers realised that the sun had just risen above the brow of the hill behind him and was shining in her eyes. She would find it difficult to identify him and he called out, 'It's all right, it's Piers Grenville. I've brought a horse for you.'

Delighted now, she asked, 'How did you know where to find me? Have you seen Ralf?'

'Yes. He's gone with Lord Airlie and an escort of Highlanders to try to catch up with the King. Colonel Trevanion is on his way to Cortachy to let Lady Airlie know what is happening. I said I'd bring a horse and come to find you.'

'Why?'

'Why?' Piers repeated. 'Because the horse you and Ralf had shared couldn't carry you both and you are on foot.'

'No, I mean why are *you* bringing the horse to me?' She had reached him now and was looking up at him, squinting into the sun. Piers thought she had a fine, strong face.

'I'm very impressed with the Highlands,' he replied. 'I thought it would be nice to ride up here and enjoy the view.'

He had a feeling that his reply disappointed her. It was only the vaguest of impressions, but before he could make up his mind she said, 'If you are really interested in the scenery and are in no hurry to get to Cortachy we could follow Glen Cally northward for a while, then take a sheep track back over the hills to Glen Clova again. The view from up there is something you will never forget.'

'I would like that,' Piers said, and he meant it.

Since being banned from the King's court by the Covenanters he had felt his life to be in limbo. Trying to win support for the King from Scots nobles was a frustrating experience beset with vague promises and a lack of enthusiasm. It seemed that each of them was waiting to see what his neighbour intended to do before committing himself wholeheartedly to the King's cause. Lord Airlie was more supportive than most, but such enthusiasm was not shared by his household. There would be nothing gained by hurrying to Cortachy in his absence.

Chatting to Frances as they rode together alongside a stream that tumbled down from the hills at the head of the glen, Piers found her to be an intelligent and knowledgeable companion. She quickly brought the conversation round to Sir Bevil Grenville and, as Ralf had suggested, she found Piers ready to extol the virtues of his late kinsman.

After a while, Piers asked, 'Did you discuss the battle of Lansdown with Ralf?'

'Only briefly,' she replied. 'Why?'

'Because his stepfather was seriously wounded there when he was ensign to Sir Bevil. It was because of his stepfather's service that Ralf was taken on as a page to the King when he was still Prince Charles. He has served him well.'

'Ralf speaks just as highly of you,' Frances said. 'Does he have a wife in the King's court?'

Piers shook his head. 'Being an untitled official in the court of an impoverished and exiled King hardly makes a man a good prospect for marriage.'

'Does that mean you too are unmarried?' Frances tried to make the question sound entirely innocent.

'It does,' Piers replied, giving Frances a sidelong glance that let her know she did not seem as ingenuous as she would have wished. 'But we have talked enough about me. I have heard rumours that *you* have led a most

204

interesting life. If they are true perhaps you'll tell me something of the Marquis of Montrose? I met him when he came to the King's court in the Netherlands. I found him far more passionate for the King's cause than any of the noblemen I have met in Scotland.'

Piers was dismayed to see tears well up in Frances's eyes. Brushing them away in an angry gesture, she said, 'Lord Montrose was passionate about all the things he believed to be right, including his support for the monarchy — and his mistrust of Argyll. It cost him his life in the same way that trust in Argyll led to the death of King Charles the First. The present king will make the same mistake if he does not take care.'

'The King does not trust Argyll — and unless I am mistaken I feel you blame Argyll for the death of Montrose. For the record, the King sent a letter to Lord Montrose that was intended to save his life. It called on him to cease all activities he was carrying out in Scotland on the King's behalf. Ralf will verify this; it was he who wrote the letter. For some reason — that Argyll may possibly be able to explain — the letter was not delivered.'

'It sounds like Argyll's doing,' Frances agreed. 'He hated Montrose and coveted his lands. No one who supported Montrose can ever rest easily; that's why I needed to hide from the Covenanters who found King Charles at the cott of Angus the shepherd. There is a reward out for me — dead or alive.'

'Then the rumours I have heard of you are all

true,' Piers said. 'You *were* an exceptional leader. One of whom your father and my kinsman, Sir Bevil, would have been proud.'

Further conversation came to an end for a while because they turned off the path on to a sheep track that forced them to ride in single file. Riding behind the slight figure of Frances Skene, Piers marvelled that she should have been such a tenacious cavalry leader that the Marquis of Argyll had felt it necessary to put a price on her head.

He also decided that she was the most exciting and attractive young woman he had ever met.

7

Because of King Charles's determination to clean himself up before returning to Perth, the officer in charge of his escort suggested once more that they stop at Cortachy castle. Charles declined, saying that now they had ridden this far they might as well go even farther south, where Lowland comfort was greater than in the more Spartan conditions prevailing in the northern fortresses. They went on to Huntly, at Longforgan, close to Dundee, and it was here that the Earl of Airlie, Ralf and the Highlanders caught up with them.

Although the arrival of the Highlanders was welcomed by Charles, their presence was not necessary to ensure his safety. The officer escorting him was aware that the power of the Kirk had been seriously undermined by the Dunbar defeat, while the King's star was in the ascendancy. He would do nothing that was likely to prejudice his own future, should power slip from the grasp of the Covenanters.

King Charles's entry into Perth, accompanied by an impressive escort of Highlanders, was cheered by those who witnessed it. Nevertheless, the hardline elders awaiting him were determined that he should suffer for his actions. He was told that as his secretary must take some responsibility for encouraging his 'foolish escapade', Ralf would be declared a malignant and banned from the royal court, which had by now dwindled to almost nothing.

Charles objected but was told that the Kirk would provide him with a new secretary. He refused to accept their decision, and when Argyll came to his chambers to confirm the decree Charles gave the Scots nobleman his own angry ultimatum.

'You will not deprive me of a courtier who has served me well for many years. Argyll, this time you and the Kirk have gone too far. I have been forced to publicly denounce the imagined faults of my father and mother, and those of myself. I have done all that has been asked of me, however humiliating — and, indeed, often absurd. It has gone far enough. My next public denunciation will be of the elders of the Kirk — and of yourself. I have kept faith with the agreements I made with you both, but have received nothing in return. Instead, you have deprived me of my most loyal courtiers and servants and emasculated the army I was promised. By so doing you ensured that it suffered defeat after defeat at the hands of Cromwell. It is time this nonsense is brought to an end. I will make my views known and we will let the people decide who is right, and who is 'malignant'.'

Argyll was dismayed by this sudden and unexpected intransigence. Aligned for the moment with the Kirk's hardliners, he was well aware that their popularity was waning fast. Should the King publicly denounce them there were many nobles opposed to Argyll who would be delighted to throw their considerable weight behind the moderates and topple him from his present position of power.

He went away promising nothing, but that evening Ralf was told he might take his place with the King once more and over the course of the next few days Piers and Colonel Trevanion were also quietly reinstated, together with other members of the court which had accompanied Charles to Scotland.

★　★　★

A fortnight after the reinstatement of the King's courtiers, Argyll came to visit Charles again. His lean and habitually unsmiling face was uncharacteristically animated and his manner almost deferential.

'Your Majesty, I come to you with splendid news. Splendid news indeed!'

Aware that what constituted good news for the Marquis of Argyll might not necessarily be good news for him, Charles said warily, 'Oh? And what is this news, my Lord Argyll? Have Parliament and the Kirk given me an army with which to recover my throne?'

'The army will be yours when the time is right,' Argyll said. 'We still have the Western Association Army. It will claim the throne of England for you — but it will be a Scots army, led by the crowned king of Scotland.'

The Western Association Army, based in the south-west of Scotland, was controlled by Covenanter extremists. Its loyalty to Charles could not be guaranteed, and he had serious doubts about its fighting qualities — but it was Argyll's last statement he questioned now. 'The army will be led by the crowned king of Scotland? What is your meaning, my lord?'

Looking smug, Argyll said, 'I have persuaded Parliament to agree to your coronation. If Your Majesty agrees, the ceremony will take place at Scone on the first day of the new year.'

This was startling indeed. Although the Covenanters had eased their iron grip on him in recent weeks it was a major step forward. However, since the news came from Argyll, Charles suspected an ulterior motive, especially as he was aware of the widening gulf between moderates and extremists within both Kirk and Parliament. He gave Ralf a quick glance and saw that his expression also was one of wariness.

'Is this a unanimous decision by all Covenanters?'

Argyll made a gesture which conveyed both embarrassment and assumed frustration. 'Not all men look at things in the same way. There are those who are not convinced that Your Majesty intends to keep your sacred oath to accept the Covenant. I have been able to convince many of them — but not all.'

'I am grateful to you, my Lord Argyll.' If Argyll was telling the truth, Charles had reason to be grateful, but the Marquis's next words showed that his motives were not entirely altruistic.

'Of course, it would be advantageous to have a queen by your side at your coronation. A Scots queen, and one devoted to the Kirk, would silence all criticism . . . '

'Especially if that queen happened to be an Argyll, no doubt?' Charles could not keep the scorn he felt from his voice, but Argyll showed no embarrassment.

'My daughter is a pious young woman from a family who has served the kings of Scotland well. The connection would greatly strengthen the ties between England and Scotland.'

'Such ties should not need strengthening,' Charles retorted. 'My grandfather was king of Scotland before he became king of England, and my father was born here. When I choose a queen it must be to forge new alliances in Europe. But that is for the future. There will be no queen by my side at my coronation and I would rather my Scots noblemen brought soldiers to my army than assemble to see me crowned, only to disappear again immediately the ceremony is at an end, leaving Cromwell with more of Scotland than I command.'

As both Charles and Argyll knew, Cromwell had been able to move at will in much of lowland Scotland after his victory at Dunbar. The only reason he did not take absolute control was that he did not yet have sufficient soldiers to occupy the whole of the area.

'That will happen in due course . . . ' Argyll began.

'When?' Charles demanded derisively. 'After

211

the Kirk has purged the army of everyone capable of defeating Cromwell in battle? I think not. The so-called army of Scotland has become a laughing stock — and you, my Lord Argyll, have allowed it to happen.'

'Mistakes have been made,' Argyll admitted, 'but the strength of the Lord is ours. He will not fail us.'

'I understand that Captain-General Cromwell goes into battle with the same faith in the Lord,' Charles retorted, 'but *he* ensures his faith is backed up by a well-trained and experienced army.'

'We can discuss the army at some other time,' Ralf said hastily. He knew that Charles was very bitter about the failure of the Covenanters to provide him with a force with which to invade England and claim his throne. He did not want it to prejudice the coronation Argyll had promised. The ceremony would do much to boost the morale of the uncrowned king and greatly strengthen his position within the British Isles and beyond. 'Let us discuss details of the coronation. It should be a memorable day for everyone involved . . . '

8

The coronation was arranged for 1 January 1651, even though not all Covenanters were in favour of either Charles or the pomp and ceremony which would accompany the crowning of the King. However, opposition to Charles and the moderates within Kirk and Parliament was to be dealt a serious blow from an unexpected quarter.

Much of the strength of the extremists sprang from their control of the Western Association Army, but on a frosty November night Oliver Cromwell lured that force into battle at Hamilton, only a short distance from Glasgow. By the time dawn broke, the Scots army was broken too. Master tactician Cromwell at the head of eight regiments of Roundheads had notched up another notable victory.

The implications of such a crushing defeat were not lost upon Charles and he was quick to point out to Argyll that unless the Covenanters faced up to reality, Cromwell and the English Puritans would soon be in control of Scotland, when the Covenant — any Covenant — would become meaningless. As a result, at a meeting of the church commissioners in Perth, it was decided that the victims of their many purges, the so-called 'malignants', would be welcomed back into the fold if they produced a certificate from their local presbytery confirming that they had made an acceptable apology for their past sins.

It meant that the battle-hardened veterans so desperately needed could once more fight for their country. Scotland could once more have a credible army.

It also had results that did not please Argyll.

When the coronation was only a few weeks away, the Marquis visited the King's chambers and was handed a list of guests already approved by the King. Most of them were Royalist nobles and their families. Many were anathema to Argyll and the Covenanters, but they were being forced to swallow their pride if they wished to retain their own brand of Presbyterianism.

However, there were some names that would be harder to accept than others — and Argyll suddenly found one of them. His finger pressing heavily upon the page, he spluttered, 'Frances Skene! What is her name doing here? There is no question of allowing her to attend the coronation. She is a wanted woman — if she is indeed a woman. No, if she so much as shows herself she will go straight to the scaffold.'

The King was reading a book on the desk in front of him, but he had been listening to what Argyll was saying and now he looked up, feigning surprise. 'A wanted woman? Why should such a charming and delightful young woman be wanted? Surely you are mistaken, my Lord Argyll?'

'You know her? How?' Argyll demanded.

'She has been presented to me by Piers Grenville, secretary to my council. She is the young woman he intends to marry. I gave the young couple my blessing. I have no doubt she will make him an excellent wife.'

'You forget there is a price on her head. Where is she now?'

'Are you suggesting I should tell you where you might arrest her and then claim a reward for so doing?' Charles asked indignantly.

'I am saying she is a malignant and will not be allowed to attend the coronation,' Argyll declared.

No longer teasing, Charles snapped, 'Frances Skene will attend *my* coronation as *my* guest . . . unless you feel the crown should be placed upon your head and not my own?'

In a bid to defuse what he realised might easily develop into a serious difference of opinion, Ralf said hurriedly, 'It is my understanding that those who had been regarded as malignants have been granted an amnesty by the church commissioners, my lord.'

'Only if they truly repent of their past conduct and receive a certificate of repentance from their local presbytery,' Argyll replied.

'Then Frances Skene has done all that is required of her,' Ralf said, concealing the triumph he felt. 'She is in possession of such a certificate; I have seen it myself.'

'It was never intended that forgiveness should

be offered to those who rode with the murderer Graham.' Argyll had always refused to recognise the Marquis of Montrose's title, referring to him only by his family name.

'My dear Argyll,' said the King patiently, 'the amnesty was granted by the Kirk, with the approval of the Scottish Parliament. Are they aware that their decision does not apply to those against whom you have a grudge, or who might have incurred the displeasure of the Campbells?' Now it was the King's turn to refer to Argyll's family name.

'This is a personal affront to me,' Argyll declared angrily. 'It will be seen as such by every Covenanter in the land.'

'Only if you allow it to appear so,' said Charles. 'On the other hand, should you let it be known that you accept the rehabilitation of Frances Skene, along with the other so-called 'malignants', it is highly probable that the Scottish nobility will be able to present a united front when an army is formed capable of ejecting Cromwell from Scotland and marching upon London to defeat those who deny the throne to their rightful monarch. However, in the unlikely event that Frances Skene is molested on your orders it will be apparent that you believe your personal authority takes precedence over king, Kirk and Parliament. I doubt whether such a presumption will be acceptable to anyone.'

When Argyll had left the chambers in a towering rage, Charles said, 'We have given my Lord Argyll serious cause for thought, Ralf

— but tell Piers to keep Frances at Cortachy until we are certain Argyll will do her no harm.'

★ ★ ★

The Marquis of Argyll was in charge of proceedings at the coronation of King Charles II, but both Ralf and Piers were involved in preparing the King and his court for the great day. Their task was not an easy one. The Covenanters were determined that Charles should spend the days before the ceremony praying for forgiveness for the sins of his parents. Charles wished it to be a memorable State occasion. As a result the coronation became a compromise between ideology and tradition. Loyal to Charles, both Ralf and Piers tried to inject as much ceremonial as possible into the service. Meanwhile the Covenanters were intent upon stressing the fact that it was primarily a Presbyterian service and not an opportunity for unseemly celebration.

On the day of his coronation, Charles sat beneath a velvet canopy wearing a princely robe, with trainbearers who were the sons of Scots noblemen. However, much of the traditional ceremonial was omitted and the crown was placed upon his head by the Marquis of Argyll. There followed an exceedingly long sermon, delivered by the moderator of the Kirk, in which he pointed out the frailty of monarchy, and even the feast which concluded the proceedings was devoid of any sense of the rejoicing that would normally have attended such an occasion.

Charles's courtiers and supporters had been rehabilitated, but those seated at the King's table were predominantly Covenanters. When he tired of their talk, Charles rose to walk around the banqueting hall to accept the homage of his other guests. The Covenanters, headed by Argyll, went with him.

After receiving the obeisance of his friends, Charles glanced towards a long table at the bottom of the hall. Here the wives and daughters of a few Kirk leaders sat with female members of noble Covenanter and Royalist families in an atmosphere that was not noticeably congenial.

'I would like to meet your ladies,' Charles said unexpectedly. 'Ralf, please ask them to come and be presented.'

Ralf hurried to where the women sat and repeated the King's request. There was an immediate excited stirring among the families of the nobles. Some of the wives and daughters of the church leaders rose to their feet too, but seeing the wives of the most senior of the kirkmen remaining in their seats, staring stonily in front of them, they sat down again in embarrassed confusion.

After only the slightest hesitation, Ralf turned his back on the seated womenfolk and escorted the noblewomen to where the King stood waiting.

As the women came to a halt, uncertain what was expected of them, Charles turned to the titled Covenanters. 'My lords, perhaps you will present your good ladies.'

Argyll was the first to hurry forward, at the

218

same time beckoning to the women of his family. The second of them to be introduced was Argyll's eldest daughter, Lady Anne. This was the daughter he had suggested Charles should marry.

Such a marriage would never take place, but as she curtsied the King took her hand and carried it to his lips, saying gallantly, 'I am delighted to meet you at last, Lady Anne. I can see for myself that my secretary did not exaggerate when he told me you were a beautiful woman . . .'

Lady Anne Campbell walked away from the King with crimson cheeks, convinced that Charles was the most attractive man she had ever met. She would later declare that she would be willing to wed him even if he had no throne to offer her.

Among the last to be presented was Frances Skene. In the end, her invitation had been issued unhindered by Argyll, and his capitulation confirmed that she was free to show herself in public. When Piers brought her forward, Charles released his grip on her hand with apparent reluctance and smiled at her.

'I am delighted to meet you once more, especially as Piers tells me you and he are to be married as soon as it can be arranged. He is a very lucky man — but you are lucky too. Piers is one of my most trusted courtiers and one who has served me well. It will not be too long before you are *Lady* Grenville.'

'Thank you, Your Majesty,' she replied and Ralf thought it was a far more demure Frances than the one who had accompanied him and the King on their abortive ride to Clova. But then, as Piers was leading her away, she startled him by giving him a surreptitious wink. He realised that she still possessed the spirit that had commanded a cavalry troop in the army of the Marquis of Montrose.

9

The wedding of Piers Grenville and Frances Skene took place in the private chapel of Cortachy castle, ancestral home of the Earl of Airlie, and the place where the illegitimate daughter of Sir Douglas Skene had found refuge.

James Ogilvy, father of the present earl, had been a dedicated Royalist and his castle had been reduced by Argyll in earlier troubles when the confused state of Scots politics and religion meant that the line between friend and enemy was so uncertain that it was likely to be redrawn on an almost daily basis.

Such feuds between rival clans were not easily forgotten and neither Argyll nor his Covenanter friends were invited to the wedding. As a result the many guests were able to revel in an atmosphere of gaiety and celebration unlike anything that had been seen for many years.

'This is the life we should be leading, Ralf.' The perspiring monarch had escorted his latest dancing partner back to her seat before returning to sit beside Ralf and accept the drink proffered by a servant.

'It's good to see you enjoying yourself, sire. There has been little to celebrate since we landed in Scotland.'

'No one would dispute that, Ralf. Who was the young woman with whom I was just dancing? She is a lively young thing. Unfortunately, I did not catch her name.'

'She is Lady Bethoc, sire, wife of the Earl of Pitloch, a man who must be at least forty years her senior, and would appear to find whisky preferable to the company of his wife. He is over there in the corner beyond the piper, looking as though he has forgotten not only where he is, but *who* he is.'

'The man is a fool to allow himself to get in such a state when he has a wife who is both young and vivacious — but the piper is playing again and if I am not mistaken Lady Bethoc is giving me a signal that I shall not ignore.'

King Charles advanced across the room to take the hand of Lady Bethoc and lead her to the centre of the hall where the dancing was about to begin. Other couples followed and the floor was soon crowded.

When the dance ended the King was not to be seen, and neither was Lady Bethoc. The Earl of Pitloch was oblivious of the buzz of interest their absence caused. He had been drinking heavily throughout the celebration and, eyes glazed, was unable to focus on anything for more than a second or two. He sat slumped in a chair, jerking out of his comatose state every now and then to tap a foot unrhythmically to the music of the piper before sinking back once more into his alcoholic stupor.

As the next dance began, a voice from beside

Ralf said, 'You look like a man who has lost a king, but don't worry. Lady Bethoc will bring him back. She has never yet lost a lover.'

It was Frances. The Countess of Airlie had claimed Piers for a dance and his bride had seen Ralf standing on his own, looking anxiously around the hall for King Charles.

He smiled at her. 'His Majesty is well able to take care of himself when a lady is involved.'

'No doubt. I understand he has a great deal of experience in such matters,' Frances said. 'Is it true he has a son by a common whore?'

Ralf knew Frances must be talking of Lucy Walter and he replied, 'He has acknowledged a young son, but the boy's mother comes from a good family, albeit one that has seen better times.'

Frances made a scornful sound. 'I believe the boy's mother has also known better times — and many other lovers.'

'No more than many other young women on the fringes of a royal court,' Ralf declared, wondering why he was defending the dubious honour of a woman he did not particularly like. 'Anyway, the King is no longer as infatuated with her as he once was — as Piers would tell you.'

'Piers defends King Charles as fiercely as do you,' Frances replied, 'but my information about Lucy Walter came from an officer who fought with my Lord Montrose. He is a kinsman of Lord Airlie and stayed here at Cortachy after being wounded. During his visit he passed on all the gossip of the court.'

'It is sad that my Lord Montrose did not live

to see this day,' Ralf said. 'He would have enjoyed seeing you wed to Piers.'

'My Lord Montrose was a truly remarkable man, who should never have met his death in the manner he did,' Frances agreed. 'But we will not talk of him today. This is my wedding day. A happy day.' Changing the subject, she asked, 'Have you never found anyone you wished to marry, Ralf?'

Her question caught Ralf off guard and for the first time in many months a memory of Brighid came to mind. 'There *was* once a girl I thought I wanted to marry.' Forcing a smile, he added, 'I was very young then and, unfortunately, she ran off with a soldier.'

Frances gave him a sympathetic look. 'Never mind. You are still young and there are many very nice girls who would make you a good wife. One is seated across the hall, in the Ogilvy party. Lady Helen is the very pretty red-haired girl wearing pale green. She is far and away the nicest of the Ogilvy girls and she has never stopped asking questions about you since we had our adventure together in Glen Cally. Come along, I'll introduce you to her properly . . . '

10

As weeks and then months passed in 1651, the position of King Charles II grew steadily stronger, while the power of the Covenanters waned. Yet, although he was now the crowned king of Scotland, Charles was monarch of a troubled country, its capital and much of the Lowlands occupied by an English army and its rulers divided by religion, mistrust and opposing allegiances.

Nevertheless, the Royalist Scots nobles were able to gather the nucleus of a growing army about the young king, and although the force controlled by the Scots Parliament was at times so fragmented that it was capable of mounting only nuisance raids against the English the two armies gradually moved closer together, although their aims were not the same. Charles wanted to lead an army into England to claim the throne he had inherited when his father was executed. The ambitions of the army which owed allegiance to the Kirk did not extend beyond the aim of driving Cromwell and his English army out of Scotland.

However, in July, when it seemed Cromwell's army was poised to conquer yet another large area of Scotland, the Committee of Estates decided something needed to be done to prevent it and they acted quickly, if not particularly decisively.

The force they despatched to deal with the situation was little more than 4,000 strong, and once again Cromwell and his soldiers inflicted a crushing defeat on the Covenanter-led Scots. Half the men in the Scottish army were killed and almost as many captured.

Cromwell's victory meant that he was now able to move his whole army northwards and achieve his objectives, while Charles and his own army were still not strong enough to face the full might of the Parliamentarian army of the north.

However, the manoeuvring of the English army had left the way open for Charles to realise the ambition he had nurtured since his arrival in Scotland a year before. He would take his army into England and march upon London, gathering Royalist supporters along the way until he rode at the head of a force capable of defeating any Roundheads that stood in its way.

★   ★   ★

'This is the moment I have dreamed of since we left England. How many years ago was that, Ralf?' King Charles put the question as they rode to the head of the marching column of soldiers, their progress cheered on by the Scots soldiers of the King's army.

'More than five years, sire.'

'Five years,' the King mused. 'So much has

226

happened in that time. So much that cannot be undone. If only I was marching into England as a prince and not a king. My father's executioners shall not go unpunished . . . but enough of such talk. Has Piers returned yet?'

'No, sire, but he should be with us before nightfall.'

Piers had been sent to tell Argyll what was happening and to urge him to march to join the King with all the men he could muster.

'Is Frances returning to Cortachy now we are on our way?' the King asked. Like Ralf, he had become very fond of the Scots girl.

'No,' Ralf replied, 'she is travelling with us. Piers wanted her to remain behind, but she pointed out that she probably has more experience of fighting than most of the men in Your Majesty's army.'

'Unfortunately, she is quite right,' the King conceded. 'I am leading an army that has yet to be seriously tested in battle. However, we shall learn quickly — and I am pleased to see that you too are wearing a sword. You should carry a pistol too.'

'I do have a pair of very fine pistols,' Ralf admitted. 'They were given to me as a present by Lady Helen, one of Lord Airlie's daughters.'

'Ah! I heard there might be a romance in the air there. Should I be congratulating you?'

Ralf shook his head, 'No, sire. Lord Airlie has made it very clear that Lady Helen will one day be married to a nobleman. Preferably a *Scots* nobleman.'

'Has he, indeed?' Charles was indignant. 'He

might one day regret not welcoming you as a son-in-law. How do you feel about it?'

Ralf shrugged. 'Lady Helen is a most enjoyable companion. I like being with her very much, but would need to think very carefully before I contemplated marriage to her — or to anyone else at the moment. I tried to make that clear to her as gently as I could, although nothing was actually said.'

'You are quite right, Ralf. Now, we are nearing the head of the column and I must consider where the army is to rest for the night. When we are in camp I will dictate a letter to my mother to tell her I will shortly be setting foot in England once more . . . '

★ ★ ★

A travel-weary Piers caught up with the King's army late that night. In reply to Charles's eager question, he replied despondently, 'Argyll will not be bringing his men to join you, sire.'

'Not . . . But I am relying on his support. He gave me his word!'

'I reminded him of his promise, but he was adamant. I fear he is offended because he has not been offered command of your army, sire.'

'It was never intended that he should have command of the whole army,' Charles said, 'but he would have been made a general. I thought he was fully aware of that.'

'I don't doubt he was,' Piers said, 'but Argyll is easily offended. It could also be that he has no stomach for battle.'

'I shall remember his disloyalty when I am able to reward those who have served me well,' Charles said. 'No matter; there will be soldiers enough for my army when we cross the border into England. That day cannot come soon enough for me. I have had my fill of Scotland and the fickleness of men like my Lord Argyll. Now I am going to my chamber. I intend that we shall make a full day's march tomorrow.'

When the King had retired, Ralf, Piers, Frances and Colonel Trevanion gathered in a room allocated to the married couple in the house where the King and his courtiers had been accommodated. Their talk was of Argyll's perfidy and how it would affect the King's cause.

'I don't think it should prove too serious,' Ralf suggested. 'We need a substantial army, of course, but there will be no shortage of loyal Englishmen eager to fight for His Majesty.'

'I wish I shared your confidence,' Colonel Trevanion said seriously. 'According to the spies who have come to me, things have changed greatly since we were last in England. Parliament has a very tight grip on the country. Known Royalists are closely watched and their freedom of movement restricted. If anyone travels any distance they are likely to be stopped by a Puritan patrol and asked to declare their business. If they are unable to satisfy the soldiers they are arrested and locked up until their reason for travelling can be verified. That could take weeks, or even months if the Puritan authorities wish to keep them that long. I don't think we will find men flocking to join the King. Even minor protests against Parliament are being put down with ruthless severity. Few will dare show allegiance to King Charles until he proves he has the beating of the Roundheads — and I doubt we have that. Our Highlanders are fierce warriors but they are not trained soldiers like those in Cromwell's army.'

'What are you saying?' Ralf asked. 'That we will not be able to gather men to fight for the King — and that our army will be beaten?'

'I am not saying that, Ralf. Victory or defeat is not decided by numbers alone — but I would be much happier if we had more troops on our side, and they possessed the experience of the soldiers commanded by Cromwell.'

* * *

The army of King Charles crossed the border into England on 6 August 1651, but a rebuff was received almost immediately when Carlisle refused to open its gates to him. He was forced to move on without the reassurance of the loyalty of this important northern town.

However, smaller towns welcomed him, albeit with differing degrees of enthusiasm, and he was proclaimed at Penrith. Nevertheless, Trevanion's gloomy predictions proved only too true. Very few men rallied to the King's banner. Those who did could not compensate for the Scotsmen who deserted the army in ever increasing numbers to return to their homes. Meanwhile, Cromwell had gathered his victorious army of the north and was pursuing the King with such speed that he was already harassing the rearguard of the royal army.

There were a number of loyal English noblemen who tried to come to Charles's aid but they were swiftly and ruthlessly dealt with by the enemy. One such supporter was the Earl of Derby who landed with a substantial force from the Isle of Man, only to be heavily defeated in a one-sided battle fought outside Wigan.

To make matters worse, Parliament had a wide network of spies throughout the land. As well as relaying the King's movements accurately and in detail, they were able to expose those he hoped would rise to join him. As a result many thousands of Royalist sympathisers were arrested and held in custody, and by the time Charles reached Worcester on 22 August he commanded no more than 16,000 dispirited, exhausted and woefully inexperienced soldiers, while Cromwell was closing in upon the city with more than 30,000 battle-hardened veterans.

Worcester was destined to witness the extinguishing of the Royalist flame of hope that had been lit by King Charles when he marched out of Scotland at the head of his army.

It was a flame that would not be re-kindled for almost another decade.

11

Within days of his arrival at Worcester it had become apparent to the generals of Charles's army that they would be able to advance no farther into England. Cromwell's army was growing stronger by the hour and now ringed the walled city that was at the very heart of England. As the Roundhead army grew in numbers, so too did their artillery and it battered the beleaguered city night and day.

Talk in the King's camp was no longer of victory, but of the chances of survival. The only man who refused to publicly acknowledge the inevitability of defeat was Charles himself. From the imposing tower of Worcester cathedral he surveyed the movements of Cromwell's troops and disposed his own men accordingly, showing considerable skill as a military commander despite his lack of years and experience.

One of the first things he did was to order the demolition of four vital bridges giving access to the town. Unfortunately, the work was not carried out as efficiently as it should have been and one of the bridges would still be available to Cromwell when he eventually mounted his attack.

On 3 September Charles was atop the cathedral tower with Ralf, Piers and a number of young Cavaliers who were employed as messengers to carry the King's orders to the senior officers commanding the Royalist regiments. Meanwhile, below, inside the cathedral, Frances was helping to tend both soldiers and civilians wounded by the Roundhead bombardment.

Still surprisingly cheerful in spite of the seriousness of the situation, Charles said suddenly, 'We shall see Cromwell open his attack upon us today, Ralf, you mark my words.'

'What makes you so certain, sire? It would be more sensible for him to continue his bombardment and starve us into submission.'

Charles shook his head. 'Are you not aware of the significance of the date, Ralf? Today is the anniversary of Cromwell's great victory at Dunbar. He is a man who attaches great importance to such portents.'

Charles had hardly finished talking when musket-fire erupted outside the city walls. Raising a spyglass to his eye once more, Charles could see a line of boats being strung across the water upriver from the city in order to attack one of the gates which had been thought to be safe when the bridge leading to it was destroyed. Roundhead soldiers were already crossing in considerable numbers.

Threatening as the manoeuvre was, it meant that the force left behind was greatly weakened. Charles thought he saw an opportunity to score a victory against the Roundhead general.

Excitedly, he cried, 'This is our chance! Come,

Piers — you too, Ralf. We will see some action today.'

Covered by his own artillery, called down in response to that of the enemy, he swept out of the gate closest to Cromwell's depleted force, at the head of his wildly cheering Highlanders.

It was not long before they were engaged in ferocious hand-to-hand fighting. Although Ralf and Piers tried to stay with the King, he was surrounded by nobles and bodyguard and it became difficult to remain as close as they would have liked. The King, although on foot, seemed totally fearless. It was a trait which inspired those about him and they fought ferociously. Many were killed or mortally wounded, including the Duke of Hamilton, one of the most senior Royalist commanders.

Charles and his Highlanders fought until their ammunition was almost spent, then, with the balance of the battle tilting in his favour, Charles sent orders for the Scots general, Leslie — the man who had lost Dunbar to Cromwell — to throw the soldiers under his command into the field to decide the issue.

Leslie failed to respond to the order.

Meanwhile, realising the danger his men were in, Cromwell had rushed to their aid, calling on three of his reserve brigades to join him.

For a while it seemed the King and his Highlanders might still save the day, but the sheer numbers of the Parliamentarians proved decisive. Had Leslie thrown his men into the battle the outcome might have been different, but he held back in a fatal state of indecision.

As a result the tide of battle turned decisively in favour of Cromwell's army. Now it was the Royalists and King Charles who were in imminent danger of annihilation. It was with the greatest difficulty that Charles was able to reach the gate and take sanctuary inside the now doomed city, crawling the last few yards on hands and knees while his bodyguard, rallied by Colonel Trevanion, bought his escape at the cost of many lives.

Ralf and Piers were among the bodyguard and it was then that Piers was struck down by a musket ball, fired at close range by a Roundhead musketeer. He would have been despatched by a pikeman had Ralf not leaped forward and run his sword through the soldier's body.

A momentary rally by King Charles's Highlanders enabled Ralf to sheathe his blade and raise Piers from the ground. The Cornishman was bleeding profusely from a chest wound and appeared to be having difficulty with his breathing. However, with the help of a Highlander, Ralf succeeded in extricating Piers from the mêlée and helping him to the cathedral.

When Frances saw Piers being helped in through the door, supported by Ralf and the Highlander, she abandoned the man she had been tending and ran to him, her expression showing the fear she felt for her husband.

There was no need to ask where he was wounded, since a large patch of blood was staining the chest of his grey tunic, but she said, 'What happened? Is it from a sword-thrust?'

Ralf shook his head. 'He was struck down by a musket ball.'

Unceremoniously ripping the shirt from Piers's chest, Frances exposed a blue-edged hole from which blood bubbled out at an alarming rate. She had witnessed more bloodletting than most women, but this was her husband's blood and it unnerved her for a moment.

Piers was drifting in and out of consciousness, his breathing laboured, and Ralf said, 'He needs to be seen by a surgeon. Where is he, Frances?'

Frances pulled herself together. 'I'll find him. While I'm gone see if you can do something to stem the bleeding.'

She hurried away and after only a moment's hesitation Ralf tore his own wide neckcloth free and folded it several times before pressing it over Piers's chest wound. He held it in place until Frances returned accompanied by a small, bespectacled man whose bloodstained hands and clothing were indicative of his calling. Hurrying behind him was a younger man, equally bloodstained, who carried a battered leather bag.

The surgeon was hopelessly overworked tending the Royalist wounded and he wasted no time on niceties. Removing the folded neckcloth, he poked a finger into the hole made by the musket ball, grunted, then said something to his assistant. The younger man opened the bag he was carrying and removed a pair of forceps which he handed to the surgeon. Almost casually, the surgeon inserted the blades into Piers's chest, causing the young Cornishman's body to arch in pain.

The surgeon's methods achieved results. Less than a minute later the instrument was withdrawn with a bloody musket ball captured in its jaws. A second delve recovered a small piece of rib bone to which was attached a fragment of cloth.

Then it was the turn of the surgeon's finger once more. His exploration completed, the man spoke to Ralf for the first time. 'The musket ball broke a rib and detached a small piece of bone which caused pressure on the lung. He will be in pain for some time, but ball and bone are out now and he is breathing more normally.'

'Will he recover?'

The surgeon shrugged in response to Ralf's question. 'He's young and strong. I have seen men recover from far worse wounds — and others die from less. I have done all within my power; the outcome is out of my hands now.' With this ambiguous prognosis he hurried away.

Ralf was refolding his neckcloth, prior to replacing it upon Pier's chest, when Frances called, 'Wait!'

She hastened to where a wounded Scots officer was drinking whisky to deaden the pain of a Roundhead sword-slash. After exchanging a few words with him, she relieved him of the whisky and carried it back to Piers. Before Ralf could question her intentions, she poured a quantity of the whisky into the hole in her husband's chest. Piers had been regaining consciousness but now he writhed in agony before lapsing into oblivion once more.

'What do you think you are doing?' Ralf demanded, aghast.

'I once saw an old woman pour whisky into the wound sustained by one of my Lord Montrose's officers. He recovered. I fervently hope that Piers will do the same.'

Ralf was not convinced, but he needed to return to the King and he left Frances tending Piers.

Outside the cathedral, although fierce fighting was still taking place, Ralf managed to make his way to the street where the King had been lodging. Finding the house, Ralf entered and was halfway up the stairs when he met Charles, sword drawn, blocking his path.

When Charles recognised Ralf, he sheathed his sword. 'I heard the door opening and did not know who it was. Worcester is lost, Ralf, and my cause with it. I tried to rally the Highlanders but they threw down their arms and ignored me. I will be lucky to escape. Colonel Trevanion is at the rear of the house with some of my officers. My brave Lord Cleveland will create a diversion in order that we may escape to the north through St Martin's gate.'

'Is there a spare horse, sire? I'll come with you . . . '

'Wait! What of Piers . . . and his wife?'

'Piers is sore wounded. Frances is with him in the cathedral.'

'Then go and see if he might be moved. If he cannot, bring Frances alone. I will tell Cleveland to delay his diversion for a few more minutes. If you miss us, then come to me at a house named

Whiteladies, near Boscobel. It is the home of Colonel Gifford, one of the officers waiting for me. I believe it lies some miles beyond Wolverhampton. They may deny I am there — as Catholics they have learned to be suspicious of strangers — but persist and ask for Gifford in person.'

Aware that there was a very real possibility they might never meet again, Ralf dropped to one knee and grasped the King's hand. 'God go with you, sire. I will pray for your safekeeping.'

'Thank you, Ralf. I value your prayers more than any offered up by the Covenanters. May you remain safe too . . . but there is little time left for any of us.'

12

When Ralf returned to the cathedral he found it in a state of chaos. Darkness was falling outside but the battle that had been fought for most of the day was not yet at an end. The wounded of both armies were being brought in and tended by the Royalist camp followers and the women of the city.

In the gloom of the interior of the building Ralf located his friends. To his great relief he found that Piers was conscious and his breathing easier than before. He related what the King had said to him, but Piers said, 'The King must escape no matter what happens to me, or to anyone else. Go with him, Ralf — and take Frances with you.'

'I will not leave without you,' Frances declared firmly. 'We will try to get you out of the city. You are secretary of the King's council — and a Grenville. Cromwell would not allow you to live.'

'You must go, Ralf,' Piers said. 'The King needs you.'

'The men who are with him at this moment are of more use to him than me.' Ralf said. 'I can do nothing more for him. My concern — and that of the King — is for you and Frances. You must get to safety.'

Even as he spoke there was the sound of musket-fire and much shouting from outside the cathedral and a cry went up: 'The Royalists are mounting an attack . . . the King is with them!'

A half-hearted cheer rose from many of those inside the cathedral and some of the less seriously wounded Highlanders made their way outside, determined to aid their king if it was at all possible.

'Surely the King is not trying to break through Cromwell's army!' Frances sounded confused. 'It is suicidal . . . '

'It's part of Cleveland's diversion,' Ralf said quickly. 'He wants the Roundheads to believe the King is with him . . . now is the time to get Piers out of the city.'

Frances looked at him in consternation. 'He's not fit to be moved yet . . . It could kill him!'

'As you just said, he'll die for certain if he remains here . . . and I have an idea. Try to find a litter while I get someone to help carry it.'

It was not difficult to find four Highlanders just outside the cathedral who were willing to help for the promise of a few shillings, coupled with a means of escape from the city.

They would leave by the river. The cathedral grounds went down to a part of the city wall which was built on the river bank. There was a doorway in the wall here. Bolted from the inside, it was too small to attract the attention of a besieging army. Colonel Trevanion had arranged for a small boat to be placed just inside the gate for the use of the King should the battle go against him and there be no other means of escape from the city.

Now the unthinkable had happened, but new plans had been made for the King. Cleveland's diversion was drawing Cromwell's troops away from St Martin's gate through which Charles was making his escape, accompanied by the survivors of the royal guard. It was also diverting Roundhead soldiers from the cathedral and in the darkness Ralf and Frances made their way to the small river gate with Piers carried in a litter by the four Highlanders.

It took only minutes to open the gate and launch the boat. When they were all aboard, they pushed off from the bank and allowed the current to carry them silently downriver. Gradually, the noise of battle faded into the distance and gentle river sounds took over.

'Where are we going?' Frances asked as one of the Highlanders pushed the boat away from the bank on a bend.

'I don't know,' Ralf admitted, 'but we need to put Worcester as far behind us as we can. When the battle is over Cromwell will have soldiers scouring the countryside for the King. Any Royalists they find will be either killed or taken prisoner.'

Once or twice they heard voices from the river bank, but it was impossible in the darkness to know whether the speakers were Roundhead or Royalist and those on board the boat either remained silent, or spoke only in whispers.

When dawn came they were drifting downriver with open countryside on either side, the quiet beauty far removed from the horrors of war they had left behind. Ralf estimated they might have travelled as far as five or six miles, but it was still not enough to feel safe.

Ralf's intention was to remain in the boat, find somewhere to hide during the daylight hours and travel with the current at night, but the Highlanders had other plans. The river was carrying them in a southerly direction and they wanted to go north, back to Scotland. They stated their intention of going ashore and making their way homeward.

Ralf tried arguing with them, pointing out that they would be hunted down long before they reached the border. Frances too pleaded with them to change their minds for the sake of Piers, but they were adamant. They had been in England following the orders of an Englishman for too long. They wanted to go home and the River Severn was flowing in the wrong direction.

Ralf's main concern was that the Highlanders would abandon the boat and leave them stranded in the heart of the countryside with a seriously wounded man. He opened his mouth to argue again, but just then Frances cried, 'Look! Up ahead on the right. It's a reed bed. If we take the boat in the Highlanders can go ashore and we might be able to find food and hide there for a couple of days until Piers is stronger.'

'It looks as though there's a hut of some sort on the far side of the reeds,' Ralf pointed out. 'That could be to our advantage . . . or perhaps not. We'll be cautious and hide the boat on this side while I find out if there is anyone in the hut.'

None of them were boatmen and for a while Ralf feared the tide might defeat their plans and take them past the reed bed. However, there was a rope attached to the bow of the boat and when the small craft bumped against the riverbank he and two of the Scotsmen were able to jump ashore and pull the boat to a break in the bank which allowed water to flow into the reed bed. From there they were able to haul the boat through the gap and hide it from view among the reeds.

Ralf made another attempt to persuade the Highlanders to remain with them and travel on when night fell, pointing out the impracticality of four Highlanders trying to walk hundreds of miles through Puritan England without being caught. But one of the men was a deer-tracker back home in Scotland. He was confident they could elude the enemy soldiers and reach home safely.

After money had changed hands and the Highlanders had departed, Ralf and Frances moved away from the boat to discuss their situation. They believed Piers to have dropped off to sleep, but they had not gone far when he weakly called them back.

When they returned to him, he said, 'You both know the dangers of staying here with me. You should be getting as far from Worcester as possible . . . No, don't try to argue with me, Ralf. Your duty is to the King, not to me — and he will have need of you. If you can obtain food and water to keep me going for a few days you must leave me — and take Frances with you. If I am well enough when the food has gone I will make my way to my family home at Stowe, in Cornwall. If I do not survive . . . well, you are my wife, Frances. You will be made welcome there and Stowe will become your home too.'

'You are talking nonsense, Piers,' Frances said, more upset than she wanted to reveal to him. 'Yes, I *am* your wife, and whatever Ralf decides to do I will remain with you until you are fit to be moved, so we will have no more talk of doing anything else. I very much look forward to seeing Stowe — but it will be with you.' Turning to Ralf, she asked, 'You heard what Piers said about your duty to the King, Ralf. What do you intend to do?'

'The King left Worcester with men who can help him far more than I,' Ralf replied. 'His orders to me were to look after you and Piers, so I think the best thing I can do is find whoever lives in the hut on the far side of the reed bed and learn where their loyalties lie. I'll decide what to do then. I'll load my pistols before I go and leave one of them with you. I trust neither of us will need to use them.'

★ ★ ★

The hut was a simple, one-room building made from wood and mud, with a dried reed thatch. In a clearing in front of the small building were piles of loose, cut reeds, with tied bundles piled high to one side. As Ralf approached, a wizened little man emerged from the hut and stood in the doorway. He watched Ralf as he walked up to the hut, but said nothing.

Nonplussed by the man's apparent indifference, Ralf stopped in front of him and said, 'Hello. I wonder whether you might have some food you could sell me?'

'Would it be just for yourself?'

When the reed-cutter put the unexpected question Ralf hesitated before deciding to tell the truth. 'No, there are three of us. We came downriver during the night.'

'I know,' said the man. 'The ducks told me. They're better than a watchdog. You'll have come from Worcester, no doubt. Most of the Roundhead army must have tramped past here these last few days, heading that way. They said the King was there with an army from Scotland and that they were on their way to see that he suffered the same fate as his father. I could hear the sound of the fighting for most of yesterday but judging by the silence this morning the battle must be over. Who won?'

Ralph met his eyes. 'Worcester is in the hands of the Parliamentarians.'

'Then you and those with you will be King's men,' the man said calmly. 'No doubt the Roundheads are looking for you?'

'They will be searching the countryside for any survivors of the King's army,' Ralf agreed, heartened by the reed-cutter's use of the

246

unflattering nickname. He decided to tell him the truth.

'My friend is in a boat among the reeds and is badly wounded. His wife is with him. If you have food to spare I will be happy to pay you well for it.'

'You have a woman with you . . . and a wounded man? Is the boat well hidden?'

Ralf nodded. He thought it better to say nothing of the Highlanders who had been with them.

'Then you'll be safe enough for the time being,' said the man. 'As for food . . . I set a net for fish last night. There'll be something there — and I picked up a couple of loaves from the miller's wife yesterday. I'll cook the fish and bring them down to you, with the bread. Stay in the reeds and keep quiet. Sound carries some distance around here. I don't want to get on the wrong side of any Roundheads.'

When Ralf began to thank him, the man cut him short. 'Go back to the others. I'll find you when the fish are cooked. You haven't asked me, but I'll tell you: I'm neither for Parliament nor against it, but what they did to King Charles was unforgivable. I wouldn't hand anyone over to the justice they mete out.'

★ ★ ★

When Ralf returned to the boat hidden among the reeds Frances was concerned that he might have placed too much trust in the reed-cutter, who had given his name as Samson Burton.

247

'It's always possible,' Ralf conceded, 'but I don't think so. I believe his sympathies lie with the King. Besides, we have to trust someone, Frances. There is no way we can survive without help.'

Despite his assurances to her the next hour was fraught with thoughts of what might happen if Samson Burton decided to report them to Parliamentarian authorities. And later, when someone was heard moving towards them through the rushes, both Frances and Ralf had their pistols cocked ready to shoot if the newcomer proved to be an enemy.

It was Samson and he was carrying bread and cooked fish as well as a half-flagon of ale.

Ralf and Frances were very hungry but Piers merely picked at his portion and Samson watched him with increasing concern. 'He's obviously received a very nasty wound,' he said eventually. 'Has anyone suggested any treatment?'

'The surgeon in Worcester took out a piece of bone and a musket ball,' Frances said, 'but there were so many wounded men he had very little time to spend on Piers. Is there a surgeon hereabouts who could be trusted to help him?'

Samson shook his head. 'I know of no surgeon I would trust to treat a Royalist without informing the Roundheads, but there is a woman living nearby who delivers all the local children and is called in whenever someone is hurt.'

'A woman?' Frances queried. 'Does she have knowledge of medicine, or surgery?'

'As far as I know she has never worked with

any surgeon,' Samson admitted, 'but she has saved more lives in this part of the country than anyone I have ever known.'

Frances was sceptical, but Ralf asked, 'Can she be relied upon to say nothing about Piers if we call her in to treat him?'

'*I* would trust her,' Samson replied. 'Her son was killed fighting for the King. She hates Cromwell and the Roundheads and was once imprisoned for expressing her views of them.'

'Then I can see no harm in having her look at Piers,' Ralf said. 'Could you bring her here?'

'I'll go and find her this morning,' Samson replied, concerned for Piers. 'She could be here before midday if there's no other call on her services.'

Ralf looked briefly at Frances, who was still looking doubtful, then turned back to Samson. 'Very well. Ask her to come here and look at Piers — but she is to say nothing to anyone else. The Roundheads would dearly love to have Piers in their hands.'

When Samson had gone, Frances asked, 'Do you think it was wise to let Samson know that Piers is someone of importance? What if he goes to Cromwell's men and claims a reward for telling them our whereabouts?'

'If he is a Roundhead supporter he will inform on us in any case,' Ralf said, 'and there is nothing we can do about it — but I don't think he is. Anyway, we have to trust him. All the same, we'll keep a keen look-out to see who might be heading this way, just in case.'

Maudie Porter was a stooped, small-framed woman in her late sixties who would have passed unnoticed in a crowd. However, when she shifted her gaze from the ground at her feet there was an intensity in her expression that was unnerving.

Piers was helped to the reed-cutter's hut where she examined his wound with a thoroughness that made Ralf and Frances wince and caused Piers great pain.

When the examination was completed to her satisfaction, she said, 'You owe your life to the surgeon who treated you first, young sir. You were lucky. Most army surgeons are a sexton's best friend. You will be as well as you have ever been if you dress that wound with a salve I will make up for you.'

'I'll see that his wound is dressed regularly,' Frances said, thankfully. 'I am his wife.'

Maudie gave Frances one of her disconcerting looks, 'Good — but you have your own health to attend to. How many months pregnant are you?'

Startled, Frances would have lied to anyone else, but there was something about this astute old woman that prevented her from denying her condition.

'Three . . . possibly four months,' she said.

'I'd say it's at least four,' Maudie replied, 'but you're a healthy young woman; you'll carry it well, come what may.'

Piers had been listening in increasing astonishment to the conversation between the two women. He struggled to sit up now, but failed.

Lying back once more he looked accusingly at Frances and asked breathlessly, 'Why haven't you told me about this before? You should never have been following the army . . . '

'*That's* why I never said anything to you,' Frances said. 'Besides, you had enough to think about, and I wanted there to be no fuss.'

'But . . . after all that has happened — and could still happen . . . '

'All the more reason for you to make certain *you* get well quickly,' Maudie said. 'Do as you're told and you'll be able to take care of your wife when she most needs you. Now, I need to go and gather a few herbs if we're to make the right salve for you. In the meantime I suggest you go back to your boat and move it farther into the reed bed. The Puritans are out seeking the King's men and would rather kill those they catch than take them prisoner — and you have much to live for.'

★　★　★

The news that Frances was expecting their baby provided Piers with the incentive he needed to speed his recovery. Maudie came to visit him every second day and in little more than a week his wound was healing well. He was able to walk, albeit stooped and hunch-shouldered in the manner of a man three times his age.

During this time a troop of Roundhead cavalry visited Samson's cottage and made a half-hearted search of the area around the perimeter of the reed bed, despite the strong protests of the reed-cutter who complained that the hooves of the cavalry horses were costing him money by trampling the stalks. When the Roundheads left, he waded to where the nervous trio greeted him with two cocked pistols.

'It's all right, they've gone now,' he reassured them. 'I doubt if they'll be back. From what they were saying they are satisfied there are none of the King's men in the area, so I think it's time we moved you downriver.'

'Where did you have in mind?' Ralf asked.

'That's very much up to you,' Samson replied. 'I often take reeds to a thatcher in Tewkesbury and I've been as far as Gloucester when the price was higher there.'

'How will you explain having three of us on the boat with you?' Ralf asked. 'Surely that will make any Roundheads we meet suspicious?'

'They won't see three of you,' Samson explained. 'You and your friend will be hidden in a space in the middle of the reed bundles. His wife will be my daughter, coming to help me along the way.'

'I suppose you couldn't take your load as far as Bristol?' Ralf suggested. 'We might be able to catch a boat from there to take us to France. It would be even better if you felt able to carry us as far as the Cornish coast.'

Samson shook his head. 'That would excite attention for certain. They grow good rushes in the Somerset marshes. No one in his right mind would carry Worcestershire reeds to the west country. I daren't take you very much farther than Gloucester.'

Ralf conceded that what Samson said made sense. Besides, there were many Royalists in the Gloucestershire area with whom he might make contact. Then Piers entered the conversation for the first time and asked Samson whether he would consider going as far as Berkeley, which was approximately halfway between Gloucester and Bristol.

When Samson looked doubtful, Piers explained, 'I have kinsmen who live there, close to the castle. They would certainly help us.'

'I know the area you are talking about — indeed, I once worked there,' said Samson. 'They grow reeds. They're not as good as mine, but they have no reason to bring thatching in from outside the area.'

'Nevertheless, a boatful of reeds wouldn't look out of place,' Piers persisted, 'and if there are any Roundheads around to query your presence you can say they are better quality than the local reeds and have been especially ordered by my kinsmen.'

'That might satisfy the Roundheads,' Samson conceded, 'but I have a living to make. When I sell my crop I usually try to sell the boat as well. Then I make my way home with enough money to live on and spend the quiet months building another boat. If I can't sell the boat I need to buy a horse to tow her back and sell the horse when I get here. Either way I need to make enough money to keep me until the next crop comes round.'

'There will be no problem about your money,' Piers said excitedly. 'I will make certain you are given a good price for your reeds — and the boat as well, if you want to sell it. What's more, I will pay you well for taking us downriver — and we'll leave our boat here for you to use, or to sell, as you see fit. I guarantee you will earn more money from this one journey than in four or five years of more mundane work. Will you take us there, Samson . . . please?'

Looking vaguely uncomfortable, Samson said honestly, 'I would have taken you for no more than the price of the rushes — but anything extra will be very welcome. Very welcome indeed.'

'Good man!' Piers exclaimed, more animated than Ralf had seen him at any time since the Battle of Worcester.

Frances too was pleased to see his enthusiasm, but she was looking at him through different eyes. Uppermost in her mind was the fact that he looked frail and wan. She hoped he would be fit enough for the voyage that lay ahead.

13

Samson's craft for carrying the reeds was part raft, part boat and larger than Ralf had been expecting. It had a thatched shelter at the stern and an outsize oar trailing behind which acted as a rudder to steer it as it was carried along by the river's sluggish current. The oar could also be easily detached if it was needed to fend the vessel off from the bank on one of the river's many bends.

From the shelter it was possible to remove some of the bundles of reeds to reveal a tunnel which led to a cramped space in the middle of the cargo.

During the day, Ralf and Piers would remain close to the entrance to this shelter, making use of it if the need arose. At night it would serve as a private 'bedroom' for Piers and Frances.

The journey passed without incident until they reached Tewkesbury. Samson had not expected to arrive until dusk, but there had been heavy rainfall at the source of the river, in mid-Wales, which caused a rise in the water level and an increase in the speed of the current. As a result, they reached the Gloucestershire border town in late afternoon, and as they passed through it they were called upon by a party of Roundhead cavalrymen to pull in to the bank to be searched.

'Shall I do as they ask, or just ignore them?' The question was put to Frances by a worried Samson.

'We do as they say,' Frances said. 'There is no way we can outdistance them — and they carry muskets. One wounded man is more than enough; we can't risk having another ... All right! We're pulling in as quickly as we can. This is a boat, not a horse. It doesn't obey orders.'

This last was directed at the Roundhead troop commander, who had repeated his order for them to pull in to the bank, and had emphasised his command by having one of his troopers aim a musket at them.

Samson worked hard at the oar to bring the boat closer to the river bank, while Frances secured a rope to the bow of the boat. As they came nearer, she called out to the Roundheads, 'When we are close enough I'll throw the rope. You can catch it and use the strength of your horse to bring us to a halt and hold us in.'

'You can jump ashore and do it yourself,' retorted the troop commander, ' ... and be quick about it.'

'I can't hold the boat against such a current!' Frances said indignantly. 'My father might work me as hard as a horse, but I haven't the strength of one.'

Frances was giving a good imitation of the sort of girl who might be expected to work on the river. She had even adopted the accent of the countryside through which they were passing.

'Don't give me any of your nonsense,' the troop commander snapped, losing patience. 'How do you usually bring the boat to a stop when you pull in?'

Aware that she was now in command of the situation, Frances replied, 'We are either berthing at a quay, where there are bollards, or, if on a river bank, we secure the boat to a tree. Can you see a tree anywhere along this bank?'

All the trees that might once have grown along the river had long since been cut down by the townsfolk for fuel for their fires. There was not so much as a sapling along the Tewkesbury stretch.

Reluctantly accepting that he could not bring this confrontation to a dignified conclusion, the Puritan troop commander called, 'Where do you come from, and where are you bound?'

Aware that the Roundhead was acknowledging defeat, Frances replied, 'My father and I are from a small reed bed a few miles upriver and are bound for Gloucester to sell our reeds for thatching.'

'Have you seen anything of any Royalists on the river?' the Parliamentarian demanded.

'I doubt if we would recognise a Royalist if we met one,' Frances lied. 'Not unless they wanted to buy a boatload of reeds.'

'Well, keep your eyes peeled,' said the Roundhead officer. 'The son of the former king has escaped from Worcester and there is a reward of a thousand pounds for his capture. Anyone who earned that would never need to work again.'

'For such an amount I would make a crown for my father's head and hand him over to you,' Frances said, 'but I doubt if we'll meet him between here and Gloucester.'

'Probably not,' agreed the Roundhead, 'but be vigilant and report anything unusual.'

'We will indeed,' Frances said. 'Thank you, sir.'

The Roundhead officer reined back his horse, and as the reed-carrying boat edged out to the centre of the river once more he pulled his mount's head round and rode back along the river bank with his troop.

★ ★ ★

With Tewkesbury behind them, and nothing but open countryside around, Samson brought the boat gently in to the river bank and went off to relieve himself, while Piers and Ralf emerged from the hideout. Congratulating Frances on her performance in facing down the Roundhead commander, they sat down beneath the thatched shelter discussing what he had said about the hunt for King Charles.

'He has probably crossed the border into Scotland by now,' Frances said, but Ralf disagreed.

'Wherever the King is, it will not be Scotland. He never trusted the Covenanters before, and after Argyll refused to join him he would not put his life in his hands again. He is convinced he would suffer the same fate as befell his father.'

'Argyll is a scheming and vindictive man,'

Frances said. 'He would sacrifice his own mother for a parcel of land. I can never forgive him for his part in the execution of my Lord Montrose, who was everything that Argyll is not.'

'But if the King is not in Scotland, then where is he?' Piers asked, and both he and Frances looked to Ralf for a reply.

'My guess is that either the King is heading for Ireland,' he said, 'which is doubtful in view of Cromwell's successes over there, or he will try to get back to his mother in France. In which case he will most probably be making for the south coast. If he is, he will come down this side of the country rather than risk having someone recognise him in London.'

At that moment Samson could be heard returning to the boat. He had proved to be a loyal friend, but they would not discuss the possible movements of the King in front of him in case he fell into the hands of the Parliamentarians.

'We may well meet up with the King in the west country,' Ralf said quietly. 'But we will keep such thoughts to ourselves.'

★   ★   ★

When Samson's boat reached the spot where the Little Avon, which flowed past Berkeley, joined the River Severn, there were so many reed beds that Piers felt embarrassed at having suggested Samson should pull in among them with his boatload of Worcestershire reeds. Samson, however, was quite philosophical about it, smugly pointing out how superior was his own cargo to the Gloucestershire variety. 'Your kinsman will not regret buying my reeds,' he said. 'His thatch will still be keeping his home snug and warm when that of his neighbours has long since rotted away.'

When the boat was safely hidden away from prying eyes Ralf and Frances set off to find Sir John Lewis, who was the brother of Piers's mother. It was felt that the presence of Frances would help allay any suspicions Sir John might have about Ralf. These were difficult times in England for anyone with Royalist sympathies. Parliament's spies were not above resorting to subterfuge in order to incriminate those who were suspect.

Ralf and Frances walked along beside the river in a light drizzle, enveloped by a mist that hid the countryside round about. Piers had tried to convince them he was fit enough to come with them to visit his uncle in person, and this was the subject of their conversation.

'It's good to see the improvement in him,' Ralf commented, 'but there is no way he could walk a couple of miles just yet.'

'No,' Frances agreed, 'but he has all the determination of a Grenville. Had we let him he would have made the walk, even if it killed him.'

After a few moments of silence, Ralf said, 'You are the ideal wife for Piers, Frances. He is very lucky to have found you.'

'I am glad you think so, Ralf. I might very easily have married you, you know.'

Ralf did not know. 'What do you mean? I

never said anything . . . neither did you.'

'What was there to say? You are a handsome man, and close to the King. I couldn't fail to be attracted to you, but I had already met Piers. Mind you, that did not prevent my Lord Airlie from suggesting that you might make a suitable husband for me.'

'He actually told you that?' Ralf expressed disbelief. 'He certainly didn't consider me good enough for Lady Helen.'

'That was a decision that made Helen very unhappy, but it came as no surprise to me. Neither you nor I are considered to have the breeding to become a member of my Lord Airlie's family.' When Ralf made no immediate reply, Frances asked, 'Does it trouble you, Ralf? Did you really want to marry Lady Helen?'

Ralf shook his head, 'The King asked me the same question. I'll give you the answer I gave to him. Lady Helen is a very nice and very kind young woman whose company I enjoyed, but I entertained no thoughts of marrying her.'

'Did you tell her so?'

'No. The subject never came up in conversation.'

'I'm glad,' Frances said. 'She would have been terribly hurt if she believed you saw her as nothing more than a friend. She is a very nice girl and absolutely adores you.'

'I know,' Ralf said. 'She is also generous. The pistols you and I are carrying were a gift from her — a very expensive one.'

They walked on in silence for a while before Frances asked, 'What would your reply have

261

been had Lord Airlie suggested that you marry me and accept a handsome dowry?'

In an attempt to avoid giving her an honest reply, Ralf said jocularly, 'I suppose it would have depended very much on the size of the dowry.'

'Would it, Ralf? Would it really?'

He wanted to lie to her . . . but could not. 'No, Frances, it would have made no difference at all. But I realised that you and Piers are made for each other, and I love you both.'

It was far more honest than he would have wished to be, but it seemed it was the reply that Frances wanted.

'You are right, Ralf. Piers and I are very much in love — but we both also have a very special friend and I will always love you for being that friend.'

There was a slightly awkward silence between them before Frances said, 'Piers and I would like you to know that if our baby is a son, he will be named Ralf. Ralf Grenville. It is a name of which he will be very proud.'

14

By following the detailed directions given to them by Piers, Ralf and Frances easily found the Elizabethan mansion occupied by Sir John Lewis, even in the thick mist that persisted along the river. The maidservant who answered the door to them seemed extremely nervous and asked them to wait at the door while she went away to find her employer.

A tall man of distinguished appearance, Sir John was frowning when he entered the hallway and walked to the open door. He glanced only briefly at Frances before turning his attention to Ralf. Addressing him haughtily, he said, 'Your name, I am told, is Ralf Hunkyn. You will pardon me, sir, but it means nothing to me. The maid also said that you are a friend of a kinsman, but she did not know to whom you referred.'

'I crave your pardon for my unannounced arrival, Sir John, but these are unusual times. I come with news of your nephew Piers — and would like to introduce his wife, Frances.'

Startled now, Sir John said, 'Piers? But he is . . . ' He stopped short before adding, 'He is far away, and I have heard nothing of his taking a wife.'

Aware of the housemaid standing in the doorway through which Sir John had entered the hall, Ralf said, 'If we might talk in private, Sir John, I will make everything clear.'

Following Ralf's pointed glance to where the housemaid stood, Sir John said, 'I think that would be a good idea. We will go to the library.'

He led the way to a book-lined room with a window that looked out upon lawns extending in the direction of the mist-shrouded river. Closing the door behind them, Sir John said, 'Now, perhaps you will explain exactly who you are, and what your mission may be.'

'I am secretary to His Majesty King Charles the Second,' Ralf said. 'I came from Worcester with Frances and Piers . . . who suffered a severe wound in the hard-fought battle there.'

Sir John was shaken. 'You were at Worcester? And Piers . . . ? Where is he now?'

'In a boat hidden in a reed bed where the Little Avon flows into the Severn.' Frances spoke for the first time. 'He is recovering from his wound, but is in need of help.'

Ralf then told Sir John of their escape from Cromwell, and of the part played by Samson Burton. By the time he had finished talking Sir John was satisfied that he and Frances were telling the truth. 'The river between Bristol and Gloucester is patrolled by Parliament's navy. We must bring Piers to the house immediately. The mist will help us, but it is likely to lift at any time.' Belatedly, he turned to Frances. 'I must apologise for failing to welcome you to the family and not congratulating you on your

264

marriage to Piers. I will rectify that immediately by introducing you to my wife, and then Ralf, myself and a few trusted servants will set off to fetch Piers to the house.'

'I would rather come with you,' Frances declared, but Ralf said, 'I think you should remain here.'

Sir John looked at him questioningly and Ralf explained, 'Frances is four months pregnant and has already had far more excitement than is good for an expectant mother.'

'Of course,' Sir John agreed. 'Come, my dear, I will introduce you to my wife, Morwenna. As you might gather from her name, she is from your husband's home in Cornwall. You can get to know her — and my daughters too — while Ralf and I go off to fetch Piers.'

Frances would rather have gone with the men but, much to Ralf's relief, she made no further protest.

The party that set off from the mansion was small but Sir John doubted whether they were likely to meet any Roundheads unless the mist cleared. In the event, Piers was retrieved from his reed-bed hide-out without incident. While he was being conveyed to the house, Samson and his boatload of rushes were towed upriver to Berkeley.

Sir John had three daughters and it was the first time two of them had met Piers. It was an intensely loyal Royalist family and the close association that Piers and Ralf had with the King meant they were both regarded with a degree of hero-worship that took them by surprise.

The few days spent at Berkeley were relaxing for the three fugitives, but Sir John and his family found it a nerve-racking time. The search for King Charles had widened and the Roundhead commander in Tewkesbury had not been exaggerating when he said that Parliament had posted a reward of a thousand pounds for his capture. It was an enormous sum, and Parliamentary officials were searching the homes of known Royalist supporters up and down the country in the hope of claiming the reward.

Sir John was fairly confident that his servants could be relied upon to protect the unexpected guests, but it could not be taken for granted. Piers and Ralf were of sufficient importance to make their capture worthwhile to any informer. They were kept well away from any callers to the house, but after one such visitor had departed Sir John came to the room where the trio were playing cards. He was highly excited and could hardly wait to tell them his news.

'That was a trusted messenger from my brother in Bristol. The King is here, in the west country. He travelled with Colonel Lane's daughter from Bentley Hall, disguised as her servant.'

'Where exactly is His Majesty?' Ralf asked, jumping up. 'I should go to him at once.'

'I think it probably best that he does not gather a retinue about him,' Piers said, 'but His Majesty playing the part of a servant is something I would like to witness.'

'If he is nearby I would at least like him to know we are at hand, should he have need of us,' Ralf persisted.

'He travelled to Abbot's Leigh, just beyond Bristol,' Sir John said. 'It was hoped it would be possible to arrange for a ship to take him from Bristol to the Continent, but the Roundheads are keeping a close watch on the port and it was felt he should move on. I believe he has been moved to Dorset, to the home of Colonel Wyndham, whose brother was the governor of Bridgwater. It is close to the Channel ports, and a great many men who are loyal to the King live in the area. He can be passed from one to another very quickly should it prove necessary.'

'I would like to go to Dorset too,' Ralf said. 'It might be possible to cross to France with him and it would bring him some comfort to know we are safe and near at hand.'

'I agree that it is time we were moving on,' Piers said. He was now well enough to travel and was aware that every day they remained at Berkeley increased the danger for Sir John and his family. However, he still looked frail, and it was decided that he should travel as a consumptive husband who was no longer able to work and was returning to Frances's family home in Dorset, where relatives would take care of them both. Ralf would accompany them as a servant, employed for the duration of the journey to attend to their needs.

By a fortunate coincidence, there were members of Frances's family living in Dorset. It mattered little that they had been so scandalised by her birth that they had cut all ties with her mother. They would serve their purpose, should the trio need to give details of their journey to Roundhead soldiers. It was doubtful whether they would ever meet each other.

15

The fugitive trio were stopped only once on the journey to the Sherborne home of Colonel Wyndham, brother-in-law of King Charles's first mistress. The Parliamentary soldiers who challenged them were sympathetic to the sickly-looking Piers and his pregnant wife, whose condition was enhanced by a small cushion hidden beneath her dress.

As their 'servant', Ralf was the one who was questioned in greatest detail about their destination. Describing Piers and Frances as caring and considerate employers, he won considerable sympathy for their present plight and they were sent on their way to an uncertain future with good wishes from the soldiers.

Riding away, on the horses provided for them by Sir John, Frances said, 'I don't know what story you told them, Ralf, but it must have been convincing. I half expected them to open their purses at any moment.'

Ralf grinned. 'I wasn't quite that persuasive, but they are really no different from us. They possess similar feelings and sympathies. It's just that they serve a different master.'

Trent Manor, home of Colonel Wyndham, was not the easiest place to find, being situated in the heart of the countryside close to the Dorset-Somerset border, and it was dark before they arrived, after a very long day.

Piers in particular was very tired. Frances had wanted to halt and find somewhere to rest for the night but he had insisted they carry on, pointing out that they risked being reported to the authorities if they stayed at an inn and someone became suspicious of them.

Ralf understood Frances's anxiety for her husband's health, but he agreed with Piers. This was not the England he had once known, where men and women could move freely around the countryside. War and a Puritan Parliament had succeeded in generating an atmosphere of fear and mistrust.

Such suspicion was shown by Colonel Wyndham when he met Ralf in the hallway of Trent Manor while Piers and Frances saw to the bestowal of their horses. Ralf had been a young page when he and the owner of the house had last met briefly in the Bridgwater home of Wyndham's brother and he was not immediately recognised.

'Ralf Hunkyn . . . ? Secretary to the King? I know of no such person . . . '

At that moment, Frances appeared in the doorway supporting her near-exhausted husband and, trying desperately to produce a weary smile, Piers said, 'Are you going to deny knowing the secretary to the King's council too, Colonel Wyndham?'

Colonel Wyndham stepped closer and peered at him. 'Piers? Is it really you? What are you doing here? The King feared you had died at Worcester, together with so many of his friends and companions.'

'Indeed, and so I would have had it not been for Ralf and my wife.'

Finally acknowledging Ralf, Colonel Wyndham said, 'The King mentioned your presence at Worcester, but feared you too had perished. As you were not known to me I trust you will understand my caution . . . but come in. I will have some food brought for you. Have you travelled far?'

'You said the King spoke of us,' Ralf said eagerly. 'Is he still nearby?'

'Beneath the same roof as yourselves,' Colonel Wyndham replied. 'He returned here only yesterday. We had been to the coast to find a ship to take him to France. Unfortunately, all the Channel ports are crowded with Roundheads, gathering to mount an assault upon Jersey. The King was lucky to escape without detection — but he will tell you about it himself. Come, I will take you to him while food is being prepared. He will be delighted to emerge from the priest-hole where he hid when I was told there were strangers at the door. His Majesty has good cause to thank his loyal Catholic subjects for such sanctuaries!'

'After the unhappy months he spent in the company of the Covenanters His Majesty would have happily embraced *any* other religion,' Ralf said. 'He told me so many times.'

Colonel Wyndham smiled. 'I believe he has said as much to my wife . . . but come, you look very tired, Piers. You have still not fully recovered from your wound, I would guess. You shall have brandy and a rest and I will bring the King to you. He prefers not to stand on ceremony these days — and I fear you may have a shock when you see him. His hair has been shorn, his skin is darkened with walnut juice, and he wears clothes that my gardeners would scorn. However, his disguise has served him well. Come.'

★　★　★

King Charles was overjoyed to be reunited with Ralf and Piers and the evening was spent exchanging stories of their various adventures since fleeing from Worcester. It came to an end when Frances insisted that she take an exhausted Piers to bed.

When the young couple had gone, King Charles, who seemed none the worse for his recent experiences and less than regal appearance, said, 'I am truly overjoyed to have the company of yourself and Piers once more, Ralf. Frances too, of course — she is a remarkable woman. We must try to remain together now.'

'I am afraid that will not be possible, Your Majesty,' Colonel Wyndham said hurriedly. 'I understand there are already whispers abroad that I have an escaped Royalist in the house. I fear that one of the servants must have been loose-tongued. If the rumour reaches the ears of the local Roundhead commander, my house will be searched. I can hide *you* safely enough, but not four people. We already know that the Dorset and Devon coasts are too dangerous for anyone fleeing from Worcester, so I will make arrangements for Ralf, Piers and Frances to find a refuge farther to the east. It should be possible for them to obtain a boat to take them to France from there. It is where I have suggested a ship should be sought for Your Majesty too. Perhaps Ralf will make some enquiries on your behalf when he is there?'

'I am entirely in your hands, Colonel Wyndham, and will do as you say,' Charles replied. 'I will be unhappy not to have Ralf with me, of course — we have shared many difficult times together. But I will find solace in the knowledge that you are alive, Ralf, and look forward to the day when we meet again in more relaxed surroundings.'

Neither the King nor Ralf would have been happy had they known it would be many years before that meeting took place.

16

During the course of the next two weeks it became increasingly apparent to Ralf and his two companions that Royalists in this part of England, at least, were well organised.

Always heading towards the south-east coast they were passed from one loyal escort to another, pursuing an almost leisurely course, but never remaining beneath the same roof for longer than two nights. Almost every family who cared for them belonged to the Catholic faith and as such were experienced in hiding priests and deceiving those in authority who regarded them with suspicion. Eventually they found refuge in the home of a retired admiral, whose boast was that he had served four English monarchs and was proud to be of assistance to anyone closely associated with the present troubled king.

Admiral Kettle knew a great many merchants and sea captains, whose ships made regular visits to the ports along this stretch of the coast. He was able to give the fugitives the names of those whose sympathies were with the King, and who might be prepared to carry them across the Channel to France — at a price, of course.

Fortunately, money was not an immediate problem. Sir John Lewis of Berkeley had supplied his nephew with money enough to enable him, Frances and Ralf to secure passages to France and have some to spare.

Ralf was still deeply concerned about the King's safety. He felt they should be concentrating on arranging a passage out of the country for the hunted monarch, instead of trying to make good their own escape. But his misgivings were brought to an end when a jubilant message was relayed to all the senior Royalists living along England's south coast. A passage had been secured for the King in a brig, the *Surprise*, and he would soon be in France. If the information was sound, King Charles would shortly be beyond the reach of his enemies in the English Parliament.

Armed with this knowledge, and a particular name given to him by Admiral Kettle, Ralf set off for the south coast port of Portsmouth, the most important naval town in England. The admiral had suggested that Ralf should try to find a Captain Alariah Flint, who had helped many other Royalists to escape to France. Ralf was to enquire for him at an inn named the Lamb, and if questioned was to pose as the servant of a man seeking to flee the country with a young girl of good family whom he had made pregnant.

The couple would be Piers and Frances, and Ralf would travel with them. Not that such subterfuge would be necessary with Captain Flint. The fact that Ralf came from Admiral

Kettle was sufficient to ensure that no questions would be asked by the sea captain.

Portsmouth was little more than a half-day's ride from Admiral Kettle's home and Ralf made the journey on a horse whose condition was in keeping with his status as a servant. Accordingly, he was given a room above the inn's stables.

Not wishing to attract undue attention, Ralf waited until the inn was fairly crowded before he left his stable room and made his way to the tap room. The customers were a cross-section of sailors, soldiers and townsmen and the landlord was a large-bellied man with a permanent scowl on his face. Catching him when he was not surrounded by customers, Ralf ordered a drink before saying, 'I've been sent to Portsmouth by my master to discuss business with a Captain Flint. Is he here now?'

Pausing in the act of drawing ale from a giant barrel, the landlord cast his eye over the customers who occupied the noisy, crowded room. 'I can't see him, but his ship is in and he's been drinking here for the past three nights. No doubt he'll be here again tonight.'

Passing over a coin that would pay for two drinks, Ralf said, 'Have a drink on my master, landlord, and I would be obliged if you would tell me when Captain Flint arrives.

He had consumed less than half the ale in his tankard when he looked up to see a woman standing looking down at him. She was one of the many whores who were in the room quite openly soliciting the inn's customers.

Her face was blotched with drink and raddled

with the ravages of her calling, yet there was something vaguely familiar about her. When she spoke it was in an accent he recognised and a voice that he remembered immediately despite a coarseness that had not been there when he had heard it before.

'Well, fancy meeting you here, Ralf — and dressed as a servant! What happened to all the finery I made for you in the days when you were page to the Prince — who is now a king without a throne?'

Starting to his feet, Ralf looked about him hurriedly in case anyone had overheard her words, then looked at her with dismay. This was no longer the girl he had once loved, but a whore who was past her prime.

'Brighid . . . what are you doing here? I thought you had fled to the Continent with Hugo Muller!'

'Ah, yes . . . and so did I. Unfortunately, Muller turned out to be no better than any other man I ever met — with one possible exception — but what are you doing here in Portsmouth?'

His thoughts recovering from the shock of meeting Brighid, Ralf remembered his mission. 'Like you, Brighid, I've known better days. I'm now servant to a man far less exalted than the one I once served. But you . . . what are *you* doing in a place like this?'

'When I helped Muller escape from Pendennis castle I thought he was going to take me home with him. *He* was certainly heading for home, but he never had any intention of taking me with him. We reached Portsmouth and stayed here together until his wound was healed, and then, after a particularly drunken evening, I woke in the morning to find he was gone and all the money I had managed to put by had gone with him. There was the inn bill to be paid and I was told by the landlord that there was only one way to earn the amount I owed him — and it wasn't by sewing.'

Despite a certain revulsion at the degradation to which Brighid's way of life had brought her, Ralf said accusingly, 'There was no need for you to continue like this, Brighid. I had told my ma and pa about you and they would have taken care of you and given you a good life on the farm.'

Giving him a strange look, Brighid asked, 'Where did you say you have been in the years since we last met?'

'I don't think I did. It's been here and there . . . wherever life took me.'

'Well, you certainly haven't returned home yourself, Ralf Hunkyn.'

Taken by surprise, Ralf said, 'How do you know I haven't been there?'

At that moment the scowling landlord came across to speak to Brighid. 'There's one of your regulars waiting for you in the other room — one who's generous with his drinks. I suggest you get to him and be quick about it.'

Brighid stood up immediately, with an expression that might have been fear, and hurried from the room.

Turning to Ralf, the landlord said, 'You were asking for Captain Flint. That's him sitting at the table by the window. I told him you were asking for him, but he wouldn't come and speak to you while you were with Brighid. He's a drinking man, but he doesn't like whores. He says he's lost more good sailors to the pox than to pirates or shipwreck. If you're hoping to do business with him I suggest you think up some good excuse for being in her company.'

Captain Flint was frowning into his tankard of ale. Approaching him apprehensively, Ralf stood before him and said, 'Captain Flint, sir . . . I am Ralf Hunkyn and have been asked to convey Admiral Kettle's compliments to you.'

Looking up from his ale, Captain Flint's expression was stern. 'What were you doing associating with that Irish whore? She's given the clap to more sailors than any other whore in Portsmouth. I've threatened Landlord Phipps that I'll ban my seamen from coming here if he doesn't rid himself of her, but no doubt she brings more business to the Lamb than does the *Mermaid.*'

'When I last saw Brighid she was not a whore, but a seamstress — and an excellent one at that. She was also very kind and helpful to me at a time when I was in sore need of friends.'

'If she has such skills why is she leading a life that brings shame on herself and on all womanhood?' Flint demanded.

'I was asking her that very question, sir, when the landlord ordered her elsewhere. It would seem that a man in whom she put her trust stole her money and deserted her here in Portsmouth,' Ralf replied.

'Do you believe her?'

'Yes, sir. I knew the man in question and before he served her so ill he had betrayed his master in a manner that could have been fatal.'

Staring intently at Ralf for what seemed a long time, Captain Flint said, more mildly, 'I wish I could share your faith in her, but she has made some very dubious friends since she has been in Portsmouth. However, you have not come here to speak of such women. What is your business with me?'

The room was very crowded now and the noise level was high, but there were many men close enough to overhear their conversation and Ralf said, 'Is there somewhere we might go to talk in private, sir?'

'Oh, it's that sort of business, is it? I am not at all sure I wish to hear it, but as you come from Admiral Kettle . . . we will walk to the dock where my ship is moored and you can tell me along the way. It has become too noisy in here anyway for a serious drinking man.'

17

Ralf was able to arrive at a very satisfactory arrangement with Flint. The captain would be sailing from Portsmouth in three days' time in his ship, the *Mermaid*, with a cargo bound for Italy. Leaving the port on the night tide, he would anchor off nearby Southsea and send a boat inshore for Ralf, Piers and Frances. They would then be landed on the coast of France to make their way to Paris where, they hoped, King Charles would once more have his court.

When Ralf tried to explain who his passengers would be, Captain Flint silenced him. He said he did not want to know and his crew did not need to know. It was better that way. Money would change hands and the crew would receive a share. That would suffice.

The two men shook hands on the arrangement and Ralf returned to the Lamb well pleased with his evening's work. Yet there was something bothering him, something that had nothing to do with the forthcoming voyage, and he wanted to put his mind at ease before he left Portsmouth.

When the landlord had interrupted his conversation with Brighid she had given him a strange look before commenting on the fact that he had not been home to Cornwall in the years since they had last met. He wanted to know why.

The inn was even busier than when he had left it, and Brighid and a couple of other girls were carousing with a number of foreign seamen whose combined thirst was keeping the inn's landlord both busy and happy.

Not wishing to break up the party, Ralf sat in a nearby window seat and eventually, as he had hoped, Brighid spotted him. She did not come to him immediately, but when another group of seamen entered, to be greeted noisily by those around her, Brighid took the opportunity to slip away. Coming to where Ralf sat, she placed a full tankard of ale in front of him and said, 'Here, no one will miss this. Have you completed your business with Captain Flint?'

'You know him?' Ralf was startled.

'All of us who work the Lamb know him. He doesn't approve of his sailors mixing with us. He says we're more dangerous to them than Turkish pirates.'

'Oh. Yes, I've completed my business with Captain Flint, but when the landlord came to tell me he was here you were saying something about it being obvious I had not been home to Cornwall. What did you mean?'

Brighid hesitated, as though reluctant to reply. Then, suddenly serious, she said, 'You told me I should have gone to your parents' farm . . . well, I did go, a couple of years after I came here. I had a baby . . . a little girl. I named her Molly, after my stepmother — you remember her?'

Shaken, Ralf nodded, and Brighid continued,

'I had managed to put a little money by and was determined that Molly wouldn't grow up to be the same as me, but I didn't know what I could do to prevent it. Then I thought of you, and your farm. You're the only man I've ever met who was really kind to me. I thought you'd probably gone back to Cornwall and that if I could get there you would understand and help me . . . and Molly. So when I met up with some Cornish fishermen who'd come here to sell salted fish to the fleet, I got them to take me back with them and they landed me at Fowey. I found my way to your farm, Ralf, but your ma and pa weren't there any more. The man who had the farm had been a Roundhead officer. He owns the farm next to yours too. He almost had me arrested when I asked for Mr and Mrs Moyle — that was the name you gave me?'

'Yes, my mother had married again.' Ralf added, impatiently, 'But where were they? Why had they left Trecarne?'

'I'm sorry, Ralf, but before I was ordered off the farm the Roundhead told me they had been thrown off the land because your father was an unreformed Royalist. He also told me it was no use trying to find him because . . . because he was . . . dead.'

'Pa . . . dead?' Ralf stammered. 'But . . . what of my ma?'

'He didn't say anything about her, and I didn't ask. My baby wasn't well and I didn't know what to do, or where to go.'

Ralf was stunned by Brighid's news. He had

283

written to his mother and stepfather intermittently over the years. Brief, cautious letters that said little more than that he was well, telling them nothing at all about what he was doing, or where he was. He had been unable to give them an address for fear of a letter falling into the wrong hands. He wondered now how many they had received.

'Your baby . . . Molly. Where is she now?'

'She died only a couple of days after I arrived in Fowey. I had her buried in the churchyard there. I had very little money left and could see no way of earning any in Cornwall, so I made my way back here. I'll no doubt stay here until I die too — and whores don't live to enjoy old age.'

Even though Ralf was badly shaken by the news about his parents, he realised that Brighid must have been distraught at all that had happened at Fowey. He tried to offer her his sympathy, but she had caught a scowl from the landlord, and with a hasty 'Goodbye, Ralf' she left him to put his own confused thoughts in order.

★   ★   ★

Later that night, when Brighid was returning to the Lamb after spending a couple of hours on the ship crewed by the sailors with whom she had been drinking, a figure detached itself from the shadows of a nearby building. Taking her arm, he propelled her roughly to the corner where he had been lurking.

It was Lazarus Sinnett, a man with whom she

lived when he was in Portsmouth. Lazarus spent much of the year working the fairs in southern England as a labourer, pickpocket and occasional footpad. He also spent varying periods in prison, lodged there on vagrancy charges.

'There's no need to be rough with me,' Brighid said, pulling her arm free. 'I've money to share with you, if that's what you're after. If you take your hands off me I'll find it for you.'

'Never mind the money for now. Who was that I saw you talking to earlier? Him as went off with Cap'n Flint?'

Brighid withdrew her hand from the front of her low-cut dress where her money was kept. She realised Lazarus must have something very serious on his mind to brush aside an offer of money.

'He's someone I knew years ago, long before I became a whore — but what's it to you, Lazarus? Don't tell me you're jealous?'

'Don't be stupid, woman. Was he one of your royal friends? If he was, what was he doing with Cap'n Flint?'

Lazarus was aware of Brighid's previous employment as a seamstress at the royal court. He also had a one-time criminal colleague who was a seaman on Captain Flint's ship. The man had boasted to Lazarus of Flint's occasional clandestine rendezvous off nearby Southsea in order to take a wanted Royalist to France, before proceeding on his more legitimate ventures.

'Why are you so interested in him? Yes, he was with the court, but he was only a page to the Prince — as King Charles was then.'

'A page!' Lazarus seized upon her statement. 'Might he still be with the King's court?'

'How should I know?' Brighid protested. 'Anyway, what does it matter? What Ralf does is his business.'

'It could be *our* business,' Lazarus said, 'and very profitable business too. Don't you have ears to know what's going on around you? The King has been beaten at Worcester and is on the run. There's a very strong rumour going about that he's in this part of the country, trying to find a ship to take him to France. For anyone who finds him and turns him over to Parliament there's a thousand pounds reward . . . a thousand pounds! Just think what we could do with that, Brighid. We could buy our own inn! A little place far away from places like this. Where you wouldn't need to be at the beck and call of any man who wanted a woman. Where I could walk along the street and not fear meeting a constable. We could start a whole new life together, Brighid. Just you and me together.'

'Aren't you forgetting something?' Brighid asked. 'There's nothing at all to say that Ralf is trying to arrange a passage to France for the King.'

'Not if he's no longer with the King's court,' Lazarus agreed, 'but those who are close to the King tend to stay with him through thick and thin. Did this Ralf tell you he was no longer with the King?'

'Not in so many words,' Brighid said. 'In fact, he was careful *not* to tell me anything about what he was doing. What's more, I know that he

286

hasn't been home to see his ma for years. He didn't even know his stepfather was dead, which he would have known if he'd been in this country and his own man. You could well be right, Lazarus. What's more, he hadn't met Captain Flint before. It was the landlord who told him when the captain came into the Lamb. I must say that if a passage for the King needed to be arranged then Ralf would be the one to do it. He was closer to the King than just about anyone.'

'There, what did I tell you? I'm right, aren't I? I've got a feeling in my bones about this. Come morning I'll go in search of the man I know who sails with Flint. I'll buy him a drink or two and find out when his ship is sailing. Then we'll arrange a little surprise for the King. Instead of going to join his Papist friends in France he'll soon be pacing a dungeon in the Tower of London.'

In a sudden moment of conscience, Brighid said anxiously, 'Whatever happens, you'll make sure that Ralf suffers no harm. He was good to me once.'

'He'll come to no harm,' Lazarus said, 'At least, not if he's sensible, he won't, but it'll take more than a past good turn to come between me and a thousand pounds — and say nothing about this to anyone, you hear? We'll see this through together, just you and me. A thousand pounds is a fortune, but it won't be if we need to share it with others.'

18

Ralf, Piers and Frances left their horses at the house of yet another Royalist supporter who lived just outside Portsmouth, before making their way on foot to the beach where they were to be picked up by a boat from Captain Flint's ship. Ralf had reconnoitred the area before returning from the Lamb to Admiral Kettle's house, and it was ideal for the purpose, the only building being a roofless tumbledown cottage.

They had learned only that day that King Charles had finally succeeded in escaping from England, despite the high reward offered for his capture. It seemed he had boarded a boat at Brighthelmstone, a short distance along the coast, and was now safely in France, but this was still not common knowledge.

The news that the King was safe delighted the trio, but their happiness was tempered with sadness. Ralf had told Piers and Frances he would not be going to France with them. After relating what Brighid had told him, he had decided to return to Cornwall to find his mother and learn exactly what had happened to force his parents to leave Trecarne Farm. He was convinced they had not left voluntarily, and felt a sense of guilt for not doing more to remain in touch with them, but, as Frances pointed out, it was difficult to think of anything more he could have done other than write the occasional discreet letter to let them know he was still alive. His paramount duty had been to Charles, both as prince and as king.

However, the events of recent months had shown he was not indispensable and now the King was safely in France once more there would be courtiers to attend to his needs — and Piers would be able to reorganise the King's council when he re-joined the court.

As though reading his thoughts, Frances said, 'Won't you change your mind and come with us, Ralf?'

'I can't,' Ralf said unhappily. 'If what Brighid says is true then I've been away too long.'

'And if it is not true, what then?' Piers asked.

'Brighid had no reason to lie to me.'

'What if you can't find your mother, Ralf?' Frances persisted. 'What will you do?'

'If she is still alive I will find her,' Ralf said. 'She has an aunt living in Fowey who will know what has happened at Trecarne. When I have spoken to her I'll decide what to do next.'

'I sincerely hope you decide to re-join the court,' Piers said. 'The King would wish it too. He thinks highly of you, Ralf, and always has, right from the days when you first joined him as a page.'

Walking between the two men, Frances suddenly shivered. 'There's a cold wind blowing.

Is there somewhere we can shelter while we wait for the boat?'

'There's a ruined cottage at the edge of the beach. It's where the boat crew will head for. We'll shelter there and hope we don't have too long to wait.'

There was a near-full moon in the night sky, but also a great deal of high cloud, so the ruin was indistinct for much of the time until they reached it and stumbled through the doorless entrance.

Although the cottage had no roof it proved to be a good windbreak, and through a glassless window they could keep watch for the signal from the *Mermaid*'s boat. Ralf was carrying a lanthorn containing an unlit candle, which he would light once they had received the signal.

The place in which they stood was separated from a smaller room by a wall which had been reduced to no more than half a man's height. Suddenly, as the moon broke free from the cloud, a figure rose from behind the wall holding a pistol and Lazarus Sinnett called, 'Stay exactly where you are! Raise your hands where I can see them — and don't even think of escape; there are others outside and they are armed too.'

Taken by surprise, Ralf and Piers did as they were instructed.

'That means you too.' The pistol swung to cover Frances and she obediently raised her hands to shoulder height.

'That's better.' To Ralf, Sinnett said, 'I've seen you before, so . . . ' turning his gaze upon Piers, he declared, ' . . . you must be King Charles.'

'Me . . . King Charles?' Despite the serious-ness of the situation, Piers's expression was one of incredulous amusement. 'I'm nothing like the King. For a start, he's at least a head taller! What on earth made you think I was the King?'

For a moment Lazarus appeared nonplussed. Then he said, 'If you're not the King then where is he? When are you expecting him?'

'Why on earth should we expect His Majesty to come here in the dead of night?'

'Because you're a King's man . . . like him.' The pistol indicated Ralf. 'And he made an arrangement with Cap'n Flint to pick the King up here, tonight.'

'Where did you get that idea?' Ralf asked, aware that Piers had rocked the confidence of the man with the pistol and that this was not a simple case of robbery. 'Yes, I've made an arrangement with Captain Flint. He is taking my two friends out of the country to escape from her father so they can wed, but that's of no concern to anyone — except perhaps her father.'

'I don't believe you,' Lazarus said, but he sounded less certain now. 'You used to be a King's page — and no doubt you escaped with him from Worcester. Even though he's not with you tonight, you'll know where he is. No doubt Parliament's torturers will get it out of you before you lay your head on the block.'

There was a sound from beyond the gaping doorway of the cottage and from the shadows Brighid's voice said, 'That isn't what we agreed, Lazarus. You promised no harm would come to Ralf.'

'That was when we thought the King would be here with him. If he tells us where he's to be found he can still go free.'

'Don't tell me you believe him,' Ralf said. 'You've changed from the girl I once knew, but you can't have changed that much. I thought you must have had something to do with this and it grieves me deeply. Hugo Muller has much to answer for.'

'Shut up!' Lazarus Sinnett raised his gun threateningly.

'I can tell you where you can find the King.' Frances spoke for the first time and everyone looked at her.

'Where? Where is he?' Sinnett asked eagerly.

'He's in France,' Frances said. 'He left England some days ago and will now be safely in the court of Queen Henrietta.'

'You're lying!' Sinnett snapped, not wanting to believe her.

Frances shrugged. 'It will be common knowledge soon enough. Parliament has men in Paris who keep them informed of what goes on there.'

Sinnett glared at her for some moments before reaching a decision. 'Well, seeing as you know so much about King Charles, I reckon the Roundheads might be interested enough in all of you to pay good money to make you their prisoners.'

'No, Lazarus, you promised . . . ' Brighid stepped through the doorway, out of the shadows behind Ralf, and when he looked over his shoulder he saw that she too was holding a pistol.

'Don't be a stupid cow!' Sinnett snarled. 'There's no King so we've got to make the most of what we're left with. You've got rope: tie their hands — and you can start with your royal friend. Go on!'

Brighid did not continue the argument. Instead, she walked round Ralf to stand between him and Sinnett and said, 'All right, turn round and put your hands behind your back.'

When Ralf did as he was told he was facing the doorway. Leaning closer, Brighid whispered, 'When I push you, dive for the door . . . '

'What are you up to?' Sinnett had keen hearing and had caught part of her whispered instruction.

'Now!' Brighid gave Ralf a shove in the back, but as he moved there was a report from Sinnett's pistol and a gasp of pain from Brighid as she stumbled to the ground.

Almost immediately there was another pistol shot. This time it came from a weapon which Frances had held concealed beneath her cloak.

Sinnett stopped in the act of drawing a second pistol that had been tucked in his belt. Looking in agonised astonishment at Frances he dropped to his knees before pitching forward on his face to lie with his head almost touching Brighid's body.

When Ralf kneeled beside Brighid she was still breathing, and as he lifted her head she tried to speak to him. Her mouth opened and closed twice, but all that came from it was a small trickle of blood. Then her head fell back and,

293

realising she was dead, he lowered her gently to the ground.

At that moment, Frances, who was reloading her pistol as calmly as she might have done had she been shooting at a target and not taking the life of a man, paused and said, 'Look! Is that a light offshore?'

Piers, who was more shaken than his wife by what had just occurred, looked through the window. 'Yes . . . It's the signal. The boat's coming for us.'

'Then go . . . both of you,' Ralf said, successfully hiding from them the unexpected grief he felt at the manner of Brighid's death. 'Light the lanthorn and give them the signal, in case the shots frighten them off.'

'They won't have heard anything,' Frances said. 'The wind will have taken the sound off along the coast . . . but what about you, Ralf? We must help you to dispose of the bodies.'

'That won't be necessary,' Ralf said. 'Just go quickly. When you're safely in the boat I'll fire Brighid's pistol into the ground, then arrange the bodies to look as though they shot each other after a violent quarrel — but you must go before the boat's crew become nervous and think you're not here.'

'Come, Frances,' Piers said. 'Ralf is right. We need to leave.' Grasping Ralf's hand, he said, 'God bless you, Ralf. We will meet again in better times.'

Frances hugged Ralf and said, 'Come to France soon, if it is at all possible, Ralf.'

As she and Piers moved towards the doorway,

she paused a moment beside Brighid's body and said softly, 'I think you spoke of her in a conversation we had on the way to the home of Sir John Lewis at Berkeley, Ralf. Whatever she did, and whatever she became, she made up for everything tonight. Think well of her.'

BOOK THREE

1

As the fishing boat approached Fowey harbour, Ralf could see the cave in the cliff side of Lantic Bay where he and his stepfather would hide their farm animals when danger threatened from the marauding soldiers of the Parliamentary army, and for the first time for many years he felt a pang of nostalgia for the happy life he had enjoyed when growing up on Trecarne Farm.

The vessel on which Ralf was a passenger was returning to its home port of Mevagissey, a fishing port only a few miles from Fowey. He had been fortunate enough to recognise the Cornish accent of the crewmen when he met them in Portsmouth, the day after the dramatic confrontation in the ruined Southsea cottage.

The sailors had been delivering salted fish to the Navy victualling yard at Portsmouth and they readily agreed to convey Ralf back to Cornwall. At this moment they were on their way into Fowey harbour to put him ashore before sailing across the bay to their home port.

Jumping from the boat to the quayside, Ralf waved goodbye to them before setting off through the alleyways that separated the houses huddled about the harbour. He was making his way to the home of Florence Spargo, his mother's spinster aunt.

Florence lived in a tiny terraced house in a narrow alleyway that ran between the houses that fronted upon Fowey's single road and the high wall that protected Place, the manor house that was surrounded by grounds more extensive than the town itself.

Turning into the alleyway, Ralf felt a brief moment of panic. He had been away from Cornwall for more than five years, during which time much had happened. What if the ageing Florence had died and the house had new occupants? What if . . . ?

He arrived at the door of the small house, observing that it was in need of a coat of paint. He hesitated, then, bracing himself, knocked firmly upon the door.

There was no immediate response and no sound from inside the house and all his doubts returned. If Aunt Florence *had* died, would the new occupants have any knowledge of his mother?

He knocked again, and when there was still no response he lifted the latch. The door opened and, after only the briefest of hesitations, he stepped inside.

He was halfway along the passageway when a door opened at the far end and a woman emerged from the kitchen, wiping flour-powdered arms with a cloth, calling, 'All right, I'm coming, but it's baking day. I can't just leave everything to answer a knock on the door . . . '

It was his mother. For a moment Ralf could

300

not speak, and with the light behind him Grace did not immediately recognise her visitor.

Suddenly, she stopped, and seeing the uncertainty on her face Ralf managed to croak, 'Hello, Ma. It's me . . . Ralf.'

Her face registered first shock, then disbelief, and, finally, uncontrollable emotion.

'Ralf . . . Oh, my love, tell me I'm not dreaming! Tell me it *is* you!'

'It's me, Ma. I've come home to find out what's been happening while I've been away.'

Grace threw herself at him and as he held her close she began crying. Holding her even more tightly, he said, 'It's all right. Don't cry . . . please. Just tell me what's been going on. Why you're here.'

Trying hard to regain control of herself, Grace said brokenly, 'So much has happened, Ralf . . . So much unhappiness . . . but you . . . ? What of the King? The word is that he suffered a dreadful defeat in battle and is being hunted down by Cromwell's soldiers. I feared you must be with him.'

'I was with him,' Ralf said, 'but I met someone in Portsmouth who told me a Roundhead had taken over Trecarne, so once I knew the King was safely back in France I came here to find out what is going on.'

There was a faint sound from upstairs and Grace said, 'That's Aunt Florence. I'm hoping she's going off to sleep for a while. Come into the kitchen and we'll talk.'

They walked together down the passageway, Grace keeping a tight grip on his arm, as though

301

frightened he might disappear if she let go. In the kitchen she automatically swung a blackened kettle over the fire to heat, explaining, 'There's fish stew in there. I prepared it for Florence, but the cat eats more than she does. Not that I blame her. Fish stew day after day may keep her alive, but there are only so many things you can do with fish. What she really needs is some good strong meat broth inside her, but I can't remember when we last had meat in the house. Mind you, we wouldn't have fish if it wasn't for the kindness of Digory Lobb. He's a fisherman and the husband of Blanche, who was Florence's friend as a child . . .'

'Ma!' Words were tumbling from Grace's lips at an alarming speed and Ralf brought her outpouring to a gentle halt. 'I have money. Enough to give Florence whatever she needs for a while, but I'm more concerned with what's happened to you, to Pa and to Trecarne.'

Tears welled up in Grace's eyes once more and began to course down her cheeks. 'Joseph was a good man, Ralf. Good to you and so good to me. He didn't deserve to be treated the way he was.'

'Tell me about it, Ma. What happened to make you leave Trecarne? I've been writing to you whenever I could. Discreet letters, not saying where I was, or what I was doing, brought to England by men and women I knew I could rely upon. I addressed them to Trecarne and it wasn't until a week ago that I heard you were no longer there — and that Pa had died.'

'He's been dead for three years now, God

bless him. Who told you about it?'

'That doesn't matter right now, Ma . . . '
Ralf's mind conjured up the image of Brighid as
he had last seen her. He did not want to dwell
upon the memory. 'Tell me about Pa and
Trecarne.'

With tears never far away, Grace told Ralf the
story of the loss of Trecarne Farm and the tragic
effect it had had upon Joseph Moyle.

When the Roundheads secured their victory
over King Charles I they exacted retribution
upon those who had been most active in their
opposition to Parliament. Joseph Moyle had
fought in the King's army and served with
distinction, but he was by no means a Royalist of
any great importance, so it came as a shock
when the Cornish county committee, appointed
to punish men of rank who had supported the
King, ordered him to appear before them to
answer for his actions.

At the hearing, Joseph argued that he had
done no more than many thousands of others in
carrying out his duty as he saw it, by serving as
the lowest ranked commissioned officer in the
King's army. Nevertheless, seizing upon the fact
that he was an *officer* in the Royalist army, and
the fact that he was a landowner, albeit in a very
small way, the committee declared him to be a
'delinquent' and ordered him to pay a fine equal
to half the value of his house and lands. It was
no use Joseph protesting that he was a working
farmer and not a great landowner. He was
ordered to pay the fine, or suffer sequestration of
his land.

When Joseph returned to Trecarne he learned that his neighbour had been dealt with equally harshly, his 'delinquency' being no more than to supply the King with a number of the very fine horses he bred on his farm. Both men pleaded in vain to have their punishment reduced, and were equally unsuccessful in trying to borrow money from the local gentry, many of whom had suffered in a similar fashion for their support of King Charles I, but most of whom had sufficient funds to pay their fines.

Notice was served upon Joseph that he and Grace had to be out of the farmhouse by a certain date, owing to Joseph's inability to pay the fine imposed upon him by the Cornish county committee. Trecarne, together with the neighbouring farm, had been given to a former Parliamentary army captain named Oliver Pym, as a token of Parliament's esteem for his services in the west of England.

Refusing to believe that his eviction would actually be carried out, Joseph did nothing, despite Grace's pleas that they should accept the inevitable and leave their home. He was a stubborn man and convinced that injustice would not prevail. He was unaware at the time that Oliver Pym was the brother-in-law of the chairman of the Cornish county committee.

Shortly after noon on the day Joseph and Grace had been told to leave Trecarne Farm, two large horse-drawn wagons entered the farmyard. In them were the wife and four daughters of Oliver Pym, together with their household possessions. Pym himself was riding a horse ahead of the wagons — and with him were six Roundhead cavalrymen.

The new owner of Trecarne was angry that Joseph had not moved out and Joseph was equally angry that he was being forced from the farm that had been home to many generations of Moyles. When Pym ordered the Roundhead troopers to begin clearing the farmhouse of the Moyles' possessions, Joseph hurried to the doorway to prevent them from carrying out their orders.

Suddenly, he stopped. His face contorted with pain, he dropped to the ground. Screaming, Grace rushed to him, but he was dead before she reached him, victim of a seizure brought on by the trauma of having his home and livelihood taken away from him.

His death failed to move Oliver Pym to show compassion, but his wife was able to persuade him to give Grace a week in which to bury her husband and make arrangements to find somewhere else to live. When the silent cavalrymen had carried Joseph's body to his bedroom inside the farmhouse, Oliver rode away, taking his wife and weeping daughters away from their future home.

It was a brief reprieve for Grace, one that Joseph had been able to achieve only in death.

★　★　★

When she reached the end of her story, Grace needed to be comforted by Ralf until her sobbing subsided. His own thoughts were in

305

turmoil and he blamed himself for not being home to help at such an unhappy time, even though he was aware that he could have done nothing to prevent the eviction.

When Grace had regained some control of herself, Ralf asked, 'Where is Pa now, Ma? Where is he buried?'

'He's in the Churchtown cemetery and he has a fine gravestone. The stonemason at Polruan served with Joseph in the army and he made it for him. He said it was his way of paying respect to one of the bravest soldiers he ever served with.' The tears returned as Grace added, 'I haven't been able to get across there for a long while, what with Aunt Florence being so ill . . .'

'Don't you upset yourself, Ma. I'll go across in the next day or two and tidy the grave up. Then I'll stay with Aunt Florence while you make the journey. I'm home to stay now, so things will be easier for you, I promise.'

2

Some days later, when Ralf was following a footpath beside Pont Pill, a creek off the River Fowey, on his way to the Churchtown cemetery, he thought of the promise he had made to his mother and hoped he had not been overly optimistic.

He had sounded out a few prospective employers in Fowey but their responses had not been promising. There was little work to be had in the town itself and with winter in the offing it was not a good time of year to be looking for work on the surrounding farms.

The problem was not yet urgent. Ralf still had money left from his time with the King and it had been supplemented by the generosity of Piers with the money given to him by his Berkeley kinsman. However, it was apparent to Ralf that his mother and her aunt had very meagre means and now he had returned to Cornwall he would need to support them both.

Walking along the bank of the tidal inlet, Ralf remembered the last time he had been on this path. It had been with his stepfather and Captain, now Colonel, Trevanion and had resulted in the meeting with King Charles I and

Ralf's appointment as a page to the then heir to the throne.

Since that day much had happened to everyone affected by that meeting. Ralf wondered how different life would have been had the meeting not taken place.

When he reached the churchyard where Joseph Moyle was buried, he followed the directions given to him by his mother and quickly found the grave of his stepfather in a quiet corner of the churchyard. He spent some time tidying the mound, then kneeled by the graveside and quietly recited a prayer for the stepfather he had loved as though he was his natural father.

Leaving the churchyard, Ralf hesitated at a fork in the narrow lane. Then, instead of returning the way he had come, he took the lane that led to Polruan — and passed the farm that had been his home for so many years, where Joseph had died.

He was going to take a nostalgic look at Trecarne Farm.

★   ★   ★

Ralf battled with mixed and confused emotions when he first glimpsed the thatched roofs of the farmhouse, but he carried on until the buildings themselves came into view.

The lane passed by at a little distance from Trecarne, yet close enough for Ralf to see that, outwardly, there had been little change during the years since he had last seen the house that he

308

would always regard as his home.

It gave him a strange feeling, almost as though all that had happened since he left might have been a dream — albeit at times a nightmare — and that now he was within sight of Trecarne once more he would wake to see his stepfather working in the farmyard and breathe in the smell of cooking from the kitchen where his mother would be humming happily, or even singing, as she baked something for them in the cloam oven.

Ralf slowed his gait, feeling the pain of being near to a place that held so many memories for him, yet reluctant to walk on and admit that he no longer belonged here.

He had passed the farmhouse when he heard the unmistakable bellow of a bull from a nearby field. He was unable to see into the field because the hedge had not been cut back, but the gate was not far along the lane and, curious to see what type of cattle Trecarne's present occupier was keeping, Ralf hurried to the gate and saw a number of cows in the field. With them was a fine, deep-bodied, short-legged bull.

He saw something else in the field too. Something which horrified him. A small girl of about seven years of age was seated on the grass, talking seriously to a wooden doll she held in her hands. Strewn about her on the close-cropped grass were a number of items of doll's clothing and other pieces of coloured cloth, made up to form a bed for her toy.

But it was not only Ralf who was looking at the girl. The bull had spotted her too. Throwing up its head, it began lumbering towards her.

Thoroughly alarmed, Ralf vaulted over the gate and ran to where the girl sat oblivious of the danger she was in.

The bull, enraged at the sight of *two* intruders, was gathering speed now and as Ralf reached the girl she looked up at him and the fear in his expression frightened her. Wasting no time in explanations, he scooped her up so hurriedly that she dropped the doll and immediately began screaming loudly.

There was no time to attempt to comfort her, or retrieve the doll. As he ran with her to the gate Ralf could hear the hooves of the bull drumming on the hard earth of the field with the sound of a charging cavalry horse.

At the gate, Ralf dropped the girl into the lane, then scrambled over in such a hurry that he fell to the ground beside her as the bull came to an angry and frustrated halt within touching distance on the other side of what now seemed to Ralf to be the frailest of safety barriers.

When the thoroughly aroused animal began butting the gate, twisting its head this way and that, Ralf feared its horns might become caught up in it and lift it from its iron hinge pivots. Rising to his feet he picked up the young girl and carried her back towards the farmhouse.

Struggling in his arms, she began to cry. 'I want Dolly,' she sobbed. 'You made me drop her.'

'I'm sorry about that,' Ralf said soothingly, 'but if I hadn't got you out of the field that nasty old bull would have hurt you — and Dolly too.'

He might as well have saved his breath. 'I want Dolly,' she wailed, and Ralf realised that not only was she very upset, she was probably simple too.

In a bid to bring her loud crying to a halt, he said, 'We'll go back and find Dolly in a minute. Before we do, why don't you tell me your name?'

At that moment a tall, thin man ran into the lane from the farmhouse, closely followed by a heavily built woman who looked frightened.

'What are you doing with Primrose?' the man demanded. 'Put her down . . . put her down, I say!'

Obediently, Ralf lowered the girl to the ground and she ran not to the man but to the woman behind him, who held out her arms to gather the child to her. Behind the woman three other girls of various ages between about ten and seventeen had put in an appearance.

'He made me drop Dolly and wouldn't let me go and pick her up,' Primrose wailed to the female members of her family as they gathered about her.

'I repeat, explain yourself, or as the Lord is my witness I will beat it out of you with this before I hand you over to the magistrate.' The man was carrying a heavy walking-stick which he waved threateningly at Ralf.

'If you care to come with me there will be no need of explanations.' Ralf turned his back on the angry man and walked off towards the gate of the field in which he had found Primrose.

'Come back here, do you hear me? By the Lord, Mary, if he tries to run away I'll strike him to the ground with this.' The man chased after

Ralf, but slowed his pace when Ralf looked back over his shoulder at him without uttering a word.

Hurrying to catch up with her husband, Mary said breathlessly, 'I don't think it is his intention to run away, Oliver. If it was I doubt whether we could catch him.'

Even as she spoke Ralf reached the gate. Inside the field the bull was nuzzling Dolly while inquisitive cows gathered around him, investigating the numerous clothes and pieces of cloth strewn about the doll.

At Primrose's loud wail of 'What are they doing to Dolly?' the cows, startled, stampeded away. Only the bull stood its ground, staring belligerently in the direction of those at the field gate.

'*There's* the reason I was carrying Primrose. Had I happened along a minute or two later I would have had a body in my arms. If you are as concerned for your daughter's well-being as you profess to be, I suggest you don't allow her to play in a field occupied by a bad-tempered, one-ton animal. Now, I have no doubt you have work to attend to so I will be on my way. I trust Dolly will not be too badly gored.'

With this, Ralf turned and walked away. He realised he had been talking to Oliver Pym, the Roundhead who had taken over Trecarne Farm and, in so doing, had been responsible for Joseph Moyle's death, albeit inadvertently.

Ralf had no wish to prolong the meeting.

3

'Wait!' It was not Oliver Pym but his wife who called to Ralf as he walked away from Trecarne.

He would have ignored her, but she ran after him with Primrose still clutched in her arms. Catching up with him, she reached out to detain him, saying, 'Stay, sir, I beg you. I fear we have done you a grave injustice. You deserve our heartfelt thanks, not accusations of wrongdoing.'

'If you wish to give thanks to anyone, then direct them to the Lord. He set my feet upon a path I have not travelled for many years and, as I thought, without reason — until I saw Primrose with her playthings attracting the attention of your bull.'

'I will not forget to thank Him for sending a brave man to do his work,' Mary Pym said, 'but will you not come into the farmhouse and have a drink with us — and some food, perhaps?'

'Thank you, but no. I have only recently returned home after many years away. My mother fears I will leave again. She is caring for a very sick kinswoman and I have no wish to add concern for my whereabouts to her other worries.'

While they were talking Oliver Pym and his

daughters had moved closer and now, less aggressive than before, the man said, 'I didn't think I had seen you in the area. What is your name?'

'Ralf Hunkyn,' was the short reply.

'You say you have been away? Where were you and what were you doing?'

Ralf thought of telling Pym it was none of his business, but he realised that, whatever his thoughts about him, Oliver Pym must have considerable influence with many of the Puritan officials who governed Cornwall. It would be both stupid and dangerous to antagonise him unnecessarily. He gave Pym the story he had decided upon to cover his protracted absence.

'I was at sea for a while but fell ill when we were in the port of Amsterdam and was left behind when the ship sailed. When I was well again I went to work on a farm in the Netherlands. I enjoyed the work so much I remained there until there was an incident at sea between English and Dutch men-o'-war. Many of the seamen who were killed were from the region where I was working and my presence there was no longer welcome. I made my way to France where I found a British fishing boat and joined the crew. One day we met up with a Mevagissey fishing boat and I decided it was time I returned to Cornwall, so I came back with them.'

Even though Ralf felt very strongly that he owed his questioner nothing, least of all the true story of his life, there was an element of truth in much of Ralf's story. Because of his farming roots he *had* taken an interest in the methods used and crops grown on Dutch farms, and he *had* returned to Cornwall on board a Mevagissey fishing boat.

'Where are you working now?' Pym asked.

'Nowhere,' Ralf replied, 'but I've only been home a few days. I'll find something when it becomes necessary.'

'Have you ever done any ploughing with horses?'

'With horses and oxen, and I can plough as straight a furrow as any ploughman in Cornwall,' Ralf boasted, on more certain ground now. It was a task he had mastered as a young boy on this very farm. He knew every irregularity and gradient of the land that belonged to Trecarne. 'Why do you ask?'

Ignoring his question, Pym asked, 'Is there someone who can vouch for you?'

'Why should I need anyone? You asked me what I've done and I've told you. I don't care very much whether or not you believe me.'

'I'm asking you because my ploughman left me last week, at the very time when he is most needed. I'm looking for someone to take his place.'

'Why did he leave?' Ralf asked, aware his question could be considered impertinent, but he felt no inclination to be polite to this man.

Sure enough, Oliver Pym took immediate offence. 'Why he left is none of your business,' he snapped. The ploughman had been dismissed for becoming too friendly with Ronwen, Pym's oldest daughter, but it was a matter that would not be discussed outside the family.

Ralf shrugged nonchalantly. 'As you say, it's none of my business.' Turning away, he spoke to Pym's wife. 'Good day to you, mistress. I hope the bull has not caused too much damage to Dolly, but it might have been much worse. It could have been Primrose.'

'Wait!'

Once again Ralf was brought to a halt, but this time it was Oliver Pym and not his wife who called to him. Pym was not a man in the habit of pleading with anyone to do his bidding, but his need of a ploughman was desperate. He had ambitions of becoming a country squire and needed his first farming venture to succeed. 'I'm willing to offer you work as a ploughman.'

This was a most unexpected development and Ralf was not certain it was one with which he could cope. There was nothing he wanted more than to be back at Trecarne — but as a farm-worker with no claim to the farm . . . ? Besides, he had good reason to hate Oliver Pym. It would be difficult working for the man who had stolen the farm — *his* farm — and caused the death of the man he loved.

Nevertheless, Ralf thought it would be an intriguing situation — and he needed to find work.

'What do you pay?' He told himself he was asking the question out of no more than idle curiosity.

'Five shillings a week — five and sixpence if you're as good as you claim to be.'

'Five shillings a week?' Ralf was scornful. 'I

can earn six shillings as a labourer. A skilled ploughman is worth seven and six. No wonder your last ploughman left you.'

Pym flushed angrily. He had in fact been paying his ploughman six shillings and sixpence. With a show of great reluctance he said, 'All right, I'll make it six shillings and sixpence.'

Ralf shook his head. 'I think I'll probably go fishing. In a good week I can make three times that sum.'

'And nothing at all in a bad winter week,' Pym retorted. 'All right, we'll say six shillings and ninepence, with good wholesome food and your own room above the stable.'

Ralf knew the 'room' above the stable. It was little more than a loft. A place where his stepfather had kept the tack for the horses, together with the tools that were in regular use around the farmyard. All the same, it could be made quite comfortable.

Nevertheless, he said, 'I have good food at home with my mother and no need to share my quarters with horses.'

Oliver Pym looked furious and, convinced he had pushed the Puritan farmer too far, Ralf turned to go.

'All right.' Pym forced the words past clenched teeth.

Turning to face him once more, Ralf said, 'You'll pay seven and sixpence?'

'Yes . . . but I will expect value for my money. You'll put in a full day's work and plough at least an acre a day. You'll also see the crops through from sowing to harvest — and I shall expect my crops to turn in a profit.'

'Neither you nor I will have any control over the market for your crops,' Ralf retorted, 'but you'll not do worse than any of your neighbours. I'll work six full days a week, but go home on Saturday night and come back to Trecarne on Monday morning.'

Pym seethed that Ralf not only had forced him to pay more than he had intended, but was now setting out the terms of his employment. He bit back the words that would send Ralf on his way. Without a ploughman there would be no crops and his hopes of becoming a successful and prosperous farmer and landowner would suffer a severe blow. 'When can you start work?' he asked.

'I'll start on Monday,' Ralf said.

It was now Thursday. His mother would have time to accept that he would be working away from home for six days a week — but it would take longer than that for her to accept the fact that he would be working at Trecarne for Oliver Pym.

4

Grace Moyle's reaction to the news that her son had accepted work from the man she believed to be responsible for her husband's death, on the farm that rightly belonged to him, was all Ralf had anticipated it would be.

'How can you even think of such a thing?' she demanded incredulously.

'Can you suggest an alternative?' he replied patiently. 'We need to have money coming into the house and there is no other work to be had around Fowey at this time of year. In a week or two most of the fishermen will be looking for something to tide them over until the spring.'

'That's as may be,' Grace said, 'but to work for *him* at Trecarne . . . Why, you'll be seeing the ghost of your poor pa in every corner of the place.'

'I don't doubt it,' Ralf agreed, 'and I'll never forget or forgive what Pym has done. He would realise that himself if he ever learned who I really am, so we must make certain he never finds out the truth. Fortunately, I had very little to do with anyone on this side of the river before going off to serve Prince Charles. He won't learn anything from here — and the only close neighbours we had at Trecarne have gone too, so there's no reason why he should associate Ralf Hunkyn with Joseph Moyle.'

'Maybe so,' Grace replied, 'but you're playing a dangerous game, and I don't like it.'

Grace's reaction to his employment by Pym as a ploughman came as no surprise to Ralf. It was what he had expected. However, despite the memories that working at Trecarne would inevitably conjure up, he found he wanted to work there. He would carry a lasting hatred for Pym and the part he had played in the death of Joseph Moyle and would always regard him as a usurper at the farm, but by working there Ralf felt he was retaining a link with what should have been his inheritance, no matter how tenuous it might be.

★　★　★

Ralf's employment at Trecarne did not get off to a propitious beginning.

On his second day there, Ralf returned from the fields at midday, having spent the forenoon ploughing. He settled the horses he had been using into their stalls, and then went to collect his food from the kitchen. Contrary to the accepted practice, which was for farm labourers to eat with the family, Pym had insisted that Ralf eat in his room above the stable.

When he had finished eating, he was about to prepare the horses he would use in the afternoon when Enid, Pym's ten-year-old third daughter, entered the stable. A lively, likeable young girl, she had a ready smile and a genuine love of the animals kept in and around the farm.

After watching Ralf for a while, she asked, 'Is there something I can do to help?'

'Yes.' Ralf was glad of the offer. He wanted to get back to the field he had been ploughing in order to have it completed by nightfall. 'Perhaps you'd like to go up and throw down some hay for the two horses I've been working this morning. I think they've earned it.'

Eagerly, Enid climbed the ladder to the platform covering half the area above the stalls. She had not been there very long when someone came to the stables and stood in the doorway, cutting off much of the light. Looking up, Ralf saw Ronwen, Pym's seventeen-year-old daughter.

'Hello,' he said politely. 'Would you mind stepping away from the doorway so I can see what I'm doing?'

Ronwen did not move. 'You're only a hired hand, so don't tell me what to do.'

She spoke with the haughtiness of a young woman who was aware of her position as daughter of the landowner — and also knew she was attractive to men.

Ralf had met women in the courts of Europe who were even more arrogant than the daughter of Oliver Pym. 'I wasn't telling you what to do,' he said patiently. 'Only asking you to move, so that I might see to do what your father is paying me for — getting the horses ready to plough Trecarne fields. The only light in here comes through the doorway and you are blocking it.'

'Don't you dare to argue with me!' Ronwen said fiercely. 'If I tell my father you've been impertinent you'll not only be dismissed but you'll be punished too. The Council is determined that Cornishmen should know their place . . . '

Before she could say more there was an interruption in the form of Oliver Pym himself.

Brushing Ronwen aside, he spoke angrily to Ralf. 'What do you think you're doing? I pay you to work on my farm, not to waste time in conversation with my daughter.'

'I was not talking to her,' Ralf replied, surprised at Pym's anger, which seemed out of all proportion to such a trifling incident. 'She came to the stable and . . . '

'He was insolent to me,' Ronwen said, adopting an air of feigned distress. 'I came to check on my mare and he told me to go away. I was very upset.'

'Is this true?' Pym rounded on Ralf once more. 'Were you rude to my daughter?'

'No he was not!'

The unexpected reply to Pym's question came from an indignant Enid who now showed herself in the hayloft above the stalls. 'Ronwen is trying to get Ralf in trouble because you sent Daniel away.'

Ralf knew that Daniel had been the last ploughman. From the little he had learned about him, he had gathered he had been dismissed for being a little too friendly with Ronwen. It explained why Pym was unduly sensitive about having his eldest daughter speaking to him

— and why Ronwen resented him.

Scrambling down the ladder, Enid continued defending Ralf to her father. 'Ralf asked her very nicely if she would move away from the doorway because she was blocking the light. Ronwen was the rude one. She said Ralf was only a hired hand and couldn't tell her what to do.'

Taken aback, Oliver Pym did not address the complaint Ronwen had made against Ralf. Instead he directed his anger at Enid. 'What were you doing up in the hayloft?'

'Enid is very good with animals.' Ralf spoke in defence of the girl who had diverted her father's wrath from him. 'She came in while I was preparing the horses for the afternoon's ploughing and asked if there was anything she could do. I suggested she might throw down some hay for the horses I was working this morning. She must have heard every word that was spoken between Ronwen and myself.'

Ignoring the original reason for his anger against Ralf, Pym said, 'I brought my daughters to Cornwall so they might learn to behave like ladies, not to carry out chores on a farm.'

'I am sure Enid will one day be as fine a lady as you might find anywhere,' Ralf said, 'but for now she's just a young girl who is eager to help out with everything on a farm. It's fun.'

'I'll decide what is and what is not fun for my daughters,' Pym declared. 'In the meantime . . . ' He looked around for Ronwen, but she had gone. 'In the meantime . . . get on with your work and stay away from my daughters.'

'All I've done is to do what I'm paid to do,'

Ralf retorted, angry that Pym seemed determined to criticise him unfairly. 'As for your daughters . . . if you don't want them to involve themselves with farm work I suggest you take them back to wherever they come from. No one, boy or girl, can live on a farm and not involve themselves with what goes on around them.'

By speaking in such a manner to his employer, Ralf was aware that he was being insolent, but at this moment he did not particularly care, although he hoped that Pym needed his services too badly to take any action against him.

Pym was also aware how much he depended upon Ralf just then. 'I don't intend that Trecarne should be their home for ever,' he said, controlling his fury. 'I intend building a house at Lantewan.' This was the neighbouring farm he had taken possession of with Trecarne. 'When it's done I'll be putting a manager in here and no doubt he'll be having his own ideas on how to run the two farms — and whom to employ. In the meantime, you've been warned. Stay clear of my girls if you want to stay out of trouble.'

Ralf's anger flared up again and, throwing caution to the wind, he retorted, 'Ronwen made it perfectly clear she has no intention of accepting even the most polite request from me. It is for you to tell your daughters what they might or might not do, not me. You've employed me as a ploughman and you'll have no complaint about my work if I'm allowed to carry it out without hindrance.'

Oliver Pym glared at Ralf for a long time and Ralf thought he had gone too far. Then, turning away suddenly, Pym growled at Enid, 'Come with me, you. Your sister has some explaining to do.'

Enid followed her father from the stable. When she reached the doorway she paused and, looking back, gave Ralf a brief surreptitious wave of her hand.

5

Although his relationship with Oliver Pym was never a comfortable one and there were more incidents when Ralf felt he was about to be dismissed, the Puritan farmer came to realise that his ploughman knew what he was doing about the farm and Ralf was still there a few years later when Oliver took his two older daughters, Ronwen and Winfred, to Cambridgeshire.

The two girls were going to visit their grandfather. James Pym was a minor member of the county's gentry and, more significantly, a friend and neighbour of Oliver Cromwell — a fact which had influenced the Cornish county commissioners when they had given the farms of Trecarne and Lantewan to his son.

Oliver Pym's intention was to become a gentleman of influence in Cornwall, but he believed his daughters would be able to make better marriages in Cambridgeshire.

Ralf felt his decision had also been influenced by Ronwen's partiality for men much lower down the social scale than suited the ambitions of her father. She had made it clear on more than one occasion that any advances made towards her by Ralf would not be unwelcome, but he remained wary of her, remembering their first encounter. She had also caused a scandal by being found drinking with some of her father's casual farm labourers when they were celebrating the gathering of the summer wheat harvest.

It was almost a relief when Pym took his daughters off the farm, although Ralf was aware that he would miss Winfred, the Pyms' second daughter. Much more serious and studious than her sister, she was also far more discreet. She would occasionally lend one of her books to Ralf and have a long conversation with him about its content, but she would never have such a discussion if there were any chance of her father coming upon them.

Although Ralf was sorry to see Winfred leave Trecarne, there was a much more relaxed atmosphere on the farm during Oliver Pym's absence and he was away for some months. As well as settling his daughters in with their grandparents, he spent time socialising on their behalf, using the family's acquaintance with Cromwell to ensure they would meet with suitable prospective husbands.

During Pym's absence Ralf had his meals with the remaining family and the two younger girls were quite relaxed in his company. He had long since won the trust of Primrose by carving a new doll for her which soon proved to be a much-loved successor to the unfortunate Dolly, and in the absence of her husband Mary was quite content to allow Enid to help him about the farmyard.

As Oliver Pym's absence continued from winter into a new spring, Mary wrote to her husband asking him for instructions on what he had planned for Trecarne for that season. His reply was so brief and vague that Mary was left in a state of despair until Ralf took pity on her. He had little liking for Oliver Pym, but his wife was a kindly woman and Ralf did not like to see her upset. He drew up a plan for the work on the farm, explaining the reasons for each of his suggestions.

Mary accepted Ralf's ideas gratefully, but when he suggested they needed to take on another man to help with his programme she demurred. It was one thing to accept his ideas, but quite another to justify spending money to employ another farmhand.

However, she was aware that Ralf could not possibly carry out the extra chores that the improved weather brought with it. She said she would take on some of the tasks in and about the farmyard and delegated to a delighted Enid the responsibility for feeding the livestock.

Mary Pym did her best with the additional duties she had taken on — with the dubious 'assistance' of Primrose — but she lacked a great many of the qualities that were required by the working wife of a farmer. Fortunately, Enid's enthusiasm and a natural aptitude for farm life made up for many of her mother's shortcomings and Ralf admitted that she was a genuine help, even though there were occasions when he would have welcomed the presence of another man to help with the more onerous jobs.

328

Ralf enjoyed Enid's company on the occasions when they worked together. She was both sensible and cheerful and had a sense of humour that constantly amused him. But she was also naturally inquisitive and he needed to field a great many questions about his life before he came to work for her father at Trecarne.

One evening she was helping him settle the horses in their stable after a long day spent cutting up a fallen tree and bringing the logs to the house. Suddenly, Enid asked, 'How old are you, Ralf?'

'Twenty-three — coming up twenty-four,' he replied, aware that he was about to be subjected to another of Enid's question times.

'Most men are married by the time they're as old as that,' she declared. 'Why aren't you?'

'Because I've never met the right girl, I suppose,' he replied. Even as he spoke he remembered Brighid and realised it had been a long time since she had last entered his thoughts.

'Yet you must have met some girls you liked,' Enid persisted.

'I've met a great many I liked,' Ralf replied, humouring her, 'but some didn't like me — and I've never liked anyone enough to want to marry them.'

'Do you like Winfred?' Enid asked unexpectedly.

'Winfred? I really hardly know her,' he replied tactfully.

'Well, she likes you.'

When Ralf protested that Enid must be mistaken, she shook her head, 'No, it's true, she

329

told me so. She told Ronwen too — and *she* told Father. That's why he took Winfred with her when she went to stay with Grandfather. It was mean of Ronwen to repeat what was supposed to be a secret, but she's like that. I never tell her any of *my* secrets.'

Ralf remembered how Ronwen had lied about him to her father in an attempt to get him into trouble and silently agreed with Enid's assessment of her eldest sister's character. He also wondered what might have happened had Winfred revealed her feelings to him. It was probably a good thing she had not, because it was evident that Oliver Pym realised that Ralf was unaware of them. Had he not, Ralf would have suffered the fate of his predecessor.

6

It took Oliver Pym far longer than he had anticipated to achieve his ambition of transforming the farmhouse at Lantewan into the small, albeit impressive, manorial house of his dreams, but he soon realised that it took more than a fine house to gain acceptance into the ranks of the Cornish gentry. There was a very thin sprinkling of their number among those who attended the party he threw to celebrate the completion of Lantewan 'Manor'.

However, Pym was not unduly disappointed. The Puritans now had a firm grip on England and his acquaintance and one-time Cambridge neighbour, Oliver Cromwell, had been sworn into office as 'Lord Protector of the Commonwealth of England, Scotland and Ireland'.

It meant that Cromwell was now the country's ruler. King in all but name, and it was time for men like Pym, who had been among his closest supporters, to reap their reward. Advancement was not long in coming.

Cromwell appointed a number of major-generals to rule over particular areas of the new Commonwealth and the man appointed to govern the west country — Cornwall, Devon,

Somerset, Dorset, Wiltshire and Gloucestershire — was Major-General John Desborough.

Desborough had been a distinguished soldier during the Civil War — and he was also Cromwell's brother-in-law. Oliver Pym had served with him and was rewarded by being made a local commissioner, one of Desborough's deputies. In addition, he was made a Justice of the Peace, his magisterial powers adding to his influence.

Ralf had hoped he might move into Trecarne farmhouse when the Pym family were finally settled in Lantewan, but when he broached the subject with his employer he was curtly informed that Pym had plans for the farmhouse which did not include his ploughman. He would be expected to remain in his room above the stable.

Enid provided some of the few bright moments in Ralf's life. With the increasing absence of Oliver Pym, she spent more and more time at Trecarne helping Ralf and he became very fond of her. Now fourteen years of age, Enid was on the threshold of womanhood and Ralf felt she would eclipse Oliver Pym's other daughters in both looks and personality. She was also uncompromising in her views and when these clashed with those of her father he would become extremely angry with her.

Early in 1655, Oliver Pym rode to Looe, a busy fishing port on the coast to the east of Trecarne, where he was to preside over a committee called to decide a dispute between the fishermen of that port and the local landowner. The dispute was in respect of the tithes which the landowner had purchased from the Church.

Contrary to the evidence presented at the hearing, Pym decided in favour of the landowner and the fishermen disputed his decision noisily, both inside the building where the hearing took place and also outside as Pym left.

On the way back to Lantewan Enid, who had accompanied him to Looe, argued their case with her father. In truth, Pym's decision was not as impartial as it might have been. The owner of the tithes, although a well-known Royalist supporter, was also one of the most influential landowners in Cornwall. Oliver Pym's ruling had been greatly influenced by his own ambition to become an accepted member of Cornish society.

Enid was fully aware of this and she was both indignant and vocal about his finding. She and her father were sharing a horse on a double saddle because her own pony was heavily in foal. He was therefore unable to distance himself from his daughter and her loudly voiced views as they followed the cliff-top path that led from Looe.

'How could you possibly rule against the fishermen?' Enid asked for the umpteenth time as they neared Lantewan.

It had been drizzling for much of the ride, but the drizzle had now turned into heavy rain and Oliver Pym was in no mood to put up with his daughter's tirade any longer.

'I have told you, Enid, I made my decision on the facts of the case, not on emotion.'

'I don't believe you,' Enid said heatedly. 'Right

333

was on the side of the fishermen. They would have happily paid to support the Church, but the tithes had been sold to a man who supports neither the Church nor Parliament. Their cause was just . . . as you knew full well.'

'I am not prepared to argue with my own daughter on a subject about which she knows nothing,' Oliver Pym said angrily. 'Now shut up, or you can get off and walk home.'

Enid's anger was not to be cooled by the elements. Wriggling her foot clear of the stirrup behind him, she said, 'Then set me down. I would rather get wet than ride with someone who would see the families of fishermen starve rather than risk losing popularity with so called 'gentry' by doing what is right.'

* * *

Oliver Pym stomped into Lantewan shedding water from his clothing and in a towering rage. He was still angry at the manner in which Enid had spoken to him — but he was also feeling guilty about leaving her on foot in the driving rain on the cliff-edge path. However, he was not ready to concede that it was *his* actions and not those of Enid which had resulted in their parting company in such an acrimonious manner.

In answer to Mary's concern about Enid's whereabouts, he snapped, 'She was unforgivably insolent and said she did not want to ride home with me. I left her on the cliff path. A long walk in the rain might help to bring her to her senses. She is in sore need of some discipline. If I were able to spend more time at home I would ensure it was given to her. Unfortunately, I need to spend a great many of my days away and it is becoming increasingly apparent that you are incapable of taking her in hand. I will write to my father and ask him to take her beneath his roof with her sisters.'

Dismayed by his words, Mary said, 'It's unfair to blame me for anything Enid has said. She is not a bad girl, Oliver. It is just that she thinks very deeply about things — about people. Please don't send her away. I miss Ronwen and Winfred so much. I don't think I could bear to lose Enid too.'

'You should have thought of that before allowing Enid to get out of hand,' Oliver Pym said callously. 'But forget Enid for now. I have a meeting this evening in Lostwithiel, and I need dry clothes. I trust I have some . . . '

7

His chores completed for the day, Ralf returned to the loft above the stable to change his wet clothes. It had ceased raining now but an easterly wind was blowing at near gale force and, as was usual with a wind from that direction, it seemed to find every crack in the old farm buildings.

Ralf had been living above the stable for some years now and during that time he had constructed a stone fireplace and chimney in a corner of the loft in a bid to make it more habitable. He had a wood-fuelled fire crackling away and a kettle just coming to the boil when the stable door opened, fanning the fire and setting the candle-lantern swaying on the cord on which it hung from a ceiling hook.

Moving to the top of ladder which rose to the loft from the stable, Ralf saw a dishevelled Mary looking up at him, clutching Primrose by the hand.

Before he could question her presence so far from home, Mary asked, 'Ralf . . . is Enid up there with you?'

Treating the question as an accusation, Ralf replied, 'No, of course not. Why should she be?'

'I was hoping . . . hoping she might have

called in to see you.' Aware that she owed him an explanation, Mary added, 'Enid went to Looe with her father today. On the way back they had an argument and he left her to walk home. I thought . . . I was hoping she might be here with you.'

'I haven't seen her.' Thinking quickly, he asked, 'When did Mr Pym leave her?'

'I don't know,' Mary replied unhappily. 'But it was almost five o'clock when he arrived home and then he had to change to attend a meeting at Lostwithiel.'

'You mean . . . he left Enid on foot in this weather to make her way home along the cliff path when it was getting dark? Where was she when he left her?'

'I don't know,' wailed the distraught mother.

Ralf looked at Mary in disbelief. The path that followed the cliff edge was dangerous at the best of times. Made treacherous by rain, and with a strong easterly wind blowing, it was a place to be avoided.

'Do you know how far she and her father had come when he left her?' he asked.

Mary shook her head. 'He was in no mood to be asked any questions when he came in. He had been to Looe to settle a dispute between the fishermen and the owner of the tithes. Enid was angry because she felt Oliver had made a wrong decision — and she can be extremely forthright when she feels deeply about something . . . '

'Spare me the details of the rights or wrongs of what went on,' Ralf said. 'The coastal path is no place to be on foot in this weather, especially when it's getting dark. I'll take a lantern and go to see if I can find her. Are there any men at Lantewan who can come out to help me?'

'Only Jeremy — oh, yes, and old Tom.'

Tom was in his seventies and not a man to take along on a search of the cliff edge, but Jeremy was a boy of perhaps sixteen or seventeen, who was employed as a manservant at Lantewan. He was a first-class house servant but, because of his age, Pym did not have to pay him the wage his skills deserved. It was a situation that suited Oliver Pym well.

'We'll go to Lantewan now,' Ralf said, reaching down a coat from a peg as he spoke. 'You and Primrose had better stay at the house in case Enid should return. Jeremy and I will take lanterns and search along the cliff path to Looe.'

Thoroughly alarmed by the urgency in Ralf's voice, Mary asked, 'You don't think something might have happened to Enid?'

'I'm trying not to think of what might have happened,' Ralf said bluntly, 'but the cliff path is no place for a young girl in the weather we've had today. Her father should have realised that.'

★   ★   ★

The light from the lanterns carried by Ralf and Jeremy cast only the feeblest illumination and was constantly threatened by the strong wind that hampered the pair's progress along the cliff-top path.

Ralf was extremely concerned for Enid's well-being by now, but it was impossible to hurry. The mud of the path made it necessary for them to proceed with the utmost caution and they progressed ever more slowly as Ralf paused every few paces to raise his voice against the wind and call Enid's name, straining his ears in the hope of receiving a response.

They progressed in this manner for almost an hour, and Jeremy had just repeated an earlier opinion that they were wasting their time and that Enid had probably found her way back to Lantewan by another route, when Ralf suddenly came to a halt.

Stooping, he held his lantern closer to the ground. 'Look! Something — or someone — has slipped here . . . see? The marks go right to the edge of the cliff.'

There were certainly distinct marks to be seen in the mud of the path, but Jeremy said, 'They might have been caused by anything. An animal, perhaps, or even the rain? Besides, they could have been here for days.'

Ralf shook his head, 'No, the rain would have washed them away. These marks have been made since the rain ceased.'

'Even so, it could have been a sheep, or any other animal,' Jeremy persisted.

Ignoring him, Ralf advanced cautiously to the edge of the cliff and called, 'Enid? Enid, are you there?'

He called twice more without receiving a response and Jeremy was about to suggest they move on when there was a sound from somewhere beneath them.

'There! Did you hear that?' Ralf demanded.

'I heard *something*,' Jeremy admitted, 'but it could have been anything. A gull, perhaps . . . or the wind.'

Even as they spoke there was a temporary lull in the latter and they both heard the sound again.

'It's her!' Ralf cried. 'It's Enid.'

He advanced cautiously to the edge of the cliff and held his lantern as far over the side as he could, but its light was not sufficiently strong to see more than the fact that the cliff was not sheer at that point — at least, not immediately beneath where he was standing. It gave him some hope that if Enid had fallen here she might not be too severely injured.

He had not been along this path since he was a boy and he tried to remember it. 'How well do you know this part of the coast?' he asked his companion.

'I've been along here a few times,' Jeremy replied. 'Why?'

'If I can find a way down there, could I make my way along the foot of the cliff? Is there any sort of beach?'

In the dim light from his lantern Ralf could just make out the negative movement of Jeremy's head. 'There's no beach, but if the tide's out you might be able to scramble across the rocks.'

Ralf's hopes dropped. He had hoped that if Enid had slid down the steep cliff side she might have landed on sand and be perhaps trapped, but unhurt.

'Do you know what the tide is doing?'

Once again Jeremy shook his head and Ralf

said, 'It doesn't matter. If it was high this wind would be throwing spray up here. I'm going down there.' He had remembered a place, not far back along the path, where the cliff dipped almost to sea level. 'You stay here and keep waving your lamp as far out over the cliff as you can to guide me here . . . '

★   ★   ★

Returning along the way he and Jeremy had come he found a place where he was able to scramble down to the shoreline. The rocks here were wet, whether from the sea or the rain he could not tell at first, but as he scrambled across the boulders an occasional wave would crash against them and envelop him in spray.

There were other places where seawater surged between the rocks as he clambered over them and it seemed a long time until he thought he could hear Jeremy's voice above the sound of wind and waves.

He could not see any light from the lantern, but the sloping cliff, terminating as it did in a sheer drop, meant that he would not have spotted it no matter how far out Jeremy held it.

'Enid . . . Enid, can you hear me?'

There was no immediate reply, and for a moment Ralf thought that perhaps Jeremy had been right, and it had been an animal that had left the marks on the cliff path.

Nevertheless, he called again and again — and suddenly his persistence was rewarded.

'Help . . . Help me.'

341

The cry was very faint, but he thought he recognised Enid's voice. Moments later he found her, and was appalled by her condition. There was blood on her face and she had grazed herself extensively but it was not this that alarmed him. She was lying on a large rock, and although she was not trapped in any way she seemed unable to move any part of her body as she greeted him tearfully. 'I was beginning to think no one would ever find me. How did you . . . ?'

'Your mother came to see if you were at Trecarne and told me what had happened. I came looking for you with Jeremy from Lantewan. He's at the top of the cliff and guided me to you.'

'I've been lying here, praying that Mother would go to Trecarne to find you. I knew you would do something. Didn't my father offer to come with you?'

'I believe he had to go to a meeting somewhere . . . but enough talking for now. I see you've got a nasty graze on your head, and there's blood running into your eye. Let me clean it up for you.'

As he worked, Ralf was deeply concerned by her inability to move her body, especially as spray was coming over the rocks more frequently now and he realised the tide must be coming in. Enid needed to be moved — and quickly.

Leaving her, he backed away from the foot of the cliff until he could attract Jeremy's attention. With great difficulty, he managed to convey instructions to move back along the path to the place where it dipped down to the shore. Then, promising a fearful Enid that he would return to her in a few minutes and carry her to safety, he made his way back across the rocks to meet Jeremy.

He told the boy to return along the path to a spot where a triangle of sheep hurdles had been placed in position to fence off a deep and crumbling-edged hole that had been caused by water tumbling down the steep slippery slope. A cow, sheep or horse coming down the hill would be upon the hole before they saw it and unable to stop. Jeremy was to detach one of the hurdles and bring it to the spot where Enid lay.

'What shall I put in its place?' Jeremy asked. 'It's dangerous there and the land belongs to old Farmer Collins, who's well known for his evil temper. If one of his animals was to hurt itself because of us there'd be hell to pay!'

'If that happens he can take it up with Oliver Pym,' Ralf retorted. 'Enid's badly hurt. Go and get a hurdle — and be quick. I fear she might have broken her back. The tide's coming in and she can't move so there's not a moment to be lost.'

Satisfied that Jeremy had grasped the urgency of the situation, Ralf made his way back to where Enid lay. She was embarrassingly relieved to see him again, but she was also shivering with cold.

Taking off his coat, he put it over her. It was doubtful whether it made very much difference because both she and his coat were too wet for warmth, but Ralf felt he was doing something. He would have made a pillow for her with his jerkin, but she screamed in pain when he tried to move her head, so he put the jerkin back on again and stroked her hair gently instead.

It seemed an age before Jeremy put in an appearance with the hurdle and there was a hint of panic in his voice when he said, 'The tide's definitely rising, Ralf. It was washing over some of the rocks I had to scramble over. We might already be cut off.'

'We'll make it,' Ralf declared, with more confidence than he felt. 'You did well, Jeremy, but you're right, we do need to hurry. The trouble is, her body seems to be paralysed and it was agony when I moved her head. If you put the hurdle down beside her I'll lift the top half of her body on to it as carefully as I can while you support her head. Then we'll move the bottom half and pack our coats around her neck to try to prevent it from moving.'

Slowly and gingerly they succeeded in placing Enid on the hurdle, but not without causing her great pain. However, once she was in place the structure of the hurdle, coupled with the support of their coats, helped prevent her head from moving. Then began the nightmare of moving her across the rocks.

The tide was definitely on its way in and once a wave came over the rocks on which they stood and threatened to sweep them all into the sea. Soon afterwards Jeremy fell into deep water between two more rocks and lost his lantern.

At last, they reached the spot from which they were able to manhandle their burden on to the cliff path and out of reach of waves and spray.

Here they set Enid down in order to take a brief, much needed rest.

'How are you feeling?' Ralf asked her anxiously.

'My neck hurts, and my face too, but I can't feel a thing anywhere else — and I still can't move. What's happened to me, Ralf? Why am I like this?'

'That's something only a doctor will be able to tell us,' Ralf replied gently. 'We'll get you to one as soon as possible, but we can't carry you all the way to Fowey like this.'

'I've heard that the curate over at Lansallos used to be an army surgeon,' Jeremy said. 'I know he sometimes treats some of the villagers. We could take her there.'

They were probably less than half a mile from Lansallos right now, while Lantewan was three times that distance — and a doctor would still have to be summoned from Fowey.

'Do you think you can help carry Enid that far?' Ralf asked him.

While they were struggling to carry Enid across the rocks, Jeremy had come to realise the seriousness of her injuries and now he declared, 'I'll carry her as far as we need to. I think she's being very brave.'

'So do I,' Ralf agreed. 'But the sooner we have her inside and away from the rain the happier we'll all be. Let's go.'

8

Curate Robert Elderton was taking temporary care of the parish of Lansallos. He had come to the Church late in life, having been a surgeon with the Parliamentarian 'Model Army' during the late civil wars. When Ralf and Jeremy carried Enid into the rectory and Ralf explained what had happened, he displayed the organisational skills that had made Cromwell's army well-nigh invincible.

A fire was lit in one of the rectory's bedrooms and, under the curate's supervision, Enid was carefully lifted on to a wooden bed from which the mattress had been removed in order to provide a firm base on which she could lie. Here, after Ralf and Jeremy had been ushered from the room, she was carefully undressed by the curate's wife and a maidservant.

Meanwhile, Curate Robert despatched a manservant to Lantewan House to inform Mary Pym of what had happened to her daughter. The servant was then to ride on to summon the doctor from Fowey.

The curate explained to Ralf that as Enid was so seriously hurt he wanted the diagnosis of a regular doctor, but that was not his only reason.

He was aware that Oliver Pym was an important man in the county, and he wanted no undue criticism to be levelled at him over his treatment of Enid — especially as he was doubtful whether she could survive her injuries.

Mary Pym reached the Lansallos rectory long before the doctor, having left Primrose in the care of a maidservant and walked — and run — through the rain from Lantewan House. She would have gathered Enid in her arms and hugged her, had the Reverend Robert not prevented her.

'You may kiss her,' he said, gently yet firmly, 'but she must be kept as still as possible until the doctor has seen her and, I suspect, for a long time after that too.'

'Why?' a distressed Mary queried. 'What exactly is wrong with her?'

Not wishing to discuss Enid's condition in the hearing of the still conscious girl, the Reverend Robert led Mary from the room. When there was a closed door behind them, he said gently, 'I am more used to dealing with the wounds of war than with accidents such as Enid has suffered, but I very much fear she has broken her neck. We will know for certain when the doctor from Fowey examines her.'

Both distressed and bewildered, Mary asked, 'But . . . what does that mean? It will heal . . . she will get better?'

The curate shook his head sadly. 'It is very doubtful. Indeed, it is surprising she survived the fall over the cliff, and she would certainly not be alive now had it not been for the courage and common sense of the two young men who found her and brought her here.'

'Where are they now?' Mary asked.

'They are being cared for in the kitchen. We found dry clothes for them and Cook made them some hot food. But, come, shall we return to Enid now? She is a very brave girl, but I don't doubt that she will be longing for her mother.'

★   ★   ★

Dr Carminow, the physician from Fowey, confirmed Robert Elderton's diagnosis of Enid's condition. She had indeed broken her neck, and in so doing had caused serious damage to the nerves controlling the rest of her body.

In answer to Mary's tearful question he was unable to predict whether Enid would ever regain the use of her limbs, saying, 'It is impossible to assess the extent of the damage caused by such a fall. I have known some who have recovered at least a modicum of movement; others who remain paralysed for the remainder of what is usually a very short life. But what was a young girl doing alone on the cliff path in such vile weather?'

Mary tried to gloss over the reasons why Enid had been left alone on the cliff path, but when Oliver Pym reached the rectory an hour later he was castigated for his irresponsibility by Dr Carminow, leaving him in no doubt whom the Fowey physician believed responsible for Enid's accident.

It was doubtful whether any other man in

Cornwall would have dared give Pym such a fierce tongue-lashing, but Dr Carminow had little to fear. Among his patients was Hugh Peters, a prominent member of one of Fowey's most eminent families and a fiery preacher who had been chaplain to the Parliamentarian army and, later, chaplain to Oliver Cromwell and the Council of State. Peters was also a signatory to the death warrant authorising the execution of King Charles I — a fact that would one day cost him his own life. But for the moment Dr Carminow could bring more influence to bear than could Oliver Pym. The farmer was forced to accept the physician's scathing criticism, but it did not improve his temper.

Later that night, after Dr Carminow had decreed that Enid should remain at the Lansallos rectory, at least until she had recovered from the trauma of her fall, Pym was returning to Lantewan with Mary when he suddenly turned on her. 'Who told Carminow that I had left Enid to find her own way home along the cliff edge?'

'I tried to avoid laying any blame upon you,' Mary replied unhappily. 'I merely told him what Enid would have said, had he asked her.'

'It was not necessary for you to say anything at all,' Pym snapped back at her. 'If word goes around that my daughter is paralysed because I abandoned her in a storm it could seriously damage my reputation in the county, just when my authority is beginning to be respected.'

Mary was usually very careful not to anger her husband, but at that she stopped short. 'Do you value your reputation more than the well-being of your daughter who is lying back there paralysed and possibly dying?' Choking on her words, she added fiercely, 'Whatever was said to Dr Carminow, it *is* your fault and nothing you can say will change that. You behaved in a totally irresponsible and bad-tempered manner, yet all you can think of is your reputation! Had it not been for Ralf I would be telling the story — the *true* story — to a coroner and your reputation would be in tatters. And while we are on the subject of Ralf, this is the second time he has saved the life of one of our children. I think it is time you rewarded him in the manner he so richly deserves.'

9

Far from rewarding Ralf for his part in rescuing Enid, Oliver Pym seemed to go out of his way to find fault with his work. When the plough broke, he accused Ralf of carelessness, even though Ralf had pointed out in the previous ploughing season that it would soon need to be replaced. It was as though he did not want to remember what had happened and that Enid's tragic accident had been largely due to his own actions.

Mary could not forget, and she was finding it increasingly difficult to care for her invalid daughter. Eventually, after much correspondence between Cornwall and Cambridgeshire, Winfred came home to help take care of her sister — against the wishes of Oliver Pym.

At eighteen years of age, Winfred was an intelligent, resourceful and strong-willed young woman, who had managed to persuade her increasingly feeble-minded grandfather that she had her father's consent to return to Cornwall. He had suggested that Ronwen should accompany her, but Ronwen took after her father. Whatever she wanted took precedence over anyone else's needs or wishes. At present she was being courted by the heir to an earldom and she had no intention of absenting herself long enough for anyone else to take her place in his affections. She wanted one day to be Countess Ronwen.

Winfred would have been perfectly content to travel to Cornwall on her own, but such a thing was unthinkable for a young woman. Instead, she was taken to London by one of her aunts. In the capital city another relative provided a maidservant to accompany her on board a ship bound for the West Indies.

The vessel anchored off Fowey and Winfred and the maid were conveyed ashore. When Winfred arrived Oliver Pym was attending a meeting of Major-General Desborough's commissioners in Plymouth and by the time he returned to Lantewan Winfred had been home for three days.

When he entered the house and she greeted him with a cheery 'Hello, Father', his expression was one of utter disbelief.

'Winfred . . . What are you doing here?'

'I am delighted to see you too after all this time, Father,' Winfred replied sarcastically. 'I am home because of what has happened to poor Enid. I wanted to be here to help Mother care for her.'

'Had your mother needed any help I would have employed another maidservant,' Pym said angrily. 'As for you, I had hoped you might have found a husband by now, but I doubt whether any father would wish to see his son married to such a wilful young woman. Furthermore, unless you mend your ways you will end your days either as a cantankerous old maid, or married to a man who'll beat some obedience into you.'

'I will have no man who would dare lay a hand on me,' Winfred declared defiantly. 'And now, as you have no welcome for me, I will go back to Enid. She at least can raise a smile for me, despite her tragic injuries.'

The heated conversation had taken place in the doorway of Oliver Pym's study, within the hearing of Ralf, who was standing in the hallway, waiting to speak to either Mary or Oliver Pym.

Enid's pony had foaled successfully and he had been hoping to deliver the news of the happy event to her, in the belief that it would cheer her up. However, with Oliver Pym in the house and evidently in a bad mood, Ralf knew there was no chance of passing the message on personally. Despite his rescue of Enid, Pym could rarely find a civil word for him.

Ralf believed that Pym would have liked to dismiss him, but the Puritan farmer was aware that he would be unlikely to find anyone either with the skills that came from knowing Trecarne so well — though Pym little guessed how well — or who would be prepared to accept the Puritan's constant criticism.

For Ralf's part, he was content to be working on the farm he loved, especially now that Pym's duties kept him away from home for a great deal of the time. While he was away, although Ralf had been refused permission to live in the empty farmhouse, he could wander through it at will, and he was also a welcome visitor to Lantewan House.

But today was not one of the days when he would be greeted with pleasure. He doubted whether the last word had been said on the subject of Winfred's return to Cornwall and he had no wish to be caught up in a family argument.

He was heading away from Lantewan when he was brought to a halt by a voice calling out his name. Winfred had seen him from a window and was hurrying after him.

When she caught up with him, she said breathlessly, 'Ralf . . . it *is* you. Why did you leave the house without at least saying hello to me? It must be three years since we last met — but you haven't changed a bit!'

'You have,' Ralf said. 'You're no longer the young girl I could call upon to help me with chores around the farm.'

It was true. Winfred was a young woman with an assured air that had deterred many of the young men of whom Oliver Pym would have approved. Ralf felt slightly in awe of her now.

'I could still do the work if it needed to be done,' Winfred declared, 'and there have been many times while I have been away that I wished I was back at Trecarne, doing all the things I enjoyed. But what are you doing here at Lantewan?'

'I was hoping to see Enid,' Ralf said. 'To tell her that her pony has had a foal, a very pretty little filly. I thought the news might cheer her up a little.'

'Of course it will! So why are you leaving without telling her about it? Come back to the house and speak to her. She enjoys your company, she told me so, and she adores her pony. Poor Enid, she needs anything that might bring a little joy into her life. Come along.'

'I'd rather not,' Ralf said, embarrassed. 'Your father doesn't like me coming to the house. I would rather you told her.'

Winfred looked at him in disbelief. 'Doesn't like you coming to the house? You saved Enid's life . . . In fact you've saved the lives of two of us now. You're not telling me that you two still don't get along after all these years of working together?'

'We don't see a great deal of each other,' Ralf explained. 'Your father is a very busy man these days, and he doesn't often visit Trecarne. I go about my work and he sees that I'm paid for what I do. It works well enough for both of us.'

'But you have just said you are not welcome at Lantewan. Why?'

'Probably for the same reason I heard you and him arguing a few minutes ago,' Ralf said. 'We each prefer to go our own way and are too outspoken about our views on things.'

'All the same . . . '

Winfred never completed the sentence. Oliver Pym appeared in the doorway of the house and demanded in a stentorian voice, 'Winfred . . . Hunkyn . . . What are you doing out there?'

As he emerged from the house, Ralf could see from his tense posture that Pym was still angry. Aware that Winfred was in the mood to continue her argument with him, he said quickly, 'I've just returned from the blacksmith's with two of the

Lantewan horses and wanted to pass the news on to Enid that her pony gave birth to a foal during the night.'

'And I suggested that he came in and told Enid personally,' Winfred said. 'I don't doubt she would welcome visitors — especially one who saved her life.'

'She'll have had enough excitement with your return home,' snapped Oliver Pym, 'and now you've been told about the foal you can tell Enid.' Returning his attention to Ralf, he went on, 'There must be plenty of work waiting for you at Trecarne, Hunkyn. I don't pay my workers to socialise, so be on your way.'

Before Winfred could say anything to further anger her father, Ralf said, 'Of course, but I'd like you to come to Trecarne sometime, to discuss what we should do with the two lower pastures.'

'I'll come when time permits,' Pym said. 'In the meantime do whatever you think is best — and I don't want to find you wasting your time here at Lantewan.'

10

A week after his visit to Lantewan House, Ralf was replacing tiles blown from the wall of a barn during a recent storm when Winfred appeared, riding the pony that had belonged to her before she went away. It had been ridden only infrequently since then and, after greeting his visitor, Ralf commented on its plumpness.

'I will soon ride that off,' Winfred said. 'There must have been a great many changes at Trecarne since I went away. Why don't you come riding with me and show me all that's been happening?'

'I doubt if your father would approve of that,' Ralf said ruefully. 'Besides, I have too much work to do.'

'Surely you are not expected to do everything at Trecarne on your own?' Winfred said incredulously. 'Don't you have anyone here to help you?'

'Your father takes on extra help at certain times of the year, but this isn't one of them. I'm on my own here — so I doubt very much whether your father would approve of your visit.'

'There would seem to be very little that he *does* approve of these days,' Winfred agreed, 'but he's been called to London, so you have no need to worry. Talking of which, Enid has been asking for you and Mother says you are welcome to call at Lantewan whenever you wish.'

'That's very kind,' Ralf said. 'Tell her I'll come as soon as I am able. Unfortunately, there are a great many chores I need to do at Trecarne first.'

'They will be done far more quickly if I help you,' Winfred said, slipping from the saddle. 'What shall I do first?'

'You can't involve yourself with farm work.' Ralf was startled. 'You're not a young girl any more, Winfred. You're a woman . . . a *gentle-woman*.'

Winfred smiled wryly. 'That's something else on which you and my father would disagree and, much as I hate to admit it, he is quite right. I was always happiest when I was able to work here at Trecarne. Far happier than living in my grandfather's house and trying to pretend I am a lady.'

'But you *are* a lady,' Ralf insisted. 'Your father is one of the most important men in Cornwall . . . perhaps in the whole country, and you're his daughter.'

'Don't you start talking like everyone else, Ralf Hunkyn!' Winfred said with a sudden display of passion. 'My father may be quite as important as you say — and *he* certainly believes he is — but that doesn't change the person I know I am and I want to be accepted as that person, not have people pretend to like me because of what my father is, or have them invite me to parties because they think I might be a good marriage

358

prospect for their sons.'

Winfred glared at Ralf, daring him to argue with her. When he chose to make no comment, she relaxed. 'Good! Now we understand each other again, what needs to be done about Trecarne?'

★ ★ ★

For the remainder of that day Winfred worked so hard on the farm that before dusk Ralf was forced to agree that he could afford the time to go to Lantewan to visit Enid. Before leaving, he went to his quarters above the stable and collected a book from a shelf he had built there.

When he came out of the stable Winfred was standing holding the reins of her pony. Seeing what he carried, she asked, 'What do you have there, Ralf?'

'It's a book of John Donne's poetry,' he replied. 'I take it to Lantewan sometimes and read it to Enid. She seems to enjoy it.'

'Yes, she always enjoyed poetry. I used to read it to her when she was smaller and as she grew older and learned to read she would borrow my books and read it for herself.' Suddenly close to tears, she added, 'Poor Enid. There is so much she can no longer do for herself. May I look at the book, please, Ralf?'

When he handed the leather-bound book to her she opened it at the beginning and saw written on the flyleaf the inscription, *For Ralf, with thanks for your patience and loyalty.* It was signed, *Christabelle and Hesta.*

Reading the inscription, Winfred said, 'This is a very special present, Ralf. Are Christabelle and Hesta very good friends of yours?'

Ralf did not like lying to Winfred, but he could hardly tell her the truth. With a smile, he said, 'Hesta is a dog. I used to take it for walks and care for it sometimes. Christabelle was its owner and the lady friend of one of my employers.'

After scanning through the book, Winfred handed it back to him. 'I would not expect to find a leather-bound book of poetry in the possession of a man who labours on a farm. I always thought you a most unusual farmhand, Ralf. Sometime you must tell me about the life you led before coming to work at Trecarne.'

'Yes, sometime,' Ralf agreed equivocally. He knew that even after so many years he must remain on his guard and be careful not to reveal details of his past service with the exiled king of England. It was a long time since anyone had wondered about his earlier life — and Winfred was far too easy to talk to.

They made their way to Lantewan with Ralf leading the pony and Winfred happily chatting about the work they had done that day, and of the animals that were currently being kept at Trecarne.

'The farm animals were among the many things I missed at my grandfather's home,' she said, adding with a short laugh, 'It's strange that more than once when I was seated with the cream of Cambridgeshire society I was wishing I was here in Cornwall, feeding horses and cows, or even cleaning out pigsties. Perhaps my father is right when he says that I don't deserve a place in society and should be married to some farmer who would give me a hard life and make me carry out farmyard chores whatever the weather.'

'There are worse ways to live,' Ralf commented. 'It's just that your father is ambitious for his family.'

'So he always told us,' Winfred retorted, 'but I sometimes wonder whether his ambitions are really only for himself and all he is concerned about is that his family do nothing to let him down.'

Ralf was in no doubt that Winfred was right, but decided to say nothing. They walked in silence for a while, as the sun sank slowly beneath the far horizon of the sea.

Suddenly, Winfred asked, 'Why have you never married, Ralf?'

He smiled. 'That's a question Enid once asked me. I'll tell you the same as I told her. I have never found the time to marry. Besides, I've had no chance of meeting any eligible young women at Trecarne.'

'But you are not there every day of the week. What do you do on Sundays, when you go home to Fowey? Don't you know any women there?'

'Not really. Certainly no one I feel I'd like to marry.' Not wishing her to ask any more questions, he decided he would ask about *her* life. 'How about you? You must have met a great many interesting men in Cambridgeshire. Men who are close to Cromwell.'

'Those who are really close to Cromwell are older men,' Winfred said. 'Either they are already married, or they have killed their wives with constant childbearing and are looking for a young wife to repeat the process. That sort of life is not for me. Some of them do have sons of marriageable age, of course, but if they are close enough to Cromwell they hope to marry them into noble families or rich ones — or preferably both. Ronwen has managed to find herself an admirer from a titled family, but they have no money and I think Grandfather has promised to give her a considerable dowry to bring them up to scratch. Anyway, I don't think I have had a single intelligent conversation with any of the men I have met. They all try to outdo each other in talking about fighting, religion, or politics. If I were to mention John Donne to any of them they would look puzzled, and then, not wishing to appear ignorant, would probably make up something like, 'Do you mean the John Donne who served in Ireton's regiment, or is there another . . . ?' As for William Shakespeare . . . if I were to mention his name they would be totally bemused!'

'I'm afraid I have never heard of him either,' Ralf confessed, relieved that Winfred had dropped her questions about his life in Fowey.

'Oh, good!' Winfred said. 'Now I can tell you all about him. He's a wonderful poet, and a playwright . . . '

She was still extolling Shakespeare's talents when they arrived at Lantewan and went inside to Enid's room.

The next few days were among the most pleasant Ralf had spent since his return to

Trecarne. Winfred would spend the mornings at her home, then come to the farm and help with the chores. When these were completed the two of them would walk back to Lantewan and spend some time with Enid before being given a meal by Mary.

On two occasions, Winfred walked a short distance with Ralf when he returned to Trecarne. They were very comfortable in each other's company, but Ralf was aware it could not last. When her father returned from London he would put a stop to Winfred's visits to Trecarne and forbid Ralf to call on Enid.

However, before Oliver Pym returned, another visitor came to Lantewan. One who would cause an unexpected upheaval within the Pym family.

11

Ralf and Winfred were on their way from Trecarne to Lantewan in the late afternoon when they saw a young woman walking towards them along the narrow lane that linked the two properties. She was wearing a strict Puritan style of dress not often seen in this part of Cornwall.

It was equally unusual to see an unknown young woman alone in the countryside and the two companions fell silent as she approached until, suddenly, Winfred exclaimed, 'Why . . . it's Clarice!'

Startled, Ralf came to a halt as Winfred left his side and ran towards the stranger. When the two women met they embraced warmly and instantly engaged in an animated conversation.

Ralf was uncertain whether to continue on his way and join the women, or turn and return to Trecarne because his presence might be an embarrassment to Winfred if the stranger was a friend of the family. Then Winfred turned and beckoned for him to come and join them.

He advanced uncertainly, not knowing whether he should behave as befitted an employee, but it was Winfred who solved the problem by saying, 'Ralf, come and meet Clarice. She was my best friend in Cambridgeshire and she has walked all the way here. Clarice, this is Ralf. He works on my father's farm at Trecarne and is my very best friend in Cornwall.'

Ralf thought there was something vaguely familiar about Clarice, but immediately dismissed the thought. There was no way he could possibly know anyone from Cambridgeshire, and Winfred's next words put the thought from his mind.

'Clarice is in trouble, Ralf. She and her father belong to the Society of Friends — the Quakers. Her father came to Cornwall to preach their message, but he was arrested and thrown into prison in Launceston castle. When Clarice was told about it she hurried to Cornwall to try to help him. Because she knew my father is a Justice of the Peace, she came to Lantewan to plead for his help in freeing her father, but, of course, my father is not here. What can she do?'

While Winfred was talking Clarice had been gazing at Ralf without speaking, and he found her attention disconcerting. Now she spoke for the first time in a quiet but firm voice. 'The reason I came to Cornwall is because I heard my father is in poor health. Unless I can do something to help him I fear he will not survive. They call the place in which he is imprisoned 'Doomsdale' because so many prisoners have died there.'

'What can she do, Ralf? How can she help her father?'

Ralf had no answer to the problem and he said so, adding, 'While I sympathise, your father is the only one who might be able to do anything practical, Winfred.'

'Yes, you are right, of course,' Winfred agreed. 'But let us get on to Lantewan. Clarice and I can discuss what to do once we are there.'

'I have already been to Lantewan,' Clarice said, 'but your mother and I have never met and she seemed uncertain what she should do with me. She told me you were at Trecarne Farm and I was on my way there when I met you.'

'Well, now you've found me and you will stay with us at Lantewan until we've decided what we might do to help. If my father were here I am certain we could secure your father's release. I remember him well and have heard him preach. All he tries to do is help people to find God. There is nothing unlawful about that. This will prove to be no more than an unfortunate misunderstanding. We will soon have it sorted out, I have no doubt.'

Ralf was less confident. Even if there had been a miscarriage of justice — and having experienced the bigotry of Scots zealots Ralf was far less convinced than Winfred of religious tolerance — he very much doubted whether Oliver Pym would interfere if there was the remotest chance he would be criticised for his actions — or unless there was something to be gained for himself by so doing.

'Shall I return to Trecarne and leave you to go on to Lantewan together?' he asked.

'Of course not,' Winfred replied positively. 'Enid would be very disappointed if you were not there to read poetry to her. Besides, I have never before been lucky enough to have *both* my favourite people with me at the same time. I want you to get to know each other.'

★ ★ ★

Clarice was still a guest at Lantewan on the next two occasions when Ralf visited the house, but on the third evening neither she nor Winfred was in the house and Mary Pym was extremely concerned for them.

'They've been away since dawn,' she told Ralf. 'Clarice has been increasingly worried about the health of her father, and last night she made up her mind to return to Launceston and make another attempt to see him. Winfred decided to go with her and they both went off together. I did not want her to go, but you know what she is like. Once she has made up her mind about something not even her father can make her do anything different. She said they would be back by nightfall, but it's dark already and there is no sign of them. I am worried about them, Ralf, I really am. Winfred is wilful, but she is not irresponsible, and she knows how concerned I will be about her. I should never have allowed her to go. It is a long way to travel to Launceston and back in one day. Something must have happened. I dread to think of her father's reaction to my stupidity.'

Ralf was deeply concerned. The girls' route would take them over Bodmin Moor, which was notorious for its bogs and unpredictable weather. Nevertheless, he tried to reassure Mary. 'I'm sure there's a very good reason for their not being home yet — and there is still time for them to return. As you say, she isn't irresponsible, and she does have Clarice with her. I'll come back at dawn and if she still isn't home I'll take a horse and ride to Launceston. But I'll need someone to feed the animals at Trecarne for me.'

'Thank you, Ralf. I knew I could rely on you. I'll send Jeremy to feed the animals.' Then, changing her mind, she said, 'No I won't. It will give me something else to think about. I will leave a maid to care for Enid for a while and take Primrose to Trecarne with me.'

★　★　★

It was a crisp, clear day and the ride through Liskeard and on to Launceston town brought back many memories for Ralf. These were lanes he had travelled with the then Prince Charles and the King.

He had hoped he might meet up with Winfred and Clarice along the way, although there were a number of other routes they might have taken to return to Lantewan. He was worried about them, and hoped they were still together. There was always the possibility that Clarice had decided to remain at Launceston to be near her father, leaving Winfred to ride home alone. It was not something he wanted to dwell upon. Bodmin Moor, in particular, was remote and lawless. It was no place for a girl to be travelling on her own.

He was relieved when Launceston came into

view. The castle, which was perched on top of a hill dominating the town, was a grim, forbidding building and Ralf had no doubt that 'Doomsdale' would be an apt name for any dungeons that the building contained.

Securing his horse in the courtyard, Ralf found a turnkey and explained that he had come to enquire about two young women who had left their home the previous day to visit a Quaker prisoner being held in the castle dungeons.

The turnkey gave Ralf a strange look before saying, 'I think you'd better speak to Mr Black, the head gaoler. He only returned to the castle an hour ago and is having a meal, but I'm sure he would want to see you.'

There was something about the man's manner that made Ralf feel uneasy. He felt the turnkey found the situation amusing. However, he needed to find Winfred and the head gaoler should know whether she arrived here and, if so, when she left.

Climbing a winding set of stone stairs in the wake of the turnkey, Ralf arrived at a stout wooden door. The turnkey knocked on the door and opened it without waiting for a command to enter.

There were three men seated at a table in the room and they were dining well. A man who appeared to be the most senior of the trio looked up scowling at the interruption.

'What's the meaning of this? I've had a tiring ride and said I didn't want to be disturbed.' The man spat out some of the food in his mouth as he spoke, and his accent was not that of an educated man.

'I thought you'd want to speak to this one,' said the turnkey. 'He's come asking after Charles Thomasson.'

The three men at the table exchanged glances and Ralf sensed an increased interest among them. Head Gaoler Black swallowed the remaining food in his mouth and laid his knife on the table beside the pewter plate. Looking up at Ralf unsmilingly, he said, 'Well now, what is your name — and what is Thomasson to you?'

'My name is Ralf Hunkyn and Thomasson is nothing to me,' Ralf said. 'We have never met. Indeed, I had never heard his name until the turnkey just mentioned it.'

Frowning, Black looked from Ralf to the turnkey and back again. 'If you don't know him, what are you doing here asking after him?'

'I am not,' Ralf replied, aware from the attitude of all the men in the room that it was important he not be considered a friend of Charles Thomasson. 'I came here looking for the daughter of my employer. She and a friend rode here yesterday to visit the friend's father, who I presume must be this Thomasson of whom you speak.'

The head gaoler looked at the turnkey who said, 'Two young women did come here yesterday asking after Thomasson. I did what you told me to do if anyone came looking for him. I locked them up until you had time to speak to them.'

Before the head gaoler could comment, Ralf

said, 'You cast Winfred and her friend into a cell! Why?'

'Because Thomasson is a threat to the Commonwealth,' the governor said pompously, 'and anyone claiming acquaintance with him is also suspect.'

'I doubt very much whether Commissioner Oliver Pym will agree with you,' Ralf said angrily. 'In fact, I have no doubt he will decide to appoint a new head gaoler for Launceston gaol.'

'It was Commissioner Pym himself who said that any visitors to Thomasson should be detained and questioned,' Black declared. 'He called at the castle on his way to London.'

'I doubt if he intended that you should throw his own daughter into gaol,' Ralf said, 'and that is what you've done.'

'His daughter?' The head gaoler suddenly lost his appetite. Pushing his plate away, he stood up and demanded, 'What nonsense is this?'

Ralf shook his head. 'It is not nonsense. Winfred Pym rode to Launceston yesterday in company with her friend Clarice, to visit Clarice's father who is locked up here. When they did not return home last night, Mary Pym, Winfred's mother, asked me to come here today to find out why. I hardly expected to learn that she had been thrown into gaol — on your orders. I will return home and inform Mistress Pym of your actions. Unfortunately, Commissioner Pym is still in London. When he returns I have no doubt he will have a great deal to say. In the meantime I expect Mistress Pym to have a letter sent to

371

their friend the Lord Protector. But I would like to speak to Winfred first, to ask what complaints she might have about her treatment.'

Ralf was aware that it was now he and not the head gaoler who was in command of the situation. His view was reinforced by Black's next words.

'If what you say is true then there has been a dreadful mistake — but I am not to blame. I was absent from the castle.'

'Nevertheless, you left orders that resulted in Winfred being thrown into gaol.'

Seeking a way out of his predicament, Head Gaoler Black said, 'How do I know you are telling the truth? This could be no more than a ruse to have the girl released.'

Ralf shrugged. 'It matters little to me whether or not she's released,' he lied. 'I am only her father's ploughman who will return to tell Mistress Pym what has happened here. But if you don't believe me then why don't you go and speak to Winfred? She'll tell you who she is. I believe she's also related to Major-General Desborough . . . '

The mention of Desborough clinched the matter as far as Black was concerned. He was the head gaoler of Launceston castle, but his power was nothing when compared with that of the regional governor — and he did not relish the very real possibility of exchanging his comfortable lifestyle for incarceration in his own dungeons.

To the turnkey, he said, 'Who locked these two

young women away?'

'I did,' the bewildered turnkey replied, 'but your orders . . . '

'My orders have obviously been misunderstood,' Black said. 'Go and bring them here immediately.'

When the turnkey had hurried away, the head gaoler glared at Ralf. 'I hope for your sake that you have told me the truth. If you haven't you'll find yourself in Doomsdale — and very few men have left there alive.'

Ralf made no reply and a few minutes later the door opened and Winfred and Clarice were ushered into the room. They were both dirty and dishevelled, but Winfred's expression was one of delight when she saw Ralf. 'I was certain you would come and find us, Ralf. I told Clarice so.'

'Silence!' Black ordered. 'We have some facts to ascertain. What is your name?'

Winfred's chin came up in an expression Ralf recognised immediately. He hoped she would not antagonise the gaoler too much. They were all still in his hands.

'I have no doubt Ralf has told you who I am,' she declared, refusing to be cowed by his authoritative manner.

'I want to hear it from you,' Black said.

'Very well. I am Winfred Pym of Lantewan House, daughter of Commissioner Oliver Pym — as I have no doubt you already know.'

From Black's expression, Ralf could see the head gaoler had been hoping that he had been lying to him. To Winfred, Black said, 'What are you doing here, in Launceston gaol?'

'That is the question I should be putting to you,' Winfred retorted. 'For the past twenty-four hours Clarice and I have been lying in one of your stinking dungeons — and for no other reason than that we came here to ascertain the well-being of my friend's father, Charles Thomasson.'

'Thomasson is a danger to the State,' said the gaoler, not meeting Winfred's eyes. 'We need to check on those who come to visit him. However, there appears to have been an unfortunate misunderstanding on the part of my turnkey. You should never have been put in a cell.'

Speaking for the first time since she entered the room, Clarice said scathingly, 'Are you saying that the state is so insecure that its existence is threatened because a man of God refuses to take off his hat in the presence of a magistrate? Because that is the reason my father is being held in your foul prison.'

'The reason why a man is sent to prison has nothing to do with me,' the head gaoler said. 'My task is simply to ensure he is kept safely under lock and key when he is put into my care by the courts. A regrettable mistake has been made in your case and I will take the appropriate action to punish those concerned. You are free to go.'

'I am not going!'

Clarice's statement took everyone by surprise and Head Gaoler Black demanded, 'What do you mean, you are not going?'

'Exactly what I say,' Clarice said. 'I came here to see my father. I have been told he is in a cell that is not fit to house the filthiest animal, is in a

374

feeble condition and fears for his very life. I am not going until I have seen him. If he is as sick as I am led to believe, I will remain with him until he is released.'

'That will not be possible,' Black said. 'My orders are that he is to see no one.'

'Then I will remain here until those orders are revoked.' With that, Clarice sat down on the stone floor, clasping her hands about her knees, to the obvious amusement of the two men who had been sharing the head gaoler's meal.

'Get up this instant,' Black ordered. 'You are being a stupid girl.'

'Then I will be stupid too,' Winfred said, following her friend's example and seating herself on the floor. 'We came here to see Clarice's father and will not leave until we have.'

Head Gaoler Black was disconcerted by this display of feminine intransigence and was reluctant to order that the daughter of the Cornish commissioner be manhandled from the office. Appealing to Ralf, he said, 'This is quite ridiculous. Make them see sense.'

Ralf shrugged. 'Commissioner Pym employs me to take care of his farm, not of his daughter and her friends.'

Winfred threw Ralf a glance which told him she appreciated that he was supporting her stand.

'But . . . I'm only the head gaoler, not a magistrate. I have to obey the orders that are given to me. I certainly can't order the release of a prisoner on the say-so of a young woman, no matter how important her father may be.'

375

'What action do you take when you realise that a prisoner is so ill that unless he is released he will die in your custody?' Winfred demanded.

'I usually send for Magistrate Lower,' said the unhappy head gaoler. 'He lives in Launceston and will come here to examine the prisoner. If he feels the man is indeed very ill he will probably make an order that he is to be released.'

'Then I suggest you send for this Magistrate Lower to examine Clarice's father,' Winfred said firmly. 'Until he arrives Clarice and I will remain where we are — and you will be a witness to what happens, Ralf. Should Head Gaoler Black or any of his men lay a hand on us you will tell my father and ensure that Black is thrown into the Doomsdale. I have no doubt at all that he will receive the welcome he deserves from those he has sent there.'

12

Four hours after Ralf's arrival at Launceston Castle he was riding westward across Bodmin Moor with Winfred, Clarice — and Charles Thomasson.

Magistrate Lower had not even checked the condition of Clarice's father. The stench from the Doomsdale was so overpowering that he had accepted without question Clarice's report on the state of his health and ordered his immediate release.

His decision would have been no different had he examined the Quaker preacher. Charles Thomasson had never been a robust man and the time he had spent in the appalling conditions of the Doomsdale had taken a heavy toll.

He was now riding Winfred's horse, a concerned Clarice at his side to support him whenever he slumped in the saddle. Winfred shared Ralf's horse and he was acutely aware of her presence as she sat behind him, her arms about his waist for support.

It was far too late to attempt the ride back to Lantewan that day, even though Ralf knew that Mary would be even more distressed by the absence of her daughter for a further night. They were heading for the moorland hamlet of Trewint, where Charles Thomasson knew a fellow Quaker who would give them accommodation.

Tomorrow, the preacher and Clarice would part company with Ralf and Winfred, riding northwards to the home of another Quaker where Charles Thomasson would be able to recuperate from his sojourn in Launceston castle's notorious Doomsdale. Ralf and Winfred would strike across Bodmin Moor in the opposite direction and hope to be at Lantewan some time in the afternoon.

★   ★   ★

Before leaving Trewint, Ralf had an experience that was quite unexpected, and temporarily unnerved him. He was alone in the stable behind the Quaker's house, saddling the horses while Winfred completed her morning toilet, when Clarice entered the low, thatched building.

After watching him for a few minutes, she said, 'You know, Ralf, you and I have met before.'

'I don't think so,' he said.

'Yes, we have. I don't expect you to remember, but it is something I have never forgotten.'

Ralf was searching his memory for where he and Clarice might have met before when she explained.

'I thought I recognised you when we first met, but felt I must be mistaken. I could not believe that you would be working in such a menial

378

occupation for such a prominent and unforgiving Puritan as Oliver Pym.'

Uneasily, Ralf said, 'I really think you must be mistaken, Clarice. I would not have forgotten you had we met before . . . '

'No, I am not mistaken,' she said in her usual gentle voice. 'I am so certain that I am going to give you something I have been carrying with me for many years, in the firm belief that I would one day be able to give it back to you.'

Taking his hand, she dropped something into it. When he looked down, he saw it was a half-crown coin. Puzzled, he looked to her for an explanation.

'You gave it to me in Lostwithiel,' she said, as gently as ever. 'You had just pulled me from the river . . . ah! I see you remember it now. It has not always been easy to save the half-crown for you, Ralf. There have been many occasions when I had need of money, but I would remind myself that it was not mine to spend. It was rightfully yours. Mind you, I never expected to find you working as a farm labourer. You were in much more exalted company then and wearing the tabard of a royal page. What happened to change your life, Ralf — and does Winfred know of your past?'

Ralf's initial reaction was to deny that he was the person Clarice claimed to have recognised, but he realised that might make her all the more determined to prove he really was her rescuer.

'Times change, Clarice, and so do fortunes. I am a farm labourer and, no, Winfred does not know of my past. I beg you not to tell her.'

Raising her eyebrows, Clarice asked, 'Why not, Ralf? Do you think she would disclose your past to her father? I can assure you that she would not. She is far too fond of you.'

'All the same, I would rather Winfred did not know.'

At that moment a shadow came between the rising sun and the interior of the stable. It was Winfred — and she had heard Ralf's plea to her friend. Curious, she asked, 'What is it you would rather I did not know, Ralf?'

While he was struggling to think of a reply, Clarice said, 'Ralf was being his usual modest self, Winfred. You see, Enid's and Primrose's are not the only lives he has saved. Many years ago he saved mine too. I was not certain until this morning, when I saw him in a certain light and knew he was the one who pulled me from the river in Lostwithiel after the women of the town attacked the camp followers of Lord Essex's defeated army. I was among them with my mother and, had he not done so, I would have drowned.'

'Is this true, Ralf?' Winfred asked.

He nodded. 'The Lostwithiel women behaved in an appalling manner — but they had suffered a great deal at the hands of Essex's soldiers.'

'Why did you not say something when we first met Clarice?' Winfred asked.

Once again it was Clarice who replied. 'He said nothing because he did not recognise me,' she said ruefully. 'It is hardly flattering, but as I said, saving lives seems to be a commonplace occurrence for him — although it is something

380

for which I will always be grateful. Thank you, Ralf. You have always been in my prayers, but now I have a name for you.'

Changing the subject, she said, 'I really do feel we should be going now, Winfred. I want to get my father to the house of his friend before he tires too much. I am most grateful for the loan of your horse. I will return it, with mine, to Lantewan at the earliest opportunity, but I realise it means leaving you with only one mount between you.'

'We will manage,' Winfred said cheerfully. 'Ralf and I are quite happy riding the same horse. I am not particularly heavy and we have no intention of pushing the poor beast too hard.'

Ralf was grateful to Clarice for saying nothing about his being in the service of Prince Charles when he had pulled her from the River Fowey in Lostwithiel. Nevertheless, he did not breathe easily until they parted company with Clarice and her father, the Thomassons riding north to their fellow Quaker and Ralf and Winfred continuing to follow the track that split Cornwall's moor in two.

★   ★   ★

Ralf found it disconcerting riding with Winfred behind him, clasping him for support and occasionally resting her head against his back. He was reminded of what Clarice had said about her friend being far too fond of him ever to tell her father he had once been part of the royal court; and he also recalled that, many years before, when Winfred had been taken to Huntingdon, Enid had told him it was because Oliver Pym was aware of her feelings for him.

If it were true, he had to admit that the attraction was mutual, but Ralf had no illusions about Pym's reaction should he have the slightest suspicion of a growing affection between his daughter and his ploughman. The Puritan liked Ralf no more than Ralf cared for his employer. Ralf had worked at Trecarne for so long only because both men had their own reasons for continuing the arrangement: Pym because he knew he employed an outstanding ploughman, Ralf because he loved Trecarne and was left to work there much as he would have had the farm still belonged to Joseph — or to himself.

13

Ralf and Winfred had been travelling in silence for a while when Winfred, who was resting her head against his back, stirred herself and said, 'I can hear a horse coming along the track behind us.'

Turning his head, Ralf saw a horse cantering towards them along the track they had just travelled. When he came alongside, the rider slowed his mount to match their pace.

'Good day to you, young sir — and to you, mistress. I think you might be seeking me.'

Puzzled, Ralf asked, 'Seeking you? Why?'

'I presume you are making for Temple church, and I am the parish clerk.'

Ralf nodded acknowledgement of the information, but asked, 'Why do you think we are making for Temple church?'

'To get married, why else?' was the reply. 'It is the reason why young couples — yes, and older ones too — come to the church. Temple is outside the jurisdiction of the bishop, so although a marriage at Temple is as binding as any in the land we can arrange it with far less formality. It is of no consequence whether or not the parent or guardian of either party consents

. . . but why am I telling you this? You already know. Why else would you come seeking Temple church, sharing the same horse?'

Behind Ralf, Winfred's arms tightened about him and he could feel her body shaking with laughter. Suppressing his own amusement, he said, 'I am sorry to disappoint you, sir, but the mist on the moor has caused me to lose my bearings. I was seeking Temple church only because it is a landmark with which I am vaguely familiar. Once I have found it I think I will be able to find the path to take my master's daughter home.'

'Oh!' The parish clerk was unable to hide his disappointment. 'Then I hurried after you in vain.' He continued to look downcast for a while before, in a sudden change of mood, he said, 'Never mind. The Lord works in strange ways. It could be that one day one of you may choose to make use of my services. Should that occur you need only ask for Merryweather Hooper and I will delight in being of service to you. You will find the church no more than half a mile on your left as you follow this track. I bid you a safe journey.'

With this, the disappointed would-be marriage-maker jerked his horse's head about and set off back the way he had come.

When he had disappeared in the mist, Winfred said, 'What an extraordinary man. I wonder how many couples he marries each month?'

A little later, when they had found the track that would take them in the right direction, Ralf felt her body shaking with mirth once more.

'What is it, Winfred? What is amusing you?'

'I have just had an evil thought,' she said. 'What do you think my father would say if we arrived home and I said, 'Hello, Father, Ralf has just had me freed from gaol — and, by the way, we were married at Temple church on the way home!''

Ralf smiled. 'I somehow don't think I would live to enjoy my married status for very long. If I did, I would be contemplating it from the Doomsdale in Launceston castle.'

After riding in silence for a couple of minutes, Winfred asked, 'Do you think you might enjoy being married to me, Ralf?'

Taken aback, Ralf replied, 'That's hardly a fair question, Winfred. For a start, we both know your father would never agree to such a marriage. Besides, if I said yes, we could never meet without you remembering that I have said I would like to be married to you. If I said no it would be even worse. You would then believe I didn't really like you very much.'

'I did not ask whether you wanted to marry me, Ralf, only if you thought you might enjoy being married to me. I have often thought I would be far happier married to you than to any of the men my father and grandfather think would be suitable husbands for me.'

Had Winfred been one of the ladies he had met at the court of King Charles he would have believed she was playing the coquette with him, but Winfred did not play such games. The knowledge excited him and he was sufficiently emboldened to reply to her with an honesty he

385

would otherwise not have shown.

'Well then, yes, Winfred, I am quite sure I would enjoy being married to you. I am happy in your company, feel pleasure whenever I see you — and I missed you a great deal while you were away.'

She was silent for so long that he began to believe he might have been a little *too* honest. Then her arms tightened about his waist and she said, 'I am glad you feel that way about me, Ralf. I missed you too while I was away . . . very much.'

There was something in her voice that made him bring the horse to a halt and turn his head to look at her. Their faces were very close together and the kiss was inevitable — and stirred strong emotions that each of them felt in the other.

When he drew his head back, Ralf said shakily, 'I think we had better get on our way, Winfred.'

She nodded and, although she did not speak, her eyes told Ralf that come what may there could be no turning back now, for either of them.

Some minutes later, raising her head from his back, she said, 'Ralf?'

'Yes?'

'Are you quite certain you don't want to go back to find the man who told us about Temple church?'

Turning to look at her again, he said, 'If I wasn't aware of how worried your mother is about you I could very easily take your question seriously. As it is . . . . I might one day remind you that you suggested it.'

Later that afternoon it seemed that Ralf's only half-humorous prediction that Oliver Pym would have him lodged in Doomsdale for undue familiarity with Winfred might come to pass, even without the benefit of a marriage ceremony at Temple church.

They were nearing Lantewan when Ralf saw a horseman riding along a track that converged with their own. There was something familiar about the manner in which the rider sat his horse and, as they drew closer, Ralf saw to his dismay that it was Oliver Pym. After his initial astonishment, a very few minutes' reflection told him that the Puritan farmer must have voyaged by sea from London to Plymouth and set off on horseback for Lantewan at dawn that morning.

Ralf slowed his own horse in the vain hope that Pym might draw ahead without noticing him. Unfortunately, the change of pace disturbed Winfred, who had been half dozing with her head resting against Ralf's back. In a carrying voice she queried, 'Why are we slowing, Ralf? Are we nearing home?'

The sound caused Oliver Pym to look in their direction. Giving a start of recognition, he dug his heels into the flanks of his startled horse and turned the animal across the ground between the two tracks in order to intercept the young couple. Before Ralf had time say more than 'It's your father . . . ' to Winfred, Pym was upon them.

'You, Hunkyn . . . Winfred, what do you think

you are doing? Where have you been together . . . and look at the state of you, Winfred! What have you been up to? By the Lord, I'll have the truth if I have to thrash it out of the pair of you!'

'Father, stop being so dramatic. We . . . '

Oliver Pym rounded on her furiously, 'Dramatic? Dramatic, you say? I find my daughter on a horse with a farm labourer, her arms about his waist and her head resting against his back as though they were lovers and you tell me not to be dramatic . . . This is too much. You have gone too far this time, Hunkyn.'

'*Father!* Before you say something you regret will you please be quiet for long enough to allow me to explain?'

Oliver Pym was not used to being told to be quiet, and as he spluttered in fury Winfred went on, 'Very well, if you are determined to think the worst of me without giving me an opportunity to explain, then I will give you a good reason to be angry. I am with Ralf because he rode to Launceston to secure my release after I was arrested and thrown into Launceston gaol — on your orders!'

'You were in gaol . . . On my orders . . . '

Ralf thought his employer was about to suffer an apoplectic fit and he said hurriedly, 'It's not as bad as it sounds, Mr Pym. Winfred did nothing wrong. It was all a mistake.'

'No, it was no mistake,' Winfred contradicted him. 'I said it was your fault, father, and so it was. Did you not give instructions to the head gaoler at Launceston castle that if anyone tried to visit Charles Thomasson they were to be

388

locked up too? Well, I went to visit him with my friend Clarice, from Huntingdon. She is his daughter and was rightly concerned about him.'

'You went to visit Thomasson?' Oliver Pym seemed to be having difficulty taking in Winfred's words.

'That's right, and we were arrested and thrown into a filthy cell, because that is what the gaolers were told they were to do. Had Mother not asked Ralf to come and find me I would still be there.'

Pym glanced briefly at Ralf, but quickly returned his attention to Winfred. 'Did the gaoler know who you are?' he asked.

'Not until Ralf arrived and told him. The turnkey who locked us up would not have taken any notice had we told him. He had been drinking.'

'Who else knows?' Oliver Pym demanded.

Winfred looked at her father scornfully. 'For just a moment I thought you were upset that I had been forced to spend the night in a disgusting cell in Launceston castle. I should have known better. Your only concern is for your reputation. As long as that remains intact it would not matter if I were still there, or whether Charles Thomasson died. Well, perhaps you have cause to be concerned. Clarice and I refused to leave Launceston castle until a magistrate was called to rule on the state of her father's health. He decided that Charles Thomasson was so sick he should be released immediately and, as he was too ill to walk, I lent him the horse on which I had ridden to Launceston — your horse.

389

Charles Thomasson rode to freedom on *your* horse.'

Oliver Pym had control of his anger now, but Ralf thought he was probably even more dangerous as a result. Pym said, 'We will discuss this further at Lantewan, not here, in the presence of a farm labourer. Hunkyn, get off the horse and let Winfred have it. You can walk to Trecarne. I will come there tomorrow to check on what work has suffered as a result of this escapade. There were others who could have gone to Launceston to find Winfred. I will want to know why you were sent and not they.'

Ralf dismounted and, despite Oliver Pym's disapproving gaze, helped Winfred seat herself more comfortably. In defiance of her father, she smiled at him. 'Not all Pyms are ungracious, Ralf. I thank you for securing my release from Launceston gaol and I have no doubt my mother would wish me to convey her gratitude too. Thank you.'

She flicked the reins of the horse and rode off without a glance at her father, who spurred after her, deliberately ignoring Ralf.

Watching them go, Ralf knew there would be a furious row when father and daughter reached Lantewan. He wondered whether he would ever be allowed to talk to Winfred again.

14

All the next day Ralf was on tenterhooks in anticipation of the promised visit from Oliver Pym. It did not come and by the end of a week he had relaxed and settled down to the everyday routine work on Trecarne Farm.

On the eighth day, ploughing one of the farm's south-sloping fields with a pair of horses, Ralf was concentrating on keeping the horses and plough working in a straight line on the field and had little thought for anything else until he reached the end of the furrow.

Turning, he looked up to see Winfred, mounted on a horse, watching his progress. Bringing his pair to a halt he hurried to her and was happy to see that her smile matched his own.

'Winfred . . . I'm delighted to see you. I've been very concerned about you. I thought your father might have sent you away again.'

Dismounting from her horse, Winfred smiled happily at him. 'You underestimate the power wielded by women, Ralf — and I am not speaking only of myself. Mother accepts Father's authority within the family without question only until he does, or says, something with which she

391

strongly disagrees. Then, like me — and I am told it is where I inherited my stubbornness — she will make a firm stand. When it happens, even my father knows he will never persuade her to change her mind so he accepts defeat. She did not necessarily agree with what I did in going to Launceston castle with Clarice, but said it was for the right reasons. As for your part in what happened . . . Mother said she would trust you implicitly with her own life and that of any member of our family. She hinted to my father that if you went she would go too!'

'What did he say to that?' Ralf was heartened by Mary Pym's trust in him but did not like to feel that he had been the cause of an argument between husband and wife.

'He huffed and puffed for a while,' Winfred replied, 'but he knew Mother meant what she said and they had settled their differences by the time I went to bed.' Suddenly serious, and looking unhappy, she added, 'There is just one thing, though, Ralf — and my father would not be moved on this. He said I am not to see you again. If I do and he finds out I will be sent away, once and for all.'

Her words distressed Ralf, but he pointed out that Winfred had come to Trecarne in defiance of her father's ultimatum.

Winfred smiled at him. 'Father has gone to Plymouth. As you well know, he is often away from Lantewan. Mother would never say anything that might cause you trouble, so we need not stop seeing each other — although we will need to be careful.'

Ralf was silent for so long that Winfred eventually said, 'What is the matter, Ralf? Would you rather we did not risk incurring the wrath of my father? I will try to understand if you say yes. After all, you run the risk of being dismissed and losing your livelihood.'

Choosing his words carefully, Ralf said, 'I enjoy working at Trecarne more than you know and I don't want to be forced to leave, even though as a good ploughman I could find work elsewhere — but I wouldn't want you to be sent away again because of me. I think I know how much you enjoy living at Lantewan.'

'I was just as happy living at Trecarne, Ralf — happier even. My happiest times of all have been when I was allowed to work here with you, talking about the farm, the animals . . . about poetry. Just talking, or being with you, I suppose.' She hesitated for a moment, and then asked, 'Don't you feel the same way, Ralf, or did I make a complete fool of myself on the way home from Launceston?'

'Of course you didn't,' Ralf said. 'But your father is a Cornish commissioner, a Justice of the Peace and a very important man. I have tried not to allow myself to dwell too much on the way I feel about you.'

'We both know what my father is, Ralf, and no one knows better than I of his ambitions for the future — but I was not talking about him. I have told you honestly how I feel about Trecarne and about you. I already know how you feel about Trecarne. I was hoping you would give me an honest answer about your true feelings for me.'

'An honest answer? That isn't as easy as it sounds, Winfred. Your father must never know how I feel about you. If he had even the tiniest suspicion we would both suffer as a result. But . . . you are probably the most important thing in my life and you have been for a very long time. When you are with me I am happy. If you are not . . . I miss you. Does that give you an answer?'

Looking at him, Winfred had to fight a hard battle with her emotions. 'Yes, Ralf, it does. I don't necessarily agree with all you say, but that is not important. The way you feel is. I take great heart from that. But now, see if you can teach me how to plough. At least you will have your arms about me . . . '

★   ★   ★

For the next few months the routine at Trecarne continued very much as Winfred had predicted it would. She was able to help Ralf at the farm during the many absences of Oliver Pym, and Ralf would make frequent visits to Lantewan to read to Enid.

Then one day, later in the year, Jeremy rode to Trecarne with tragic news. Enid had unexpectedly died during the night.

The death came as a shock to everyone and Ralf paid a visit to Lantewan to express his sympathy to his employer, Mary and Winfred, but under the watchful eye of Oliver Pym Ralf had no opportunity to talk privately with Winfred before Enid's funeral.

The ceremony took place on a cold drizzly day in the Churchtown cemetery, attended by many of Oliver Pym's fellow county administrators and all his servants and workers.

Enid was laid to rest close to the grave of Joseph Moyle and when the mourners had departed as hastily as was polite from the wet and windy churchyard, Ralf hung back. He had laid a sweet-smelling posy of late-flowering lavender beside the open grave. It had been planted in the Trecarne kitchen garden by his mother many years before and now, as the last of the mourners passed from view, he broke off a sprig of the perfumed flower and moved a few steps away to place it on the grave of Joseph Moyle.

Winfred had also hung back outside the churchyard, but before she could have a word with Ralf she was challenged by her father, who had seen her falling behind the others.

'What are you doing, girl?'

'I was just taking a last look back at Enid's grave,' she replied.

It was unfortunate that Ralf should come from the churchyard at that moment, and Oliver Pym scowled. 'Enid's grave . . . or my ploughman?' Then, with a shrug, he added, 'Not that it matters. With Enid gone there is nothing to keep you in Cornwall now. You will be accompanying your mother and me to Huntingdon next week, to celebrate the betrothal of Ronwen to Alasdair Manning, nephew and heir to the Earl of Yarnton. It's a far better marriage than you are likely to make, young lady, until you raise your eyes from the gutter — or the furrow,' he added maliciously.

'I seem to remember that Ronwen was once more interested in ploughmen than noblemen,' Winfred retorted, 'but if you are alluding to Ralf, then yes, I was hoping to speak to him. I wish to return the book of poetry he lent me to read to Enid. I have it here.'

'A ploughman reading poetry? I would like to know how he came by such a book.'

'It was given to him by a friend of the man he once worked for,' Winfred explained. 'It is inscribed to him here, in the front of the book.'

'It is not the sort of present that is given to a farm labourer,' Pym said. 'Perhaps I should have enquired more closely into his background before taking him on.'

'Why? You have had no cause to complain of his work,' Winfred said. Then, not wishing to anger her father any more, lest he turn his anger upon Ralf, she said, 'I will give him his book, then return with you to Mother and Primrose. Poor Mother . . . '

*　*　*

Ralf did not see Winfred again until the day before she was due to leave for Huntingdon, when he was alarmed to see her riding openly up to Trecarne.

Looking around to make certain no one was watching, he hurried outside and helped her from her horse, saying, 'You shouldn't have come here, Winfred. Jeremy was here yesterday and he said there had been an awful row at Lantewan and your father had forbidden you to say goodbye to me before you left for Huntingdon.'

'That's right,' Winfred said with a defiant lift of her chin that Ralf had come to recognise as a sign that she was going to do, or say, something that might not meet with the approval of her father, 'but I would have come anyway. However, I have no wish to get you into trouble, so I have waited until he needed to go to Fowey to check on the ship that is to take us as far as London. I just couldn't leave without seeing you again, Ralf. Meeting you whenever it has been possible has made me very happy these last few months.'

'I'm glad,' he replied honestly. 'I'm going to miss you far more than ever before, but I spoke to your mother the other day and she says you'll all be back here again in two or three months' time.'

'I hope so,' Winfred said, 'but I know my father will try to make me remain there when the others return.'

There were a few moments of unhappy silence before she asked, 'Are you really going to miss me, Ralf?'

'Very much.'

'I'm glad,' she said, 'because I am going to be very sad knowing there are so many miles between us.' Stepping forward, she kissed him, and when she would have moved away from him he held her close and this time the kiss lasted for a very long while. When she eventually pulled back from him she was flustered but happy.

'Think of me often, Ralf, and you'll know that I will probably be thinking of you at the same time.'

'There will be few moments when you aren't in my thoughts, Winfred,' he said.

'If you really mean that then no one, neither my father nor anyone else, will ever be able to come between us. I must go now. I don't want to upset Father and cause Mother more unhappiness than she is feeling at the moment.'

15

During the absence of the Pym family Ralf worked hard, and although he missed Winfred he was happy at Trecarne. One day he brought his mother to the farm to see how it was being kept. Grace shed a few tears, but despite her misgivings of earlier years she declared that Joseph would have been proud that Ralf had maintained the standards he himself had set during the time Trecarne had belonged to him.

Partly due to exceptionally bad weather in eastern England, where the Pym family were celebrating the betrothal of Ronwen, they did not return to Lantewan until the spring of 1658 — and Winfred was not with them.

It was not until a few weeks later, when Ralf paid a visit to Lantewan during one of Oliver Pym's absences, that he learned from Mary that Winfred had been left behind at the Huntingdon home of her grandparents much against her will. It had been Oliver Pym's decision, his intention being that Winfred should find a husband among the sons of Cambridgeshire's Puritan elite.

Ralf was alarmed to hear the news and tried not to allow his feelings to show. Nevertheless, Mary was quick to let him know that, in her opinion, Winfred would not accept any of the suitors who were likely to be presented by her grandfather, adding significantly, 'It is my firm belief that her heart is here, in Cornwall.'

★　★　★

Ralf worked hard that year and although bad weather meant the harvest was going to be late, it showed every promise of being a good crop and there seemed little to upset the pattern of rural life.

Then, in the first week of September, startling and unexpected news swept the country. Oliver Cromwell, Lord Protector and iron-fisted ruler of the country, had died suddenly of natural causes!

His death threw into disarray the constitution of the republic he had created — and it happened during the month when the Pym family had returned once more to Huntingdon, this time for the wedding of Ronwen and the heir to the earldom of Yarnton.

It had been predicted that the wedding would be the social occasion of the year in Huntingdon, graced by the presence of the Lord Protector himself. His untimely death cast a pall over the celebrations, but Ronwen resisted all suggestions that the ceremony be postponed. She had already sensed a waning in the enthusiasm of the prospective bridegroom for marriage and was determined there should be no other candidate for the future title of Countess of Yarnton.

The wedding went ahead as planned, but

immediately after the ceremony Oliver Pym rode to London where Cromwell's son, Richard, had inherited his late father's title. Unfortunately, Richard Cromwell had neither the charisma nor the political ability of his father and there was the promise of a fierce power struggle among his followers. Pym wanted to ensure that his own position in the west of England remained secure. His family could make their way to Cornwall later.

* * *

Oliver Pym arrived back in Cornwall before his family, satisfied that his post of commissioner for Cornwall was as secure as it could be — but Ralf was soon to learn that his own future was far from settled.

The weather had improved and Ralf had provisionally hired help to bring in the harvest more quickly. He was concerned that Pym might not approve of his action, even though it was essential that the wheat be harvested before the weather deteriorated once more, so the morning after his employer's return he was relieved to see him riding into the Trecarne farmyard where he was sharpening the scythes that would be used in the harvesting. Now the responsibility could pass to him.

However, Pym voiced an angry and unreasonable criticism before Ralf could say a word. 'Why is the wheat still standing in the fields? It should have been cut and brought in weeks ago.'

'I agree,' Ralf said. 'Unfortunately, I have no

401

control over the weather and we've hardly had two fine days together since you went away.'

'Nonsense!' Pym said. 'The farmers around Huntingdon have had no problems. Most have not only cut their crop but threshed it too.'

'They must have had better weather than we've had here,' Ralf said with more patience than he felt. 'The other farmers in Cornwall are just as late as we are, but I've taken on a couple of men to help and I'm confident that between us we'll succeed in gathering a harvest that will more than match that of other years.'

'You've taken on extra labourers without my permission? Dammit, Hunkyn, I'm not paying good money for what's probably no more than your laziness in getting things done. If you've hired them then you'll pay them. I've got more expenses than I need right now. That reminds me, you'll need to find somewhere else to sleep. My new son-in-law is coming to Trecarne with Ronwen. They'll be occupying the farmhouse and converting the stables to make living quarters for the farm manager they are bringing with them.'

'A farm manager from upcountry, here . . . at Trecarne?' Ralf looked at Pym in disbelief. 'The farm isn't large enough to support a manager. Does he know anything about Cornish farming?'

'If it needs to be larger we'll merge Lantewan and Trecarne into a single farm, and I doubt whether Cornish farming is any different from farming anywhere else.'

Ralf was aware that Pym had never taken any real interest in the land. Had he done so he would be aware that working a farm so close to the sea was quite different from working an inland farm, but Ralf made no attempt to point this out to him. Instead, he said, 'Even if Trecarne and Lantewan are merged they will only support a working farmer, not a gentleman with a farm manager. What sort of place does your son-in-law think he's coming to?'

Flushing angrily, Oliver Pym said, 'That is no concern of yours. All you have to do is move whatever you have at Trecarne and find somewhere else to stay. Perhaps, in view of your remarks, you should also be looking for somewhere else to work. I have shared my thoughts about you with Alasdair, and Ronwen has told him how rude you were to her when we were living here, so I don't think you will last long — especially if his manager is as efficient as he is reputed to be.'

Oliver Pym was gloating over the impact his revelation had made and it was this obvious enjoyment that decided Ralf upon a course of action he might otherwise have put off, in the hope that matters might right themselves and because of the association that Trecarne had with his own family — and with Winfred.

Collecting the scythes he had been sharpening, Ralf said, 'Very well, Mr Pym, I will gather my belongings and leave. It shouldn't take me long; I don't have much at Trecarne.'

It was Pym's turn to be taken by surprise. 'You'll do no such thing,' he said. 'You'll work until the end of the week if you want to be paid.'

It was Tuesday. If he left now Ralf was aware

403

he would lose two days' pay, but it no longer mattered. Nothing mattered very much any more. He was aware that he would also need to leave the area in order to avoid victimisation by Pym, but that would be no real hardship. Aunt Florence had died a year before, leaving his mother the house and a small amount of money. Added to what he had been able to save from his wages she would be able to manage quite comfortably without him.

His only concern was Winfred's reaction when she returned to Cornwall and learned he had left Trecarne. She would be very hurt. He would need to find some way of letting her know where he was and why he had left. One thing was certain: with Ronwen and her husband at Trecarne, meeting Winfred would have been well-nigh impossible even had he remained in the employ of Oliver Pym.

'I'll not stay for the sake of a couple of shillings, much as I enjoy working at Trecarne,' Ralf said, 'I will go elsewhere and look for work.'

'You won't find it about here,' Pym said angrily. 'In view of your failure to carry out the tasks that should have been completed during my absence, and walking off without giving me due notice, you need not expect to go away with a reference from me.'

'I wouldn't ask for one,' Ralf said, 'but for those who know Trecarne, the condition of the farm today is reference enough. Goodbye, Mr Pym. I hope the weather holds to allow the new farm manager to bring in your harvest, but no doubt his knowledge of farming will enable him to overcome whatever problems it may cause.'

A surprisingly short time later, Ralf was walking towards Fowey with a bundle of his belongings, mainly clothes, held on his shoulder. He was sad to be leaving Trecarne, but now the break had been made he felt a certain relief in the knowledge that he would no longer have to work with Oliver Pym's criticism and scarcely disguised dislike hanging over him. Only the knowledge that he might never see Winfred again was hurtful.

★   ★   ★

When Ralf broke the news to his mother that he was no longer employed at Trecarne, her tears had nothing to do with the loss of earnings coming into the household. In addition to the money she had put by, she had recently been employed as an assistant housekeeper at Place, the Fowey home of the influential Treffry family, so she would be able to manage quite comfortably.

Her distress was due to Ralf's break with the home they had both loved for so long and the knowledge that he would be going away once more. Like Ralf himself, she knew that in order to find work he would need to go far from Fowey and Oliver Pym's immediate influence.

Ralf decided to leave the area as quickly as possible. If Ronwen, her new husband and the man who was to be Trecarne's farm manager did not arrive soon the harvest would be lost and Pym would be certain to lay the blame squarely upon Ralf. He might even accuse him of deliberately failing to reap the wheat and have him arrested.

He had already decided he would head for north Cornwall and the home of the Grenvilles, Piers's family. He would make a decision about his future when he learned what his friend was doing . . . and he would find some way of getting a message to Winfred.

16

Setting off from Fowey, Ralf had no way of knowing whether he would ever return, so before heading for the home of the Grenvilles, at Stowe, near Kilkhampton, he took the ferry across the river and made his way to Churchtown to visit the grave of his stepfather for what might very well be the last time.

With him he carried a small bunch of flowers picked by his mother, with her employers' permission, from the garden of Place, and he followed a path that avoided Trecarne farm. He had no wish to risk a meeting with Oliver Pym.

Arriving at Churchtown, he kneeled by the side of Joseph Moyle's grave for a long while, then glanced to where Enid's grave was marked with a new and elaborate headstone. In a reversal of the last occasion when he was in the tiny graveyard he removed one of the flowers from the posy on his stepfather's grave and placed it on that of Enid, before kneeling and saying a prayer for her.

While he was on his knees with his eyes closed, a soft voice said, 'Enid would be deeply moved to know you have not forgotten her, Ralf.

I wish I might say the same about your thoughts of me.'

Startled, Ralf opened his eyes to see Winfred looking down at him.

Struggling to his feet, his first reaction was one of joy, mingled with a certain amount of apprehension. 'Winfred! I had no idea you were home — and there was no way I could come to Lantewan to ask. You will have heard that I was forced to leave Trecarne?'

'That isn't what I have been told. My father is saying you left him in the lurch when there was a harvest to be gathered in. I realised there had to be another explanation, but it was not possible to learn the truth.'

'I don't doubt it.' Ralf spoke bitterly. 'But let's find a place where we can't be seen by anyone who passes — and might know your father.'

They eventually settled for the church porch. Here, after a moment's hesitation, Ralf kissed her. Failing to respond, she broke away from him, saying, 'Tell me what happened to make you leave Trecarne, Ralf.'

Seated beside her on the cold slate slab seat in the porch, Ralf repeated the conversation that had passed between himself and her father.

When he ended his story, Winfred said, 'I was aware that Ronwen and Alasdair would be moving into Trecarne, but I knew nothing about their manager. If it is the man I believe it to be then you and he would not have got along with each other. He is a thoroughly horrible man. You were right to leave, but . . . ' Pointing to his bundle of belongings, she said, 'Were you really going to go away without leaving word for me of your whereabouts?'

'I could think of no way of telling you before I left,' Ralf replied. 'As for where I am going . . . I am not at all certain myself. I might seek the help of some of those I have known in the past.'

'That means nothing to me,' Winfred declared. 'You have never divulged details of your past, have you, Ralf — at least, not to me. Indeed, I have sometimes found it hurtful that whenever I have raised the question you have successfully avoided giving me an answer. However, I have recently succeeded in gaining information from others and, although I now understand why you would say nothing, I still find it hurtful that you did not feel able to trust me.'

Warily, Ralf replied, 'Before I say anything more, perhaps you'll tell me what it is you have heard about me.'

'I know who you really are, Ralf.'

'You have always known,' he said. 'I am Ralf Hunkyn. I have never lied about that.'

'True,' Winfred agreed. 'In fact, I don't believe you have actually lied about anything — but I wonder if you would have told me the whole truth had I not seen you take a flower from the posy at Enid's funeral and place it on the grave of Joseph Moyle? At the time I thought it was no more than a kind gesture. A flower from Trecarne for the man whose home it once was. Then, when I returned from Huntingdon and learned you had left the farm, I went to Fowey to try to find you. I soon discovered that nobody knew you! Then I met an old lady who remembered that Widow Moyle had a son by her first marriage to a man named Hunkyn — and suddenly everything fell into place and I understood the reason for your secrecy. Had my father learned who you really are he would have found some reason to have you thrown into gaol. He would certainly never have allowed you to work at Trecarne: your home, which he had seized. But how could you have worked for him for all these years, Ralf? Although it was never intended, he is responsible for the death of your stepfather. You must hate him very much — and me and the others too. We have taken your home away from you!'

'I will never be able to forgive your father for what he has done,' Ralf agreed, 'but I have never blamed your mother, or any of your sisters. In fact, I became very fond of them — and I have no need to tell you how I feel about you.' He made a helpless gesture. 'In time I found I was able to put the knowledge of what your father had done out of my mind for days at a time because it meant I was able to stay at Trecarne — and spend time with you whenever the opportunity arose.'

'Yet now you would leave without a word to me! My father has behaved abominably towards you and never acknowledged what you did to save the lives of Primrose and Enid, but do you really have to go right away, Ralf?'

'Your father left me no alternative, Winfred. He told me I had to leave my room above the stables and made it clear that the manager employed by Ronwen's new husband will have

410

his own ideas about running Trecarne. He made it very plain that I was not likely to be employed there for very long and pointed out that no one else in the area would dare to take me on.'

'I believe you, Ralf. My father is determined to become one of the most important men in Cornwall. He thinks that if Alasdair inherits his uncle's earldom while he is in Cornwall, *he* will instantly be accepted by the country's gentry. It's an ambition that is more important to him than anything else — even his own family. But what about us, Ralf? You and I? Do you intend going out of my life for ever?'

'It's not something I want to do,' Ralf said unhappily. 'But can you honestly believe that with his ambition to be accepted as a gentleman, your father would allow you to marry a farmhand — an out-of-work farmhand — even if we were not sworn enemies now?'

'I will reach my majority soon and he will not be able to prevent me from doing whatever I wish,' Winfred said defiantly, 'and . . . there is another way, Ralf.'

'Tell me,' he said disbelievingly.

'We could find that man who chased after us on Bodmin Moor when we were returning from Launceston. We could ask him to marry us at Temple church, just as he has married all the other couples he was telling us about.'

'Do you really believe your father would accept that, Winfred? He would have me arrested, saying I carried you off and married you for the money you will no doubt inherit one day. Looking at the facts, there isn't a court in

411

the land that would find in my favour. Even if they did, how would I keep you? I will be hard put to fend for myself!'

Keeping a very tight hold on her emotions, Winfred said, 'I was so much looking forward to returning to Trecarne, Ralf. I thought that after pretending to others — and to ourselves too for much of the time — that we were no more than casual friends, we might finally find a way to show the world how we felt about each other . . . ' Silencing Ralf when he was about to protest, she went on, 'Perhaps I've been deceiving myself, but I was convinced that love would find a way to overcome our problems — and I do love you, Ralf. I love you very much, but I believe your heart is really in Trecarne.'

Deeply touched by her declaration of love, Ralf said, 'My heart is in Trecarne, yes, but not only in the land, Winfred. I love you too. For that very reason I couldn't live with myself if I married you and brought you to a state of poverty because of it.'

'I would not care, Ralf — truly. Not if I knew that you truly loved me.'

He shook his head. 'No, I want more than that for you, Winfred.'

'So you are saying you will not marry me? That this is the end for you and me?'

'No, I am not saying that. I . . . ' Outside, a sudden clap of thunder interrupted what he was saying and the rain that had been threatening since early morning began to fulfil its promise. It was Winfred who spoke again when the thunder rumbled away into the distance.

412

'Ralf, please tell me honestly whether or not you see any future for us.'

'Very well,' he said. 'First of all, I want to assure you that I really do love you and have for a very long time, even though I have never dared take it any further than we already have. But if you are really certain about your feelings for me and it's more important than anything else to you, there might just be a way we can work things out.'

If Ralf had been in any doubt about her sincerity, it would have been dispelled by the look she gave him now. 'Do you really mean that, Ralf? I will do anything — and promise I will be deliriously happy, even if you decide to lead the life of a tinker, just so long as you take me with you.'

Ralf smiled at the thought of Winfred leading the life of a tinker. She was certainly not as vain as her older sister, but she still enjoyed wearing good clothes and having many of the comforts of life.

'I don't think that will ever be necessary,' he said. 'But I have another confession to make about the life I led before you met me.'

He saw the apprehension in Winfred's expression as she wondered what he was about to disclose, and he continued, 'I was in the service of the King for a long time. In view of your father's devotion to the Puritan cause, I don't know how you feel about a King's man?'

Her relief was evident and she said, 'There is nothing wrong with having served the King. Many men were Royalist soldiers, but the war has been over for a long time and they have put the past behind them. You can easily do the same.'

'I was not a soldier, Winfred, but a member of the court of the Prince — now *King* Charles. Clarice knew this. I was with the Prince's party when I pulled her from the river in Lostwithiel. I was also with him at Worcester.'

It took some moments for Winfred to digest what he had disclosed. Then she said, 'What has this to do with us and our future, Ralf?'

'I intend calling on the family of a friend who still serves the King. They are men your father would have no hesitation in arresting as enemies of the state, but I am going to speak to them with the intention of regaining a place in the King's court.'

Winfred seemed to be having difficulty in taking in what he was saying. 'But . . . Charles is in exile in France!'

'That's right — and that's where I will go if I am accepted back into his service.'

'But what of me . . . of us?'

'If the King will take me back into his service I will find some way of contacting you and asking you to come and join me. If you agree, we can get married there.'

'You want me, the daughter of a Parliamentary commissioner who was a friend of the late Lord Protector, to marry you and live in the court of King Charles?'

'I know it's asking a great deal of you, Winfred,' he said, 'and life in the court of an exiled king is not easy, but . . . '

Winfred silenced him by flinging her arms about him and hugging him so fiercely it took his breath away. Then she kissed him more passionately than ever before, saying, 'You apologise for offering me marriage and life in a king's court? Ralf Hunkyn, you are the most extraordinary man I have ever met — or will ever meet. I don't care if you once served the devil — and there are many who believe that Oliver Cromwell had a pact with *him* — but you had better hurry and find your place in the court once more and send for me, otherwise I will be obliged to come and find you, wherever you may be . . . '

★   ★   ★

Leaving Winfred and Churchtown behind him, Ralf made his way back to Polruan, to take the main road northwards to Bodmin Moor and the Kilkhampton home of Sir John Grenville.

As he paused on the hill above the riverside village, the morning sunlight was suddenly reflected on a window in the village and Ralf's thoughts returned to that day, many years before, when he and his stepfather had sat their horses on this very spot, looking down upon a royal cavalcade — and a scene that was about to change his life for ever . . .

BOOK FOUR

1

After spending three days on the road from Fowey and three nights sleeping in hedgerows, Ralf was aware that his appearance was decidedly unprepossessing. As a result, he approached the manor house of Sir John Grenville with considerable trepidation. He had cleaned himself up as much as possible in a stream just short of the Grenville mansion, but he was aware that he still looked like one of the many vagabonds who trod the lanes of Cornwall.

He had come here to enquire after Piers, but he realised it was necessary to proceed with great caution. This had been the home of Sir Bevil Grenville and his dependants and it was his son Ralf was coming to see.

Sir Bevil had been one of the great heroes of the late civil war and, in common with Joseph Moyle, the family might have had their house and lands sequestered by the Parliamentarian authorities. Even if that had not happened, it was likely they were keeping a low profile in order not to draw attention to their earlier Royalist affiliations. Should that be the case it was highly probable they would refuse to speak to him.

These and many other worrying thoughts

crossed Ralf's mind as he approached the house, to be faced with a further dilemma. Hesitating for a moment before the imposing building, he wondered whether he should perhaps go to the rear of the building, to the servants' entrance?

He dismissed the thought immediately. He was coming as a former courtier in the court of King Charles, even though he no longer looked the part. If the Grenville family had retained the same fierce loyalty to the English throne that had made Bevil and Piers such outstanding supporters of the King, many men like himself would have come to the door of the mansion. If they had not, the worst they could do was to tell him to go away.

Nevertheless, Ralf's spirits sank when the servant who answered the door looked him up and down disapprovingly and promptly called the butler. A tall, imposing figure, the butler eyed Ralf with the same distaste the lesser servant had displayed.

'What are you doing at the front door?' he demanded. 'The back door is for beggars and those seeking work, but anyway you are wasting your time. We need no further help in the house or grounds, and if we did we would employ a local man, not a vagabond.'

'I am not seeking work,' Ralf said, 'and I am no vagabond. I wish to speak to Sir John Grenville. Is he at home?'

Taken aback by the authority Ralf had managed to summon into his voice, the butler sked, 'What possible business could you have ith Sir John?'

420

'Family business,' Ralf retorted. 'I will save any further explanations for Sir John.'

The butler was reluctant to accept that this unkempt man could possibly have business with Sir John, but there was something about Ralf that caused him to stop short of ordering him from the house. Leaving Ralf in the hall, under the watchful eye of a footman, he went in search of Sir John Grenville, son of the late Sir Bevil.

Sir John was no more impressed with Ralf's appearance than his butler had been.

'My butler tells me you refuse to leave the house without speaking to me. Kindly state your business, and do not waste my time. I am a very busy man.'

'I am a friend of Piers,' Ralf explained, trying not to be put off by the manner of Sir John Grenville's reception. 'I have come here seeking news of him.'

'*You* are a friend of Piers?' Sir John was still sceptical. 'My cousin has been out of the country for many years. When and where was this friendship, and what is your name?'

'Ralf Hunkyn,' Ralf replied. 'My stepfather served your father as his ensign. As a reward for his service, the late king appointed me as page to the then Prince Charles. I later became secretary to His Majesty.'

'Ralf Hunkyn?' Sir John peered at Ralf more closely. 'Good God! It *is* you! My cousin wrote to me after Worcester, telling me how you had helped him and Frances make good their escape — and now I remember seeing you when I visited the Prince in Bristol. What have you been

421

doing — and where?'

Suddenly aware that the butler, together with the footman, had remained in the hall to be at hand should Sir John have trouble with his unkempt visitor, Sir John dismissed them before leading Ralf to his study. Once there he poured a large brandy for himself and one for Ralf before asking his uninvited guest what a former secretary to the King was doing dressed as a farm labourer.

'Because that's exactly what I have been working as since soon after Worcester,' Ralf said, and gave Sir John an outline of his life since leaving the King's service.

When he ended, Sir John commented, 'You were wise to leave the area after your altercation with Pym. He is a vengeful man who has been given more power than he can properly cope with. He would have found a reason to have you thrown into prison.'

'A reason was closer than he knew,' Ralf said. 'I and one of his daughters intend to marry when she is of age.'

Staring at Ralf in disbelief. Sir John suddenly let out a peal of laughter. 'I can understand why you and Piers are friends,' he said. 'You both seem to enjoy living dangerously. But what do you intend doing now?'

'I thought I might find Piers and see if there were some task I might perform about the court.'

Sir John looked at Ralf speculatively for a while before saying, 'If it is your wish to serve His Majesty, and in view of your service in his court, I think I might find more gainful

422

employment for you than kicking your heels in a foreign country. I have received a secret letter from the King. It speaks of a planned uprising by a Royalist group calling itself the Sealed Knot. They have given him a date for their proposed insurrection and asked him to come to England to lead them. It is his intention to do so — *but he must be stopped at all costs.* The Sealed Knot has a spy in its midst, a gentleman named Willys. Not only is he aware of the King's plans, but His Majesty is quite out of touch with the situation in the country at the present time. An uprising at this early stage would be disastrous for everyone involved in the King's cause — not to mention a great many who are not. Unfortunately, I fear it will take more than a letter to convince the King that such a venture at this time is doomed to failure. Were he to bring a foreign army with him in order to give battle to Englishmen the whole country would rise against him. If he bides his time, with a little patience and careful planning Englishmen will flock to his banner. They have had enough of Cromwellian cant and the ineptitude of Parliament. But such a message needs to be given to the King verbally, by someone he knows and trusts, especially as the spy in the ranks of the Sealed Knot is someone he knows and who served his father well.'

'Are you suggesting I should be that person?' Ralf asked incredulously. He was aghast at the thought of the awesome responsibility of such an assignment.

'I am not suggesting anything,' Sir John replied. 'It is your duty — if you have any love for your king and country.'

'But I know nothing about the Sealed Knot, or of the plot and its possible consequences.'

'Stay here at the manor for a few days and I will tell you all I know, and why the King must stay where he is for now.'

Ralf was still dubious about his ability to successfully carry out such an important mission, but Sir John said, 'Sleep on it, Ralf. You will come to see how important it is. In the meantime I will arrange for a bath to be prepared for you and some respectable clothes found. Then you shall meet my mother and over dinner tell us more of your incredible adventures.'

2

Although England had been ruled by Parliament for a decade there was still a very efficient network of Royalist supporters across the length and breadth of the country and Ralf was passed from one to another on his way to the coast and the boat that would take him to the Continent. Eventually he found himself once more enjoying the hospitality of Admiral Kettle.

To Ralf, the old admiral appeared little different from the man he had known in 1651, although the old sea dog's memory was not what it had been. He did not recognise his clandestine visitor, but it shook Ralf when he was told he would be sailing with the same Captain Alariah Flint who had ferried Piers and Frances to safety when they were fleeing from Worcester.

The arrangement for Ralf's passage to France was disturbingly similar to that of all those years before, although on this occasion Ralf's companion as far as the rendezvous was a servant of the old admiral, a former sailor who had once served on a ship commanded by him.

They waited for the *Mermaid*'s boat in the same ruined building where Ralf had sheltered with Piers and Frances.

That eventful night had been many years before, but the building had not changed and Ralf's memories of that night were evoked by his companion. The one-time sailor carried a shuttered lantern and with this he nervously explored all possible hiding places in the ruined building.

When Ralf asked him what he was doing, the servant said, 'I'm checking that no one is hiding here, sir. Many years ago there was a dreadful happening in this very place. A woman of the town and a well-known rogue killed each other. It's said their ghosts haunt it still.' Observing Ralf's scepticism, he added, 'I've met honest men who claim to have seen apparitions here after dark. Mind you, because of that there's little fear of us being discovered. I know of no one from the town who would venture here after dark.'

It was with mixed feelings that Ralf thought wryly that the death of Brighid had haunted him for long after her demise. It would appear he was not free of her yet.

Fortunately, no apparitions appeared, although Ralf was relieved when the boat from the *Mermaid* signalled its presence.

On board the ship, Captain Flint recognised Ralf immediately and repeated the story of the deaths of Brighid and Lazarus Sinnett, adding, 'It must have happened soon after I took young Grenville and his bride to France. Since then I have taken many such passengers. Indeed, although there is legitimate travel between England and the Continent now, there are many, like yourself, who don't want it known that they have business there, although now that Cromwell is dead the trade will no doubt come to an end.'

'Do you really think so?' Ralf asked.

'No doubt about it,' said Captain Flint. 'There are already so many English nobles and gentry scuttling across the Channel to seek favour with the King that there are probably more of them in France than in England — and they usually know which way the wind is blowing.'

When Ralf was set ashore on the French coast he quickly learned that King Charles was in the Low Countries where, by dint of devious alliances with leaders of minor European states, he had managed to gather a small army. Ralf set off to find him.

He eventually located the exiled monarch and his court in Brussels. The King's motley 'army' was made up of many diverse nationalities, but the household guard were soldiers drawn from the countries of the British Isles — and Colonel Trevanion was still their commanding officer.

He gave Ralf a genuinely enthusiastic welcome before escorting him to the chamber where King Charles was consulting with his council.

Charles did not immediately recognise Ralf, but when he did he greeted him warmly, declaring that he had believed him dead when nothing was heard from him after Piers and Frances joined him in France. 'Where have you been, and what have you been doing?' he demanded.

'It is a very long story, Your Majesty,' Ralf said, pleased with the King's welcome, 'and one I will be delighted to tell to you in due course, but first I have a message to deliver to you from one of your most loyal supporters in England — and I have strict instructions to tell it to no others.'

Taken aback, the King said, 'This is my council, Ralf. I trust its members implicitly. However, as your message is obviously of considerable importance we will go to my chambers — although I insist that Piers comes with us.'

Piers, delighted at Ralf's unexpected arrival, now hurried forward to embrace him, saying, 'You have never been out of the thoughts of Frances and myself, Ralf. We will have much to talk about — but first we will learn your reason for coming here.'

Once in the King's chambers, Ralf revealed that he had come with a most urgent message from Sir John Grenville.

Delighted, Charles said, 'Sir John is one of my most loyal and staunch supporters. It is encouraging news, I trust?'

Aware that the King had been hoping for news that would hasten his return to England, Ralf shook his head unhappily. 'I am afraid not, Your Majesty. Sir John has sent me here to urge you not to attempt to return to England just yet. The country is not ready to welcome you and Parliament's spies have infiltrated the hierarchy of the Sealed Knot. Because such spies occupy important posts Sir John would not commit his message to paper — and he requests that his name be not mentioned, even at your council meetings, for fear he should be arrested and executed. He is deeply involved in moves to restore Your Majesty to your rightful role as ruler of the British Isles, but it would be disastrous should any attempt be made too soon.'

'But I understood that all was ready for my landing and that the country would rise for me,' said Charles, dismayed.

Ralf shook his head. He had been well briefed by Sir John and had the answers to most of the arguments the King was likely to put forward in favour of an early landing in England.

'The mood of the people is certainly moving in your favour, sire, but the movement is not yet strong enough for your loyal supporters to take on the might of the Parliamentary army. It also requires strong leaders — and Parliament have arrested many whose names can only have been given to them by one of their spies from within the Sealed Knot. The time is not yet right — but it soon will be, Your Majesty, and Sir John will ensure you succeed. In the meantime, the army is not happy with the leadership of Richard Cromwell; Parliament is jealous of the power wielded by the generals and the people of your country have had enough of Puritan killjoy rule. They long for change. Sir John is following all that is happening very closely and begs you to have patience for a while longer.'

The King looked unhappy and turned to Piers for advice. 'What say you, Piers? Do you agree?'

'Sir John is my kinsman, sire, and the son of Sir Bevil. He is as wise as his father was brave. His views must be discussed with your council, of course, but the very fact that he has sent Ralf and would not commit his views to paper is an indication of the seriousness of the situation. We should at least wait until we have confirmation of the arrest of those upon whom we would need to rely.'

After remaining silent for a long time, King Charles said, 'You are right, Piers. We must not risk a second Worcester. We will speak to the council right away. Thank you, Ralf. We will talk again soon and you will tell me all you have done since we last met . . . '

3

'Ralf . . . *darling*!' Frances's reaction to seeing Ralf when Piers ushered him into the house they occupied in Brussels was overwhelming. She quite literally threw herself at him, hugging and kissing him with a warmth that startled her six-year-old son and momentarily shocked the French nursemaid who held a two-year-old girl in her arms.

Entering behind Ralf, Piers took the small girl from the nursemaid and smiled benignly at the enthusiasm of Frances's welcome for their unexpected guest. 'I knew you would be delighted to see him,' he said. 'But I think you had better explain to *young* Ralf that this is the very special man after whom he is named.'

Ralf shook hands gravely with his serious young namesake and said to Frances, 'I can see he is going to be a very fine young man, like his father and his late great-uncle.'

The name of the small girl was Rose. Piers had already told Ralf that it was in honour of the great Scots nobleman for whom Frances had once led a cavalry troop, the Duke of Montrose.

'It is truly wonderful to see you again, Ralf, but where have you been for all these years

— and what are you doing here, in Brussels?'

Replying for him, Piers said, 'Ralf has been working on his stepfather's farm, which, unfortunately, has been sequestered by a friend of the late Protector — he will tell you all about it over dinner. He is here because he has brought the King an important message from my cousin, Sir John. But we must allow him time to clean up and relax. He has ridden here from Calais. There will be much time for talking. I have insisted that he stay with us until his return to England.'

'But of course,' Frances said. 'Where else would he stay? I trust it will be time enough to introduce him to some of the eligible young ladies of the court — or are you already married, Ralf?'

He shook his head. 'No, but I have an understanding with one of the daughters of the man who sequestered my stepfather's farm. Fortunately for me — and for Winfred — he knows nothing of the arrangement. If he did he has the power, as a Puritan commissioner and Justice of the Peace, to have me thrown into gaol. Something he would not hesitate to do.'

'I am thoroughly intrigued,' Frances declared. 'But I must not keep you talking. Piers is right, you must be weary and hungry. Tonight we will have our own very private celebration. Piers will tell you, there have been few weeks when I have not wondered aloud what you were doing. He owes his life to you and I will for ever be in your debt for the great happiness I have known as his wife.'

'I am delighted for you both,' Ralf replied, with true sincerity. 'I look forward to hearing the story of your lives since we were last together — and to getting to know your charming young children.'

★ ★ ★

That evening there was much to talk about. Piers and Frances had followed the exiled king on his wanderings between the capitals of Europe, forced to rely for the very essentials of life upon the sometimes grudging generosity of more secure monarchs.

Having experienced a similar way of life in the years before Worcester, Ralf was aware of the hardship and humiliation they must have endured. The fact that they remained so happy together said much about their love for one another.

Pressed to tell them what he had been doing, Ralf gave them details of life on the farm that should have been his own.

Frances was outraged at the treatment meted out to him by Oliver Pym, but was intrigued by the attraction that had developed between Ralf and Winfred. 'Does she know of your past duties in the King's court, Ralf?' she asked.

'She didn't,' Ralf replied, 'but I told her just before I left for Stowe.'

'And it made no difference to the way she felt? She is still as keen to marry you?'

'She told me she would be just as happy to be my wife were I a penniless tinker,' Ralf said, his thoughts returning to the farewell between them in the porch of the small church near Trecarne.

'Then she must be a very special young woman,' Frances declared. 'I suggest you hurry back to Cornwall and marry her before someone else comes along and recognises her qualities.'

'I would like nothing better,' Ralf replied. 'But I would need to take her to a place where her father could not catch up with us — and where I could support a wife and the children who would no doubt come along in a year or two.'

'You could bring her here,' Piers said. 'We would find a place for you both and the King would be delighted to have you back with him.'

'Of course he would,' Frances agreed. 'You served him well in the past. He sets great store on loyalty and enjoys rewarding those who have stood by him in adversity. There may be few luxuries for those who follow an exiled king but we have managed well enough, even though it hasn't always been easy. You and Winfred would never starve, Ralf.'

'Winfred could certainly come and stay with us and be very welcome,' Piers said, 'but I doubt if Ralf will be able to become part of the King's household just yet. It is not impossible that the King will return to England at some time in the not-too-distant future, but in the meantime his reinstatement is being opposed by many of those Puritans who have much to lose. They will fight to remain in power and with so many of their

434

spies among the Royalists there will be a need for a trustworthy courier to carry verbal messages back and forth across the Channel. I believe you have been chosen to fill that very important role, Ralf.'

4

Ralf remained in Brussels with Piers and Frances for three weeks. During this time news began to filter through from England that there had been no arrests made among the leaders of the Sealed Knot. The King began to feel he had been fed false information by Sir John Grenville.

It was now that Edward Hyde, the seasoned adviser to both Charles I and Charles II, gave his considered opinion.

It was not only Parliament which was adept in spying. Hyde had his own informers among those who occupied Westminster. He told the King that Sir John had most probably been right, but that the Parliamentarians were deliberately not arresting those who were plotting against them, in the hope that it might lure Charles from the safety of Europe.

At present the army of the Protectorate was quite capable of defeating any army the exiled king might bring with him and Charles would inevitably suffer the same fate as his father.

King Charles did not always accept what his future Lord Chancellor advised, but on this occasion he did. Sir John Grenville was highly esteemed by Hyde, Piers and Ralf and reflected a great deal of his father's glory. Charles decided he would accept what the titled Cornishman had said. He would put off his proposed invasion of England until the time was deemed propitious. Ralf was instructed to return to England to pass this information on to Sir John.

★ ★ ★

The ship on which Ralf took passage from Antwerp, the closest port to Brussels, was bound for Truro, in Cornwall, to take on a cargo of tin and here Ralf purchased a horse and decided he would call in upon his mother in Fowey before going to Stowe.

He took some comfort in the fact that it was dark when he reached the small seaport. He would rather not meet anyone who knew him. Oliver Pym would still not have forgiven him for leaving Trecarne when the wheat crop needed to be harvested and might have ordered his arrest.

Leaving his horse at one of the town's stables, Ralf made his way to his mother's house to be overwhelmed by her welcome. It was not until she had seated him at the kitchen table and placed a hot meal in front of him that she said, 'Oh, I had a visit from one of the daughters of that man you worked for at Trecarne. It was the day before yesterday, I think . . . yes, that's right . . . or was it the day before?'

Ralf paused with a spoonful of food halfway to his mouth. 'A daughter of Pym? It must have been Winfred. What did she want?'

'She wanted to speak to you. Said it was urgent.'

'How urgent? Didn't she say anything else?'

'She didn't tell me what it was all about, but said I was to tell you that she goes to someone's grave at ten o'clock every day. She did tell me the name of who it was but I can't remember. It might have been Edith . . . something like that.'

'Enid?'

'Yes . . . it might have been. What's it all about, Ralf? Why should one of that man's daughters come here to the house looking for you?'

'I don't know,' Ralf said, 'and I can't find out immediately. I need to take a message to someone tomorrow. If possible I'll be back tomorrow night, but it will more probably be the day after. If she returns to the house tell her that I will meet her at the place she suggests as soon as I possibly can.'

He spent the remainder of the evening worrying about the reason for Winfred's call upon his mother. It must have been something important, but he had the message from the King to Sir John Grenville to deliver before he could deal with personal matters.

★   ★   ★

Unfortunately, much to Ralf's frustration, he was forced to remain at Stowe for a whole week. A great deal of ever-changing information was reaching the house from London.

A fierce power struggle was taking place in the

438

capital between the army and those Parliamentarians loyal to the new Lord Protector — and Richard Cromwell was losing. Sir John wanted to have positive information to send to the exiled king and Ralf was kept waiting until it arrived. When it did, Sir John briefed Ralf on its implications.

It was now inevitable that Cromwell would be forced to admit defeat and resign. When that happened, the army, although faced with its own internal differences, would take over the running of the country. Chief among the army leaders was John Desborough, the major-general who had administered the south-west of England and raised Oliver Pym to his present importance in Cornwall.

However, another very powerful army figure was deliberately remaining in the background, and he could not be disregarded. General George Monck, commander of the army occupying Scotland, controlled an experienced and well-disciplined force that could dictate the outcome of the power struggle if Monck so wished, but the wily general was content for the moment to remain in Scotland and not become involved in the struggle for power in London.

The Grenvilles and Moncks were kinsmen, and Sir John had reason to believe he might be able to persuade General Monck to shift his allegiance and support the restoration of the monarchy. The Reverend Nicholas Monck, brother to the general, had been appointed rector of Kilkhampton by Sir John some time before. Now Sir John intended to use him in a bid to influence his brother and win him to the cause of King Charles.

That was the exciting news that Ralf was to convey to King Charles, stressing the need for the King to do nothing that might upset the still delicate negotiations.

Ralf set off on his mission, having told Sir John of his intention of taking a boat from Plymouth after calling on his mother — and Winfred — first.

★ ★ ★

After spending the night at his mother's house, Ralf collected his horse from the Fowey stable and, the tide being low, crossed the River Fowey at a ford some distance above the town on his way to the Churchtown cemetery. There was a horse tethered outside the churchyard gate and Ralf recognised it as being one of the mounts stabled at Lantewan belonging to Oliver Pym.

He proceeded cautiously, but his mount whinnied at the sight of the other horse and before he reached the churchyard gate Winfred had appeared on the other side.

'Ralf! You got my message.' Running to him she hugged him, saying, 'It was so long ago I thought you must be away and would not be given it in time. Your mother said she had no idea when she would see you again.'

'I arrived home only last night,' Ralf said, kissing her. 'What's happening? I'm absolutely delighted to be with you again, but why is it so urgent? Where is your father?'

'He has been in London,' Winfred said. 'There's a serious crisis there. John Desborough is leading a movement that intends to topple Richard Cromwell and allow the army to take over the country.'

Her information about Desborough added nothing to what Ralf already knew, but she had more to say. 'He isn't due back for a while — but when he does come home he intends to see me married.'

'Married?' Ralf echoed. 'To whom? You have never mentioned anyone to me.'

'How could I . . . I hardly know him! It's a man named Ebenezer Sawyer who must be almost three times my age. I have only met him twice — and then he was married to someone else. She died in childbirth about three months ago and he spoke to Father about me a couple of weeks ago. Father agreed I should marry him and says the marriage will take place as soon as he returns from London. I can't go through with it, Ralf. I love *you*! I would rather kill myself than marry anyone else.'

'There is no need to talk like that,' Ralf said, his thoughts reeling at Winfred's revelation. 'You won't marry him, I'll see to that. When is your father likely to get back?'

'I don't know,' she said. 'It could be in a few days, or it might not be for weeks. What can I do, Ralf?'

'What does your mother think about your marrying this man?'

'She is almost as upset about it as I am,' Winfred replied. 'She and father had a big

441

argument about it, but she couldn't change his mind. This man is a Justice of the Peace, like Father, and has a large house and a great deal of land. Father says it will be a good marriage, but he means it will be a good marriage for him and his ambitions, not for me. It really doesn't matter to him what I think about it.'

Even as she was talking Ralf arrived at a decision. 'You're not marrying him,' he said. 'When can you be ready to come away with me?'

Startled, Winfred said, 'I . . . I am ready right now . . . but where will you take me?'

'First of all we'll go to Temple church. After that we'll go to stay with married friends of mine. I have told them about you and they said we are welcome to go and live with them. You'll be perfectly safe staying with them whenever I have to go away.'

'Go away where . . . what are you doing, Ralf?'

'That doesn't matter . . . are you willing to marry me and trust me to take care of you?'

'You don't need to ask me that, Ralf. I suggested it to you ages ago. Yes . . . yes . . . yes! I will go with you right now, if that is what you want.'

'We both have a few things we must see to first.' Excited at the thought of what they were about to do, he kissed her and her response excited him even more.

Drawing apart, he said, 'We'll leave first thing tomorrow morning. I'll meet you with a saddled horse on the lane that runs past Lantewan. By tomorrow night we will be man and wife.'

'It will be a dream come true, Ralf — but

442

there's no need for you to bring a horse for me. I have mine here.'

Ralf shook his head. 'Your father wouldn't hesitate to accuse me of stealing both horse and saddle. We won't give him such an opportunity. There is a gypsy camp upriver from Fowey and they deal in horses. I'll buy one from them today, together with a saddle. We'll ride to Temple tomorrow, then travel on after we're married — if you're quite certain it's what you want.'

'If it's what I want . . . ? I have thought of little else since the days when we used to work together at Trecarne Farm.'

'Then we will both be happy,' Ralf said. 'But what about your mother? Will you say anything to her?'

'I shall tell her I am going away but will be well looked after and she has no need to worry about me. Is that all right? I couldn't just go off without saying anything. It would make her desperately unhappy. Besides . . . ' Winfred gave Ralf a sidelong glance, 'I think she has a very good idea of the way I feel about you, Ralf, and unlike my father I really don't think she disapproves. I know for a fact that she is far fonder of you than of Alasdair, Ronwen's husband. She will probably realise I have gone away with you. She might even use my disappearance to further her wish to return to Huntingdon. She has been trying to persuade my father for a long time that we ought to go back there, where she would have a great many of her family about her. But may I tell her where I am going?'

443

Ralf shook his head, 'I'm afraid not, Winfred. There is always the chance that she might let something slip to your father. If he realises you have gone away with me he will move heaven and earth to find us. I can't afford to allow that to happen.'

Not fully understanding what he was saying, Winfred said, 'I wouldn't want it to happen either, Ralf. I love you and just want to be with you — whether you decide to marry me or not.'

'We will be married,' he promised. 'By this time tomorrow you will be Winfred Hunkyn. Just be sure to be outside Lantewan at dawn.'

5

The plan almost foundered before they got under way. The next morning, when it was still barely light, Ralf was riding along the lane that led to Lantewan, leading the saddled horse he had purchased from the gypsies. Approaching the house he had slowed the animals to a gentle walk when he was suddenly confronted by a stocky, ruddy-faced man carrying a sporting gun.

Although taken by surprise, Ralf would have ridden past him, but the man stood in the centre of the narrow lane, forcing Ralf to bring his mount to a halt.

'What are you doing here at this time of day?' the man demanded, his finger finding the trigger of the long-barrelled weapon resting carelessly in the crook of his arm.

'Minding my own business,' Ralf snapped back at him. 'What are *you* doing?'

'Don't be clever with me or you'll find yourself standing in the dock in front of Magistrate Pym,' said the man.

While he had been talking, Ralf had seen a movement on the other side of the low wall that separated the gardens of Lantewan from the lane. Guessing it must be Winfred and that she could hear what was being said, he raised his voice to make it easier for her to realise what was happening.

'If you continue to delay me it will be you who will incur the wrath of Oliver Pym. I am here with a saddled horse to escort Miss Winfred to Falmouth, where she is to take a ship to London. I am late enough already.'

Taking her cue from Ralf, Winfred appeared at the gate carrying a bag. Crossly, she said to Ralf, 'What are you doing wasting time talking to Smith? At this rate we are never going to reach Falmouth in time.'

'I am sorry, Miss Winfred,' Ralf said, 'but this man held me up, demanding to know where I was going.'

The man in question was immediately apologetic, 'I beg your pardon, Miss Winfred. I am only looking after your father's interests. Important men like him have many enemies. I had come out early to see if I could bag a couple of rabbits when I saw this young man. He's a complete stranger to me and, for all I know, he might have been stealing the horses.'

'You are employed as the farm manager of Trecarne, not as a parish constable,' Winfred pointed out. 'Now you can help me mount, then go about your business.'

'Certainly, Miss Winfred. Please accept my apology for delaying you.'

Leaning his wheel-lock weapon against the wall, the farm manager helped her to the saddle of the horse Ralf was leading before passing the package she had been carrying up to him. Ralf took it without a word, then wheeled his horse and set off after Winfred, who was already heading away along the lane.

Catching up with her, he said, 'That was an anxious moment, Winfred. Had you not been waiting I think he might have taken me to the house in order for me to identify myself.'

'It would have been far worse than you realise,' Winfred declared. 'Father returned unexpectedly from London last night. It seems General Desborough intends to make his move against Richard Cromwell and sent Father back to Cornwall to ensure there is no trouble here when it happens. He is calling out the militia and has been up most of the night writing his orders. I feared he might still be working when I wanted to leave the house. Fortunately, he went to bed about an hour ago, but it means he will know of my disappearance much sooner than we had hoped — and he will have the militia to call upon to help search for us. By tonight there will be a hue-and-cry throughout the county. Had Smith not seen us Father might have believed I had gone off to stay with one of my friends — not that I have many here, in Cornwall — but when he speaks to Smith he'll know I have eloped.'

Suddenly, despite the seriousness of their situation, Winfred's body shook with an involuntary quiver of delight. 'It is very exciting to actually be eloping with you, Ralf, it really is.'

'I am very happy at the thought of being married to you too,' he replied. 'But perhaps it's

447

going to be more exciting than I would have wished it to be! We must hope the Trecarne farm manager doesn't learn of the elopement too soon — and that when he does he sends everyone on a wild goose chase to Falmouth.'

★ ★ ★

There was a lot of riding to be done that day, but although Ralf and Winfred could not push their horses too hard they were still able to reach Temple church by mid-morning. As good luck would have it, they found Merryweather Hooper, the parish clerk, just about to leave the tiny church, having conducted a wedding there earlier in the morning.

He recognised Ralf and Winfred immediately, and when they informed him of the reason for their visit he chuckled happily. 'I knew I wasn't mistaken when I saw you the first time. I'm a romantic and I know when a young couple are in love as soon as I set eyes on them — but it will cost two pounds in gold coin, paid in advance. I trust you have the money?'

Amused by the clerk's blend of romanticism and astute business sense, Ralf handed over the required sum.

He and Winfred stood before the clerk as he produced a book, saying, 'Before the Protectorate, this duty would have been performed by a clergyman, but now the authority is vested in me. Nevertheless, you will be as legally married as you would be if you were married in a cathedral — and at a fraction of the cost.'

At a certain point in the wedding ceremony it was discovered that the bridegroom did not have a ring to present to his bride in order to put a seal on his vows, but once again the resourceful clerk came to the rescue, producing a small box of plain gold rings, each costing only two crowns.

It was not the most romantic of services, but it was brief and that suited the young couple in their present circumstances. Ralf, in particular, was concerned that Oliver Pym might already have discovered that Winfred had run away from Lantewan, and have organised a search for her. In fact, it was not until late afternoon that he enquired after the whereabouts of his errant daughter, but Ralf could not know this.

'Where are we going now . . . husband?' Winfred asked as they prepared to mount their horses once more.

'Plymouth,' Ralf replied. 'There I hope we will find a ship to carry us to the Low Countries.'

'You are taking me to Europe?' Winfred asked, wide-eyed.

'That's right,' he replied, 'and once there I will introduce you to King Charles.'

Winfred looked at him uncertainly. 'Truly, Ralf? You really do know the King well enough to introduce me . . . as your wife?'

Aware of the awe in her voice, Ralf said, 'I was with him for some years — momentous years.'

'And yet you were content to leave such a life behind and work at Trecarne, spending your nights in a stable . . . Why, Ralf? Why did you leave the King's service?'

'After the battle of Worcester I made my way

to the south coast and was waiting to take passage to France when I was told that my stepfather had died and Trecarne had been sequestered by a former Roundhead officer — your father. So instead of returning to France with the King I went home and learned it was all only too true.'

'Who told you?'

Winfred's question conjured up the image of Brighid once more. 'Someone who used to be part of Charles's household when he was a prince.'

'Was it a man or a woman?'

'A woman. She had been one of the Prince's seamstresses.' He tried to sound casual, but did not quite succeed.

'Had you escaped from Worcester together?' Winfred persisted, aware that Ralf was discomfited by her questions and wanting to know why.

'No. She had left the Prince's service some years before, when he was retreating through Cornwall. She went off with a mercenary soldier believing he was going to marry her. Instead, he abandoned her when she was expecting his baby. After it was born she came to Cornwall seeking help from my mother and stepfather, only to learn that he had died and that my mother was no longer living at Trecarne.'

Silent for a while, Winfred said suddenly, 'I can remember a young woman coming to Trecarne not long after we moved in. I must have been about nine or ten. She was an Irish girl and her baby was sick. Mother sent me outside with some milk for it but I remember the baby seemed ill and unable to take the milk. Mother would have taken her into the house, but my father forbad it.'

Taken aback by the fact that Winfred had actually met Brighid and trying not to think too much about the picture of Brighid and her baby she had conjured up, Ralf said gruffly, 'The baby died and is buried in a pauper's grave in Fowey.'

'Were you very fond of her, Ralf?' Winfred asked quietly.

'She was very kind to me when I first became a royal page and everything was strange to me,' Ralf said non-committally, adding, 'We became very good friends.'

Winfred realised that he was not comfortable talking about Brighid and she decided it was a subject she would not bring up again. Edging her horse closer to Ralf, she said, 'I can't think of anything I would rather be doing on my wedding day than riding off to begin a new life with my husband. Tell me, Ralf, where will we be staying when we reach the Low Countries — and what will you be doing there . . . ?'

6

Settling Winfred in a Plymouth inn late that evening, Ralf set off for the harbour to see what ships were in. In a waterside tavern he sat drinking on his own for a while, watching the other men around him and listening to the languages they spoke.

Eventually, he moved to where a wizened old man dressed in faded seamen's clothes was also seated alone. 'Mind if I sit here?' he asked, pointing to the empty space on the bench beside him. 'Perhaps I could buy you a drink?'

Eyeing him up and down, the old sailor said, 'Well now, I'm not one to refuse a drink when it's offered — but I like to know first what's expected of me in return.'

Ralf smiled. 'Only your conversation. There is a table over there which seems to be occupied by ship's captains from various countries. I just thought you might be able to tell me about some of them.'

'Well now,' said the other man, 'I've been coming in here for so many years that I know all the regulars by sight and one or two of the others by reputation, so I suppose I *could* tell you something about them — but it's likely to take more than just one drink to loosen my tongue, especially if you're perhaps thinking of taking passage with one of 'em.'

'If I am then it will be money well spent,' Ralf said, 'so we'll call for the first right away.'

While the drink was on its way, Ralf told the other man his Christian name and he replied in kind, saying that his name was Jan and adding that he had recognised Ralf's accent and that he too was a Cornishman, but from the north coast.

With this settled and the drink on the table before him, Jan proved that Ralf had chosen the right man to tell him about the other customers drinking at the waterside tavern.

Ralf became particularly interested in a man Jan called Captain Paynter. Jan knew him as a one-time ship's captain in the Navy of Charles I, who had left the Navy when Cromwell took over the country and was now the English captain of a Dutch ship with a home port in the Lowlands, adjacent to the territory where King Charles and his court were currently accommodated. It was rumoured that he had commanded a Dutch man-of-war in the late war between the Netherlands and Cromwell's Commonwealth, so Ralf knew he must have little time for the Puritan regime.

Ralf remained talking to Jan until he saw Captain Paynter bid farewell to his companions and leave the tavern. Hastily thanking the old seaman for his company, Ralf hurried after the sea captain, catching up with him a short distance along the torchlit harbour front.

'Captain Paynter . . . may I have a word with you, sir?'

Casting a quick glance in his direction, Captain Paynter said, 'Why didn't you speak to me in the tavern? I saw you glancing across at our table often enough. If you're proposing something illegal I don't want to know. I can find enough trouble for myself.'

'It's nothing illegal, only . . . if you're sailing for the Netherlands I would like to book a passage with you, for me and my wife.'

'Nothing illegal, you say? Then why not take passage in an English ship? There are enough of them trading with the Netherlands these days.'

'Because I like what I hear about you, sir.'

'You don't want to take too much notice of anything old Jan tells you. He's a well-known gossip and will tell anyone what they want to hear so long as they set a pint of ale in front of him.'

Disappointed, Ralf said, 'So there is no chance of taking passage with you, sir?'

'I didn't say that. This 'wife' of yours . . . is she pregnant?'

'No!' It sounded too positive and Ralf explained, 'We were only married today and I was hoping to take her to the Low Countries to stay with some friends I have there.'

'Only married today and you are taking her out of the country? You would seem to be a very impulsive young man . . . unless, of course, there is another reason why you should want to be taking your 'wife' out of the country in such a hurry?'

Aware of the implication in Captain Paynter's words, Ralf said, 'We were properly married, sir, in a church, albeit the service was conducted by the parish clerk.'

Captain Paynter glanced at Ralf once more. 'Do you have money for a passage to the Netherlands?'

Scarcely able to contain his delight, Ralf said, 'Yes, sir. I can pay whatever you ask.'

'I sail the day after tomorrow for the Netherlands. My ship is the *Abraham*, berthed close to the entrance to the harbour. Bring your wife on board tomorrow, after dark. There will be a cabin ready for you.'

★   ★   ★

It was by no means a peaceful night for the newlyweds at the Plymouth inn. There was a celebration going on downstairs involving a number of the residents, and at one stage Ralf was forced to leave the matrimonial bed and resort to physical force to deter a drunken man from breaking into their room, convinced that it was his and someone had locked him out.

There were also a number of noisy fights taking place in the street outside and, although this was far less disturbing for the two lovers, it did distract from their lovemaking.

It was not until morning that they learned that Richard Cromwell — 'Tumbledown Dick' — had been forced to resign and that most of the revellers had been soldiers. It seemed the factional army, nominally led by Major-General

455

John Desborough, was now in control of the country.

This was something that had been predicted by Sir John Grenville and now Ralf would be able to give a first-hand report to the King that it had come to pass.

Ralf and Winfred spent the whole of the next day in their room until darkness fell, when they made their way to the harbour to board the *Abraham*.

Captain Paynter was there to welcome them and it was immediately apparent that he was taken with Winfred. He explained this to Ralf later by saying that she reminded him of the daughter he had lost, together with her mother, from smallpox, many years before.

Ralf had hoped that the *Abraham* would sail on the morning tide the next day, but loading had not been completed and the ship would not be leaving Plymouth until the late evening.

The young couple felt it would be safer to remain in their cabin until the ship sailed, just in case a hue-and-cry was out for them and they were spotted on deck.

The precaution proved to be very wise.

Winfred was looking out of the cabin port when she suddenly exclaimed, 'A troop of militiamen have just arrived at the harbour — Cornish militia!'

Peering over her shoulder through the porthole, Ralf saw a small band of men dismounting beside the ship. The sight sent a shiver through him but he said to Winfred, 'How do you know they are Cornish?'

'I recognise their captain,' she said fearfully. 'His name is Sawle. He lives in a manor house not far from Lantewan and has had meals at the house on many occasions. He must be searching for me and will recognise me immediately . . .'

At that moment, Captain Paynter walked down the gangway from the ship and, approaching the militiamen, shook hands with the officer in charge. The two men talked for some time and Ralf was perturbed when it appeared that Sawle was about to come on board the *Abraham*, but at the last minute Captain Paynter said something to him and, shaking hands once more, the militia captain mounted his horse and rode off at the head of his men.

It was not until later that night, when the *Abraham* had sailed from Plymouth and was heading out into the English Channel, that both Ralf and Winfred went out in the darkness to stand beside Captain Paynter on the upper deck.

Ralf spoke of what they had seen earlier through the porthole, adding, 'Winfred and I thought for a while that they were going to come on board to search the *Abraham*.'

'Was that cause for concern?' Captain Paynter asked.

'It was,' Ralf confessed. 'You see, although Winfred and I really are married, it was without her father's consent. We eloped.'

'I gathered as much from the officer,' said Captain Paynter. 'I also gathered that Winfred's father is a very important Puritan official in Cornwall and sent the militia out to search for her. Fortunately, he was looking for a couple who were seeking a boat to take them to London. I told him I was bound for the Netherlands and would not be going near London.'

After Ralf had thanked the captain for not informing the militia that they were on board his ship, Winfred said, 'My father certainly believes he is important, but he has treated Ralf abominably.'

'That is something he may well regret one day,' Captain Paynter said, surprisingly. 'You may have gathered that I do not have a favourable opinion of the Protectorate, or the Commonwealth, or whatever it may be called at the moment, and unless I am very much mistaken you serve a very different master, young man. If I am correct then perhaps you will send a loyal greeting to the one you serve. You may remind him that he once sailed on my ship and spent a very enjoyable hour at the helm. I hope it is a pleasure I may one day be able to repeat.'

* * *

Piers and Frances were delighted to welcome Ralf and Winfred to their home after their long journey and were thrilled to learn that they were now married, despite the many obstacles that had been in their path. Winfred liked Frances immediately and was quite happy to remain with her while Ralf went with Piers to report to the King.

Charles was delighted to hear Ralf's account of the deposing of Richard Cromwell and of the celebrations at the inn to mark the event. 'My people will have had enough of Puritanism,' he declared happily. 'It will not be long now before I am asked to return to take my throne.'

The message Ralf carried to the King from Sir John Grenville was more cautionary, but it had been given before Richard Cromwell had been toppled and Ralf did not dwell upon it. There had been little cause for celebration in the King's life for so long that Ralf felt he deserved to enjoy this moment of hope, at least.

When Piers informed Charles that Ralf had married whilst last in England and had brought his wife with him to the Low Countries, the King insisted that Winfred be presented to him immediately and a messenger was sent to fetch her.

She arrived at the court more flustered than Ralf had ever seen her, but Charles could be utterly charming to women, especially attractive young women, and within minutes she was chatting easily to him. She was delighted when he made her a wedding gift of a lace-edged handkerchief embroidered with the royal cipher and promised to find a place for her in his court.

Knowing the King as well as he did, Ralf was less enthusiastic about Winfred's becoming a member of the court, but he said nothing. Besides, Piers had informed him that the King was now totally infatuated with the latest in a long string of mistresses. A cousin of the Duke of Buckingham, Barbara Villiers — as she was still called — was married to a Royalist named Roger Palmer, a fact which seemed to bother neither her nor the King in the least.

7

Official news from England of the fall of Richard
Cromwell was brought to the King in a letter
two days after Ralf's arrival. It came from the
Sealed Knot and contained a suggestion that the
King and his court, together with his 'army',
should move closer to the Channel ports of
France, in order that he might cross to England
more quickly when the signal for a proposed
general uprising was given on his behalf.

The King was enthusiastic, envisaging crossing
to England within weeks, or even days. The court
was hurriedly mobilised and a few days later set
off for Calais, placing the French authorities in a
difficult situation. Their relations with Cromwell's government had improved considerably in
recent years and they did not want to offend the
new regime.

However, the French too had their spies in
London and their ambassador was sending back
reports of the increasing chaos in the country's
government and of the growing support for the
exiled king in the streets of the capital.

Despite the optimism displayed by King
Charles and many of those about him, Ralf
expressed his concern to Piers about the King's

plan to take his pitifully small mercenary 'army' to England to help the Sealed Knot in their proposed uprising. He had already informed Charles of Sir John Grenville's considered opinion that landing an armed force — a Catholic force — on the shores of England would be playing into the hands of Parliament and set an outraged populace against him, but the King seemed to have forgotten the warning.

'I agree with you,' Piers said, 'and Hyde has already warned Charles against making such a move, but I fear he is tired of wandering around Europe and aware that he has become an embarrassment to both rulers and governments by relying on their charity for his very existence. He has reached the stage where he would be willing to risk defeat and almost certain death in order to gain some self-respect — and there is little that those closest to him can do to make him change his mind.'

'Nevertheless, we can try,' Ralf said. 'Although it is a friendship I would have neither imagined nor, indeed, countenanced before now, Winfred and Barbara Villiers seem to get along very well — and the King takes more notice of his mistress than of his advisers. I will speak to Winfred. If we can enlist Barbara Villiers we might persuade the King to curb his eagerness to invade England and wait for his people to tire of the present uncertainty. In the meantime I will go there myself and seek the advice of Sir John. Your kinsman will have a better grasp of the true situation than anyone else I know.'

Ralf was put ashore in England at the busy north Devon fishing village of Appledore. He had sailed from Calais in a French fishing boat which had been especially hired for the voyage. While Ralf made his way to the home of Sir John Grenville, a comparatively short distance to the south, the boat would spend a couple of days fishing in the Bristol Channel, returning each night to Appledore to sell its catch, and convey Ralf back to France when he was ready to leave England.

Sir John was alarmed at Ralf's news of the King's determination to land in England with his tiny force of mercenaries when summoned by the leading Royalists in the Sealed Knot.

'What on earth is His Majesty thinking of?' he exclaimed, agitatedly pacing back and forth across the carpeted floor of his study. 'Have you not passed on my warning that there is a highly placed Puritan spy in the Sealed Knot? The government — such as it is — knows every decision that is made. What is more, they have been warned of the planned uprising and have quietly gone about the business of arresting leading members of the organisation — and this time my information is accurate. So accurate that the uprising has had to be cancelled. Unfortunately, so many senior Royalists have been arrested it is doubtful whether the order to abort will have reached every commander. There will still be spasmodic risings throughout the country and they could be enough to convince

His Majesty that it is the signal for him to invade England. It is also possible that the Parliamentarians will arrange to have a false message sent in a bid to persuade him this is so. Either way, if the King sets foot in the country before the time is right he will suffer the same fate as his father. You must return to France right away — tonight — and warn him.'

'I will of course do as you say, Sir John, but His Majesty has suffered so much humiliation during his years on the Continent that I fear he is in no mood to listen to those who preach patience. Hyde and your kinsman Piers are among those who believe he might sail for England, come what may.'

Ceasing his pacing, Sir John slumped into a leather-bound armchair and looked intently at Ralf before speaking again. 'I think I can understand His Majesty's wish to move matters forward as quickly as possible, but what I am about to tell you may well stay his hand. I had hoped to avoid saying anything until my plans were in a more advanced state, but if we are to avert disaster he must be told now. The present Parliament in London is in chaos, its members appointed by factions of the army who cannot agree among themselves. It spreads more confusion with every day that passes. I have been in contact with General Monck, in Scotland, and firmly believe he is not averse to the thought of restoring the monarchy, if only to bring order back to our country. But Monck is not a man to be hurried. He will only act when he believes the time to be right — but when he does, his action will be decisive and I have reason to believe His Majesty will then be asked to return to the country. However, should the King be foolishly precipitate, all will be lost. Monck will use his army in support of the people — and it is my firm belief that there is not an army in the whole world capable of withstanding him.'

There was much more talk in a similar vein, and by nightfall Sir John Grenville was satisfied that Ralf would be able to put a very strong case to persuade King Charles to bide his time for a while longer.

Before Ralf left, Sir John stressed to him that this was probably the most important mission he had ever undertaken. The whole future of the English monarchy could rest upon his ability to persuade the King that the course he advocated was the right one.

He also had a word of warning for Ralf himself. 'I believe you ran off with the daughter of Commissioner Pym when you were last in Cornwall. Has she returned home yet?'

Surprised that Sir John should know about him and Winfred, Ralf replied, 'No, and she will not. We were married in Temple church on Bodmin Moor on the day we went off together. She is now in Calais, staying at the King's court with Piers and Frances.'

'I doubt if that news will do anything to appease Commissioner Pym. I don't know how he learned it was you she ran away with, but he named you when he raised a hue-and-cry and used the militia in a bid to find you. You must keep out of his way. You are far too important to His Majesty to allow yourself to be arrested.'

After thanking Sir John for the warning, Ralf set off for Appledore accompanied by an armed Grenville servant.

8

When Ralf returned to Calais he found the King's small army paraded and ready to embark for England. A letter had been received declaring that the Royalists of the land were ready to fight for his cause and would rise in his support as soon as he set foot on English soil once more.

Ralf immediately declared the letter to be a forgery and repeated the warning given to him by Sir John as forcefully as he dared. However, the King was eager to lead his mercenary force in pursuit of his crown and it took the combined persuasive skills of Ralf, Hyde, and Piers to persuade him to defer the voyage for forty-eight hours in the hope that information might be received that would either confirm or refute Sir John's account of the situation in England.

Fortunately, it came the following evening in a written message from one of Hyde's London spies. Sir John Grenville had been right to warn the King against landing in England. Many of the men who should have been prominent in the uprising had indeed been arrested and brought to London where they were currently lodged in the Tower.

There had been sporadic risings thinly spread

throughout the country, led by minor leaders who had not received a message deferring the uprising. One such leader, Sir George Booth, actually succeeded in securing parts of Cheshire and Lancashire for the King, but his success was short-lived. A Parliamentarian army was quickly on the scene and Sir George was routed and forced to flee.

King Charles was deeply disappointed by the news, but he was not a fool. He realised that had Sir John not sent Ralf to warn him in time he would now be dead, a monarch who had never ruled his country.

After spending only a week with Winfred, Ralf was sent back to Cornwall to take the King's thanks to Sir John. It was the beginning of many months of to-ing and fro-ing across the English Channel as the personal courier of King Charles. During this time, Charles, despairing at the protracted and highly secret negotiations between Sir John Grenville and General Monck, made one more attempt to move matters forward on his own terms.

France and Spain, after years of bitter war, had called a meeting close to the French-Spanish border to discuss a peace between the two countries. King Charles decided he would travel there to appeal to both countries to provide him with a joint army with which to regain his throne. His appeal to the more settled monarchs fell on deaf ears, but the news coming out of London meant that he was treated with more deference than he had been used to in recent years.

Then the court received cheering news from England via Sir John Grenville and Ralf. The government in London was now in utter chaos and rumour had it that General Monck and his army were on the move from Scotland, determined to restore order and government to the country.

Ralf reported this to Hyde, who had not travelled with the King to meet the French and Spanish leaders. He immediately sent a message urging Charles to return, and on the day after Christmas 1659 King Charles rode into Brussels where he had already spent so many frustrating years.

Early in January, news was received from London that Monck was indeed on the move with a formidable army, his stated intention being to restore a representative Parliament. He had not yet openly declared support for the restoration of the monarchy and Ralf was despatched to Cornwall to consult with Sir John Grenville yet again.

Ralf arrived at Stowe to find him entertaining a clergyman who was introduced to Ralf as the Reverend Nicholas Monck, brother of Parliament's most powerful general.

'You have come at a most opportune time, Ralf,' Sir John said, after the introductions had been made. 'Nicholas is going to London tomorrow to speak to his brother, to see whether he will now publicly throw his weight behind the King and set the wheels in motion to hasten his return.'

'That is the reason His Majesty has sent me

468

here,' Ralf said. 'All the indications are that General Monck will support him, but the general has made no firm commitment.'

'My brother is a very cautious man,' said Nicholas Monck. 'His first aim is to restore stability to Parliament. Not until that is achieved will he consider his next move — but all the indications are that the country needs a monarch to stand behind Parliament. That is certainly the opinion of the people and my brother is determined that the will of the populace will dictate his actions.'

'His Majesty will be very pleased to hear that,' Ralf said. 'But he would like to have the general's own views on the future of the monarchy.'

'Well, why don't you come to London with me tomorrow? Then you can return to the King and give him a first-hand account of my brother's thinking.'

'That sounds a splendid idea,' Sir John said. 'The King trusts your opinion, Ralf, and you will be able to give it to him at first-hand. It is a wonderful opportunity.'

It was something with which Ralf could not argue and he said so.

'Good!' said Nicholas Monck. 'We will set off at first light tomorrow. I look forward to having your company, Ralf.'

★　★　★

When Ralf and the Reverend Nicholas Monck arrived in London they learned that General Monck had taken up residence in an army

469

barracks, guarded by trusted men of his own army. They were escorted to the office where he was working and General Monck greeted his brother warmly, declaring it had been far too long since they had last met. He was less friendly when it was explained who Ralf was.

'You say you *were* the King's secretary? Why did you leave his service? Because he was forced into exile?'

'No,' Ralf replied. 'We did not part company until after Worcester and it was my intention to return to the Continent with him. Then I learned that my stepfather had died and my mother had been turned out of her home, so I returned to Cornwall to see what I could do to help. I re-entered the King's service last year and am currently employed as a trusted courier.'

'A trusted courier? What does that mean? Are you a spy? Have you brought a spy here to meet me, Nicholas?'

Before the cleric could reply, Ralf said, 'I am not a spy, sir. The King employs me as his personal courier because I have served him loyally in the past. I will continue to serve him loyally, but I love my country as well as my king.'

Monck glowered at Ralf in silence for a full minute before asking, 'Have you ever been a soldier?'

'No, although I was present at Worcester and at various battles fought between King Charles the First and the Parliamentarians. My stepfather was the soldier in the family. He was wounded at Lansdown when he was ensign to Sir Bevil Grenville.'

470

General Monck's expression softened and he visibly relaxed. 'Sir Bevil was my kinsman and a very brave soldier. His death was a sad blow to the whole family. But why are you in England now?'

'Because King Charles is of the same mind as yourself. He wishes to see an end to the troubles of the people and believes he has an important part to play in the future of the country. I was sent to England to consult with Sir John Grenville — and, hopefully, ask if you might consider the King in your plans to bring sound government back once more.'

Frowning once again, General Monck commented, 'You speak more like a courtier than a courier, Hunkyn. How can I be certain there is no more to your visit than you say?'

'As a page to the King I was taught the language and the ways of the court by a good tutor and an even better friend. He is another kinsman of yours, sir. Piers Grenville.'

'He is still with the King?' Monck's expression lightened once more.

'He is indeed. He, his wife Frances and their two children are all close to the King.'

Shaking his head sadly, the general said, 'The troubles we have all lived through these past two decades have divided not only our country, but families too. Piers was but a young lad when our ways parted . . .'

Nicholas Monck and Ralf remained talking to the general for more than an hour, and although Ralf left the army barracks with no firm promise for the future of the monarchy, General Monck had suggested that King Charles should write to him with his thoughts on how best a monarch might serve Parliament and the people. He also suggested that the King move away from the protection of Catholic monarchies and take up residence in a country whose religion was more in keeping with the Church that was favoured by those he hoped to rule.

Ralf went away with a high regard for Monck. The general had already succeeded in doing what no other man could have done. Brought order out of the chaos that had ensued after the abdication of Oliver Cromwell's son. Furthermore, Ralf believed he had not acted for self-aggrandisement, but out of a genuine love of his country.

If King Charles could somehow convince Monck that his return would benefit the country, then Ralf believed that the general was the man to secure his throne for him.

9

An indication that General Monck had taken Ralf's visit seriously was that he gave orders for Ralf to be taken to the Low Countries from the naval dockyard in Chatham in a man-of-war — an arrangement which did away with the need for subterfuge. In Brussels once more, Ralf repeated his conversation with General Monck to the King, Hyde and Piers. All were highly delighted, none more so than the King himself.

'You have done splendidly,' he said. 'General Monck has opened the door to my return. When I am on the throne I will see that he is suitably rewarded — and you too, Ralf.'

'Ralf has carried out his duties in an exemplary manner,' Hyde agreed, 'but we have not yet arrived at a stage where we can begin to plan your coronation. General Monck has suggested that Your Majesty write to him. It must be a very, very carefully worded letter if it is to succeed in prompting an invitation to return to London as ruler of the kingdom, and not plunge the country into civil war once more.'

'You are my Lord Chancellor, Sir Edward, and probably the wisest man in the kingdom. Between us we will find the right words to persuade General Monck to support my return to the throne.'

★   ★   ★

The letter to General Monck took almost a fortnight to compose, the reason being that it was probably the most important letter ever written by an English monarch. The future of both King and country depended upon its wording.

While the letter was being carefully composed Ralf was able to spend more continuous time with Winfred than at any period of their married life so far. It was a very happy time for them both, but not until their last night together in the house they shared with Piers and Frances did Winfred disclose a secret she had been keeping from him until now.

They were lying in bed together, looking out of the window to where a full moon was climbing high into the star-spangled sky, above the rooftops of the ancient city.

Suddenly stirring in Ralf's arms, Winfred said, 'Don't you think that little Ralf is the image of his father?'

'Yes. He even tries to imitate Piers's gait and gestures — and Piers loves him very much.'

'It must be very special for a man to have a son,' Winfred said.

'Piers certainly thinks so,' Ralf agreed, 'but he is equally fond of Rose and she really is a delightful little girl.'

'Yes, I take her out with me often,' Winfred

474

said. 'She is adorable.'

'Well, one day we will have children of our own,' Ralf said. 'Both boys and girls.'

'Would you really like that?'

'I would like it very much, but I hope that by the time they arrive we will be settled in a peaceful England once again, and have a settled future.'

'I hope so too,' Winfred said, 'but peace will need to come fairly quickly, Ralf.'

He was in a happily drowsy state and it was some moments before he realised what she meant. When it dawned upon him he sat up in bed and looked down at her in the light of the moon that shone through the window.

'Wh . . . what are you saying, Winfred?'

'I am pregnant, Ralf, almost three months pregnant, so I hope the return of the King is settled soon.'

Ralf was stunned by her revelation. 'But . . . why have you said nothing to me before this?'

'You have been so busy travelling back and forth to England on the King's business I did not want to worry you. Besides, I had to be quite certain before I said anything to anyone.' She hesitated. 'You are not angry, Ralf? You really do want me to have your baby?'

'Angry? It's wonderful news, Winfred. I just feel sorry that we are unable to tell your mother and mine. They would both love to be able to share our happiness.' As an afterthought, he asked, 'Do Frances and Piers know?'

'Frances suspects, but I don't think she has

said anything to Piers.' Suddenly hugging him fiercely, she said, 'I am so glad you are pleased about it, Ralf. I was concerned it might not be what you want.'

'It's probably something I want more than anything else in the world,' Ralf said, 'What's more, I don't care whether it's a boy or a girl. After all, sooner or later we will have both.'

★ ★ ★

The following day Ralf left the court and made his way to London carrying with him a letter from the King. It was addressed to General Monck.

Ralf felt that the delivery of the letter was an historic moment and should, perhaps, have been made with due ceremony. In fact, it was something of an anticlimax.

Ralf was shown into General Monck's office but there were others in the room, mainly army officers, and Ralf could say merely, 'I am carrying a letter for you, sir. I have instructions to give it to no one else.'

Monck took it from him. 'Thank you. I will read it later. Should it be necessary to reply I will arrange a trusted messenger.' The general spoke without a hint of recognition, but Ralf was aware that Monck knew very well who he was — and who had written the letter.

Leaving the barracks, Ralf knew it made no sense to remain in London. He wandered along the Thames river bank while he tried to decide whether to return to Brussels and Winfred, or go to Cornwall and report to Sir John Grenville. He was still contemplating the issue when he came upon some seamen manhandling a number of heavy church bells from a quay beside the river to a small ship moored alongside.

Stopping to watch the proceedings, he became aware that the accent of the seamen was Cornish. He moved closer and asked a man who seemed to be the captain of the ship where the bells were bound.

'I'm taking them to Cornwall,' he was told. 'That's if we ever succeed in getting 'em on board.'

'I could tell that's where you come from,' Ralf said. 'I'm from there myself. Which church are they for?'

'I couldn't tell you exactly,' the ship's captain replied. 'I know they're from the Whitechapel bellmakers and I'm to deliver them as close to Tregony as I'm able to make it up the River Fal, but where they're bound from there I couldn't say. Mind you, the way things are going, I doubt we'll have them on board in time to catch the next tide.'

'I'll give you a hand,' Ralf said, arriving at a sudden decision. 'I'll help unload at the other end too if you'll give me a passage to Cornwall.'

The captain was desperate for assistance and Ralf appeared strong enough to make a significant contribution to his small crew. 'I'll accept your offer as long as you don't eat too much on board,' he said. 'Before leaving Cornwall I took on only enough victuals to last my crew for the return voyage. I'm not buying more, not at London prices — and your passage will be in lieu of any pay.'

'I'll try to curb my appetite,' Ralf said, 'and I never expected any pay. Getting to Cornwall will be reward enough.'

'Then you can start by putting your weight to the bell they're trying to swing on board now. We'll need to speed things up a lot if we're to get off with the tide.'

The voyage to the River Fal took four days in indifferent weather, but the church bells were eventually landed at a spot where a road ran beside the river within sight of Tregony town. It was as far up the River Fal as even the smallest ship might sail.

With the exception of one of the seamen, Ralf had felt perfectly at home with his fellow Cornishmen. The man who was the exception had taken an undue interest in Ralf's movements, wanting to know where he had come from, what he was doing in London, and his eventual destination in Cornwall.

The questions made Ralf uneasy and he said very little to meet the seaman's curiosity, disclosing only that he was going to Fowey to pay his mother an unexpected visit. This did not entirely satisfy the seaman, but Ralf would not tell him exactly where in Fowey his mother lived.

★ ★ ★

Grace Moyle was delighted to see her son again, but she became upset when she learned he had married without letting her know. She was even

478

more upset when he told her that his wife was one of Oliver Pym's daughters. 'I don't know what the world is coming to when a woman's only son goes off and weds without a word. Was Pym at the wedding? I can't see him giving you his blessing if he knows who you are.'

'He doesn't know, Ma. We didn't tell him we were getting married either. We ran off and got married at Temple church, up on Bodmin moor. It's out of the jurisdiction of the Church, and it's the parish clerk who does the marrying there since the Puritans came to power. He can marry couples without banns being called — and, more important to Winfred and me, without the permission of any parents.'

Suddenly remembering the girl who had called at the house asking for Ralf, Grace asked, 'This girl . . . is she the one who came here saying she needed to speak to you urgently?'

'That's right, Ma, but she isn't 'this girl'. Her name is Winfred and she's now my wife — and your daughter-in-law.'

'Had you got her into trouble?' Grace demanded. 'Is that why she came here for you?'

'No, Ma, she was not in trouble, but we are expecting a child in about six months' time — and don't take against Winfred before you even know her. She's a very nice girl and we are very happy together. She's also very unhappy about the way her father took Trecarne from us.'

'So she should be,' Grace said, determined not to accept Ralf's marriage to Winfred just yet. 'Where is she now?'

'She's staying with two of my friends.'

Grace sniffed her disapproval. 'I don't know why you never found a girl you could marry in a normal fashion, the same as everyone else.'

'Because times *aren't* normal, Ma. All sorts of things are going on in the country, but one day you'll understand and will learn to love Winfred just as I do.'

10

Ralf was arrested the day after his return to Fowey. Mary had gone to work at Place and Ralf decided he would stroll to the quayside, in order to purchase fish from the boats which landed their catches.

He was arrested by the town constable, accompanied by the seaman who had asked so many questions of Ralf on the voyage from London.

The constable, a large, self-important man, took Ralf by surprise. Coming from behind he took him by the arm and said, 'You . . . is your name Hunkyn — Ralf Hunkyn?'

'What if it is?' Ralf demanded, at the same trying unsuccessfully to free his arm from the town constable's grasp.

Behind them, the seaman said, 'It *is* him. I should know, I've just sailed with him from London.'

Ignoring him, the constable said to Ralf, 'You'd better come with me. You can stay in the lock-up until your name is confirmed.'

'What is it I am supposed to have done?' Ralf queried. 'I've broken no law as far as I know.'

'We'll let the magistrate decide on that,' said

the constable, adding with a chuckle, 'but as he's the one who's complained that you've abducted his daughter, I doubt if he'll be inclined to deal kindly with you.'

Ralf was alarmed. He had nursed a faint hope that his arrest might have been a mistake. Now he realised it most certainly was not.

'I tell you it *is* him,' the seaman kept repeating as the trio walked to the lock-up. 'When do I get the reward?'

'First we need to have him properly identified,' the constable declared pompously, 'then, if he *is* the wanted man, you'll need to apply to the magistrate — Commissioner Pym.'

★ ★ ★

Oliver Pym did not come to the lock-up until that evening and his satisfaction at finding Ralf in chains was evident. 'So you've come back, have you, Hunkyn? Have you brought my foolish daughter with you?'

'If you're speaking of Winfred, she is now my wife and is perfectly safe and happy staying with friends.'

'Your wife? What nonsense is this? Winfred is not yet old enough to marry without my permission. If she is not here in Fowey, then where is she?'

'We are lawfully married,' Ralf repeated, 'and she is perfectly happy where she is.'

'Very well, if you refuse to tell me her whereabouts I shall have you committed to Launceston gaol until you change your mind. I doubt whether that will take very long — although I am inclined to hope it might.'

Ralf was conveyed to Launceston castle the next day, Oliver Pym signing the committal order without bothering with the formality of a court appearance. Ralf was relieved to discover that the head gaoler he had met when Winfred and Clarice were incarcerated for a night was no longer in charge of the castle prison and he was placed in a communal cell occupied by four other prisoners. Three were vagrants, the fourth had murdered his wife and two children and was quite obviously mentally disturbed.

The tormented ranting of the demented murderer meant that there was little sleep for the other occupants of the cell. The situation continued for another ten days, until the murderer was taken out to be tried by a Judge of Assize. He returned to the cell a convicted man and the next morning was taken out and hanged, his torment brought to an end.

Ralf spent a month in the communal cell, at the end of which time all his fellow prisoners had been released and replaced by others. Then one day Ralf was brought out of the cell and taken to the remembered office of the head gaoler. Here, Oliver Pym sat behind the table with the new prison head at his side.

During his weeks in prison, Ralf had been given no access to a razor and he had an irregular growth of beard that made him appear both unkempt and older.

Oliver Pym viewed his appearance with obvious approval, saying sarcastically, 'I can see that prison life is bringing out the real you, Hunkyn. Perhaps you would now like to tell me where I might find my daughter? I am of the opinion that she deserves all you have brought her to, but my wife does not agree and wishes to have her return home.'

'You may thank Mistress Pym for her concern,' Ralf said defiantly, 'but my wife is well cared for and will continue to be, whatever happens to me.'

'I see you have learned nothing since leaving my employ,' Pym said angrily. Turning to the head gaoler, he said, 'You treat your prisoners too well, Mr James. Hunkyn has failed to repent the error of his ways since he has been in your care. I suggest you put him somewhere to contemplate his behaviour. Is the Doomsdale empty?'

'No,' replied the head gaoler. 'We have a Quaker in there — on your own instructions.'

'Yes, of course. Preacher Entwhistle. They will be good company for each other. Put Hunkyn there. I am on my way to London now. When I return I will come back and see if the Doomsdale has taught him anything.'

Head gaoler James did not seem entirely happy with Pym's orders. 'When do you think you might return from London, sir? Since the recent unfortunate deaths in the Doomsdale Magistrate Lower has said that a prisoner is not to be held there for longer than fourteen days.'

'Magistrate Lower is a very compassionate man,' Oliver Pym said, tight-lipped, 'and no doubt there are prisoners who are worthy of his compassion. Hunkyn is not one of them. He will remain in the Doomsdale until I return and say he is to be released. You have your orders, Mr James. Obey them!'

Minutes later Ralf was pitched into the stinking windowless dungeon that was feared by every prisoner who was committed to Launceston castle gaol. It was filthy in the extreme, the straw that covered the floor heavily soiled and seldom changed. The smell alone was enough to make a strong man feel faint.

In the darkness Ralf heard the rustling of straw and a weak voice said, 'I will not bid you welcome, friend, but to me you are. I have spoken to no one for almost a week. Are you one of us . . . a friend? A Quaker?'

'No,' Ralf replied. 'My only crime is to have married the daughter of Commissioner Pym — but I came here some years ago to help secure the release of another Quaker. A man named Charles Thomasson.'

'You knew Charles!' There was delight in the other man's tired voice. 'He was a wonderful man, his faith unswerving. Sadly he died soon after being released from this very prison. But his daughter has returned to Cornwall. She visits me whenever she can — and when the gaoler on duty allows me to have a visitor. But allow me to introduce myself. I am Richard Entwhistle. A humble member of the Society of Friends,

485

though we are perhaps better known today as Quakers.'

Reaching out a hand that was grasped weakly by the other man, Ralf said, 'I am Ralf Hunkyn — and I am known to Clarice. I look forward to her next visit to you.'

11

Clarice came to visit Richard Entwhistle eight days after Ralf had joined him in the Doomsdale. She did not immediately recognise Ralf, but it was hardly surprising. Untouched by water or brush, his face was so dirty and his beard so tangled that she did not believe it was him.

'If you really are Ralf Hunkyn why are you here?' she asked.

Ralf grimaced. 'Because I had the audacity to marry Winfred without asking permission from Oliver Pym.'

'It is you — and you and Winfred are married! I always believed you would be one day. Tell me about it . . . '

Ralf recounted his story, but, as always, told her only that Winfred was 'with friends'.

'Does she know you are in here?'

'No . . . and it's just as well,' Ralf said. 'She is expecting a baby. I would not want her worrying about me. And I don't want her coming back here to face the anger of her father.'

'I don't think anyone need fear the anger of Oliver Pym for very long,' Clarice said. 'Oh — of course, you will not have heard . . . the rule of the Puritans is over. Pym's friend John Desborough has fled the country and the King is expected in London any day now, invited to return by Parliament — and General Monck.'

'That is wonderful news,' Ralf said. 'Absolutely wonderful!'

'Most people would agree with you,' Clarice said. 'He has promised that everyone may worship according to their own inclinations. It means that you will soon be released, Richard . . . but what can we do to help you, Ralf?'

For the last few days Ralf had found logical thought difficult, but now he concentrated. 'If the news of the King's return is true then I would like you to get word of my whereabouts to Sir John Grenville, at Stowe, near Kilkhampton. Once he knows where I am he will get me out of here.'

'Kilkhampton? That is less than twenty miles away. I was there last week. I will ride there immediately. If he is as influential as you say you will be out of here very quickly — and it will not be a minute before time. You are both sick men . . . but I will have a word with the head gaoler before I leave. Despite his position here he is a more compassionate man than the gaoler who was in charge when Winfred and I were imprisoned. But I will waste no more time. I have brought some food with me: take it, and look forward to your release.'

When Clarice had hurried away, intent upon her errand, the two men sat down on the filthy straw and shared the bread, butter and cheese she had left them. As they ate, Richard

Entwhistle said, 'Clarice spoke of being a prisoner here. What did she mean . . . ?'

★   ★   ★

The fact that they were not immediately moved from the Doomsdale to a normal prison cell was a disappointment, but the spirits of both men remained high. They agreed that the head gaoler would hardly listen to the pleas of a girl — and a Quaker girl at that. He had been given express orders by Pym that Ralf was to be kept in the Doomsdale, and he shared Pym's dislike of Quakers.

For the next few days they thought that every sound outside their dungeon might be the footsteps of Sir John. But as the days became a week, they began to lose hope. Perhaps things had gone wrong in London. Perhaps Monck had lost control of the country and something had happened to prevent the return of King Charles.

Questions to the turnkeys who brought food once a day elicited no answers. News was always slow in reaching Cornwall and the turnkeys neither knew nor cared what was happening in the rest of the country.

As the end of a second week approached, the spirits of both men had sunk so low they no longer wanted to talk, while life itself had become a matter of an hourly rather than a daily battle for survival. They lay on the filthy straw not speaking to each other, yet afraid of the thoughts they were keeping to themselves.

Then one day there was the sound of footsteps

outside the Doomsdale, followed by the grinding of a key in the complaining lock.

'Good God! What a stench!'

It was a moment before Ralf recognised the voice.

It was Piers!

Struggling to his feet, Ralf tried to speak, but his voice seemed unable to produce intelligible words. He would have embraced his friend, but Piers did not immediately recognise him and kept the filthy, stinking figure at arm's length.

'Piers . . . it's me . . . Ralf.'

'It *is* you! My God, what a disgusting state . . . Someone will pay for this. Come along, we'll get you out of here and cleaned up.'

'Wait . . . ' Ralf turned and indicated Richard Entwhistle, who was attempting to rise to his feet without success. 'He's a sick man. He must come too.'

'Of course.'

Piers snapped an order to the head gaoler and the turnkey who was with him. Only the turnkey moved forward to lift the feeble Quaker but Piers rounded on the gaoler. 'Help him . . . and be quick about it. The stench in here is turning my stomach.'

The two men were helped up the stairs, flinching as the light from the windows hurt their eyes. Piers had them taken to the head gaoler's own quarters, where he made the staff prepare baths before he sent them to the town to find clothes.

As soon as he was able to think clearly, Ralf asked, 'What are you doing here, Piers? How did

490

you know . . . and where is Winfred?'

'She is in London with Frances and the court. The King is there too and so is Sir John. That's why it has taken so long for someone to get here. Winfred would have come with me, but I felt it unwise to allow her to travel in her condition. I am glad I insisted. I fear that if she had seen you in this state she would have lost the baby.'

'You are a good friend, Piers,' Ralf said gratefully.

'And you are a loyal servant of the Crown,' Piers said. 'The King is taking a great delight in rewarding those who have served him well in his exile, and you will not be forgotten. We will go to London as soon as you are well enough to meet him again. It was His Majesty who personally signed the warrant ordering your immediate release from this place.'

'I am well enough now,' Ralf declared, belying the statement by tripping and almost falling to the ground.

'I can see you are!' Piers said drily. 'But you will be in a couple of days, and then we will make our way to London and you can enjoy the life of a courtier once more — only this time you will be well rewarded for your services.'

'I am not certain it is the life I want,' Ralf said unexpectedly. 'My happiest days were at Trecarne, especially when Oliver Pym was away and Winfred was there to help me.'

'Ah yes, Mr Pym. He will be a lesser man now he no longer has the protection of Desborough — and he will surely pay for what he has done to you and your family.'

'I have no love for the man,' Ralf said. 'No love at all, but he is still Winfred's father.'

'Were Winfred to see you in this condition she would disown him, Ralf. Let us talk of happier things. You will be much better by the time we reach London and Winfred will be the happiest woman alive when she sees you again. Prospective motherhood suits her. She is the picture of health.'

12

It was another ten days before Ralf and Piers reached London, by which time Ralf, although thinner and still pale from his time spent in the dark dungeon of Launceston castle, was almost his old self: clean shaven, well dressed and eager to be with Winfred once again.

They met in the suite of rooms she was sharing with Frances and when he entered the room where she was playing with Rose, she did not immediately look round.

When she did, and saw him, her eyes widened and she swayed as though she was about to faint. Ralf rushed across the room immediately and when he took her in his arms she burst into tears.

While Ralf was trying to soothe her, Frances entered silently and carried her daughter from the room, closing the door behind her.

★ ★ ★

Much later, Ralf, Winfred, Piers and Frances were enjoying a meal together when suddenly a flustered maid burst into the room and said breathlessly, 'It's His Majesty, sir . . . madam.

He's here to see Master Hunkyn.'

As the four friends rose to their feet, King Charles swept into the room. Seeing Ralf he advanced towards him, closely followed by a smiling Colonel Trevanion. As Ralf was about to drop to one knee, Charles said, 'Wait, Ralf.' And before Ralf knew what was happening he was being embraced by the King.

'I am both happy and relieved to see you safely back with the court again. Piers has told me of your suffering in Launceston castle. We must make amends . . . *now* you may drop to one knee.'

When a mystified Ralf obeyed the command, Charles turned to Colonel Trevanion, who had unsheathed his sword. He handed it to the King hilt first. Taking the sword from him, King Charles tapped Ralf gently upon the shoulder with the blade, then, handing the weapon back to Trevanion, said, 'Now you may rise . . . Sir Ralf Hunkyn.'

Ralf was aware of Winfred's gasp from behind him, then the King was embracing him once more, but only briefly this time. Beaming happily at the other occupants of the room, Charles said, 'Unfortunately, I am unable to stay, but we will meet again tomorrow and decide how else I may reward you for your services.'

A few moments later the King had gone and a still bewildered Ralf was being congratulated by his hosts. When their congratulations were over, Ralf looked at Winfred. 'Well? Don't I get a kiss from Lady Hunkyn?'

He duly received his kiss, but after they had all

drunk toasts to the King and his newest knight, Winfred suddenly choked on her wine.

Concerned, Ralf hurried to her side. 'Are you all right? Is something the matter?'

To his relief, when she looked up at him he saw she was laughing. When he asked for an explanation, Winfred said, 'Oh, you don't know the irony of this, Ralf. Do you remember how my father despised you, and how he told me that while I was casting my eyes on a farm labourer Ronwen was making a marriage that would give her a title?'

Ralf nodded but he was still puzzled, so Winfred explained. 'As soon as I arrived in London I wrote to my mother — chiefly because I wanted to know whether she had any news of you. I had a letter by return, and she told me that the wife of the uncle from whom Alasdair expected to inherit the earldom had died and within weeks of her death the Earl had married a woman half his age. Within six months of the marriage she had given birth to a son — and *he* is the heir to the title and not Alasdair. It means that Ronwen will not now be a countess, while I am Lady Hunkyn. She will never speak to me again!'

'That is not your only news, is it, Winfred?' said Piers. 'Why don't you tell him the rest — and then I might add something to it of which you are unaware.'

'You mean about Ronwen and her husband leaving Trecarne?'

'They have left Trecarne? Why?' Ralf asked.

'Because Alasdair told my father that he had

495

brought him to Cornwall under false pretences and that he had not left Huntingdon in order to become a poor farmer. He said the land would raise no crops and there was no social life to be had anywhere around. He went back to Huntingdon taking his manager with him. Of course, Ronwen had to go too, even though things are not good between them. I think the truth is that Ronwen did not marry Alasdair because she loved him, but because she wanted a title . . . And now *I* have one,' she ended happily.

'That is not all you have,' Piers said. His smile embraced both Winfred and Ralf. 'When I spoke to King Charles immediately after our return today, he asked me what he could possibly give Ralf as a reward for his services. I told him of his love for Trecarne and how your father took it from him as the result of a Puritan sequestration. After a few more questions he sent for Hyde. The result is that Trecarne — and the farm next to it, where Oliver Pym built his new house — is to be taken back . . . and given to you, Ralf.'

Ralf was finding it difficult to take in all that was happening. 'I am very happy to have Trecarne given back to me — it is rightfully mine — but I can't accept Lantewan. That's the home of Winfred's mother and Primrose.'

'True, it is at the moment,' Winfred said, 'but if you remember, I told you that my mother hates it there. Her greatest wish is to return to Huntingdon where all her relations are — Ronwen too, now. It will be no hardship, Ralf, not even for my father — although his pride will certainly be hurt. He will one day inherit my grandfather's house and a small estate — although I doubt whether he will be the same again when he learns of your knighthood.'

'I really can't take all this in,' Ralf said, close to tears as the full import of all that had happened this evening came home to him. Looking apologetically at Piers, he said, 'I am very, very grateful to you, Piers — and to His Majesty — but I really don't think that court life is for me. All I want to do is return to Cornwall and farm for a living — especially now Trecarne is mine.' Turning to Winfred, he said, 'I'm sorry, but that really is how I feel.'

She reached out a hand to him. 'I am very glad, Ralf, because that is the way I feel too . . . ask Frances. I told her so a long time ago. I suspect she mentioned it to Piers — which I think is why he had the King return Trecarne to you.'

Piers nodded. 'There will also be a pension awarded to you, Ralf — and that suggestion was made by neither the King nor myself. Before we returned to England Hyde had you added to the list of those who are to receive one. I don't think anyone will try to stop you if you wish to return to Cornwall, but there will be a proviso. You may go back to farming for a couple of years, but then you must consider whether you wish to return to court.'

'I will need to think very carefully about that,' said Ralf. 'But by then I think there will be one or two young Hunkyns about Trecarne. It is a wonderful place in which to bring up children — and you must admit that I should know . . . '

Books by E. V. Thompson
Published by The House of Ulverscroft

THE DREAM TRADERS
CRY ONCE ALONE
BECKY
GOD'S HIGHLANDER
THE MUSIC MAKERS
CASSIE
WYCHWOOD
BLUE DRESS GIRL
THE TOLPUDDLE WOMAN
LEWIN'S MEAD
MOONTIDE
CAST NO SHADOWS
MUD HUTS AND MISSIONARIES
SOMEWHERE A BIRD IS SINGING
SEEK A NEW DAWN
WINDS OF FORTUNE
THE LOST YEARS
HERE, THERE AND YESTERDAY
PATHS OF DESTINY
TOMORROW IS FOR EVER

THE RETALLICK SAGA:
BEN RETALLICK
CHASE THE WIND
HARVEST OF THE SUN
SINGING SPEARS
THE STRICKEN LAND
LOTTIE TRAGO
RUDDLEMOOR
FIRES OF EVENING

THE JAGOS OF CORNWALL:
THE RESTLESS SEA
POLRUDDEN
MISTRESS OF POLRUDDEN

We do hope that you have enjoyed reading this large print book.

Did you know that all of our titles are available for purchase?

We publish a wide range of high quality large print books including:
Romances, Mysteries, Classics
General Fiction
Non Fiction and Westerns

Special interest titles available in large print are:
The Little Oxford Dictionary
Music Book
Song Book
Hymn Book
Service Book

Also available from us courtesy of Oxford University Press:
Young Readers' Dictionary
(large print edition)
Young Readers' Thesaurus
(large print edition)

For further information or a free brochure, please contact us at:
Ulverscroft Large Print Books Ltd.,
The Green, Bradgate Road, Anstey,
Leicester, LE7 7FU, England.
Tel: **(00 44) 0116 236 4325**
Fax: **(00 44) 0116 234 0205**

Other titles published by
The House of Ulverscroft:

TOMORROW IS FOR EVER

E. V. Thompson

For Alan Carter the greatest personal sacrifice of the Great War of 1914-18 is being called up after only one week of marriage. Leaving his new bride is even more painful than the wound that, months later, sends him to Cornwall to convalesce. For, there, he has time to think about Dora and about the career as a writer that he secretly nurtures. A career that seems possible when he finds himself accepted by the established colony of Newlyn artists. There is one artist in particular — Vicky Hazelton — who encourages Alan's leanings towards the arts. And she stirs other feelings: inappropriate and impossible ones. For Vicky and her set inhabit a different world from Alan's. He belongs to London's East End — and to Dora.

PATHS OF DESTINY

E. V. Thompson

Cornwall, 1854: Alice Rowe was rescued from the workhouse by the Reverend Arnold Markham, the parson of the tiny village church in Treleggan. He employed her in his parsonage as a housemaid, so when he dies of a sudden heart attack, Alice faces a fearful and uncertain future. But as one chapter in her life ends, another begins. For as she discovers the Reverend's body in the woods, she meets Gideon Davey, a 'ganger' who is laying a nearby stretch of railway line. Gideon helps her to recover the body and returns to Treleggan for the funeral — and also to see Alice again. Then, just as their friendship hints at something more serious, Gideon is given an offer he can't refuse: to travel to the Crimea, to build a railway to help the British troops . . .

HERE, THERE AND YESTERDAY

E. V. Thompson

In this collection of short stories by E.V. Thompson, there are tales of the sea: Prunella the cat is in trouble when she's found by the captain of the ship she's hiding on; every time a galleon appears off West Cornwall, a member of the St Gerard family dies — now only Wendy is left, and the galleon reappears . . . And there are stories about criminals: in Arkansas a man is mugged on his way home; three gangsters turn up at the shop of West End fence Elijah Fink to claim their dues . . . And there are other pitfalls: a man, lost on a walking holiday in Ireland, arrives at an isolated house on the moors — and discovers that it's haunted . . .

THE LOST YEARS

E. V. Thompson

Cornwall, 1914: Nineteen-year-old Perys Tremayne arrives at St Austell to stay with relatives at Heligan House, hoping to use his family connections to start a military career. Perys is a Tremayne, but only just: his illegitimacy brought disgrace to the family. The Tremaynes of Heligan are distant relatives, and remain so. His cousin Edward takes an instant dislike to Perys, and uses his influence to dash any hopes of his becoming an officer. Perys finds favour and friendship with the servants and locals. But just when his relationship with farm girl Annie Bray promises to flourish into romance, war breaks out and he leaves to join the Royal Flying Corps . . .

WINDS OF FORTUNE

E. V. Thompson

Thomasina, a maid in a nineteenth century Cornish household, is forced to flee when she is violated, then falsely accused of theft by a titled member of the family. Reunited with Jeffrey, her charming but immoral, childhood sweetheart, she embarks with him on a brief but lucrative career of highway robbery on the roads of Cornwall and Bristol, and remains undetected, protected by her sex. But what is the connection between Thomasina and the young boy shipwrecked and rescued unconscious from the cruel rocks of St Michael's Mount, the island home of the St Aubyn family?